Middle2
from Somewhere Small

. . . .

By Karin J. Eyres

FriesenPress

Suite 300 - 990 Fort St
Victoria, BC, Canada, V8V 3K2
www.friesenpress.com

Editor: Amelia Gilliland
Editor: Terri Wingham
Editor: Charlene Wood

ISBN
978-1-4602-5256-7 (Hardcover)
978-1-4602-5257-4 (Paperback)
978-1-4602-5258-1 (eBook)

1. Fiction

Distributed to the trade by The Ingram Book Company

Dear Nikki,

Here's to many deep conversations
we'll do around Trout Lake.

I'm so pleased to meet you.

xo Karin.

ACKNOWLEDGMENTS

Without the encouraging words of my friend, whom I affection-ately call my Chief of Operations and Planning (COP), this book might have remained an idle fancy rather than a completed manu-script. During lunch on a drizzly Friday afternoon, I read her the first two chapters, and she told me to get busy and finish it. She needed to know how it was going to end. I told her I didn't know how the book was going to end either, but I'd figure it out. Sherry Reid, thank you.

And without the reviews of the two early drafts by a wise and honest friend, the book would not vibrate with the emotional depth I wanted to create. This friend is the one who suggested I write it while we were sitting at her neighborhood pub, enjoying a glass of wine on a scorching summer day. Terri Wingham, thank you.

Several individuals provided important feedback during the editing process. I include a heartfelt thank you to the following:

Amelia Gilliland
Charlene Wood
Clare Hoyle
Sharon Tamaro
Wendy Robb

PART I:
SOMEWHERE SMALL

CHAPTER 1

THE BIG RIVER

People in small towns, much more than in cities, share a Destiny.
Richard Russo

Acid. That's what filled the air in Somewhere Small and what made skeletons of the trees along the banks of The Big River running through it.

In the 1960s, Somewhere Small churned out toxic smoke from the lead and zinc smelter that employed at least one member of each family in the town, including Dad and both of our grand-fathers. As effluent grew, so did affluence in Somewhere Small. Families easily achieved The Good Life, but not necessarily the simple one. The divorced, the widowed, and the otherwise unhappy hearts sought refuge in the extra shifts that multiplied their bank balances. The surplus was the soothing salve that paid for drinks during lonely nights spent at the Crown Jewel on Main Street. While the barren banks along The Big River choked on the acid spewing from the smelter above it, the number and size of homes along MerryAnna Crescent grew with the bustling economy in Somewhere Small. At the heart of The Good Life was the gospel that preached there was no problem money couldn't solve.

I must have screamed, "Let the adventure begin!" on the first day of spring in 1963 as the less than five pounds of me squeezed out of Mom a month early. My sisters, Eldest and Middle1, had already arrived; Youngest was Mom and Dad's last child when she appeared twenty-eight months after me. Mom and Dad's combined reproductive power leaned toward the creation of females, as The Powers That Be blessed them with four girls in five years, minus seventeen days.

Our parents were physical and psychological opposites. Dad was a snake charmer. When he walked into a room, people noticed. When he talked, people leaned forward and listened intently. But Mom was the solitary flower in the farthest corner of a garden. She blossomed with only the birds tweeting their delight as her petals unfurled. Mom's dad couldn't tell her how beautiful she'd become. It would have made him cry because of how she reminded him of the woman he had met thirty years before and had loved ever since.

Hands on hips, Dad rarely hid his biceps, even from the most rugged coworkers at the smelter above Somewhere Small. But Mom was uncomfortable wearing dresses that crept above her knees. Dad flaunted more than his biceps. He rarely wore white t-shirts that didn't cling to every muscle of his torso. Mom wore white too, but her matronly collars never hung below her collarbones and her skirts hid her widening hips. Dad used Brylcreem, whereas Mom resorted to haphazardly placed bobby pins to keep her strawberry-blonde tresses in place as best she could. But she wasn't concerned about the few unwieldy strands. She seemed to know early on that life could be like wayward threads.

Mom's mom died unexpectedly from a blood clot after an operation to fix a herniated disc in her lower spine. Perhaps the strain of giving birth to seven children and the heavy impact of chasing The Good Life were enough of a burden to break her back. Mom's dad didn't shed a tear when his beloved died — not publicly, anyway. He grew up in the era when good Scotsmen didn't cry. They got back up, put on their armour, and headed back to war. But his inability to cry gave him a chronically ruddy complexion.

The sudden and unexpected death of my grandmother awoke his memories of the fragility of life he had acquired during his soldier days in WWI. Tears turned inward become stones in a tempest, the sparks igniting an inferno within the soldier, one that can only be extinguished by his tears. After the death of his wife, Mom's dad obsessed about the safety of his girls. He paced throughout the house several times a day, surveying as far as his eyes could see through the windows, as if he were still a soldier looking for clues from enemies who could be lurking anywhere. The only enemies in the house were the ghosts that brushed up against his arm after the recliner creaked "welcome back" when he dropped himself into it at the end of each day. Grandpa found it easier to fall asleep in his favourite chair since Grandma died. But soon enough he became restless in his reliable resting spot because he sensed the imminent arrival of the next ghost. And this ghost would be different than the ones that hovered and darted about while he dozed. It would haunt him every waking moment for the rest of his life.

Although Mom's dad had weathered many traumatic events in WWI, the swift and unpredictable loss of the love of his life made him vigilant. When Grandma died, his strict control and enforcement of his girls' schedules was the only way he could dictate the outcomes of an otherwise uncertain world. When the familiar is shattered, its rubble buries us until we have the strength to emerge from it with a new blueprint in hand. Grandpa didn't have one after his wife died—and wouldn't again, even though he remarried a woman he didn't really love. But he needed a companion, and although he never admitted it, he really was an old romantic who couldn't let Grandma's side of the bed stay cold for long. He towered above most men in Somewhere Small like a grumpy oak tree, but he needed a woman like the oak tree needs the wind to prevent it from getting too stiff in its old age.

When Mom and her twin sister turned fifteen, they begged Grandpa to let them go to a community dance. He growled and stomped in protest, but their moping faces at the breakfast table and downturned lips at dinner softened him. Sitting in his chair in the quiet of the night, he knew his girls had each other. With the uncanny connection bridging the hearts and minds of twins, he knew that if they became separated and one was in danger from the inappropriate advances of a young man, the other would know it and find a way to help her.

Mom and her twin stood practically as one in a dark corner for most of the night at the community dance, while Dad twirled, laughed, and carried on with the prettiest girls. But unbeknownst to Mom, Dad's glance never left her for long. He took advantage of the intermissions when the roaming spotlights gave him a glimpse of her. Each time the lights passed over her, she had still been in the same place, and the sight of her sent a shiver through him as if she had been running her fingers up and down the nape of his neck.

The sisters danced together to songs even the shyest person could swing to, like "At the Hop." A carefree joy filled them as they jived, leaving no room for past troubles or thoughts about the future. Dad smiled at the sight of his moonflower in all her sweet glory. But as the night progressed, so did his anxiety. Would he be the first to ask Mom to dance the final slow song of the night, or had there been another bee circling his flower when he wasn't looking? Dad had caught Mom's eye that night too, long before the last dance, but he moved too fast for her to keep track of him for long. She doubted he would save the last dance for her when he could pluck any of the more colourful and fragrant flowers around him.

But Mom watched him approach her when the last dance was called and the host ordered the boys to "find their favourite girl and hold her tight" as he changed the vinyl to the Everly Brother's "All I Have to Do is Dream." As she rose to take his outstretched hand, she tripped on the hem of her skirt and fell hard on her right knee. Dad bent down to take her hand and whisked her onto the dance floor. When Dad cupped his arm around her waist and pulled her close to him with the other, their union was as natural as The Big River hugging the banks of Somewhere Small.

Mom had certainly seen Cinderella by then, and like most fifteen-year-old girls whose hearts haven't been broken yet, she likely viewed Dad as the mythical prince with whom she would find forever after. Her prince had found his way to her, with the divine guidance of The Powers That Be. How could their meeting be otherwise explained? Within a day of Mom's dad releasing his grip on his girls, Mom met the man who would shape her destiny.

Dad's dad hadn't let the other side of his bed get cold for long either. He remarried quickly after my grandmother died, which had no greater effect on my Dad than a few droplets of rain falling on The Big River. A torrent of emotions had been swirling inside his heart for years, like The Big River whose banks swelled from spring runoff. Dad had really lost his mother years earlier because of the prolonged sad spells she suffered after her youngest son died in the basement of their house when he was two years old. The apparent cause of death was accidental strangulation from the washing machine hose. I suppose a toddler could find his way into the basement to satisfy his need to explore the workings of the world around him. But raised eyebrows, pursed lips, and scornful looks from the neighbours hinted at another story one of Dad's brothers told Middle1 several years later. Apparently Dad's mom had taken the boy to the basement while carrying a basket of laundry in one hand and holding his hand in the other. She claimed the boy must have played with the hose as if it were a snake while she was distracted. But my grandmother's personality changes led to rumours that had nothing to do with an accident or parental inattention.

No one could blame Dad's mom for being depressed after the death of her child, but there appeared to be something more sinister taking hold of my grandmother. No one knew exactly what was wrong with her, but she was moody and temperamental — one day social, the next reclusive. When she died unexpectedly at the age of forty during heart surgery to fix her valves that had become diseased during a bout of childhood rheumatic fever, she took not one, but two secrets to her grave.

My parents shared a common pain from having lost their mothers when they were teenagers, and as a result, the landscapes of their irises had become dark and murky in the same places by the time they met each other. Without the need for words, Mom and Dad spoke a language they both knew well: the language of pain. They only needed to look into each other's eyes to be unmistakably understood.

As a young man embarking on The Good Life in Somewhere Small, Dad unabashedly flaunted his Ford Corvair by driving too fast and too far on most nights. Mom waited patiently for Grandpa's postprandial snoring to begin within minutes of sinking in to the recliner before tiptoeing to the door and racing to the Ford with Dad at the wheel. The big car, big dreams, and big passions inflamed their first few months together. Presumably, they became acquainted with one another in the back seat of the Ford as "Put Your Head on My Shoulder" and "I Need Your Love Tonight" played on the radio while the engine purred. My parents didn't crave alcohol to distract them from their shared sadness at having lost their mothers. They became utterly intoxicated by the mere sight of each other.

The beginning of my parents' love affair was no different than the thrill all the kids felt with their first leap into The Big River coursing through Somewhere Small. Eyes closed and backs arched with their hearts exposed to the sun, harbouring thoughts about getting burned or drowning was the job of their parents. The young hearts filled with joyful anticipation had no room for tragedy, but logic became important when a few unsuspecting divers found themselves gasping at the river's surface, having survived the unexpected vacuum of an undertow.

My parents hadn't become scared and breathless after surviving a Near Death Experience when one of the undertows of The Big River tried to swallow them. Their fear stemmed from life, not death, with the unplanned but hardly unexpected pregnancy that led to the birth of Eldest and the decision to get married shortly thereafter.

CHAPTER 2

THE LITTLE HOUSE AND "THAT HOUSE"

Love is a fire. But whether it is going to warm your hearth or burn down your house, you can never tell.
Joan Crawford

With the birth of Eldest, Mom and Dad moved into The Little House with two bedrooms and a basement in a hilly community above Somewhere Small. Mom had dreamed of being a doctor but settled into family life easily. She loved being pregnant, and even though the pill had become commercially available for sale in 1960, the same year Eldest was born, she proceeded to have more children. She didn't work outside the house, and perhaps Dad had cinched the purse strings as a way to control her. Maybe they couldn't afford the cost of the prescriptions, or maybe she surrendered to the little voice that spoke to her in the still of the night, convincing her of the merits of young motherhood. Taking care of four young children kept Mom busy and distracted her from nagging and worrisome thoughts. Being a wife and mother also cured her loneliness following the death of her mother, but the cure was a drug that led to serious side effects.

Although exhausted from life as a mother, her brow hadn't started to crease yet. That only happened when confusing problems arose suddenly, like spiders octo-creeping from behind brooms and dustpans.

Dad was temperamental and his moods were unpredictable. They blew through the house like halothane, temporarily paralyzing us until he snapped out of them as if he had awoken from a bad dream. Dad's gloom cooled and darkened the house as if it was in the shade of a heliotropic evil tree whose size and shape also changed to prevent the sun from ever shining on it. When he was at work, Mom anxiously surveyed the goings-on outside while we played in the yard. Gazing up at the sky from the screen door, on more days than not, I thought the dark clouds moved too fast; later in childhood, I realized they had been the first in a series of dread-and-doom moments.

Even after having four children, Mom's frame was still petite and frail for a young woman. Photos of her in her early twenties also revealed a drooping smile. She held us a little too tightly, which maybe meant she suffered from neuroses or premonitions. She certainly had reason to be neurotic when I first learned how to walk and discovered how to escape the house and seek the sun. Perhaps I already knew the adventure I'd begun in The Little House was going to be a little rough. I needed to get out of there early and often as a way to reduce the likelihood of being present if a particularly nasty storm accompanied Dad's return from the smelter. I frequently wandered into the streets without looking left or right for cars, and on one occasion, I got a close-up view of the tread of the front tire of a Volkswagen van. Years later as a teenager, I was still plagued by near misses with vehicles, and I often wondered if I had an unconscious desire to tempt fate into returning me to The Great Unknown, as if The Powers That Be had made a mistake giving me life as Mom and Dad's daughter in Somewhere Small.

We all took turns hiding from Dad under the stairs in the basement of The Little House when behavioural modifications became necessary. His eyes became a little darker and his chin dimpled during breakfast on the days when it was my turn for a private visit after he got home from work. I was taking too much time to go to the bathroom properly, so I needed discipline to encourage speedier progress. And as the roosters cock-a-doodle-doo to signal the dawn of a new day, I knew when to make my way to the basement and hide from him under the stairs as soon as mom lit her fifth cigarette since lunch, signalling Dad was only minutes away from walking in the door. When he arrived, the thumping of his steel-toed boots across the kitchen floor sounded like dull claps of thunder, followed by squeaky thuds as he made his way down the wooden stairs. I seemed to lack imagination because I always went to the same place under the stairs. Going underneath the stairs wasn't really hiding. It was just a way to delay the inevitable. Dad failed to develop effective disciplinary methods because I could never recall what happened between the appearance of his boots through the space between the stairs and my retreat into my second hiding place.

I sought refuge in the unfinished basement bathroom each time and twisted my torso to see my reddened backside, which I interpreted as needing to do better and be better. Achieving both would certainly make my Dad proud of me someday. My Dad knew most definitely the difference between right and wrong, good and bad. I must have been bad and therefore deserved the punishment required to put me on the path to being a good and proper girl. Mom never came to visit me in the basement bathroom. She was probably anticipating her own disciplinary action the following day, with her treatment taking place in their bedroom. Or maybe she was afraid of basements too.

Middle1 often spoke about the nights when Dad grabbed Mom's hair and dragged her across the living room floor during their most heated arguments. I have no memory of Mom letting her hair hang down her back. Instead, she sported a tight bun, as a stiff librarian might wear Monday to Friday, nine to five. If she wound it tightly enough and used more pins than necessary, perhaps she thought Dad would grow impatient at the effort required to untangle it and use it as a rope.

Dad's physical abuse and jealous rants escalated. An odd set of circumstances had apparently catapulted Dad's ego onto one side of a teeter-totter, with his insecurities metastasizing on the other. Dad's older brother had become involved in a romantic affair with the neighbour's wife, whose husband ultimately found out about it. In a confrontation with Dad's older brother, the scorned man vowed to destroy the family. He decided to enrage Dad by telling him Mom would frequently entertain male guests while he was at work. How Mom could "entertain" guests with four small children clambering around her would have been quite a feat, but I suppose anything was possible.

No one is really sure what the tipping point was for Mom, but she eventually decided to leave Dad. His medical records contained written evidence of his threats to kill her before the final breakdown of their marriage. Maybe she concluded that if he was going to kill her, it wouldn't be in the same house where her children had been born. And rather than wait around for him to come home and make good on his promise, she committed to rebuilding a life on her own. The prospect of changing her socioeconomic situation as a single mother of four young girls must have haunted her like a voodoo mantra that drummed "unlikely." Mom told everyone in the family about Dad's threats. Her dad made visits to the local police department, imploring them to do something, anything, to protect her. Every officer told him threats were just that, and enforcement could extend to a restraining order, which in many cases has been as effective as expecting a lion to leave an injured water buffalo alone.

We moved to "That House," which was a few miles away from Dad. I have vague memories of Mom being skittish. She was a cat aware of the coyotes watching her every move. "That House" was situated in a busier part of town, as busy as Somewhere Small could be with its population of a mere fifteen thousand. We were forbidden from playing outside even though I remember yearning to explore my new neighbourhood, which made me feel tentatively hopeful. I was a hummingbird desperate to sip the nectar of flowers it couldn't reach from an enclosed porch. I couldn't figure out how the trees could turn pumpkin orange and pomegranate red as the days grew shorter. What did this change mean? The orange in the leaves was like the yield signs, and the red like the more serious stop signs as part of the safety lessons Mom repeated. I didn't have thoughts about whether I should be concerned about the fiery colours outside because of the warm temperatures inside "That House." I didn't know about fires yet and that warmth came from both embers and newly lit fires. I learned later that several fires had been in progress on the day we moved into "That House." Some had been in the ember state and others were just getting started.

The System allowed Dad to visit us weekly, with conditions in place to protect Mom. She used to have her dad come to "That House" before Dad's arrival, in keeping with the restraining order. I do not recall any of the visits with Dad, except for the last one, which is difficult to classify as a visit. The part of my brain holding memories of prior calls appeared to be guarded with a no trespassing sign that included a tagline: "Remembering would be hazardous to your health."

The apocalyptic void associated with memories of Dad was no doubt associated with the bizarre changes in his mental health, which had deteriorated to the point where he had been admitted to a psychiatric hospital in The Urban City a few hundred miles west of Somewhere Small. Dad's Dad had been convinced there was nothing wrong with his perfectly fine son, and consequently decided to make the sixteen-hour drive to rescue him and bring him home to soak up the acidic air around Somewhere Small, a remedy capable of dissolving any ailment. Dad's Sister's Husband completed the mission with my fiercely-proud-and-in-denial grandfather. Many years later, as he recounted the drive to and from the psychiatric hospital in the month before our last visit with Dad, he lamented the frenetic driving to The Urban City and Dad's frenzied desperation to reunite with the woman he believed yearned for him.

After dinner on the Friday night eight days following my fifth birthday, Eldest, Middle1, Youngest, and I were playing in the living room of "That House." The spring weather had been clear and glorious that day in Somewhere Small. Mom was in her room getting ready to go out on a date, and we could hear her laughing while talking on the phone to Dad's Sister. Dad bolted into the house looking half-crazed while Mom was still in her room talking to his sister. I felt a girlish glee at the sight of him until I remembered he wasn't supposed to be there yet. He gave each of us a chocolate bar. Mine was the one made by Neilson's with eight squares, each containing a different filling. I don't recall whether I had a particular penchant for that candy bar, but I felt delighted that he had brought it just for me. But the girlish glee turned into anxiety when he left the living room and headed for Mom's bedroom, because he had been wearing the clothes of a hunter and the crazed look in his eyes didn't subside as it used to do after spending a few minutes with us.

Mom's chatter continued in the background while our little fingers excitedly opened the chocolate wrappings. Without warning, her voice waned just before we heard her bedroom door slam. The internal camera recording the moments of my life switched into slow motion in the several minutes that followed. The chatter ended but was quickly replaced by thumps, thuds, and Dad's voice yelling "Shut up! Shut the fuck up!" We could hear Mom's chorus of whimpers and pleas. I swear I could hear the branches of The Evil Tree crackle as if a vicious storm were tangling them into a knotted mess.

Eldest grabbed Youngest and placed her on the top bunk in our bedroom, the most sensible solution a girl of seven could think of to protect her two-year-old baby sister. She ran out of the house with Middle1 to find help. I ran between Mom's bedroom door and the living room screen door separating me from the outside world, one that was deaf to her screams. Peering beyond the tiny squares, I hoped something could see into the horror unfolding in

"That House" during the early evening hours of a radiant spring day. I clung to a trio of hopes I heard as scrambled verses: if I could just see clearly through one of the mesh squares and wished hard enough while gazing up into the vastness of the sky, Mom's Dad's car would magically appear. Once in the house, he would wrestle Dad to the floor; he had been a soldier after all, and he could enter any battle with a fierce resolve, particularly in one to save his daughter's life. My third longing was that no matter what state she was in, he could save her. As I sent my wish list through the square mesh up to the sky where Heaven meets Earth, The Evil Tree had stopped howling and so had Mom's screams. In that instant, Dad flew out her bedroom and into the living room. I searched for reassurance from him that Mom's silence meant she was in a quiet state like Somewhere Small experienced after spring storms. The spirit of The Evil Tree had wrapped itself around Dad and demonized him, turning his eyes into bulging black balls that spun and causing him to shiver as if he was outside in summer clothing on the coldest day of winter. He raced by me and fled out the screen door, down the stairs, and toward his car.

As I watched him leave, an ache I'd never known radiated from my chest and stagnated in my feet. The ache made them as heavy as the lead the smelter produced in Somewhere Small. By the time he had reached his baby blue station wagon and sunk into the driver's seat, his form had turned to black and his outline blurred, making me wonder if he would disappear altogether. He did just that as the car tore away and turned left at the end of our street. In that moment, sadness rained down on the underside of my breastbone, like a barnacle that had found its rock. Outside, the sun had dropped behind the mountains, but the sky was still blue. As soon as Dad's car disappeared, silence enveloped "That House" and wrung all the joy out of it.

To reach Mom's bedroom, I had to walk through the kitchen. On the counter to my right, I gazed at the half-eaten birthday cake with its smooth white icing and fallen blue borders. My stomach churned, breaking the news as gently as it could to my heart: Mom would not make my sisters or me another birthday cake again.

To the left of the kitchen, Mom's bedroom beckoned me with an eerie, ghostly chant: "Yes, child, it's time to come." I didn't want to, but a warm, invisible hand had settled in the middle of my back, nudging me forward. As I turned into the room's entrance, death had been painting a red background underneath and around Mom's lifeless body. As it soaked into her silken camel slip, I yelled, "Stop, stop, stop!" I wanted to run away as fast and as far as I could. Perhaps if I were no longer a witness to the scene before me, it would cease to be real and true. And when I returned home to "That House," Mom's Dad would have arrived and made her whole again. But the lead in my feet prevented me from moving anywhere very quickly. Besides, fleeing would have been pointless because the timeless and ageless part of me knew Mom had been a flower flattened in a flash flood of violence. No amount of exposure to the sun would make her rise again, and the blood pooling around her marked the beginning of the decay of her petals.

The phone was in the middle of the bed, and the receiver hung helplessly over the side farthest from me. The line was dead. But what had Dad's Sister overheard during the last fight between my parents? One thing was certain: she didn't know Dad had slit Mom's throat with a knife. Mom hadn't put her hair up in a bun

Youngest was the first of us to leave Dad's Sister's and Her Husband's house. A family a few miles from Somewhere Small wanted her. They already had three children of their own—two boys and a girl—and decided a family of four children would make the perfect family. The sister of Youngest's adoptive mother decided to exercise a less-committed form of altruism by taking in Eldest and me to her home as foster children. She was married with two daughters and they lived in the part of Somewhere Small where most families were living The Good Life. On the day we left Dad's Sister and Her Husband's house with our new foster parents, I rested on my knees and stared out the car's rear window to see no trace of either of our temporary parents. Their sadness and desperation had made them grim reapers in their home.

Many years later, I discovered I had shunted away the most important memories of my final day at Dad's Sister and Her Husband's house. Some of the gaps in the memories of our lives get filled many years later through unexpected encounters with people from our past. When I returned to Somewhere Small for Youngest's twenty-fifth wedding anniversary, I visited with her adoptive dad, my favourite person in what had become her family. He was a gentle, generous, and kind man, someone I had always felt safe with as a child. The day following her anniversary party, she and I enjoyed an early morning hike before I needed to board a plane back to The Urban City. No sooner had we returned to her house did we hear a knock at the door. There he was, Youngest's adoptive dad, in time for a morning coffee break and what I presumed would be idle conversation, having not seen him for decades.

I talked openly about that day back in the spring of 1968. He talked about the day that he and his wife had come to fetch

Youngest to bring her to their home, her new and safe home. He told us about how much I cried when they took my baby sister away and how I begged for them to take me too. He also explained how they couldn't take me because the social worker warned that my presence in the home would be too disruptive and damaging to the psyche of the biological daughter they already had. During the party, I thought I had returned to Somewhere Small not only to participate in Youngest's happy milestone with her husband and their friends, but also to silently celebrate coming home to my birthplace without the need to visit the burial sites of my childhood. And despite the clean air that residents of Somewhere Small breathed, as I took a deep breath after that conversation, my sinuses and lungs burned.

CHAPTER 3

ALCOHOLIC FOSTER PARENTS

Alcohol is the anesthesia by which we endure the operation of life.
George Bernard Shaw

After Youngest left Dad's Sister and Her Husband's house, it didn't take long for a shiny navy blue Cadillac to arrive at our doorstep. Clearly, our new foster parents were enjoying The Good Life; the glossy exterior of the car most certainly represented the character of its occupants. At the very least, I knew we would be travelling in style around Somewhere Small. Although even the most polished surfaces have imperfections only visible from certain angles. And if a couple had a shiny car, it was not an indicator of their suitability as guardians of Eldest and me. In fact, we had become wards of a very troubled state.

Our new foster parents had undoubtedly coated themselves with a thick layer of varnish before the interview with The System to assess their ability as foster parents, and the interview occurred during the day while their demons slept. They arrived at noon wearing wide and warm smiles, which remained perfectly intact as they piled our belongings into the Cadillac. We had finally been blessed with the beginnings of The Good Life. Oh, mercy me, sweet Jesus, The Evil Tree had become a horror from the past! Our fortunes had changed with the arrival of our smiling guardians who drove a fancy car.

Eldest was still the oldest of four girls in our new home, but I became Middle1. Our new foster dad was a German disciplinarian and owned his own painting company, while his wife was a waitress with a chronically aching back. They had two of their own biological children and I was puzzled about why they decided to bring two more girls into their house, particularly since their marriage was as stable as their gait after their nightly binges, another by-product of The Good Life they had been enjoying. By the time we arrived, they had decorated their living room with a polished oak cabinet displaying many varieties of ornate crystal glasses and expensive liquors.

Oh, they worked hard! And they had earned many postprandial visits each night to the cabinet and the treats sitting on the dustless shelves behind the perfectly transparent glass doors, a mandatory requirement of the design. With a quick glance, they could take stock of the inventory in case replenishment was required on the short drive home during the weekdays. They may have been exhausted at the end of most days, but they were never too tired to take the requisite detours to maintain the inventory. From the living room downstairs, we knew the unmistakable sounds of Alcoholic Foster Father's return from work, not from his happy hellos when he opened the door at the top of the stairs above us, but from the crinkling of opaque brown paper bags whose contents were hardly a mystery with the clinking of glass bottles as a merry accompaniment. His grand entrance ended with the clap of car keys on the kitchen table upstairs, a step that freed his hand to unpack his purchases as gleefully as a child who has found the hidden stash of candy in a cupboard.

For Alcoholic Foster Parents, the best part of the day had begun, as had the worst part of ours. They weren't the so-called happy drunks. After dinner, while we watched television downstairs, their moods turned fouler with each drink. Most evenings ended in thumping brawls, which increased in both frequency and duration as the months passed. But the early builders who had taken up residence in Somewhere Small were master craftsmen who knew the importance of constructing solid homes that meant we couldn't hear the tinkling of the glasses in the cabinet or the clinking of the ice cubes in our Alcoholic Foster Parents' tumblers. I fantasized that I was the triumphant matador and they were the angry bulls I taunted while working the capes.

But thank goodness for the arrival of Christmas and the gift of freedom bestowed on me in the name of Jesus. I really had to thank Him since my most precious gift had come in the form of a little green bicycle that ultimately provided me with an escape from the house where evil grew. I must say, I wondered about Santa's plan for delivering it to me. Surely he must have parked it at the front door, because the house didn't have a chimney, and even with one, the noise of metal on brick would have jarred us out of our slumber that Christmas Eve. Well, at least it would have jarred me or one of my sisters from the sleep we desperately needed, even though we were all still less than ten years old. And thank goodness we still believed in Santa, because Christmas was a particularly merry time for The Alcoholic Foster Parents.

Consequently, I doubted they could have heard Santa's difficult logistics that would have been necessary to deliver the bike from the rooftop. But perhaps there had been letters between the Alcoholic Foster Parents and Santa, and in a moment of self-awareness, Alcoholic Foster Father submitted a request to Santa to simply leave the bike at the door for him to plant beside the Christmas tree.

My green bike hadn't been wrapped in a red bow, but I didn't care because my escape routines could begin in earnest after I mastered the balance and braking techniques required to prevent me from crashing into one of the many streetlamps lining MerryAnna Crescent. Mr. and Mrs. King down the street kept close watch on me from their gargantuan living room window during the unsteady period. Each time I collided with one of the street lamp posts and I couldn't breathe long enough for them to wonder if I too would be joining Mom in The Great Unknown, they appeared looking down at me from behind their bifocals, which made them look like aliens. Thank goodness I had inherited Dad's athleticism: through will and practice, my bike gave me reasons to spend as little time as possible in the Alcoholic Foster Parents' house by the time I turned seven.

Their house was only about a mile from "That House" where Mom made her ascent into The Great Unknown. Dropping my bike in the same spot the blue station wagon had been parked on that day in March 1968, I would walk up the sidewalk and stand below the stairs that rose to the entrance. I was never too far away from my bike in case the sighting of a ghost warranted a speedy departure back to MerryAnna Crescent. I hoped ghosts existed, particularly if Mom had become one, yet I still harboured too many fears about my survival in Somewhere Small to cope with the possible existence of otherworldly beings. The human ones I had been dealing with in Somewhere Small were already proving to be enough of a challenge.

With each visit to "That House," I wondered if every occupant saw her, heard her, or smelled her presence, particularly in what had been her bedroom? Could anyone ever feel at peace when they walked through the entrance door of "That House"? Once inside, did the people always feel a vague or subtle anxiety without quite knowing why? And who bought the house after we left? Had it become a revolving door of owners and tenants who found the ambiance there unsettling? If the residents had known about its history before moving in, obviously they weren't the superstitious or easily spooked types. Instead, they must have taken a purely pragmatic approach to being in a home with a morbid history. A fresh coat of paint and new flooring in Mom's bedroom would have covered evidence of the violence that had taken place there. Real estate listings, of course, don't include a bulleted list of unusual events, or more specifically, murders, that have occurred on the property, but "That House" was in Somewhere Small where everyone is a next-door neighbour. On each of my many visits over the years, I never once saw a person inside or around the house, but the lawn had always been green and finely manicured. At the very least, the yard had a caretaker.

I suppose Mom's death explained my early fascination with mediums claiming to channel the dead. Losing her at such a young age, I wanted confirmation that the dead still lived and that there were special people who had an uncanny ability to access the dimension of the departed. I longed for the day when I could sneak into "That House" accompanied by my own psychic medium to see if Mom's spirit still floated about. And I didn't care if she was still dazed and confused, which would be perfectly understandable, but I hoped she wasn't trapped in some kind of harrowing and hellish bardo.

I doubted anyone could be at peace in The Great Unknown when they died from acts of violence. Therefore, I decided she must have still been hovering over "That House," and damn it, I was going to find a way to communicate with her. I didn't have to look for ideas beyond the floor-to-ceiling bookshelves along the living room walls of the basement in the Alcoholic Foster Parent's home. They were lined with novels—as well as *Life* and *Time* publications of a mostly technical nature—but I found the few covering mystical topics such as spirits, ghosts, and reincarnation. If I studied the books long and hard enough, I could learn the language that would permit me to talk to her. I knew it couldn't be English, otherwise she would have been talking to me during my days at Dad's Sister and Her Husband's House and when I walked to and from school on the days I was alone.

During my spiritual apprenticeship, Mom never did communicate with me, and by her silence, I concluded I was on a solo journey. I was disturbed that books detailing such fraudulent drivel could be published, but if The Alcoholic Foster Parents could bring two minors into their home under the guise of being capable of taking care of them, anything was possible. They were just two different examples of deceit.

Without Mom's spirit to love and protect us, I needed to find something else to believe in. Eldest and I, with the two daughters of The Alcoholic Foster Parents, often spent the after-dinner hours in the basement watching television. The adults' drunken brawls were our after-dinner mints, which contained enough menthol to numb us until bedtime. Television sometimes distracted us from the thumping, which for me happened only during the annual broadcast of "Cinderella" starring Leslie Ann Warren. By the time I was twelve, I prayed hard to The Powers That Be for a prince—my prince, The Prince, who would one day rescue me from The Alcoholic Foster Parents. I really hoped he was out there and heard me, but was simply waiting for me to grow up before making his grand entrance. As the years passed, the prince failed to appear, but I reasoned that I wasn't big enough yet to sit on his horse. Furthermore, my arms weren't long enough to wrap around his waist, which would prevent me from falling off our trusty steed as we galloped into the sunset. This notion sat perfectly poised in my list of assumptions about my romantic fate. I decided the prince and The Powers That Be had made a pact because they wanted me to be safe. In the meantime, I needed to cultivate patience, hard work, and persistence before being granted an exit pass from Somewhere Small.

The family pets in The Alcoholic Foster Parents' home were the only continuous source of joy for me and they assuaged my aching loneliness, particularly at night before going to sleep when I contemplated my place in the universe before I was born. I remember shortly after becoming part of their family, a new Collie puppy arrived who looked like a miniature Lassie. I hadn't yet seen the movie when our dog joined the family so I didn't have fears she would suffer the same fate.

She became the love of my life within a day and shone a beacon of hope on an otherwise desperately dark house. Her joy, playfulness, and spontaneous affection calmed the gnawing anxiety that wormed its way through me on a daily basis. The light she brought into my world shone long enough to provide a flicker of optimism about love, but not long enough to calm my fear of its impermanence. Within a couple of months, she was hit by a car and died.

Although I wept for days, we also had a cat, which we had christened with the particularly ingenious name of Kitty. She lived with us for a few years and then one day disappeared. Somewhere Small had a host of predators that could have made a fine meal of her, but we never found out what happened to her. Post-Kitty, for a brief period, we took care of a stray cat more creatively named Tippy because of his bright orange-tipped paws, ears, and tail on an otherwise white coat. This cat was more affectionate than Kitty, who was aloof and remote yet still utterly loveable. She used to stare at me with her enormous blue eyes as she sat atop her regal post on the armrest of the couch. Tippy, on the other hand, had the adorable habit of wrapping his entire body around my head every night during the brief time he made us his family. Maybe The Powers That Be had sent him to the house just long enough for me to feel some modicum of affection to sustain me for a while. If Mom's spirit had dissolved into the universe, surely to goodness some other form of help assisted me through my life journey. Perhaps that help came in the form of pets. I wanted proof of otherworldly assistants one way or another. The notion sat patiently in a quiet place in my imagination for many years. While I waited for the truth about the mystery to be revealed, my two beloved pets provided joyful companionship during the chaotic years in my first foster home.

Alcoholic Foster Father exhibited an odd habit, which still amuses me, and I'm certain it contributes to my predilection for corpses and crime. For as long as I lived in his home, whenever the phone rang, he picked up the receiver and answered, "City Morgue." I never understood what possessed him to do this, but it seemed rather appropriate given the incurably somber mood in the house, which stunk of death and decay. Everyone who phoned knew the house was filled with the dead, or at the very least dying, and perhaps he decided to dispense with appearances since after a certain point the evidence speaks for itself. Naturally, the Alcoholic Foster Parents' marriage did eventually end but not until the thumping upstairs got louder and longer, the thuds a little heavier, and the arguing voices more threatening. Did this happen over the course of weeks or months? I'm not sure, but I do recall the final straw, which in this case turned out to be a few empty bottles and a man. Alcoholic Foster Mother left Alcoholic Foster Father for another drunk. At least he was a happy, calm one, which an objective bystander could reasonably call progress in her relationship trajectory. They would routinely pick us up for visitations The System prescribed, with her new lover at the wheel and she beside him in the passenger seat. It didn't matter how long or short the drive was or what time of day they arrived to collect us. He inevitably had to make a pit stop within the first fifteen minutes to barf somewhere along the road that paralleled The Big River.

The visits could have more accurately been called a taxi service with a drop-off at the house of Alcoholic Foster Mother's mom, who epitomized the role of loving grandmother. Whether we were in the custody of Alcoholic Foster Mother and her drunken lover or Alcoholic Foster Father, her home was a safe house and her love our respite from the "City Morgue." She had made her living as a hair stylist for several years, and as an almost sixty-year-old, she still worked twelve-hour days. She lived in a humble apartment across The Big River from her hair salon and doted on us as if we were the best gifts she had ever received. In her tiny apartment, we feasted on our favourite food of macaroni and cheese pasta. Afterwards, we sat on her lap, sang songs, and ate an assortment of candies as if it had been Halloween all year long, minus the scary costumes, witches, and ghouls. We all snuggled up to her, like puppies that had been separated from their mom for days. With her, I could sleep, feeling safe in her bed. Her affection and warmth were as pure and calming as the security an infant feels nuzzled up against its mother's bosom, feeding from her breast, and dozing to the lullaby of her steady heartbeat. This taste of adoring love fed me throughout my childhood and provided me with faith in the possibility of experiencing it again.

My surrogate grandmother radiated love and gentle kindness, yet all her children were either alcoholics or drug addicts. She had been married at one point, but her husband and his story remained a mystery for my entire childhood. What had happened to him? And was he the cause of their misery? Had he been a cursed man, either through bad genes or horrific circumstances that made him a mean, angry father to his children and an abusive husband to his wife? And did they become such dysfunctional adults through some combination of heredity and absorbing the impoverished spirit of the most important man in their lives?

Shortly after the Alcoholic Foster Parents separated, Alcoholic Foster Father seduced Young Pretty Foster Mother, who became his second wife and our maternal replacement. Alcoholic Foster Father must have thought he'd won the lottery when she agreed to marry him. Undoubtedly, the civil servant who performed their simple marriage ceremony hadn't read her the list of inherent promises she was making to Alcoholic Foster Father during the particularly romantic 'til-death-do-you-part segment: I will love you no matter how many days a week you get drunk; I will stay with you no matter how many nights a week you berate me in front of the children during dinner; I will cook, clean, and be an honourable mother to all four of your children, even though I have no capacity to love them because my spirit is broken and I don't even know it.

Alcoholic Foster Father was a dedicated disciplinarian. His methods were severe but didn't prevent us from getting into trouble repeatedly, which resulted in prolonged periods of purgatory in the confines of our bedrooms. My need to challenge authority could not be suppressed no matter how many times I was sent to my room, spanked, ridiculed, and mocked, with Alcoholic Foster Father's unspoken conviction that repeatedly shaming me would correct the bad behaviour.

As I got older, the urge to sneak out of the house at night when I was supposed to be in my bedroom doing homework was the grand coup until I pursued more creative endeavours with my widening circle of friends. On one occasion, we sat around someone's kitchen table scouring the phone book for what we considered appropriate surnames that merited a response to a question we would ask of the person who answered the phone. We rewarded our brilliance with candy bars from the local corner store after we located "Titsworth" in the phone book and deemed it only natural to ask the man who answered how much his wife's tits were worth. We made a bit of a tactical error on another occasion when we called the house of a woman who recognized our voices and threatened to call our parents unless we came to her house to have "a little chat." She even served us tea and cookies while lecturing us about our most unladylike conduct. She told us it was disrespectful to all concerned, including ourselves, and that someday when we were mature, we would look back on our behaviour as appalling and too embarrassing to expose to anyone.

My friends and I then went through a period of pyromania that involved setting garbage cans on fire, but it ended when one of the local physicians chased us down an alley in his station wagon after a particularly lively fire broke out when we lit his bins. He was an obese man, which is why he needed to resort to the car chase, but fortunately for us Somewhere Small was filled with many escape routes lined with bushes and trees and many other things to hide behind.

The consequences of my behaviour became more severe on a day Alcoholic Foster Father ordered me to take out garbage bags from the kitchen and dump them in the bins outside in time for garbage collection the next day. When I opened the lids to find the containers full, I decided to toss the bags over the fence behind the shed of the neighbours' house, whose occupants I found cranky and stone-faced, even though their daughter had become my friend and often invited me to their house to indulge in the frozen foods section of their freezer. But the man of the house happened to be working in the shed when he heard the thud of the garbage bags as they made their way to what I thought would be their final resting place. On the bright side, I worked my way through several Nancy Drew mystery novels as a consequence of my lengthy confinement doled out by Alcoholic Foster Father. At least my bad behaviour didn't extend to drugs and alcohol. I was afraid the altered reality they induced would be worse than the one I was living without them.

Getting on the seat of my little green bike was the drug that excited my adventurous spirit. I obeyed the rules of restricting my rides to MerryAnna Crescent until I decided that my silent eff-yous to the adults in my life finally needed some form of tangible expression. Since they seemed to lack the discernment to do what was good for them, I concluded they probably didn't know what was good for me either, which was when I made the decision to ride up the switchbacks along gravel roads above MerryAnna Crescent. Although Alcoholic Foster Father had forbidden me from leaving the paved roads, my opinion was at odds with his. I was old enough to begin making my own decisions, and surely I couldn't do anything that would be more harmful than the ones the System or its employees had made on my behalf. Each time I reached the third turn, I saw Somewhere Small from an elevated perspective. It was nestled in a valley surrounded by alpine meadows and pristine lakes, and the mountains bred a striking beauty in all seasons. Wildflowers painted the meadows with fiery reds and yellows in the spring, and the shade from the evergreens provided a cooling respite from the scorching summers. The fiery hues returned in the autumn when the leaves turned to the orange of pumpkins and the red of pomegranates in a final display of glory before falling to the ground. I had made the right decision about following my impulses to deviate from the paved roads in Somewhere Small. Like the seasons that changed every three months, Somewhere Small would also change, perhaps just not as quickly. My little green bike gave me many options to survey the valley from an elevated position. I could leave Somewhere Small.

Although Young Pretty Foster Mother's personality was as tender as a lamb's, she was also the dog who ignored its owner when its needs weren't being met. I would never have believed I could disappoint her so much when I couldn't find the right Christmas present for her when I was eleven. I didn't think she'd notice that I hadn't wrapped anything pretty or practical for her and put it under the tree. After Christmas presents were opened, she asked me where her present from me was and I told her I couldn't find one I thought she'd like before Christmas and lied by saying I thought I'd buy her something in the new year when I found the perfect gift. She didn't respond and instead refused to talk to me or even look at me for what seemed like an eternity but had really only been two weeks. Her silence was no different than the sting of bees that swarmed around Somewhere Small every summer. I just learned to avoid them, and when I did get stung, I quietly withdrew and waited for the pain to subside.

Young Pretty Foster Mother's mother terrified me, not only because of her size, but also because of her venomous temper. She was what historians might call a robust Doukhobor. She spoke English well but had a thick Russian accent. She was as round as she was tall and as tempestuous as the violent July thunderstorms.

Surprise! Her second husband was also an alcoholic who sat like a statue in front of the blaring television all day, every day. His only movements involved shuffling to the kitchen fridge to get another beer. My impression of Mrs. Robust was reduced to a single word (crazy) when she hauled me out onto the porch one afternoon, accusing me of being a husband stealer because I had been sitting on Stoneman's lap while we watched television. I was a mere eleven years old and really didn't have any conception of what it meant to be a husband stealer, but since her face mutated into that of a snake as she hissed the accusation, I knew it wasn't good and that it had to do with what she thought was happening while I sat on her beloved's lap.

Within the next couple of years, I began to go through puberty and wondered how it was possible to develop C cups within a year. The attention accompanying the new curves baffled me since I was still quite content to get on my bike and ride into the mountains with the boys in my neighbourhood. But I was no longer one of them. As soon as the C cups appeared, the boys became clumsy, inexplicably fidgety, and tongue-tied around me. I was confused by their change in behaviour, but the mystery was short-lived. They wanted to spend less time on the bikes and more time inside the tents we pitched during our forays into the hills. Their teasing progressed from throwing things at me, to pinching me, to joking about kissing me, and doing it. The early discoveries about how to kiss and be kissed up in the hills above Somewhere Small was my natural evolution from a tomboy to a girl. But like all change, the passage included some tricky parts.

Young Pretty Foster Mother worked as a lab technician; she often invited one of her lab technician friends and her fiancé to family dinners, which evolved into taking vacations with the couple. The Lab Technician had a wild, curly red mane, and her fiancé's personality matched her hair. We all found him hilarious and fun-loving, and he was warm and attentive to everyone in his company. He played with us tirelessly, whether it was swimming in the lake, playing card games, or generally horsing around.

In the summer of my thirteenth year, we rented two cabins at a lakeside a few hundred miles from Somewhere Small. Our foster parents stayed in one cabin, and the rest of us shared the other. On one particularly sweltering day, the Lab Technician spent too much time in the sun while sprawled out in the canoe that had rocked her to sleep in the middle of the lake. By dinnertime, she had rehydrated herself and taken a sleeping pill before collapsing on one of the two double beds in the cabin.

Later in the evening, my sisters and I couldn't get comfortable in our bed, and as we tossed and turned and yelled at each other to stay still, The Lab Technician's fiancé came to the rescue. He invited me into the bed he was sharing with his fiancée, who had become as still as a corpse. I was relieved, believing he would cuddle me to sleep while his fiancée recovered peacefully on the other side of him. But as soon as I settled into the bed beside him, he reached for my breasts and begin to fondle them through my flannel pyjamas. "I want to teach you how to kiss," he whispered, turning my face toward his. Being only thirteen years old, I recoiled; the tiny hairs along the back of my neck became like those of a cat whose tail bristles when it senses clear and present danger. I pushed his hand away and moved to the other side of The Lab Technician, who had curled into the fetal position by then. Safely away from the groper, I drifted to sleep. Before dawn, I awoke to the bed shaking rhythmically as they had sex beside me. Before going back to sleep, I wondered if escaping the clutches of an undesirable man was simply a matter of putting a woman in his path, and if I would need to employ such a strategy in the future.

In the meantime, there was power in numbers when it came to encounters with Somewhere Small's slippery weirdos, which was how I labelled the single, divorced, or widowed men who seemed to have nothing better to do than spend too much time on their porches, waiting for a certain kind of traffic to appear. They were slippery for several reasons. If they had hair, it was normally greasy; if they looked at us for too long when we rode along MerryAnna Crescent in our bathing suits or shorts, our sweat became somewhat oily (I suppose technically *we* had become slippery in this case, but it only happened when they ogled us); and when we made the rounds to collect donations on behalf of the Salvation Army, their hands would often slip from the middle

of our backs to our lower spines or from our shoulders to the middle of our upper arms, with their fingertips alarmingly close to our breasts. Some of the men's hands shook, mind you, but I didn't interpret their problem as a neurological one because I didn't leave their homes feeling sad and sorry for their condition. At least the collections for the Salvation Army took place in the chilly autumn and snowy winter months.

Other summer vacations included the sixteen-hour drive in the Cadillac to visit Young Pretty Foster Mother's dad. Roy Orbison was her favourite singer, and "Only the Lonely" and "In Dreams" wailed in the background for hours as we headed east. I sometimes stared at Young Pretty Foster Mother in the passenger seat of the Cadillac, with her curly hair blowing in the wind. She appeared tired on vacations and I thought perhaps she preferred looking at bacteria through the lenses of microscopes to visiting her father in the Prairies. But during the first trip there, the changing landscape distracted me from Young Pretty Foster Mother's emotional state and gave me some inkling of the variety to be discovered in the geographies of the world. We climbed out of Somewhere Small along serpentine roads carved out of the alpine meadows before descending into rolling hills covered in tall yellow grasses that eventually led to a sea of multi-coloured crops in the shape of squares and rectangles.

Alcohol had not dimmed Alcoholic Foster Father's ambition. After every break, once we took our places in the plush seats, his focus narrowed to a countdown of the miles remaining. I still can't sit on a long-haul flight without checking the map on the seat monitors to see "miles from departure" and "miles to destination." No matter how fast the landscape moved outside and no matter how many cars Alcoholic Foster Father passed in a day,

38

the "miles to destination" didn't consist of numbers—it was one word: forever.

Although the cool air from the car vents wafted into the back seat, it carried blue clouds of second-hand smoke that supplied us with a steady dose of a stinky soporific. I understood why Alcoholic Foster Father and Young Pretty Foster Mother smoked. It calmed them and must have done other things to them when they inhaled directly from the butts. By the end of the two-day journey, the dizzying effects of the air we breathed provided another benefit: it also numbed the dread about what awaited us at our endpoint. Oh, I understood. Cigarettes were to them what chocolate bars and ice cream were to me. As we neared the Tiny Prairie Town, I thought about the lyrics to the old western song, "Home on the Range":

Home, home on the range,
Where the deer and the antelope play.
Where seldom is heard a discouraging word,
And the skies are not cloudy all day.

However, I doubted that the home on the range I was about to experience would live up to such lofty promises.

I prayed that the Tiny Prairie Town where Young Pretty Foster Mother's dad lived was little enough that there were no bars or liquor stores, which would make getting alcohol too difficult. But I soon learned that bars such as The Crown Jewel were only one way to satisfy the cravings of alcoholics. Everyone within a hundred miles of Young Pretty Foster Mother's dad's house was making moonshine. Fortunately, with one shot of that stuff,

Alcoholic Foster Father ended up stretched out like a corpse for hours on the couch whose fabric looked like pea soup.

I wondered about the other peculiar properties of the clear liquid that looked as benign as water. Young Pretty Foster Mother became pregnant during what would be our last trip to the Prairies, despite (or maybe because of) the moonshine. Then again, perhaps the well water contained the perfect balance of trace minerals that improved the motility of Alcoholic Foster Father's sperm and the receptivity of Young Pretty Foster Mother's egg. And maybe Young Pretty Foster Mother had become nostalgic about life in the Prairies where farmers like her father obsess about reproduction and productivity.

Young Pretty Foster Mother's dad had taught her that booze was as much a staple as the daily bread made from the wheat he grew and the butter made from the cows he milked. And life without an alcoholic man at the head of the table was as strange as a farm without a barn. Therefore, Alcoholic Foster Father easily captivated her heart. At the same time, he gained a drinking partner in her younger sister's husband, The Binge Buddy. Back home, they would alternate houses where the weekend fun and games took place. The breakfast accompaniment of tomato juice and beer became gin and tonics when the clock struck noon. Both Young Pretty Foster Mother and her sister had married drunks. Their shared choice of husbands stemmed from a flaw in their father, and even though as adults they lived hundreds of miles from him, distance had not diluted the damage they had inherited.

Midway into our "vacation," everyone piled into the Cadillac for what appeared to be a leisurely afternoon drive along a pitted dirt road. Peering outside the rear window, I watched the dust billow as the car bumped along to an undisclosed destination.

Several miles later, the car turned onto a grassy path and stopped in front of a dilapidated house. I didn't know where we were and it didn't matter. We were on an adventure and I could feel it in my still-growing bones. Even if it ended badly, we weren't at the ranch listening to party-line conversations, playing the umpteenth game of Hearts for the day, or counting the number of gooseberries we'd picked that morning.

Walking toward the house, I couldn't wait to see the treasures awaiting my discovery behind the wooden door. Once inside, I saw a spindly man sitting expectantly at a large wooden table with an unopened whiskey bottle ceremoniously placed in its centre. As we gathered around the table, the mood inside his humble home entranced me. It was dark in there, except for the flicker of an oil lamp perched on a table in the corner to my left. He studied everyone's eyes as Young Pretty Foster Mother's dad introduced each of us. A withering sparrow of a man, our host paused between introductions and bowed slightly as if he needed to absorb and pay respect to our uniqueness. His face was weathered from years spent under the unforgiving prairie sun and the countless bottles of whiskey he'd consumed with the oil lamp as his companion. I assumed he needed the whiskey to steady his sagging lower lip. His voice was raspy and his cheeks sunken after having lost his teeth decades ago. I wondered if he used to sing but couldn't anymore.

After the whiskey bottle had made its rounds a few times, Young Pretty Foster Mother's uncle disappeared for a minute to retrieve his fiddle from its sacred spot in one of the corners of the room. Mounting the instrument under his chin, he transformed from a sparrow into an eagle. He played a few melancholy pieces as if his beloved instrument were the precious hand of a lover he'd never been able to release. Without an intermission of silence to mourn her, he sprang out of his chair, playing bouncy folk tunes as he jigged around the room with the energy of a five-year-old boy. He had embraced sorrow, but it could not consume his passion for music, a world where sorrow and joy coexist. They are two sides of the same coin, and the truth is, we can't have one without the other, just like we can't divide a coin in two without diminishing its value. Despite his weathered appearance and unflamboyant home, an excitement still dwelled in him that burned as brightly and steadily as the solitary flame of the oil lamp.

A few years after Young Pretty Foster Mother joined our family, she had become like a big sister to Eldest, who by nature was a loyal and dedicated friend to all the people she allowed into her circle. But Young Pretty Foster Mother's moods became unstable around her seventh month of pregnancy. Dinner gatherings became particularly strained and she often ended up in tears by the end of many meals due to the continuous jibes from Alcoholic Foster Father. We all swallowed his tireless teasing, which burned on the way down and settled into acidic masses somewhere in the lining of our guts.

Alcoholic Foster Father took to inviting a married couple to the house for dinners, perhaps as a way to mitigate the dismal dinner hour. I had reached puberty but had not yet learned the subtle non-verbal cues that accompanied philandering behaviour. Eldest had already mastered the workings of the grapevine and had tapped into its ever-abundant source of information about the unsavoury activities going on in Somewhere Small. And in this case, the unsavoury activities revolved around Alcoholic Foster Father's whereabouts when he wasn't working or at home. I never found out how she learned about his infidelity, but what mattered was what she did with the information and the consequences of her actions. Eldest informed Young Pretty Foster Mother about what she knew, due to what she no doubt perceived to be a great injustice and disloyalty to the woman who had become an older sister. The news might as well have been a tornado that ripped us from the house on MerryAnna Crescent, carrying Eldest and me and a very pregnant Young Pretty Foster Mother away to different suburbs in Somewhere Small.

A whirlwind of activity ensued. Alcoholic Foster Father found out that Eldest had exposed his affair to Young Pretty Foster Mother and he proceeded to excommunicate her from the household. The System became involved at that point and finally declared the house unsuitable for two minors. I'm not quite sure why the previous events hadn't triggered the same conclusion, but somehow this particular drama tipped the metrics into the unacceptable range. Word got out that Eldest and I needed to be placed in another home in Somewhere Small. The news skipped the grapevine and travelled as quickly as a wildfire through parched grasslands.

Young Pretty Foster Mother purchased a house where she and her baby would live. I never saw her cry during and after the breakup of her marriage to Alcoholic Foster Father. I suppose the overwhelming circumstances of her life as a single new mother, new homeowner, and career woman meant that crying ended up last on the list of things to do, or perhaps it didn't make the list at all. Or maybe her tears ended up in the lining of her lungs underneath the tar and nicotine.

In a prolonged and pungent post-mortem analysis of our life with the Alcoholic Foster Parents, I tried to understand how two alcoholics could become foster parents, even with the liberal values of the 1960s. What were the criteria that permitted this to happen? Was there even an interview with standard questions that assessed the capabilities of these "adults"? Perhaps asking questions about the amount of alcohol they consumed on a daily basis would have been useful. And what about whether they got physical each night? Not physical in that sense, but in the bar-room brawl way. Imagine the awkward moments with this line of questioning from The System: "So tell us, folks, how many times do you punch each other on a weekly basis? Or does it depend on the kind of day you've had? Are Fridays worse than Wednesdays? And just how many beers do you consume before the fists start to fly?"

I truly believed we might have been better off as street people or members of some circus act where we would have learned how to tame animals or perform outlandish tricks for a captive audience. Certainly we would have gained some marketable skills with this fate, which might have been a path to The Good Life. The path I dreamt about would have been unconventional, to be sure, but at least it would have been better than being locked up with the kind of animals The System found for us in Somewhere Small.

A different fantasy involved spending our childhood in an orphanage where we were given our daily bread and a few pats on the head from at least one member of the staff as they made their daily rounds. Better yet, no interaction with adults might have been the ideal solution if we'd had access to porridge in the kitchen and a teeter-totter in a supervised playground. A simple placard placed above our beds with a subset of Dr. Seuss's beloved quotes converted to "The Ten Commandments of Getting Through Childhood as an Orphan" would have sufficed as the necessary preparation for my exit from Somewhere Small:

Commandment #1

"I know—up on top you are seeing great sights, but down here at the bottom we, too, should have rights."

Commandment #2

"You can get help from teachers, but you are going to have to learn a lot by yourself while sitting alone in a room."

Commandment #3

"I'm afraid that sometimes you'll play lonely games, too—games you can't win 'cause you'll play against you."

Commandment #4

"All alone! Whether you like it or not, alone is something you'll be quite a lot!"

Commandment #5

"When you think things are bad,
when you feel sour and blue,
when you start to get mad
you should do what I do!
Just tell yourself, Duckie,
you're really quite lucky!
Some people are much more,
oh, ever so much more,
oh, muchly much-much more
unlucky than you!"

Commandment #6

"You can find magic

wherever you look.
Sit back and relax,
all you need is a book."

Commandment #7
"Don't cry because it's over;
Smile because it happened."

Commandment #8
"Only you can control your future."

Commandment #9
"You have brains in your head.
You have feet in your shoes.
You can steer yourself in any direction you choose."

Commandment #10
"Everything stinks till it's finished."

For much of my stay with The Alcoholic Foster Father during his two marriages, I thought life in Somewhere Small was like the garbage I had dumped behind the neighbour's shed. But a single event that took place in a modest homestead at the end of a dusty road on the Prairies taught me my first lesson about joy that comes from expressing one's Art, and that The Good Life couldn't purchase it along with Cadillacs and crystal glasses. Cigarettes, booze, and lost love couldn't quash it in the man with the fiddle, nor could the aches and pains of old age. If Art dwelled within this man, surely it dwelled in me, and from that day forward I would seek it until I found it. Did my purpose whisper softly to me in the few hours before sunrise as a chant that went, "Sing your song"? And did its power reach a crescendo at the moment the sun peaked over the horizon, after which it faded and waited patiently for darkness to descend again, whereupon the mantra began anew? I went to bed many nights believing the mantra played while I slept. My purpose would spend many years encrypted in the songs of the morning birds, the squawks of the crows, and hooting of the owls. Important revelations are births that occur after a necessary gestation period, one that requires faith and patience and, yes, even bouts of an unbearable type of morning sickness.

CHAPTER 4

THE JANITOR AND THE
BINGO PLAYER

Government does not solve problems; it subsidizes them.
Ronald Reagan

My grade seven teacher and his wife wanted to take me in, but the janitor at the elementary school and his bingo-playing wife won the draw because they were willing to provide what The System considered a healthy home for Eldest and me. Again, I'm not sure what measures The System used to assess the competency of these prospective foster parents, but we didn't end up with my grade seven teacher and his wife, even though they didn't need the money to care for us. Instead, they needed the satisfaction of serving a cause in Somewhere Small.

Initially I thought it was a great failing of The System for us to be denied the other option, but The Powers That Be didn't make this decision as some form of punishment. In a private conversation with The Janitor during a short drive between his house and the city centre of Somewhere Small, I learned the details about why The System placed us with him and The Bingo Player. They were willing to take both of us, whereas my grade seven teacher did not want the added responsibility of a fourth child, since he and his wife already had two boys of their own. And while I had been convinced the placement with the teachers would have been more suited to my temperament, The System's social research about the benefits of keeping biological siblings together dictated the outcome, even though Eldest and I were not permitted input as individuals or as sisters who reached an opinion as a unit.

Once again, The System knew best, just as it had when it discharged Dad from the psychiatric hospital years before and when it placed us with The Alcoholic Foster Parents. The System's employees and their relatives knew what was best for us too, apparently. Early on during my custody in The Janitor and The Bingo Player's house, her sister clarified that she wasn't our "Aunt," and requested we refrain from using the term in reference to her. Calling her by first name would suffice. But our relationship was symmetric; we weren't her nieces either.

My new foster parents had two daughters, one from The Bingo Player's first marriage and the other from her marriage to The Janitor. For the third time, Eldest was still Eldest but I had become Middle1 for a time. Eldest and I shared one bedroom with their oldest daughter who had already started to develop hoarding tendencies, with her particular problem being the collection of paper. Consequently, the ten-by-ten-foot bedroom became somewhat crowded with three teenage girls, including the reams of paper for lesson plans and remedial learning materials. But when she graduated from each lesson, the paper didn't do the same by ending up in the recycle bin—the piles kept growing. If I spent too much time in the bedroom, I started to see the stacks of paper collapse around me, and when I did, I wandered into the living room where The Bingo Player was usually perched—cigarette in hand—on her vinyl throne, ensconced in a daily drone of game shows, soap operas, and talk shows.

I may not have had a choice about living with The Janitor and The Bingo Player, but I did make decisions about daily rituals I began while in their home. At the end of each day, I cherished lying in bed before sleep, reading some epic tale or another. In the morning, I got up before everyone else so I could sit on the kitchen floor vent that pumped out hot air. There I sat with a mug of hot chocolate, which was a divinely delicious breakfast on winter days. During these years, my spirit danced between midnight and dawn. No matter how difficult I found the daylight hours, I eagerly anticipated books, knowing I would always find a way to read them while the people around me slept. When I didn't feel like reading, the silence of the night soothed me as if my mother were stroking my cheek with the back of her hand with a touch as light and delicate as a feather.

Our time at The Janitor and The Bingo Player's house lasted three years. These surrogate parents were a gross improvement over the first set, but they were also one-pack-a-day smokers who spent more time indoors than out while lacking the space to accommodate two teenage girls. But they were decent people, as the saying goes. The only glee I got from moving to their home was the anticipation of a different summer holiday. I thought The Powers That Be were playing a horrible joke on me when The Janitor announced vacation plans at the dinner table one night in

June before my eighth-grade graduation. We were going to the Prairies for three weeks. He delivered the news with the excitement I would have experienced if the destination had been Egypt. Admittedly, we weren't going to the same Tiny Prairie Town we had visited with Alcoholic Foster Father, where our daily decisions involved finding ways to amuse ourselves while avoiding the adults who pickled themselves on moonshine.

The Janitor's elderly parents lived on a farm on the Prairies and The Bingo Player had an aunt and uncle in a section of the province north of the Prairies. Therefore, I concluded that my fate regarding summer vacations was getting better, if only because of different destinations in a province whose aftertaste had been considerably worse than fermented cabbage. During the first year in our new home, we visited The Janitor's parents, where the most exciting events of each day involved winning one game of Hearts and giggling about the banter over the party line during afternoon tea. We heard of tales such as Mrs. So and So's new dye job that glowed in the dark, or Mr. Somebody who was no longer a spring chicken with outstanding pecking abilities. We didn't know what "pecking abilities" entailed, but assumed Mr. Somebody's decline was uproariously funny given the thunderous laughter of the other woman on the line.

The following year, we visited The Bingo Player's aunt and uncle in the north, which was dotted with pristine lakes and white sandy beaches. The day after our arrival, The Bingo Player's uncle invited us to ride as passengers in his four-seat plane for an aerial tour of the vast land north of the Prairies. Once boarded and with our seat belts fastened, the pilot started the engines; I marvelled at the propeller blades that became barely visible as the rotation speed increased. The body of the plane trembled as the uncle steered it to takeoff, and the plane accelerated quicker than I expected.

As soon as we lifted off, I wondered if Mom had felt the same quickening when she left Earth for The Great Unknown. Even with my skepticism about spirits, I speculated that if the quickening effect happened to her, perhaps she still existed, even though I couldn't see her—in the same way I couldn't see the plane's individual propeller blades after they reached a certain speed.

At cruising altitude, glistening lakes and plump bushes speckled the rippled white sand. The miniaturization of the lakes below made me realize that if I had been down there looking up at the sky, the plane would have appeared as a dot, or I wouldn't have seen it at all if the timing hadn't been right. And that was perfectly fine. Alcoholic Foster Father had already taught me that kids should be seen and not heard. And I could think of many times when not being seen on Earth had its advantages. Being in a plane high above the glistening lakes and sandy beaches had definitely been one of them.

During this second visit to the Prairies with The Janitor and The Bingo Player, I received my first opportunity to experience a teenager's version of The Good Life. A small business in the town where the uncle lived needed teetering stacks of paperwork filed, and they decided I had the necessary skills required to put their affairs in order. The town's population was a mere five hundred, and I guessed my competition was either already gainfully employed or on vacation.

I was intrigued by the paper trail left by the employees and the story it told about them and the clients they served. I was also surprised about the bosses' decision to allow a fourteen-year-old access to the private details of the business. They conducted their operations in the middle of nowhere and I suppose they assumed a nerdy girl wouldn't do too much harm because of her association with a locally respected family. Also, as a transient member of the community, any power I wielded over them would disappear quicker than the dust cloud left by our car as we headed out of town. I wondered about the temptations of adults to abuse this power and if I would grow up to be one of them. I hoped not, and that if I made a decision to do so, it would be for the greater good.

Our lives were relatively normal during the first three years with The Janitor and The Bingo Player, but the calm ended in dramatic fashion when Eldest started dating. She and The Bingo Player were at loggerheads with each other from the day we moved into her house, and when Eldest began to break her curfews in the months leading up to her graduation, the tension escalated. Eldest hated being controlled by a woman she considered an inferior mother figure compared to Mom. Shortly after her graduation, a final confrontation about Eldest breaching the rules of the house ended in a screaming match. The breach pertained to a private matter, a matter that was none of The Bingo Player's or anyone else's business.

Although the addictive aromas wafted from the bakery each morning into the deepest recesses of Somewhere Small, making the residents sluggish from their intoxicating effects, they didn't inhibit the speed of activity along the grapevine, which still rivals the information superhighway. Privacy was an illusion in Somewhere Small, and the grapevine had delivered the news about Eldest directly into The Bingo Player's ear through a telephone call—from whom, no one knew with certainty, though I had my suspicions.

After this event, any of The Janitor's attempts to rekindle the relationship between Eldest and The Bingo Player was like trying to light a wet log. Eldest moved out of the house within one day of receiving her high school diploma. Having packed her stuff into her little green Datsun, she sped off, leaving a cloud of black smoke she hoped The Bingo Player would choke on. Eldest longed for a peaceful family life as a wife and mother, but she became a thirsty nomad who pursued a succession of pools only to discover that they were mirages once she got close enough to them.

During my last year with The Janitor and The Bingo Player, my unfortunate fate with rings began. That Christmas they gifted me with my first one, an aquamarine, the stone of my birth month. Unlike the opal, which has a long legacy of being associated with misfortune and bad luck, the aquamarine's mystical lore ushers calmness and focus, and augurs a happy marriage for a woman who wears one. Called the stone of mermaids, sailors wore them during lengthy journeys because they believed the gem would protect them from the stormy seas. Could a gem bestow its bearer with a spate of good fortune? It didn't take long for me to heave the folklore associated with the aquamarine into the heap of deplorable fiction.

Before long, stormy seas of my own were on the horizon even though I had fallen in love for the first time. Those first awkward moments of learning how to kiss and be kissed, to touch and be touched, are exciting and magical, full of primal mystery. At sixteen, I had unmistakable evidence of love at first sight as an actual phenomenon, and I was about to embark on a fairy tale of my own. The early experiences with my First Love formed indestructible crystals in my eyes, and they would be the sparkling pillars in my ashes. I even entertained the silly notion that embalming fluid and cremation practices in the future would lack the potency to disintegrate them and they would remain in the ashes I would need to claim with my next birth. How had I become such a hopeless and irrational romantic who thought the rules of love transcended those of science? The answer was straightforward: because I was sixteen and needed experience and science to dispense with stupid fantasies and irrational thinking.

My First Love and I were physical opposites, just as Mom and Dad had been. I got my first glimpse of him at the high school in Somewhere Small where I was a junior and he was a senior. I studied his gait in my periphery as he strolled down the long corridor while I pretended to organize the contents of my locker. He hung his head and his body hugged the wall as he approached the corner across from where I stood. Once his back was to me, I turned around to watch him from behind as he made his way to the cafeteria. I needed to see his hands, eyes, and lips up close to decide if I wanted to kiss him; before the end of the school year, I had the opportunity to inspect all three, which led to a quick decision and a much anticipated date. I looked forward to kissing First Love more than wrapping cotton candy around my index finger and sucking on its airy sweetness.

On our first date two months after my sixteenth birthday, we wandered through the grounds of the May fair set up in the recreation centre's parking lot at the end of Main Street. The lights from the rides and games, the smells from the cotton candy and hotdogs, and the continuous laughter of all the happy people created a mesmerizing vignette, blessing me with amnesia about the reams of paper, the droning television, and the inquiring minds back at The Janitor and The Bingo Player's house.

Whenever First Love held my hand on our first date, I felt safe and secure in a world that had been filled with uncertainty. The date ended with a ride on The Spider, which whirled and undulated as my girlish heart had done all night long. Even though I hated the spiders I often found in the shed behind The Janitor and The Bingo Player's house where the rakes and shovels were stored, at sixteen I had found a reason to like them. And I hoped that reason would last a lifetime.

We met several times under the swaying branches of The Willow Tree above The Big River that summer, with the balmy air eliminating the need for much clothing on most nights. What a relief to have finally found a context where I would not be scolded for running my hands over things that appealed to me. And how sweet it was to be ensconced in a timeless state involving lips and hands and all kinds of new and pleasant sensations in my body. The more time I spent with him, the less I wanted to leave him. With him, the past and the future dissolved because the present was brimming with joy, leaving no room for the other two. Where First Love was concerned, the most important property of time was Forever After, which is how long I wanted to be with him. But The Powers That Be had a different plan for us.

During the summer of my romance with First Love, I made a decision to take my destiny into my own hands regarding my living situation. I started to view my life as a series of problems needing solutions and I was getting old enough to become a problem solver. The most pressing and immediate concern involved finding a new home. With the problem clearly articulated in my mind, I got on my bicycle and road down to The System office where I made what I thought to be a simple and reasonable request to my social worker.

"There's no privacy or peace in that house. I want a new home."

"We need to do an assessment to determine if moving you is warranted," the social worker said. He looked tired and I wondered if that was the only way he knew how to express impatience.

"I'm telling you, I'm not happy there. I have nowhere to think, including the bedroom. It looks like a paper factory and the house reeks."

"Let me talk to them and we'll let you know what we find, okay?"

"Oh, I get it. It doesn't matter what I want. It matters what my so-called foster parents tell you about my life in their house, from their perspective, not mine. "

"No, you're here, and the fact that you want to leave them means we're going to talk to them," he replied.

I found out the outcome of the "assessment" when The Bingo Player told me after dinner one night about the visit they'd had from The System.

"Oh, you think you can do better, do you?" she asked, sneering from her throne across from me in the living room. Her forearm was raised in a victorious salute to herself, with a cigarette perched between her middle and index fingers. Striking a match across the flint on her box of matches, she lit the cigarette and dragged on it as if she was preparing to tell me some profound truth.

"You're acting like a spoiled little bitch," she yelled, blowing the smoke in my direction. Although I hated the smell, I wondered if internal combustion started this way and fantasized that it would happen to her if she smoked long enough. I used to hope the couch had a low flammability rating and that a stray butt would trigger a blaze that would cause everyone's speedy exit from the smelly house. But The Powers That Be must have deemed my fantasy as devilish, because it never happened.

"You know, you can't always get what you want in life," she added, as if she was imparting the world's great wisdom.

"Yeah, I think I've already learned that, but thanks anyway," I said, looking down at the open book in my lap.

"Oh, you think you're so clever, don't you? And stop reading when I'm talking to you!" she yelled.

I looked up and stared out the window.

"Jesus Christ, we feed you. We clothe you. We don't beat you. You don't know how good you have it here," she said, using her cigarette like a conductor with his baton.

The fact that I was being provided with the basic necessities of life—food, shelter, and decent people who didn't beat me—gave The Janitor and The Bingo Player a passable grade in the eyes of The System, the same one who placed me and Eldest with The Alcoholic Foster Parents and only showed up when Alcoholic Foster Father divorced his first wife and told him that we needed to be in a home with two parents; otherwise they would have to consider moving us. I guess The System viewed a house with two parents as optimal, regardless of their state as a couple or as individuals. And as long as they didn't beat us, everything else was a matter of inconsequential detail. Nobody's perfect after all.

If The System wouldn't help me, I needed to look beyond its borders to seek a different solution, one I would orchestrate. How hard could it be for me to find a new home? I made up my mind that I would show these people that I could actually do a better job, judging from the precedent set by the two previous placements. The bar was low because of their track record, which made me confident that my job would be fairly straightforward.

After all, I just needed a quiet and uncluttered place to eat, sleep, and study. It's not as if I was asking for model surrogate parents. I might have been young, but I wasn't stupid enough to think that was possible in Somewhere Small, given that my first two foster homes were apparently in the upscale neighbourhood of Somewhere Small. If The Alcoholic Foster Parents and The Janitor and The Bingo Player were indicators of the homes in the rich part of town, I wasn't interested in finding out what life could be like in the poor neighbourhoods.

I would have time to solve my problem during our annual trip to the Prairies since I had already learned about gooseberries and party lines, and I wouldn't have First Love to help me forget about my future. Initially, The Bingo Player and The Janitor were going to allow me to stay in Somewhere Small at their house while they travelled to the Prairies to visit his elderly parents, but they changed their minds—another nasty trick The Powers That Be played on me! I had become euphoric at the thought of having the house to myself and drinking up the kisses and affection of First Love. In hindsight, I think they thought my relationship with him was getting too serious and that I might make some bad choices while they were away, and that the bad choices would end up as unfortunate consequences, just as Mom and Dad's had several years earlier. The Janitor and The Bingo Player didn't have psychic powers. They just remembered what they did when they were sixteen.

First Love came to their house on summer days when I was home alone. My bed became the grass under The Willow Tree, and as soon as our exploration of each other continued, the time-less nature of being with him expanded to spacelessness. When I closed my eyes during our increasingly pleasurable kisses, my awareness of the mountains of paper around us vanished. Each time I saw First Love after the night at the spring fair, a burst of excitement rose in the small of my back and sprung to the top of my head, leaving me with a warm tingly feeling and unladylike thoughts about being naked with him under the starry summer sky in Somewhere Small.

The three-week vacation seemed like an eternity, even more so because the town was much smaller than Somewhere Small and the day's highlight was finding gooseberries larger than the tip of my pinky finger. I read *Lady Chatterley's Lover* and *The Catcher in the Rye*, which fed my obsessive thoughts about First Love. During the sixteen-hour drive back to Somewhere Small, I anticipated reuniting with him as much as seeing a Christmas tree light up for the first time after the tinsel had been meticulously draped evenly over all the branches. I would likely see a Christmas tree light up for the first time every year for the rest of my life, but would I kiss First Love under the mistletoe as many times? The thought was fleeting, and I didn't invite it back for another visit because I was afraid of the answer.

Back in Somewhere Small, First Love and I met in a grassy park across the road from The Willow Tree. We chose "Reunited" as our song while he clipped a silver chain around my neck. A silver heart hung from it, containing a tiny photo of him with an inscription of "Look to this day…" on the side that sat against my skin in the middle of my chest. The inscription referred to a poem he had read to me about living in the moment and surrendering to the inevitable vicissitudes of life. In keeping with the message, he revealed he'd been accepted to a university three thousand miles away; he planned to leave Somewhere Small at the beginning of September to begin his new life there. First Love was about to fulfill his vision of leaving Somewhere Small. In fact, his dreams had always been more specific than mine. In his graduation yearbook, he had unambiguously declared his goal: to leave Somewhere Small and never return.

Unbeknownst to him, I was in the midst of planning my own escape from The Janitor and Bingo Player's house as the first of many steps that would also lead to my departure from Somewhere Small. I guarded this news since my whereabouts wouldn't matter to him soon enough. That night under the twinkling stars, my heart receded from First Love's, even though the silver heart inscribed with "Look to this day" rested against my breastbone. The news of his imminent departure reverberated in my chest with the same burning ache of loneliness I'd experienced eleven years before when I watched the circle of blood grow around Mom's head.

Sitting on my bed at home later that night, staring at the little silver heart in the centre of my palm, I couldn't help but see a red pool form around it because First Love and I had mutually agreed to end our romance when he left Somewhere Small. A timid kitten longing for affection and acceptance, I could not show or tell First Love I would miss him after he left, and instead congratulated him on what was the cusp of a new and exciting life. The primal mystery of our union had become the cold truth that I was ill-prepared to be a soldier in love's battlefield. I chose to retreat instead, with my shaky promise to revisit the battle once I'd finished high school. Perhaps by then I would view love as a resplendent garden rather than a war zone.

The Powers That Be prepared me for life without First Love within a couple of days of his news when The Janitor and The Bingo Player decided to escape the heat wave in Somewhere

Small by taking a camping trip to a lake retreat one hour away. Before leaving for the lake, I paid a visit to who I hoped would be my new foster parents. During my grade ten year, I had a French Teacher who had been born and raised in Lille, France. She was the epitome of a lady who prided herself in teaching us about the culture of her native land, particularly to the eager students in Somewhere Small who craved hearing about the experiences of people who had lived in Faraway Places. I naturally assumed this respect would carry over into a personal relationship with her as my fourth and final foster mother. So off I went on my bicycle to pay her a visit.

It was a hot summer day in August and her house was only a ten-minute uphill ride from the Janitor and The Bingo Player's home. I walked up the paved path toward the stairs leading to an aquamarine door with the head of a male lion as its doorknocker. Would this house provide protection from the lion, or would it devour me? Desperation was the fertile ground for hatching intrepid plans. As far as I was concerned, everyone I'd lived with up until that moment had been certifiable (except for my Mom and The Janitor); I could only hope for sane people to be occupying the French Teacher's home. Perhaps if I spent sufficient time with the sane, I would be normal one day, as long as I hadn't inherited Dad's craziness.

My French Teacher opened the door with a swift sweeping motion.

"Hello, Madame," I said.

"Well, hello, my dear! What a pleasant surprise. Please come in," she said, welcoming me with a toothy smile.

Walking behind her, I watched her glide across the room as she escorted me into the living room.

"Please sit, dear."

I sat on a couch upholstered with a design of white peonies in full bloom on a milky aquamarine background. She was wearing a floral headscarf, a sleeveless top with a matching skirt, and two-inch-high heels. I could smell the aromas of the creams and perfume wafting from her smooth skin, while mine was dotted with beads of sweat and undoubtedly reeked from the stench of cigarette smoke that had clogged my pores from living at The Janitor and The Bingo Player's house.

"This is going to sound a bit weird: I need a place to live for the last two years of high school, and I thought maybe I could stay with you."

"Oh, my goodness. Well, where do you live now?"

"At the bottom of the hill, near the elementary school. I'm in foster care."

"I see," she said. "Darling, could you come in the living room please?" she called out.

A few moments later, a middle-aged man appeared, dressed in gardening shorts and a t-shirt, wearing glasses that rested on the middle of his nose. He lowered them to look at me. I guessed he wasn't near-sighted like I was.

He held out his hand to shake mine when she introduced us and then he sat down on a chair beside her. He crossed his legs and leaned back in his chair, waiting to find out why a young woman had showed up on their doorstep.

"Darling, this young lady is one of my students. She wants to live with us."

He was as composed and as unrattled as she was, almost as if they had been expecting me to appear on their doorstep.

"I just need somewhere quiet to finish school before I leave here," I responded. I couldn't think of anything else to say.

"We will need to discuss this together and talk to your social worker," my French Teacher's husband said.

I hope I thanked them before I got up to leave, but I don't remember if I did. I also don't remember riding down the hill back to The Janitor and The Bingo Player's house. But I did, and summer continued.

Two days later before leaving on our vacation to the lake, I also made a visit to my social worker to inform him that I'd possibly found a new home, but when I arrived at The System's office, I learned he had taken a year's sabbatical. He had spent the first part of his career rescuing sinners as a priest before he decided his skills would be better applied as a facilitator for placing orphaned and abused kids throughout The System's web. His gentle comportment, the steadiness of his light gait, and his attentive gaze told me he was sensitive, but I wondered if the coarse ways of The System were too difficult for him to feel satisfied with the outcomes. And quite possibly, "sabbatical" had been the politically correct term for what was really the beginning of his retreat from a traumatizing profession. Perhaps he had become a dripping sponge that had absorbed too many watery emotions over the years; maybe the necessary remedy was found looking into perfectly blue skies from a chaise lounge on some tropical beach where he could dry out.

His replacement was brash, boisterous, and bold. He had come from South America and he drove a gold Citroën. I tried to imagine the sequence of events ending with his placement in Somewhere Small and what compelled him to choose a French car, but I dispensed with my curiosity about him quickly, given the circumstances. Instead, I explained the status of the situation to him; unbeknownst to me, he had handled all the logistics of my move from the Janitor and Bingo Player's house to my French Teacher's house within a two-day period.

Once at the lake campground, the Paper Hoarder and I pitched our tent; The Janitor, Bingo Player, and their other young daughter settled beside us in their trailer. The August heat fuelled The Bingo Player's simmering anger about my challenge to The System about the suitability of her house as a foster home. On the second day at the lake retreat, she decided to confront me about my actions behind her back, with a how-dare-you physical attack that involved slapping me on the face and pushing me to the floor of the camper, conveniently out of the view of the prying eyes of residents from Somewhere Small, many of whom also made the exodus out of the steamy bowels of the town during the hottest two weeks of the year.

The Bingo Player's response erased any doubt about my decision to escape her tobacco-stained clutches that extended to every corner of the house, even while she was perched on her vinyl throne in the living room. An undeniable truth slapped me on the other side of the face that afternoon: she was an employee of The System and used the income to fund her habits; she was not a maternal figure fostering my care. Fortunately, by the time I was five, Mom had taught me what it meant to foster a child's development. She may not have lived a long life, but she did her job well in a short period.

On the day of the move, I met my South American social worker at The System's downtown office in Somewhere Small before driving to The Janitor and The Bingo Player's house to collect the black garbage bags they had stuffed with my belongings. Before he went in the house to talk to my soon-to-be-ex-foster parents, he asked me if I had a message for them. Clearly I had been watching too many episodes of *All in the Family*, or nervousness manifested itself in a peculiar way: I told him my desire to leave their house hadn't been a "sperm of the moment" wish. My choice of words didn't faze him—or perhaps his lack of reaction was attributable to a "lost in translation" moment, since his mastery of English had only been passable. I told him to tell them I was sorry to hurt them but I wasn't happy in their home. They didn't come to the door when the social worker brought my bags to his car. As he hurled them into the back of the Citroën, I watched The Janitor, through the living room window, hold The Bingo Player as she cried.

We drove away from The Janitor and The Bingo Player's house into the downtown of Somewhere Small to enjoy a pasta dinner before the South American delivered me to my French Teacher's house. He drove slowly along the road that paralleled The Big River. With the windows rolled down, the breeze tousled my hair and swept away some of the nervousness that had been buzzing inside me for several weeks. He remained silent during the drive to the restaurant. Engaging in superficial conversation would have been insincere and dismissive of what had just taken place, and I respected him for that. The Janitor and The Bingo Player were decent people. They filed their taxes with the System on time. The Janitor mowed lawns for the elderly widows in the neighbourhood, and The Bingo Player helped her aging parents with their activities of daily living. But even though my surrogate parents were decent, it didn't mean they were good for me. I couldn't grow in their ecosystem. Their home was a desert and my habitat was a rainforest. Optimism creates fertile ground for idyllic fantasies, and I was ever hopeful about my tenancy at the French Teacher's house. But I soon discovered I had just traded in one unsuitable environment for another.

CHAPTER 5

THE WAR BRIDE AND THE CANADIAN SOLDIER

We cannot solve the problems with the same thinking we used when we created them.
Albert Einstein

My French Teacher met her husband in Paris during World War II when he was deployed along with over a million other Canadians as part of the fight against the Third Reich. He was born in 1918 and was raised as a farm boy on the Prairies. She was a devout Catholic, he an atheist. Based on this incompatibility alone, their romance must have been extraordinary given such a fundamental difference in their values. But my French Teacher became a war bride to her Canadian soldier; they settled in Somewhere Small to begin their married life together at least three decades before I knocked on the aquamarine door of their house.

A few days after I moved in, First Love found me before leaving Somewhere Small. He had been a lifeguard at a pool in the neighbourhood where he lived and I made the grinding bike ride up the hill to see him the day before he left. When I arrived, he was chatting with one of the girls he'd known since grade school. I felt inconsequential and redundant as I stood talking to him, with his friend listening to every word. We said our goodbyes to each other without drama or desperation. Riding in a tucked-down position, my tears couldn't make the vertical route below my chin to become a dripping faucet. Instead they made an arc-shaped passage to the reservoir of my ears, making me deaf while I sped down the highway back into Somewhere Small. I had become a worn-out pair of socks with holes in them that First Love had already tossed away. It seemed as though any impression I'd left on his heart was as short-lived as a fruit fly. With that conclusion, I had only one choice, and that was to push every thought of him out of my mind, forever. I, too, was embarking on a new life. I may not have escaped Somewhere Small, but at least my last two years there were going to be peaceful and uncluttered, providing the necessary preparation for my departure from the town whose stench had become more unpalatable than ever.

Yet The War Bride's marriage to her Canadian Soldier renewed my hope in Forever After. Even after thirty years of marriage, The Canadian Soldier still swaggered a little when his French lady entered any room, as if he were remembering the first time their eyes met in a softly lit narrow cafe somewhere in a quaint quarter of Paris. The Canadian Solider read Zane Grey, worked as an employment counsellor, and exhibited an innate talent for understanding people, while The War Bride wallowed in big thoughts, having proudly read the literary works of her fellow countrymen: Camus, Sartre, Hugo, and Rousseau, among others. Frankly, it didn't matter that their literary tastes were as different as their religious values and that they'd come from opposite ends of the cultural spectrum. The War Bride and her Canadian Soldier made each other laugh every day in between their comfortable silences. She looked at him with pride from the balcony doors as he tended the garden in the summer months; he left her alone in the little library in the far corner of the house to mark student exams and write papers for courses she took to complete her degree in French literature. By the strange sounds that travelled from their bedroom to mine through the one wall the two bedrooms shared, I knew they still satisfied each other as happy husbands and wives do. Unlike the tryst that took place one Saturday night between The Alcoholic Foster Parents after they had divorced (and while Alcoholic Foster Father was married to Young Pretty Foster Mother), the strange sounds from The War Bride and The Canadian Soldier's bedroom didn't make me feel anxious. Instead, they were like a melody lulling me into a wonderland of sorts.

The War Bride's Canadian Soldier lost his sense of direction every time he gazed into his wife's big blue eyes; they were shaped like lagoons and were deep enough for him to dive into. Once immersed, he could plainly see that anything was possible. And she felt safe and secure with him. He was her Canadian Soldier, devout in his own right with his belief in her and his willingness to fight for her and them. Important causes were the two days a year he joined her to attend the church ceremonies for Christmas Day and Easter Sunday Mass. There was an unspoken agreement resolved many years before I arrived on their doorstep. She didn't expect him to experience an epiphany that somehow made a believer out of him, but they would leave the house together, both dressed in their finest. Her arm linked in his, they walked united into the house of God twice a year. I admired the compromise they made on what most people would consider a fundamental difference that has killed millions over the centuries, never mind one romantic relationship.

I couldn't believe how different my life had become as a new tenant in their house. My new foster parents were refined: we sipped cocktails and tasted appetizers before dinner and ate sumptuous three-course meals while I listened to their dialogue about books, world news, and the lives of their intellectual friends in Somewhere Small. I watched The War Bride hold her knife between her thumb and index finger (which I assumed only French women did) and gently dab the corners of her lips with a cloth napkin in between bites.

Within a short period at my new placement, I learned they had weathered a serious storm in their relationship. The Canadian Soldier had been a smoker when he met his elegant French paramour. Despite her animated protestations throughout their marriage, he continued to smoke until he was diagnosed with throat cancer. With the diagnosis, he quit smoking without pomp, fuss, or the usual moodiness, to his War Bride's self-satisfied victory, which in her mind was long overdue.

We used to visit a retired European couple whose house was an hour's drive north of Somewhere Small. They resided in a grand old house on top of a hill overlooking one of the many freshwater lakes in the vicinity of Somewhere Small. Each time I entered it, I felt as if I were walking through a portal that whirred me back in time to the Victorian era. Tiffany lamps cast a mellow yellow light throughout the halls and in each room. The hosts always presented tea in Royal York china, neatly arranged on an antique silver platter. Even though the cups revealed their age with brown veins creeping down the inside surface, the hostess's elegant presentation made me believe the cracks had been part of the original design.

During the first part of every visit, the hostess spoke quickly and brightly, even though the thick accent made understanding her difficult at times. Then without warning, she became mute, and when asked a simple question by her adoring and devoted husband, her lips quivered, which turned out to be the only response she was capable of. On the drive home, The War Bride and her husband would refer to her episodes as "drifts," with further descriptions such as "that one wasn't too bad" or "this one was a little longer, don't you think?" What on Earth was a "drift"? I wondered. The dictionary definition of "the general tendency to change" made the most sense. But this was the noun, not the verb, which connoted a certain whimsy to me, having been teased by many teachers for "drifting off to other worlds" during class. In this case, the noun meant something much more serious than the verb. Her drifts were like the snowy ones that buried things the sun couldn't reach. As time passed, the drifts would bury her mind for longer periods and eventually, spring would cease to be. I wondered if Dad was somewhere suffering from "drifts" of his own, and if he still experienced springtime.

Within a month of First Love's departure from Somewhere Small, I received a letter from him announcing he had begun dating someone else. Well, at least I had received confirmation that the length of his interest in me had been shorter than the life cycle of the Drosophila melanogaster I'd come to learn about in science class. However, I was confused when less than five months later he sent me a bunch of red roses on Valentine's Day. I thought it was odd for an ex-boyfriend to send me flowers on the day of the year that celebrates love and romance, particularly since he had started a love affair with someone else. Had First Love really fallen in love with another and spent nights skating along the frozen canal in a city on the other side of our native land? Maybe he had given her fewer flowers than he'd had delivered to me, and perhaps they were a colour other than red and had died quickly. And she may have been a skater who could glide on ice, but could she dive into The Big River?

As admirable as I found The War Bride in the classroom, her character outside it was confusing territory. She could be cruel, though I'm sure she didn't intend some of her words to have the impact they did. While I lived with her, two crushing blows happened to her family in France. Within a year after I moved into their home, her mother became very ill. The War Bride left in haste to France with the news and was away for about a week to visit her before she died. When she returned to Somewhere Small, one of the first things she decided to tell me was how disappointed and confused her mother was about their decision to bring "some orphan" into their house. Periodically, I felt like a weed in a pristine lawn when The War Bride reminded me about my checkered past with Mom and Dad and the need to be vigilant and wary of my future, given Dad's "unfortunate problem"; she believed only God knew whether I would be so afflicted. And when I wasn't the weed in the lawn, I became the solitary bluebell in a garden of pruned rose bushes. I was the interloper, the one who had taken up residence in a place I had no business being. I was the sullied orphan whose roots were as rotten as the compost in the back corner of the yard.

Despite my corrupting influence on The War Bride's family tree, I developed close relationships with three male friends who didn't see me as a weed or rotting remains. We began lunchtime rituals of eating pizza and red licorice in one of the classrooms. We enjoyed talking about our exit plans from Somewhere Small and competing to outwit each other during the witty banter about the failings of our teachers. With them I had found a safe haven that put a cast around my broken desire for romance. No romantic curiosity about each other fuelled our meetings, which in my mind only solidified the need for the pizza and licorice lunches. During my graduation year, when I was at a drive-in movie with one of them, I had put my aquamarine ring on the dash of the car because we held hands during the scary parts. I forgot about it when the movie was over and when he dropped me off later, the ring was nowhere to be found. Its disappearance was inconsequential since I had no sentimental attachment to The Janitor and The Bingo Player. And the loss of it wasn't a bad omen because I didn't believe the folklore associated with it anyway.

Years later, I connected with another high school friend through an unexpected meeting, which would provide an insight about my friendship with the pizza and licorice buddies from high school. I met an Artistic Colleague when I was an employee of a large health organization in The Urban City. On an autumn evening shortly before Christmas, she invited me to a performance starring one of her close friends whom she'd met at university twenty years earlier. Afterward, the three of us went out for a celebratory drink. As the conversation progressed and the actress began to describe her relationship with a man, I realized she was talking about one of my high school classmates. She connected me with her boyfriend who earnestly provided his own theory about my friendships with my male friends. In my coffee conversation with him, I learned that all three men were gay as adults, and the one that I had been closest to had only recently disclosed his sexual preference. My friend suggested my safe male friends had formed a circle around me, creating a barrier preventing me from mingling with other guys who would have been catalysts for the expression of my femininity and sexuality. I wondered how this friend, now a physicist, could know more about my psyche than I did, given that we hadn't had a conversation since graduation day.

After the brief romance with First Love ended, I spent the next year without a boyfriend. I wasn't interested in anyone in Somewhere Small. But during my final year of high school, a friendship developed with a smart, gentle guy, which eventually evolved into romance. Oddly, I have no concrete memory of how our friendship turned into a romance. I don't remember the first time we kissed or made love, but he was my BrotherLove, a man who was the trusted male sibling I never had. I had been unwilling to remove the cast around my heart, and BrotherLove didn't insist on it. He accepted me for who I was: a broken-hearted soldier wearing a scratched and dented sheath of armour.

Despite our lack of passion, BrotherLove made a gesture to seal our relationship as a couple by presenting me with an opal ring on my eighteenth birthday. At the time I received the gift from BrotherLove, I didn't know about the opal's checkered history. Medieval Europeans shunned the stone, designating it as "The Evil Eye" because of its likeness to the eyes of animals such as cats. In fact, opal is derived from the Sanskrit *upala* (meaning "precious stone") and later from the Greek *opallius*, meaning "to see a change of colour." They were also thought to heal the blind and make a person invisible to his enemies. Arabian folklore contends that they fell from the heavens in flashes of lightning; the early Greeks believed the stone bestowed its wearers with powers of prophecy. Caesars would often gift their wives with the gem for good luck since they associated it with rainbows. Spain's history with the gem was particularly disturbing. King Alfonso XII gave an opal ring to a succession of women, beginning with his wife, only to have them all die as soon as it was in their possession. Cholera was rampant during King Alfonso's time and they all likely died from it; however, the ring was considered the bad omen in every circumstance. And diamond cartels actively perpetuated the myth that opals conferred bad luck when Australia began marketing high-quality stones in the 1890s. Even today, prejudice remains in Southern Europe and the Middle East where some jewellers refuse to carry the opal in their inventory because the majority of their customers will not purchase them. Of course, the history of this beguiling jewel would be incomplete without a sorcery dimension. Witches used the black variety to cast spells on people they wanted to harm. I promised to focus on the positive notes in the opal's history. Besides, nothing can ever be characterized as all good or all bad. How I chose to view my acquisition was simply a matter of perspective.

Three months later, for my graduation present, The War Bride gave me the sapphire ring her mother had given her when she graduated. I was touched by her choice to part with a family heirloom, particularly since her mother had already expressed her opinion about their role as my foster parents. Ironically, sapphires are associated with loyalty, fidelity, and trust. Was The War Bride breaching an implicit agreement with her mother by giving me the ring? Gazing at the emerald-cut stone, set in a fine eighteen-carat gold band, I doubted it would bestow its purported qualities of calmness, mental clarity, and peace. But maybe it would unite me with the heavens, which is why bishops wore them. Then again, Moses had been presented with the Ten Commandments on a tablet filled with sapphires, and his fate had been somewhat mixed.

Fate constituted only one of the variables that would determine the course of my life. Destiny was not like the weather, for heaven's sake. I had a free will, regardless of the purported qualities of the stones mounted in the rings I wore. Stuffing my belongings into BrotherLove's dad's car to make the journey to begin our first year at university in The Urban City, I had consciously decided to embark on a journey in the direction of The Good Life. I was closing an opaque curtain on the first phase of my life in Somewhere Small; climbing out of the valley it was nestled in, I would decide how The System influenced me because my destiny included both fate and free will. Drawing the opaque curtain, I would no longer be able to see the past, even if the impulse to turn around fazed me for some godforsaken reason. My childhood was over, period. Leaving Somewhere Small, I adopted First Love's philosophy, but with a slight modification: I would depart from there as a young woman and return if I wanted to, not because I had to.

CHAPTER 6

REUNITED WITH FIRST LOVE – IT DOESN'T FEEL SO GOOD

I'm glad it can't happen twice, the fever of first love. For it is a fever, and a burden, too, whatever the poets may say.
Daphne du Maurier, Rebecca

First Love and I did reunite one time over the summer when he returned to Somewhere Small to work at the smelter between his first and second year at university. He made the trip over to The War Bride's house and revealed his plans to live with his girl-friend in September. As he continued describing the subjects he planned to study, I became lost in a different series of subjects about what their life would be like together as a couple: snuggling up together under a rose-coloured eiderdown, feeding each other homemade chocolate chip cookies in bed while doing other nice things for and to each other, and being the first and last person they would see each day. Thoughts are powerfully suggestive things; the overwhelming nausea that struck me with the image of the eiderdown jarred my attention back to the living room at The War Bride's house with him sitting across from me on the floral couch.

He didn't tell me about his new love to hurt me. He probably thought I had developed an immunity to the infection I acquired after our hearts were torn apart the previous summer. If he entertained such a thought, he would have been right. In the months after we broke up, I spent hours converting The Garden of Love from a resplendent garden—overflowing with flowers whose assorted colours covered the spectrum of a rainbow—into a wasteland. The conversion was necessary to build the antibodies needed for my recovery. As for sorrow, well, I couldn't have cared less, frankly. I didn't have time for tears. I needed to remain steadfast in my determination to leave Somewhere Small. Shortly after my fifth birthday, I had learned that crying was a waste of water. Only babies cried, and I was no longer one. Since my mother died, I'd started to build a dam to retain the reservoir of sadness, fear, anger, and disappointments from the growing list of adults who couldn't or didn't meet my needs. I learned to flatly accept the retaining wall as an architectural plan that accompanied my birth certificate. However, in my short-sightedness, I hadn't considered things like life expectancy and that I might have another seventy years or so of having to keep the retaining wall intact. I also hadn't thought about any congenital or acquired structural weaknesses that would make maintaining them prohibitively expensive.

It didn't take long for a serious (but not life-threatening) crack to develop when my grade ten history teacher died at the end of the summer before the beginning of my graduation year. I admired his grit, his boundless intellect, and his unshakeable will in the face of adversity. The man needed kidney dialysis a few times a week. Despite his frail physique and jaundiced skin, he stood before classrooms of bored and insolent students to teach us about our country's history and geography. During his lectures, he paced the front of the classroom with a four-foot steel pointer he used for multiple purposes:

1. To show us the exact location of every obscure lake, river, and town across the vast land we inhabited, as he walked the perimeter of the classroom with maps that were curtains for the chalkboards.

2. To break the trance of students whose minds had vacated the premises, by landing it squarely on their desks.

3. To steady his gait when his eyes were closed during a pregnant pause that ushered in a discourse about the earliest inhabitants of our country.

4. To point at the door when he called someone Mister or Miss plus his or her surname, indicating that step number two had failed and it was time for him or her to take a stroll down the hallway (or wherever, because The History Teacher had bigger problems than knowing the whereabouts of his students outside his classroom).

I still can't believe the stick never landed on my desk. My native land's history bored me, but geography lessons from west to east covering the vast and varied country we inhabited launched an imaginary reel about how I thought it looked. And The History Teacher's personality fascinated me. I wanted to know everything about him, in particular, how he could maintain his train of thought and hold an untold number of obscure facts in his head for one hour at a time, when two of him could fit in his suits, and his skin was the same colour as the apricot preserves I'd eaten for breakfast.

It probably comes as no surprise that there was no limit to the score students could achieve on his exams. Grades ranged from a few hundred to over fifteen hundred on his geography tests. The more rivers, lakes, cities, and towns we knew, the higher the score. And then came the time, many days later, when he had completed grading the exams. He would sit behind the mammoth oak desk, his diminutive and sickly body hunched over a list of our grades. He read out every result, with no visible emotional attachment to the highest or lowest numbers. Our exams were never returned to us and he did not disclose his methodology for assigning marks and bonuses. Yes, there were bonuses; I surmised that they corresponded to correct answers given for the remotest and smallest places not included in his list of "must-knows." No one dared ask him since we never quite knew how he would react to questions about his marking methodology, among other things.

He paid a few students for what most people would consider a very odd assignment. His assistants would help him with his home dialysis sessions a couple of times a week. We were basically there to provide extra hands during the insertion or removal of needles in the big blood vessels of his hands, or if a medical emergency occurred while the machine purified his blood. The occasional blood projectile during the insertion and removal of needles was the only scary situation to arise while I sat with him. And it wasn't the thought or the appearance of blood that made me nervous. More than ten years before that, I'd seen my mother's blood stream from her neck into a pool that kept growing no matter how much I'd wanted it to stop. No bloody scene in the course of my life would be worse than that. What scared me the most was the rage that spewed out of him every time something bad happened. And because he was so ill, everyone tolerated his explosive temper. But I admired his dogged determination to continue teaching until the last few months of his life, presenting himself each day in a suit and tie. Who wouldn't have become short-tempered and cantankerous in his condition? He had also been a professional athlete as a young man, and at the end of his life could barely walk up a flight of stairs. It was easy for me to imagine The History Teacher being angry about his fate, particularly after finding out that one of The System's drugs caused his kidney failure in the first place. Despite his volatility, I liked him. Or maybe I had just learned to like difficult men.

The War Bride and I attended his funeral service; the first thing I noticed when I walked into the chapel was First Love and his mother sitting a few pews in front of us. I stared at the back of his head during the entire service without hearing any of the words of remembrance spoken by the officiant. As The War Bride and I left the funeral home arm in arm, I made a mental conviction to expunge First Love from every one of my cells. The timing of my resolution seemed only fitting at the end of a funeral. During our drive home, I watched The Big River flow to the south as we travelled north. First Love had become The Big River during the short drive. He and I were moving in opposite directions. It was time for me to reinforce practical and sensible ideas about love and romance. I wasn't even sure how I'd become a hopeless romantic since I hadn't been drawn to romance novels any more than other genres. I prayed I hadn't inherited the genes for the painful disorder of incurable romantic (of the early onset variety). On the bright side, I reasoned that if I had, my heart wouldn't be able to cope with the emotional roller-coaster and I'd die relatively young.

There was another high school teacher who used to look at me somewhat sympathetically and in a warm avuncular way when our eyes met while making our way in between classes through the dark and crowded halls. In my graduation year, we ended up travelling to The Urban City together for a conference. I took one thing away from that trip, and it wasn't the subject matter of the conference. In a conversation with him over dinner on the night we arrived in The Urban City, I learned the reason why he looked at me the way he did in the hallways. He had been a good friend of Dad's years earlier. He expressed his sadness about what had happened to my parents. What followed surprised me and made me curious about the man who had been my dad. The teacher told me my dad was a "nice guy" with the most fun personality of anyone he'd ever met. He'd never been able to comprehend how he could have murdered Mom because they seemed happier than most to the outside world. I guess Mom and Dad presented the same couples' paradox as the Alcoholic Foster Parents who smiled brightly when they picked us up in the Cadillac. Married people who appear the happiest in public might be the most troubled.

During the sixty-minute flight from The Urban City back to the airport north of Somewhere Small, my mind became a beehive of activity with thoughts about my dad and the teacher with whom I had spent a weekend. My travel companion behaved like a beloved uncle toward me. I added him to the growing list of men I'd met in my childhood who instilled hope in me that trustworthy men were not an illusion. The three-man sample size was small, but I interpreted it as a promising start. Sometimes something only needs to happen once to change a belief. And I had three examples to believe in the character of men by the time I reached adulthood.

Talking to the teacher opened my mind to learning other facts surrounding my dad's destiny; I considered the ones I'd been given had been prematurely classified as such. The events at "That House" in Somewhere Small had indisputably led to Mom's death, and my dad had committed the murder, without a doubt. But how had "the nicest, most fun" guy become the opposite in such a short period? And doesn't like attract like? If my dad had been a close friend of the teacher, who appeared decent and honourable, was it not possible my dad carried the same traits? Perhaps the so-called facts merited a reclassification into the category of specious data. My thoughts about Dad had revolved around feedback from those who loved Mom and who viewed her as the grievous victim of the events that took place in "That House." My dad had been labeled the jealous ex-husband and an evildoer who had committed the most egregious and unforgivable sin.

As a result of my weekend away with the teacher, I decided to seek the truth as a journalist would. I would follow a story of personal interest but maintain objectivity uncluttered and unclouded by emotion. Notably, as often happens, once an intention is declared, providence becomes a handy helper.

CHAPTER 7

THE LORD IS MY SHEPHERD, I SHALL NOT WANT

There is no footprint too small to leave an imprint on this world.
Author Unknown

Middle1 was the last of us to be placed in another of The System's exemplary foster homes. By the time she was fourteen, she learned to turn off the light as quickly as possible after she locked her bedroom door from the inside so that she could try to fall asleep. Even when she did, on most days she woke up to what felt like a bitter wave rippling through her body. The cold spells always preceded the shivers, as if she had been submerged in icy water all night and needed to shake off the chill that had worked its way into the marrow of her bones. This happened to her even on sweltering summer nights when the heat rose and made a cauldron of her bedroom on the top floor of her foster parents' house. But at sixteen, she didn't need to lock her door, because she stopped coming home at night when she joined a group that participated in daily chemistry experiments whose sole purpose was to dissolve life as they knew it in Somewhere Small. These were self-prescribed experiments, and let there be no doubt, The System frowned upon them. While the experimentation was in progress, Somewhere Small underwent a miraculous metamorphosis: the sky remained blue and didn't get dark, because the sun never set. Predatory men became vampires, making it necessary for them to hide, otherwise risk being identified because they would sparkle more intensely than the most brilliant diamonds.

To Middle1, everyone and everything radiated an iridescent glow, making them appear otherworldly, even angelic in some cases. Moreover, her biography was no longer a sad short story. The experiments shredded it into confetti that she gathered up into her cupped hands. She threw the remains into the air, and twirled around and around while the black and white strips fell softly on her and vanished as soon as they reached the ground. Sometimes Middle1 regressed to a time before we moved into "That House," when our mother used to cradle her in a snowy blanket softer than a kitten's coat. During these experiments, Middle1 was warm again and she didn't need cigarettes to calm her chronic jitter. Middle1 had found a way to escape the town overlooking the east side of Somewhere Small where she lived with her foster family, but the more she travelled to unknown places, the more trouble she found herself in. Middle1 wanted to be a mother but not at the same age our mother had become one. Yet she gave birth to her first child before she turned twenty, and she welcomed him on the same day Dad had been born.

In October of the same year of The History Teacher's death, I developed a strong aversion to funerals when Middle1's infant child died from a congenital heart defect. I would become the antithesis of the characters in *Harold and Maude*, the critically acclaimed dark comedy about two quirky people who obsessed about death and made a hobby out of attending strangers' funerals. When I entered the church, my sight landed squarely on the casket, which resembled a white crib with a lid on it. My chin, the faucet, was about to drip, whether I liked it or not.

The pews were filled with an equal mix of strangers and some of Middle1's adoptive family. The minister began his narrative about the infant child quietly and solemnly, a mood that perfectly mirrored that of the audience. He told us the story of the baby's birth in September, followed by a sympathetic summary of the health crisis and heart surgery that could not save him. Thirty-three days after his birth, the child, whose endocardium was too thick and whose atria were unhealthy, entered The Great Unknown.

Unbelievably, the minister presiding over the service looked like a shepherd. Curly, dark hair fell softly around his cherubic face; his constitution was somewhat portly and he radiated gentleness that conveyed sincerity and perspicacity as he endeavoured to lead us to more cheerful pastures. The utterly still congregation listened to the eulogy celebrating my nephew's brief passage on this Earth, with nary a tear shed. Something happened to me between, "He maketh me to lie down in green pastures," and "He leadeth me beside still waters." I became deaf and was transfixed by the tiny white casket, knowing that the baby's lifeless body had been placed in the middle of its velvety interior. Well, I trusted the coffin had been lined that way. My chest tightened and my throat burned as I tried to control the sadness welling inside me. I even closed my eyes and imagined a dark curtain falling in front of the baby's coffin to hide it. But neither the blindness nor the deafness helped me. I'd already seen and heard too much. I began to cry uncontrollably as I envisioned velvet cushioning his three-pound-eleven-ounce body, and the deft hands that would need to wring the sadness from my sister's heart from time to time for the rest of her life. As the pastor continued the psalm, my sobbing continued and became a virus infecting everyone in my pew. We became a sobbing symphony, a sorrowful accompaniment to the shepherd's voice while he read what remained of the poem.

My nephew's life and death brought my sisters and me together to grieve, not only for Middle1's child, but also for our mother and father, who would have been grandparents for the first time. Yet another bud on our family tree would not blossom. In a conversation with Middle1 several years after the death of her first child, she told me how she coped with the loss of her newborn boy. She came to believe that God wanted her son in The Great Unknown with our mother, his grandmother. To this day, I cannot think of a better reason to believe in the possibility of The Great Unknown or God. To believe in something, anything, during an intense period of loss and mourning serves a useful purpose, doesn't it?

Middle1 blamed herself for her son's death because of the drugs she took before and after his conception, even though her doctor reassured her that the child's condition resulted from an idiopathic defect. After the death of her baby, Middle1 never took a drug again. Within two years she gave birth to a healthy daughter and left the man who was the father of her children. She had begun dating another man and moved with him to the Prairies. After that relationship failed, she met the man she would be married to for more than twenty-five years.

Eldest, Youngest, and I all attended their wedding and participated as her bridesmaids. Given the nature of the event, we enjoyed libations and dancing all evening. Several months after that day, I began to dream about Eldest, that she was drunk in various social situations. She had never been much of a drinker, except during celebrations. The Powers That Be were telling me something, but it took seven years for me to find out what it was.

CHAPTER 8

YEARNING

I love crime, I love mysteries and I love ghosts.
Stephen King

Dad's life became a mystery to me when he tore away in the baby blue station wagon after he murdered Mom. Nearly thirty years would elapse before I unraveled it, even without seeing him again. In the intervening period, I was no different than any girl who yearns to know the details of her parents' lives. I used to have a recurring dream where I approached a defunct movie theatre playing *The Life of Middle2's Dad*. I would buy a ticket from a ghostly and sullen proprietor who opened a door with peeling black paint that revealed an older red coat. Each time I passed through the door, he glared at me with an exasperated resignation. The theatre was dark and dank, and the pang of longing to know my dad and the events of his life gnawed at my core as I groped around in the dark to find my seat. I'd make my way to the highest row in the back of the theatre and plunk myself down in the seat nearest the exit sign. Since the day I found myself at the screen door of "That House" begging for help from an invisible but omnipotent being, I built an escape plan out of wherever I found myself, including places my subconscious created while I slept.

The theatre reminded me of the one at the end of Main Street in Somewhere Small, but the seats were cozier in my imaginary cinema. They had high backs with lower back support and a recline option, all of which clearly indicated the show might be long and require maximum comfort. The theatre lacked a concession, which wasn't disappointing because I never seemed to have an appetite there anyway. My palms weren't sweaty, yet I couldn't stop rolling my thumbs or turning my left foot in counterclockwise circles as I sat waiting for the film to begin. I wondered what it would show me about the story of Dad's life—when he started to walk, what his first words were, what kind of cake he hoped for on his birthdays, the neighbourhood kids he hung out with, and the mischief they got into as teenagers. But mostly, I anticipated the scenes of his romance with Mom. I wanted to know whether my fanciful thoughts about their young love were accurate, but I wasn't interested in seeing the scene resulting in my creation (or that of my sisters). And I certainly didn't want to see the filmed version of the final events at "That House" either.

The cinema was quieter than a church filled with the pious in prayer and darker than anywhere I'd ever been. But I always knew when the show was about to begin because the weighty velvet curtains shuffled, and the clicking of the projector followed shortly thereafter. The brightest light eventually shone on the screen, but no matter how long I waited I never saw opening credits or a beginning sequence with an appropriate title such as Eric Clapton's "My Father's Eyes" playing in the background. Maybe Dad hadn't experienced many happy moments in his life and the ones he did have I already knew about.

By the time I finished high school I stopped having this dream. Maybe my conscious mind had finally declared victory over my subconscious with a stop-the-torture clause. The unknown ceased to be a form of torture when I started to view it as a critical aspect of life, fuelling curiosity and wonder. Mom and Dad had become mysteries to me on the last day we were all together and the important questions about them would remain unanswered. What thoughts led Dad to kill Mom? Does karma exist? If so, would Mom and Dad need to become husband and wife again in some future life? And in that life, would Mom kill Dad this time to settle the score? Or, if in this supposed future existence, should Dad feel the impulse to kill her again but not succeed, would he end up in jail, giving her the opportunity to manifest her dreams as a liberated and fulfilled woman? And heaven help us, would Eldest, Middle1, Youngest, and I become their children again? But the laws of the universe do not have definitive answers to any of these questions. They come from the need for reconciliation. I can imagine that we live one lifetime only, and our consciousness does not survive death. But the dreamer in me entertains the possibility that my path might cross theirs in The Great Unknown, back on Earth in some future life, or in some other unimagined realm.

It's important to face the reality of my current life, since that's what I know exists for certain. And although my yearning to know my parents will continue for the remainder of my life, I have periodically received information from distant relatives and life events that have offered insights, causing my longing to wax and wane like the moon. For instance, while living with The War Bride and The Canadian Soldier, I became an employee at an optometrist's office in Somewhere Small during a summer break. One of my responsibilities involved retrieving files in preparation for patient appointments and then re-filing them once the exam and prescriptions had been filled. One afternoon, while I was re-cataloguing a stack of records, I found myself in the drawer that contained patient files whose surnames began with the letters E, F, and G. While searching for the correct location to insert a patient file whose name began with E, I found my dad's card that had been inactive for over fifteen years. It contained the details of his eyes, the eyes he used to find his way to my mom's bedroom where he killed her, the eyes that had seen his children's for the last time on that same day, the eyes that couldn't see the panic in ours as he raced away from the murder scene, the eyes that followed the highway he sped along before crashing into a utility pole, the eyes that had never seen the world whose beauty would remain a mystery to him, the eyes that would not see me and my sisters mature, the eyes that would not carry images of occasions and anniversaries inside his head to become lasting memories of a life fully and fondly lived. My dad would not manifest the dreams he'd had as a boy, dreams that had matured by the time he'd become a man and a father, because no sooner had he reached the age of maturity than did fate introduce a different plan, one that possessed his free will and hurled his dreams into a furnace, incinerating them in the blink of an eye.

Another memory, a more distant one, stoked this yearning in me when I was ten years old and still living at The Alcoholic Foster Parents' house. Two boxes appeared in the mail on a summer day in July, one addressed to Eldest and the other to me. Dad's brother hand-delivered the packages to the house during a trip to Somewhere Small where his dad and stepmother still lived. I looked at the box addressed to me and wondered if Dad had wrapped it himself, if his handprints lingered invisibly on its surface. Seeing the box scared me. I didn't want to know what was inside even though it was small. Maybe the hunting knife he used to kill Mom had been folded and neatly tucked inside. I eventually dispensed with my morbid thoughts about the contents and ripped the box apart. A Timex watch sat stiffly in the centre, mounted like a trophy, but it was small and dainty and a perfect fit for my wrist. The box addressed to Eldest contained the same gift.

Staring at the timepiece, I wondered whether Dad wanted his girls to be able to tell the time to prevent us from being late for school or getting into trouble for not arriving home before curfews. Or did he want to share the torment of his mental and physical confinement? Was it his hope that whenever we looked at the wristwatches as long as we were in Somewhere Small, we'd be reminded that it was the same time where he was, a place he could never leave? If he wished to dish out his suffering to Eldest and me like the sauerkraut we both despised, it didn't matter because Providence became the exalted father, one whose powers far surpassed his, and as such, He intercepted to protect me. Within a few days of wearing my watch, it stopped working. Even with a change of battery, it once again stopped ticking after two weeks. Yet, the gift could not be forgotten, even though I didn't wear it. After several years, I still viewed my dad like the broken watch he'd given me: a useless accessory.

I'll never know his motive for giving the timepieces to us, but one thing we do know for sure: Mom's death haunted him. Mom's twin told Middle1 he used to chant her name, as mournful as the calls of a lonesome wolf in search of its pack. Had he been beckoning Mom's spirit to come to him in order to beg for her forgiveness? Or had he experienced flashes of clarity about what he had gained and lost so quickly? Then again, maybe his cries attenuated his melancholia when it became too much for him to bear, like a recurring abscess that needs to be lanced periodically.

I wanted to have conversations with my grandfathers, because the actions of one created the circumstances for my parents to meet, and those of the other gave Dad the opportunity to carry out his threat to kill Mom. Did they sleep peacefully again until they entered The Great Unknown? Did a burning anger rage through them, making ashes of any seeds of joy? And if so, what happened to the unresolved conflict when they passed into The Great Unknown? Did it become filed in the archives of their souls under Unfinished Business on Earth, with the requirement that they resolve it somehow, somewhere in the expanding universe? I guess it's really none of my business. My job is to resolve my conflicts so that I enter The Great Unknown with a peaceful mind and a heart with cracks that have been filled.

During my childhood and much of my adulthood, I viewed Somewhere Small with The Big River running through it as inhospitable as Chernobyl after the nuclear meltdown. Admittedly, the disasters were eighteen years apart, with Chernobyl occurring in 1986 and the events in Somewhere Small in 1968 when all hell broke loose in "That House." But The Evil Tree hadn't proliferated like hogweed throughout the entire town like the human error did in Chernobyl, causing the decimation of its land and people. The people of Chernobyl needed to escape their poisoned land to find another home, another place where they experienced a sense of belonging and where evil trees couldn't grow. I also longed to find such a place, but finding somewhere to call home and the kindred spirits who dwelled there seemed as unlikely as winning the national lottery because of the events that shaped my early beliefs about what was possible. And yet, I had read the same news articles as everyone else about the elderly couple from some other small town who had purchased lottery tickets for thirty years and finally won. Someone, somewhere wins, even when the odds are thirty million to one. If the elderly couple in another Somewhere Small could win the numbers game against all odds, I would find the places and people to whom I felt connected. I just needed to act in the same ways the couple did. I needed to look for my people and places with an unwavering conviction that involved the time-tested methodology of patience, persistence, and practice.

PART II:

THE ESCAPE FROM SOMEWHERE SMALL

Leaving home in a sense involves a kind of birth in which we give birth to ourselves.
Robert Neelly Bellah

CHAPTER 9

THE WAR BRIDE NO MORE

The story was clearly over, as in juggling when the ball you throw up finds the moment to come down, hesitates as if it might not, and then drops at the same speed of that celestial light. And life is no longer good but just what you happen to be holding.
E.L. Doctorow

During the summer following my first year at university, my relationship with The War Bride came to an abrupt end. As with perishables that become inedible, there are associations with people that have an expiry date. Warning signs had appeared long before the major upheaval occurred. But warning signs can simply be a symptom in need of some remedy, just like high blood pressure is a sign of heart disease but can be managed and even reversed. And following some prescription, a stroke becomes avoidable, just like a relationship doesn't have to explode if the problems are confronted and resolved. However, my problems with The War Bride were unmanageable.

During my freshman year at university I became close friends with one of the women I had met in calculus class. When the year ended, we wrote letters back and forth throughout the summer, during which time I found The War Bride moody and impatient. In retrospect, I'm not sure if it was due to the stress of building a home they would retire in and moving from Somewhere Small out of the house she had lived in with her sons and husband for many years, her impending retirement, or other factors I wasn't aware of. Or perhaps I had become difficult. In one of my letters to my friend, I wrote about looking forward to going back to university with more than a little "alacrity" because I found living with The War Bride oppressive. I had written the letter in my bedroom and placed it under some other papers on my dresser where no one would find it unless that someone deliberately searched the pile.

Later in the afternoon, the neighbours called me to babysit their two boys who lived a few houses down the street from us. They both had curly mops of brown hair and matching eyes the shape of saucers. I took every opportunity to chase them around the back yard until they stumbled from the anticipation of my threats to gobble up their still-plump little feet for a snack. During my absence, The War Bride entered my bedroom with a dowsing rod configured to locate damning and persecutory evidence. When I returned home, she confronted me at the door as I sat on the stairs while hunched over to take off my shoes. She was mortally offended by my lack of gratitude for her maternal care and my "alacrity" about leaving her home and returning to university.

At the beginning of my second year at university, The War Bride, her husband, and her son had all moved to the new house in The Fertile Valley midway between Somewhere Small and The Urban City. During the Christmas vacation, I went to spend time with them at their new house, but The War Bride barely spoke to me, other than a monosyllabic "yes" and "no" when I asked a question.

I found this silent treatment unbearable and planned to leave the house a few days early to visit BrotherLove and his family in Somewhere Small before we returned to university after the New Year. Stretched out on the bed in the basement spare room during my last night with The War Bride, I found myself unable to take a deep breath no matter what position I was in. It was as if a blood pressure cuff was wrapped around my chest and fate was squeezing the ball to pump it up. My spirit was crushed at having failed to solidly form a relationship with the woman whose motherly love I craved. I hadn't simply wanted a bedroom and study to finish my school year, insulated from the family I lived with. I wanted them to embrace me as a family member, but no matter what, our blood types were mismatched. And despite the warmth and sense of belonging I felt with BrotherLove's family, I was certain we would not experience Forever After together because he was a brother whose romantic blood type was incompatible with mine.

When The War Bride and I bid each other goodbye with a cold yet cordial farewell and I closed the door of their new home in The Fertile Valley behind me, the tightness in my chest disappeared and I was certain I would not see her again.

CHAPTER 10

BROTHERLOVE AND A SECOND CHILDHOOD

It's never too late to have a happy childhood.
Tom Robbins

Born in France, BrotherLove's mother was German and his father Italian. His family had immigrated to my native land from Tunisia. Although I hadn't added Tunisia to my list of Faraway Places, every time I looked into the eyes of BrotherLove's grandparents, I wondered what images of the country they had taken with them. BrotherLove's parents lived in different homes in Somewhere Small but their relationship had reached an amicable homeostasis after their divorce. They had shared custody of their four boys, and when we were all together at family events, their interaction was like a room heated to a comfortable temperature.

BrotherLove's mother became a great role model for me. She was smart, adventurous, and kind, as well as practical and stable.

Being around her was like wearing a favourite knitted sweater. BrotherLove and I shared a companionable and filial kind of love rather than a romantic, passionate one, but his family provided a stability I hadn't yet experienced.

BrotherLove's dad worked at the smelter, and having come from an Italian family, the welcome mat to his house never got dusty or buried in snow for too long. He lived in a quaint house along The Big River a few kilometres north of Somewhere Small. In the winter, few days went by without the fireplace crackling, which helped me forget about the skeletal remains of the deciduous trees dressed in snowy covers that turned them into ghosts for the season. In the summer the hammocks were strung between the evergreens in the back yard with a view of the swift currents and steady flow of The Big River.

BrotherLove had a brilliant mind for mathematics and rose to the top ten students in his class. Although I scored high grades in the theory component of my science classes, I suffered in the chemistry labs on many occasions when my test tubes were filled with murky liquid instead of what should have been flawless crystals. My clothing budget also suffered in my pursuit of scientific excellence. Regardless of the length of my white lab coats, by the end of the first two years all my clothing became dotted with holes from the acid that somehow made its way to the second layer.

BrotherLove and I both lived at the university residence for the first two years of our college education. But The Good and Simple Life I had been building with him collapsed in my third year. BrotherLove found an apartment off-campus since we thought life would be more balanced if we lived in The Urban City. Our apartment was located in the Italian section of town, which recreated a comfortable familiarity after growing up in

Somewhere Small. It didn't take long for the chandelier above the kitchen table in our apartment to clink just before midnight and for my legs to feel weak shortly thereafter. Mayhem had been in progress upstairs with the unsteady life of an alcoholic duo, causing me to wake up each morning as if I were going to write an important exam and go to bed as a hyper-vigilant elderly widow living in a sketchy neighbourhood.

Just before falling asleep on many weekend nights, my heart raced as if I had been back in Somewhere Small in the basement of the Alcoholic Foster Parent's house. I left university without completing the first semester of my third year after deciding it was stupid and a waste of time and money to sit in classes without a clear purpose. I was Humpty Dumpty who'd had a big fall—but could I put myself back together, or would I continue to spin in a centrifuge of indecision and apprehension?

I returned to Somewhere Small and worked as a waitress in a busy diner at one of the local hotels. Running between the kitchen and the dining room tables while serving the locals breakfast, lunch, and dinner made my feet chronically achy but distracted me from the endless cascade of thoughts about my vacant life purpose that flooded and swirled in my mind, making me dizzy and tired. After work, when my thoughts began to whir again, I raced up the hills of Somewhere Small believing I could outrun them. They inevitably caught up to me as most unresolved things do. There's as much stagnation in perpetual motion as there is in mucky, slimy ponds.

I lived with Eldest during my time back in Somewhere Small, and she placed no psychological demands on me. But the novelty of a few months of watching television together wore off, as all new things eventually do. Although I needed a respite from the nervous exhaustion after living below the alcoholics in the apartment I shared with BrotherLove, The Simple Life in Somewhere Small made me feel duller than the soggy February days in The Urban City. Weather was temporary, but I wasn't sure my anxiety would be. How on Earth could I create my Art when I didn't know what it was or how to find it? During my walks up and down hills between the local diner and Eldest's apartment, I scoured my brain for answers; when that strategy failed, I ran a route crossing both bridges that connected the east and west sides of Somewhere Small, as if this ritual would coax insights out of their hiding place, like bats that appear out of nowhere at dusk. But my insights were extinct, apparently. No matter how many times I crossed the bridges, whether I ran or walked, and in any kind of weather, the search for my calling was a disappointing exploration.

During my stay at Eldest's, my uneasiness billowed like an opaque curtain hanging in front of the bedroom window I kept open at night. Not only could the curtain balloon with the wind, but it could also twist into a rope and wrap itself around my neck from time to time while I slept, because I frequently dreamt I couldn't breathe. At the end of the fall semester, BrotherLove decided to return to Somewhere Small to join me in The Simple Life. By the time he arrived, my clothes had been hung up in the closet and neatly stacked in the dresser drawers at Eldest's. But by Christmas I began to wake up with the distinct impression I was in a foreign place, and when I opened the closet and drawers to fetch my clothing, the first things I noticed were my forlorn and empty suitcases with wheels that had become miniature spinning globes.

CHAPTER 11

PSYCHIATRIST #1

If you break your knee, you have therapy on your knee, and it's the same for your heart.
Toni Braxton

My family physician in Somewhere Small referred me to a psychiatrist during my second year of university because of the anxiety I developed following the breakdown of my relationship with The War Bride and the existential angst about continuing my university education. Psychiatrist #1 would teach me how to navigate the adult world. While I waited to see her, I fulfilled the second part of his prescription, which involved attending a meditation class to manage stress. Each session began with the facilitator instructing us to lie down and close our eyes. Then we followed steps to tense and relax all parts of our bodies, starting with the face and finishing with the feet. After this first step, I became aware of a subtle vibration in my core and a pleasant tingling sensation in my extremities. The next step involved focusing entirely on the breath and the gentle rhythm of inhaling and exhaling. During this concentration on the breath, a bandit would often lasso and catapult me into scenes from the past or some imagined future disaster. But as I continued to practice, the lassoing waned and I discovered an important part of me awoke while my body slept. I came to know about the peace that comes from keeping my attention in the present moment. I had first become aware of the dissolution of the past and future during my nights under The Willow Tree with First Love, but this new-found experience didn't require First Love or anyone else as long as I was willing to be still and silent, and return to my breath when I realized my mischievous mind had abducted me from the present and taken me somewhere else.

Psychiatrist #1 had been one of my family doctor's beloved professors during his medical training in The Urban City. Despite her diminutive physique, Psychiatrist #1 struck me as tough as nails. She chain smoked, which I found bizarre given her physician credentials, and I often wondered what possessed her to indulge in smoking considering she had often referred to cigarettes as cancer sticks. She didn't use some obscure metaphor to deny the hazards of the habit she blatantly associated with death. Did she have a personal death wish? If so, why?

She held her patient appointments out of a spacious room of her house overlooking a lush garden. There was no couch in this unusual office, which pleased me somehow. I needed to look directly into someone's eyes to confront and resolve the difficult emotions I couldn't unravel by myself. Each week I sat with my back perfectly erect in the plush and finely upholstered wingback that bore the weight of all her patients. Most people could have curled up in the chair to make serious headway on a Dickens novel for an afternoon. That chair might as well have been a desk where I wrote the most difficult exams, because each time I sat down in it, I squirmed throughout her hour-long question periods about all the events of my childhood. When she wasn't puffing on a cigarette and searching for my eyes through the dancing smoky veil separating us, she had her head tucked into her chest while earnestly taking notes with a gold-plated pen, a saluting soldier marching along a page of my chart that sat at a forty-five degree angle on her oak desk. I wouldn't have been surprised if there had been a bottle of cognac and a few snifter glasses in the matching windowless cabinet behind her. A sip or two might have stopped my fidgeting and thawed the matter-of-fact delivery of my biography, which was as interesting as the life cycle of any of the cactus plants as far as I was concerned (I hated botany as much as history). Then again, if said cognac bottle had its secret and sacred spot in her office cabinet, perhaps it was needed when neither the cigarettes nor the garden view could take the edge off the more difficult topics of her own life.

At our last session before the summer break from university, she surprised me after I had lulled myself into the arrogant belief that telling my story to a professional would restore my wellness (or help me be well since I questioned whether I ever had been). And, as long as that professional deemed me sane, my life path would present itself to me with an unambiguous clarity as I shed the burden of my past. This emotional stuff could be mastered as easily as organic chemistry. Consequently, I thought the thing called "therapy" was a no-brainer. And the cure for my anxiety involved recounting my biography to a stranger with the necessary credentials awarded by The System. I could do that. Telling stories had been easy for me, and I actually liked it. In fact, I'd been relegated to the corner in the back of many classrooms on multiple occasions throughout my school years for doing it incessantly during class. I was pleased that something I'd been punished for as a child was beginning to serve me as an adult.

Half-way into my last session, she asked me how it felt to be "cool as a cucumber." My immediate thought was, *What does she mean, "cool as a cucumber"?* I viewed myself as sappier than a maple tree in spring. I cried at Latter Day Saints commercials. How could she possibly characterize me that way? Clearly, she didn't know me and had no insight into the fabric of my emotions, which consisted of a complex weave with embroidery! What the hell was she talking about, "cool as a cucumber"? She sensed my bewilderment at the question and recounted with an astounding accuracy of each session we'd had, the events discussed, and my calm divulgence, all in a tone she described as that of "a historian narrating a BBC World War II documentary." I wanted to ask her if my voice was as appealing as David Attenborough's but thought the timing wasn't ideal.

What did she expect me to do, exactly? Curl up in every corner I could find to dissolve into a blubbering idiot bemoaning the fact that I'd had a horrible childhood? Plenty of people had experienced awful childhoods and they weren't emotional messes. In fact, they were happy and healthy functioning adults. Wasn't I supposed to leave her office feeling uplifted and hopeful? She wanted me to leave her place with puffy eyes and a nose redder than Rudolph's for the entire world to see. And why were we focusing on my childhood, anyway? I needed someone to help me find a life path, not work through her endless supply of tissues. Jesus, I was in a crisis about my future, and she was concentrating on history. Talking about Mom, Dad, The Alcoholic Foster Parents, The Janitor and The Bingo Player, The War Bride, oh, for Christ's sake, the whole crazy lot, would only make me insane and not help me solve my current and more pressing predicament: my future was as foggy as winters in The Urban City.

I didn't curl up in the corner, but I did have a wail of a catharsis. Squeezing several used tissues into dense white balls in the palm of both hands, I made a promise to resume therapy as soon as I returned to university in the fall of that year. However, I didn't keep it until spring, when my anxiety began to flare up again due to my ongoing state of feeling without purpose or conviction in any given academic direction. By the time students reach the third year of university, many have chosen their careers and have engaged in an ardent pursuit to complete their studies and enter the "real" world, seeking a "real" job.

Existential angst continued to plague me, and no matter how hard I tried, I couldn't find it in the Diagnostic and Statistical Manual either (along with "cool as a cucumber"). Wasn't existential angst a real disorder, with the requisite acronym EA? I knew my diagnosis, but I didn't know how to cure myself. And what was worse, if I couldn't fix myself and the therapist couldn't neatly put me into one of the known diagnostic boxes with an associated treatment protocol, what hope was there for me?

When I did continue therapy with Psychiatrist #1, hope arrived with my realization that strength was a derivative of weakness, and the more I expressed my sadness and disappointments, the better I felt. In doing so, my life didn't become easier, but I learned that crying was a sign of strength. The path to wholeness had already been an arduous climb, even though I'd only reached base camp with her.

Ten years after my therapy sessions with Psychiatrist #1, a scandal appeared in the newspapers, which confirmed my odd spontaneous intuitions as I walked the path behind her house to her office. The newspapers were rife with all the sordid details of her husband psychiatrist's master/slave relationships with some of his patients. I would have reached base camp fairly quickly if my family physician had referred me to Psychiatrist #1's husband. If he had asked me to sign a slavery contract, disrobe from the waist up, and proceed to whip me during each session, I would have vacated the premises without further ado. I had already graduated from this form of therapy when the Lab Technician's fiancé tried to feel me up on the cabin bed with his sunstroke-stricken girlfriend in a coma beside me.

The story stirred many questions about Psychiatrist #1's marriage. Did she ignore obvious signs that to an outsider would have set off red flags if he or she had been observing their quotidian life? When I walked by his garden office and saw him peer through the window, an indefinable uneasiness occasionally gripped me by the shoulders and turned me away from his direction. Other times I swore I heard the hiss of a snake in the garden under his window, sensing a threat that hadn't yet touched me but was lurking in close proximity. Even if Psychiatrist #1 suspected her husband's hidden life, they had a long history with each other and he was the father of her children. And if a woman loves a man, she can be blind to his faults even when she's the most qualified person to see them. It would take many years for me to have direct experience with this truth.

CHAPTER 12

ISLAND YEARS

In theatre, they say a theatre piece is only as good as its transitions.
Reggie Watts

After BrotherLove graduated from engineering school, he secured employment on The Island west of The Urban City. I remained in The Urban City during the summer where I worked as a clerk in a small grocery market owned by a British family. One of the sons had come to Canada to manage the store and I found myself attracted to him during the four months I worked there. I didn't pursue any romance with him because I was committed to BrotherLove, but the attraction remained. Our paths crossed intermittently for several years because I'd become friends with the couple who co-managed the business. During my brief time working at the grocery store I also met a woman, and my friendship with her would last for over twenty years. She was my Wise-But-Drug-Addicted Girlfriend. Unlike me, she had grown up with her biological family throughout her childhood in The Urban City, but just like me, she had been drowning in a swamp of familial dysfunction. She had inherited the difficult trifecta: mental illness, addiction, and sexual abuse. Our friendship deepened five years after I left the grocery store to pursue my education on The Island even though she remained in The Urban City during my absence. She had cast me as cold and calculating, a characterization that didn't shock me, but it did make me laugh. Clearly I still gave the impression of being "cool as a cucumber."

After the summer job at the grocery stored ended, I left The Urban City and embarked on another attempt to find my place in the world with what I considered the best practical solution to my career options. Health and medicine had appealed to me since my days of snooping in Young Pretty Foster Mother's medical textbooks that she studied in preparation for her advanced laboratory medicine exams. An applied science dealing with the collection and management of medical information seemed like a good way to satisfy my need to work in the medical field—but not because I was talented at building databases or computers (or anything else, for that matter, given my problem with leftover pieces each time I assembled something). Instead, my decision sprung from the practicality of becoming trained in an emerging field where the demand for professionals would outlive me. I liked the idea; I didn't love it, but I figured liking something implied a promising starting point. Practicality trumped a passionate pursuit since I lacked the ability to navigate my way through the dense fog to find it. I wanted to be away from the tiring bustle of The Urban City because I'd become a pair of jeans, faded and frayed from having been washed too many times.

If there had been any family members observing my professional progress from The Great Unknown, Mom's Scottish dad would have been proud of my pragmatism; my crazy dad would have been oblivious; and his angry dad (who'd become utterly and completely apathetic) wouldn't have cared one way or the other. Mom would have remained speechless and calm no matter what I had chosen, because she embodied wisdom beyond her years. She knew the best thing she could do was avoid building expectations and let me find my way through trial and error from experience and experimentation. Maybe I had trouble finding my purpose because I didn't have my parent's expectations to rebel against in the first place.

A few days before moving to The Island, I received a phone call from BrotherLove's mom who informed me about the sudden death of The War Bride's Canadian Soldier at age sixty-five. I didn't find out how he died but suspected some new cancer had been festering inside him. Or maybe he had had a heart attack. After all, he'd enjoyed The Good Life, which included the finest omnivore diet with lots of saturated fat; and he'd been a smoker for over forty years, which would have taken its toll in places other than his throat by the time he quit. I would have wanted to say goodbye to him and thank him for having been a decent and kind foster father for a brief two-year period. He had even made valiant attempts at facilitating a reconciliation between The War Bride and me. He periodically made his way to have lunch at the Hotel Diner in Somewhere Small where I worked during the summers between university years. Even when I was not his server, we carried on an abbreviated conversation whenever I could sneak a few minutes at his table. He never forgot to extend the open-ended invitation to come to the house for tea sometime. He even acknowledged The War Bride could be a real "bitch" at times, and she did want to see me despite the persistent silence after our last goodbye. I never did take him up on the multiple offers to visit their house and see her in person, even to say goodbye to her forever after mutually agreeing we could not forgive each other. But I suppose I was as stubborn as The War Bride. I had not even had the opportunity to give my real mother a proper goodbye, which swiftly extinguished the occasional twinge to say sorry to a surrogate for being honest about my feelings. The War Bride's focus on my impolite usage of alacrity and my ingratitude for her surrogate maternal care prevented her from acknowledging any fault in her own actions. I guess I could have told her I regretted hurting her feelings, but as time passed, so did any inclination to call and tell her that.

I made the move to The Island and settled with BrotherLove in an apartment close enough to the university where I could easily take public transit to the health information sciences classes. On the second night there, I dreamt about The Canadian Soldier. He was wearing the same shirt and pants he used to garden in as he drifted toward me. He wrapped me in his arms and hugged me as if all that remained of him was his loving and open heart. He had been an affectionate man toward me, and never inappropriate, ever. Like fingerprints, everyone's hug is unique. I felt the signature of his during my dream, but this time, a feeling of love for him warmed me in a way I'd never experienced. If we'd had more time together, I would have been happy to call him Dad and meant it.

Within a week of living on The Island, I searched for the opal and the sapphire rings that I had so carefully taken care of for a couple of years by removing them before taking baths, which I did many nights of the year, even during the hot summer months. I traced my last memory of them and remembered leaving them on the edge of the bathtub during my last night at the apartment I had been renting. *Oh, my God, no,* I thought. How could I possibly have forgotten the only possessions I valued? I called the landlady immediately and she flatly denied finding any rings in the bathroom, and the new tenant had not turned them in to her.

Had my absent-mindedness been a bad omen? With the loss of the sapphire, would I lose loyalty and fidelity in my romantic life? Would I become depressed and anxious? Would a mental fog seep into my brain? And if so, for how long? But maybe the loss of the opal was instead a good omen because it was not my birthstone. For that matter, the sapphire wasn't either. I decided that the prognostications about my life after losing the rings resided in the silly domain of superstition and that superstitious people were both gullible and fearful. Entertaining such thoughts was irrational and had no bearing on the events that would come to pass in my life.

During my university years on The Island, my fascination with death became more pronounced. When the opportunity to visit The Urban City morgue arose during a workshop, I thought I could solve two problems at once. I'd get to see the literal version of Alcoholic Foster Father's "City Morgue" and I'd satisfy my curiosity about what actually happened during a post-mortem exam. Most importantly, I would finally find out what happened to Mom's corpse after her body had been removed from "That House."

When we were learning about lab systems and their operations, a study group I had been working with made an on-site visit to one of the largest hospitals in The Urban City. We toured the lab facilities and learned how bodily fluids and organ samples were processed. Of course, the entire time we were making our way through all the clinical instrumentation, I was obsessed with wanting to see the morgue. When our lab guide asked if we had any questions, I suggested a trip "down there" would complete our orientation. I don't think I've used feminine wiles much in my lifetime but I have no doubt that I widened my eyes and batted my eyelids a few times while creasing my brow to convey genuine intellectual curiosity. "Well, let me see," said the guide who went away for a few minutes to make a call. He returned with, "Let's go" as an answer to the question. The anticipation was as palpable as the private promise I had made to ride my little green bike "up there" into the mountains surrounding Somewhere Small.

Walking down the stairwell, I had visions of Jack Klugman as Quincy, with his unwavering passion to solve the mystery of how the victim of the week had died, which of course ended up being due to nefarious activities of some unlikely suspect. We entered the morgue and were instructed to put on blue cloth booties and lab coats before being allowed to enter the autopsy area. From a distance I could see two pathologists, each at a stainless steel examination table and in the process of dissecting and inspecting the internal organs of bodies. I turned to my best friend at the time and told her I was convinced they were practicing on medical mannequins because the skin of one of the bodies resembled the peachy-jaundiced colour of plastic used to make dolls I had frowned at throughout my childhood. She laughed at me and told me emphatically the bodies were real. And did I think they got out the plastic versions when there were visitors on their way to the morgue? But if the bodies were real I wanted to know why the skin looked the way it did.

My friend was right. The bodies were not plastic replicas. Arriving at the first stainless steel surgical table, the pathologist conducting the autopsy on a twenty-two-year-old woman provided us with a running commentary of her medical history while he excised her organs. She had died from Hodgkin's disease after chemotherapy and radiotherapy failed to put it into remission. The chemotherapy she had been given during the last week of her life had caused her skin to discolour. Staring at the physical shell of the young woman, I questioned whether she would have consented to strangers observing her naked body in a cold, clinical setting where we had been given the blunt narrative of the last days of her life, including her cause of death. And how was her family feeling? They were somewhere out in the world mourning the loss of a young woman they had probably adored. How would they have reacted if they had known about the strangers, even though legitimate students, who had observed the brutal medical exam? And we weren't required to sign medical consent forms before entering the autopsy site. Never were we informed of the young woman's name or other identifying demographics, but I developed pangs of guilt that our presence at her post-mortem exam was inappropriate and a vulgar invasion of her privacy.

The autopsy of an elderly woman had also been in progress at the adjacent surgical table; she had died at home, which meant hers was a coroner's case. Her exposed chest showed evidence of breast cancer, which she had suffered from many years before her death. She'd had a mastectomy on her right side without reconstructive surgery. Her skin was English pale and her body emaciated. While we were there, the medical examiner had not yet sawed open her chest to weigh her heart and lungs and examine their health through observation and clinical tests. In this woman's case, I was sorry she had taken her last breath while home alone, and none of her loved ones had been present to hold her hand before she entered The Great Unknown. We have all heard stories about people on the verge of entering The Great Unknown experiencing visions of their predecessors. Looking at the naked bodies of the two women before me, I hoped their most beloved predecessors had welcomed them during their passage to The Great Unknown. Theoretical physicists talk about death as simply the cessation of physiological processes, with no survival of consciousness. I fear they're right but hope they're wrong. Who among us does not want to reunite with the souls of our departed loved ones when we die? Well, maybe not all of them...

My inquisitiveness about death and my unwavering need to explore distant lands were related. I associated morgues with Faraway Places, not because I had to travel many miles in The Urban City to visit them, but because they were the airports for departing souls. At least that's what I hoped they were. My will and a network of airports were the only things separating me from any place I wanted to visit on Earth, and without a doubt I could satisfy any curiosity once I arrived at any of them. But I probably would never satisfy my greatest curiosity with respect to my expanded definition of Faraway Places: where had my mother landed when she took off from the airport of the departed?

CHAPTER 13

ENTERING ADULTHOOD

With adulthood comes responsibility.
Mary Lydon Simonsen

My first job after completing my health informatics studies required me to move from The Island back to The Urban City. With the transition from student to adult, my relationship with BrotherLove came to an end naturally, like maple leaves that begin to change colour in the final days of summer. I bought a package of clear garbage bags and spent two weeks filling them with things I had collected during our twelve-year relationship. The space between us grew in the bed we shared as my move date approached; and we slept back to back, not like two bookends safeguarding my favourite books, but like two voyagers looking in opposite directions. We sought solace in our private thoughts and dreams instead of in each other, and shutting our eyelids became the drapes closing our view to the uncomfortable and imminent change before us.

We avoided each other's eyes as we made multiple trips between the apartment and my rusty brown Honda Civic on the day I left The Island. When my car was stuffed to capacity, I believed my move back to The Urban City would be the hot iron that would smooth my clothes and make my life wrinkle-free. I stood at the entrance to the opened driver's door and hugged BrotherLove with one arm while I steadied myself with the other on the car door. Embracing him, my heart felt warm, as if I had moved in front of a fireplace filled with smouldering embers about to lose their orange glow. Tears welled in our eyes, even though we would later view our goodbye as a necessary sadness. We honoured and respected the support we had given each other during the transition period from high school to university and from Somewhere Small to city life. He had been my maple tree, sturdy and composed in all kinds of weather. Yet I was about to emerge from a chrysalis that had been safely nestled in the crevice of its strongest branch. But BrotherLove surprised me with some revelations before I drove away. He told me that I was wrong in my assumption that I had lost the pendant First Love had given me in Somewhere Small. He had deliberately placed it on the upper ledge of a closet before we moved out of the apartment we lived in during our third year at university. He also admitted that the next year he threw out a postcard I'd received from First Love when he checked my mailbox on the only day of a semester I was sick and had to miss classes.

I had always wanted a brother and I found him in BrotherLove. When my relationship with First Love ended, I believed I could settle for a comfortable and complacent romance. Passion created too much drama and was too hard on the heart, just like too many saturated fats in the diet accompanying The Good Life. I needed to find someone who had longed for a sister, or alternatively, someone nice enough whose heart had also been broken but who had reached the same conclusion I had about romantic love. Finding a brotherly love in a partner without the passionate connection would suffice. Passion in intimate relationships is the baking soda in pancakes, the yeast in bread, the salt in oatmeal, and the red wine in beef bourguignon. But I didn't care. I hated beef, wheat and oats made me sick, and wine was too acidic, like the water in The Big River. I worked hard to maintain my characterization of an acceptable romance as a steady state with no dramatic fluctuations. My need for passion had died with the disappearance of First Love, and I had found the steady state with BrotherLove. But after twelve years with him, it was as hard on my heart as the soaring passion I had experienced with First Love. I didn't want the arrhythmia resulting from too much drama, but I also didn't want my heart to flat-line before I found both passion and friendship with a lover.

The rumble of the ferry engines caused a quickening to course through my body as we crossed the strait to The Urban City. I had found a basement apartment within walking distance from the job I'd been offered after completing a work-study position there the previous year. With my arrival in The Urban City, I learned from my friends that the British guy I'd met at the grocery store had also been living there and that he was in the off-phase of his on-again-off-again relationship with an English woman. My friends gave him my phone number, and after a short phone call we decided to go bowling. Doing an activity on a first date was a good way to become casually reacquainted. We met at the bowling alley, and although I found him physically attractive, I had been easily distracted with thoughts about the things I needed to do to get myself settled in my new home. Leaving the bowling alley together, the crisp autumn night sent my wandering mind home to my bedroom where my new, feathered bed and John Steinbeck were waiting for me. Driving home alone and pondering the Brit, I noticed the "Dead End" road sign at the entrance to the street opposite mine.

CHAPTER 14

DARK&ANGRY

The grass is always greener on the other side, until you jump the fence and see the weeds up close.
Albert Grashuis

Within a couple of months, I began my next romantic disaster, though it was thickly coated with a syrupy goop and it took me a while to find its rotten core.

I met Dark&Angry at the gym of my newly appointed neighbourhood in The Urban City. Based on our idle chats at the fitness centre, he appeared to come from a decent family. On our first date, we went for a hike, with him leading the way in his familiar territory. We ascended one of the local mountains in The Urban City, which involved a steep climb for one and a half hours. I liked watching his backside more than looking at his face. His features were too angular and too sharp and his teeth were too white and straight. Pretty men had never appealed to me since I assumed they had gotten their way too easily in life because of how they looked rather than how they behaved.

I don't remember my first intimate night with him, other than the taste of fish oil on his lips from the supplement he had taken before he left my apartment the next morning. When he closed the door behind him, I was primarily concerned about whether the landlords upstairs heard my guest and me the night before and if they saw him leave. Making the bed tucked snugly up against the wall, I had no urge to recreate any part of the scene of being skin to skin with my new lover. Smoothing the sheets, I couldn't recall the caress of his warm breath as he kissed the nape of my neck or a tingly urgency when we kissed and touched each other. Fluffing my pillow, I didn't pick up the one he had slept on to bury my face in it to smell the scent of my new man. Meeting Dark&Angry didn't begin an insatiable curiosity about his favourite things or send me on a sentimental search for "our song." I didn't sense a budding tenderness grow in my chest, either. I shivered a bit at the thought of him, but it was winter in The Urban City and I was living in a basement suite with drafty windows.

Dark&Angry's abuse began with what he called "accidents," but they were accidents that increased in frequency over time; additionally, they were as suspicious as the events surrounding a man who becomes a widower multiple times while he proceeds to collect life insurance after the "accidental deaths" of his wives. On bike rides, he routinely spit while I was close behind him; never comfortable with me in the lead, he would often cut me off before we were a safe distance apart. Dark&Angry was my competitor, not my partner. We weren't building common goals as we snuggled up for intimate talks in the still of the night. We were roommates who didn't need romantic intimacy but wanted the pretence of it; we satisfied a mutual need for outdoor fun and adventure with a buddy, not a life partner.

Dark&Angry and I spent much of our time together outdoors. In our first winter together, we made a fifty-mile trek along a pitted and gravelly logging road into a remote mountain setting with natural hot springs dotting the river's edge. Arriving at the destination, we needed to hike down a path to the river's edge where the mineral pools were located. The surface of the snow crunched beneath my feet and then my legs sunk into the fluffy depths. Dark&Angry and I spoke very little as we worked toward the pools that were certain to warm our cold hands and feet. The river tore through the valley behind the tranquil pools where steamy ghosts rose from the surface and danced under the moonlight as we undressed. Dark&Angry and I sunk into the largest pool near the river. I was more interested in closing my eyes and luxuriating in the warmth than gazing into Dark&Angry's small brown eyes on our first romantic adventure together. The ability to gaze into someone's eyes while naked implies a certain trust has been established, but I had already experienced Dark&Angry's mean streak during a jeep excursion a few weeks earlier.

We had stopped along another pitted dirt road north of The Urban City to walk out onto a log that stretched out into a frigid lake. Dark&Angry decided I needed to cool off and pushed me in. The sting in my heart was fleeting as the frigid waters took my breath away. I guess his arm had suffered from some inexplicable twitch causing it to flail in my direction before I could catch my balance, but from that point forward, I decided he would be my exercise buddy only. He would be a companion, not a confidante, a comrade, but certainly not a trusted partner.

We cycled back to the jeep in the dark for four hours. Dark&Angry rode ahead of me for much of the way. Within five miles of the vehicle, a pack of wolves had begun to howl, and soon I could only hear one. His mournful cry echoed under the starry skies as we pedalled back to the vehicle. During the final stretch, I forgot about the spitting rocks my tires left in their wake and the ache in my shoulders from holding the handle bars to brace myself from the numerous pits on the back road. The wolf had called me into the wild, with an affirmation that my journey with Dark&Angry would be a solo one.

Two years into my relationship with him I ended my contract in The Urban City. I had stayed too long at an unfulfilling job that had whittled my self-esteem to the size of a crumb. Dark&Angry reminded me every day about my unemployment status and smirked while he asked me just where my adventures would take me. What I should have done was charge him my hourly rate for writing his English essays as part of a course requirement to apply for teacher's training.

Walking along the paths, my gait steadied and my breath slowed; I put one foot in front of the other, even though periodically I couldn't resist kicking as many rocks as I could until my legs got tired or I started to cry. I finally stopped fretting about the future because anything beyond the present moment was too troubling. The trails looked different each time I walked them, and a theme would focus my attention while I walked. Sometimes it was the mossy moustaches hanging from the evergreens; on other days, it was the variety of leaves and my awe at the many shades of green, yellow, and red when the light shone through them; at other times it was the animal images I saw in the twisted knots of tree trunks and branches. Perhaps I needed to view life the same way—I needed to decide what to focus on. I had quit a job that bored me but had chosen to be with Dark&Angry. I needed to solve one problem at a time. My first problem was to re-enter my profession by finding an interesting project.

I accepted a short-term position to cover the maternity leave of a staff member in The Trauma Registry at one of the large hospitals in The Urban City. It didn't take long for me to become acquainted with the forensic pathologist whose office was a few floors above the registry. On a Friday afternoon, when no one else was around, he popped in for a visit. After explaining some of the cases he had been investigating and answering my barrage of questions, he invited me to view some of the forensic evidence associated with them. When we walked into his office, I couldn't believe it—every wall was covered with graphic photos of death scenes. He proceeded to methodically describe each case, working in a clockwise direction, starting with the wall to the left of the office entrance. I asked him how he could sleep after spending all day surrounded by such gory images. He explained in a matter-of-fact manner that the pictures weren't of his friends or family—they were people who had met a gruesome death and he considered it his service to humanity as a provider of truth culminating in justice. The truth shatters illusions. Lies never do that. They don't liberate anything and they bury beauty and light. His job was to unveil the truth. In that moment I understood why I was attracted to pathologists.

While I was working at the registry, Dark&Angry and I planned a nine-hundred-mile bike trip along the Pacific Coast Highway, beginning in Astoria, Oregon and ending in San Francisco. My trainer thought the goal was too ambitious for a woman with weak wrists but he vowed to help me make them and my shoulders stronger to improve my chances at completing the ride in twelve days. For the second time in my life, I had found a goal that mattered to me. Completing it with Dark&Angry was a matter of logistics only, since finding Forever After with each other was as likely as a jaunt to Mars. But no matter how weak my wrists were and no matter how many hills we had to climb in the last half of the trip, I saw myself at the crest of the Golden Gate Bridge on day twelve as a matter of fact; it didn't matter whether I walked, limped, or crawled to get there. I would do the bike trip within our goal, whether my trainer thought I could or not. This achievement was not a matter of fate. It was a matter of will. And fate was not its master. I was.

We made full use of the meter-wide bike lane for all five hundred and ninety-five kilometres of the Oregon coastline. But the difficulty of the trip changed as soon as we crossed into California. The trainer was right about the last half being the hardest. The elevation climbs into the mountains in the north lasted for hours and we had to endure searing heat that melted my confidence and determination. Despite being in prime condition during these mountain passages, at times I didn't have the horsepower in my legs to pedal the steepest sections. Instead of complaining about lacking the physical strength to cycle the hills, I dismounted the bike and pushed it until I was ready to ride again. The hills could have been a punishing behemoth about to kill me, but I didn't care. At least I'd die moving and not in the clutches of one of The System's health care facilities, where I lacked the physical or mental strength to escape.

The heat in the mountains and the wind along the coast delayed our schedule, which meant we needed to cycle over two hundred miles on the last two days. On the last day, we treated ourselves to breakfast at a local diner on a bay glistening under the morning sun. I had already declared victory when we sat in the shade on a lawn as tidy as a golf course to eat granola bars and suck on our chocolate milkshakes. After the morning feast, I lay on the grass and stared into the vastness of the blue sky while the warmth of the sun sank into my aching thighs. Dark&Angry and I didn't walk hand in hand to the waterfront and embrace each other while whispering about how proud we were of each other and how we would celebrate our shared victory as a couple once we checked into our hotel. Strangers observing us from a distance might not have realized we were a couple, let alone travelling together.

By noon I realized I had declared victory prematurely. We underestimated the degree of difficulty of the ride between a sea-level beach community and a city that led to the Golden Gate Bridge. The route led us into a series of switchbacks that, if viewed from a map, would have resembled the crisscross pattern of a garland on a Christmas tree or the snowy tracks of the Grinch's path to Whoville. I desperately wanted to curl up into a shivering ball on the Grinch's sled for the last five hours of the ride due to the growing nausea from the indulgences at breakfast and my malfunctioning thermostat.

With each mile, my attitude oscillated like a metronome that went from *You can do it* to *I think I'm going to die*. And my actions followed suit: one moment I was sitting beside the road crying and refusing to move (and thinking, *Yes, it would be symbolic to die right now since it's close to sunset and the sun and I can go down together*); the next moment I was muttering something about not caring how long it took me to get to the bloody Golden Gate Bridge, even if I had to walk the rest of the way. Once I returned to The

Urban City, I would stuff what remained of my cycling shorts in the bastard of a trainer's mouth who counselled me to be happy with the attempt but unattached to completing my goal.

But Christmas did come on that July evening as we dropped from the garland under California's Christmas tree and caught a glimpse of the Golden Gate Bridge, which resembled a garnish on a sunset cocktail. I dismounted my bike at the crown of the pedestrian path and Dark&Angry continued riding. Holding onto the railing, I looked down and saw a mesh drape that looked like a gigantic hammock. But it wasn't a resting place. I knew it was there to catch desperate souls, and I hoped it also caught their dreams and restored them before The System's rescuers arrived. I looked up and closed my eyes. My body buzzed from the many days of over-exertion, but the wind from the bay whisked it away, leaving me bodiless and floating above the bay before it was dark enough to see the stars. The chilly air made me shiver and told me I had arrived, but it was time to go. Gazing out at the Pacific Ocean to the west, night had begun to put the bay to sleep with a blanket of fog that was working its way toward us. Cycling to the entrance of the city shook me out of my sweaty delirium. By the time I had reached the other side of the bridge, Dark&Angry was standing in front of a locked gate. San Francisco didn't want us. Fortunately, a security guard had still been in the process of closing the day's business in a rickety booth hanging precariously from the iconic bridge. He granted us access into a city I wished had been flat. I had grown tired of hills and climbing them with someone who was challenging to be around most of the time. Yet I had become a stonecutter with the sun and wind acting as my chisel and hammer that chipped away at doubt while I rode for twelve days. I could succeed at a goal through determination and grit. And perhaps my prior lack of commitment had more to do with the things I pursued rather than from a deficiency of will. I just needed to identify things worth my investment and commitment. Whatever directions I followed in my future, completing the bike ride was my jewel cap that held the compass needle of my life intact. It was the strength that came from knowing I could complete something hard, as long as it mattered to me.

Once settled in our hotel at the midway point of the longest street in San Francisco, Dark&Angry and I showered separately. I crawled into bed and rested on my side with my back to my travel mate. I had never been more grateful for the comfort of an inanimate object but couldn't say the same about the living one beside me.

CHAPTER 15

THE TRUTH ABOUT DAD

Death is no more than passing from one room into another. But there's a difference for me, you know. Because in that other room I shall be able to see.
Helen Keller

My next job assignment was at a cancer clinic in the valley south of The Urban City. Within a few weeks of my arrival, one of the pathologists found his way to my office, which gave me ample opportunity to once again delve into the real-life stories of the morgue. He made a point of calling me downstairs when he was working on interesting or unusual cases. The first time he called, I couldn't resist the offer, despite the recurring guilt about privacy. The patient was an infant who had died shortly after her birth. Seeing the baby, I gripped the gurney with both hands to prevent myself from fainting. She was perfect and beautifully whole, but still. I became weak, as if all the arteries and veins in my body had disintegrated and every drop of blood had flooded my feet. I envisioned the mother in a hospital bed somewhere above us while the medical examiner spoke about her history, including four abortions and a miscarriage. The baby had been birthed using forceps, and the pathologist's job was to determine whether the procedure or a congenital problem had caused her death. My friend took gentle care of this baby during the autopsy, even though the procedure is harsh and gruesome. I was awestruck by the utter perfection of each of the baby's organs as my friend removed and examined them according to protocol. The exam did prove the baby had died from a fatal brain hemorrhage as a result of the forceps procedure. I still wish I didn't know the truth about the baby's death and that two women would suffer for an indeterminable amount of time: the mother who carried her for forty weeks, and the women who birthed her and accidentally caused her death.

On July 23, 1995, not long after the baby's autopsy, I received a call from Island Aunt.

"I have some bad news," she said in a barely audible voice. She was silent for a few moments, which gave me the opportunity to take a deep breath and sit down on the green leather couch. I put a pillow on my thighs to rest my elbows on, but my legs still shook as if I had just sprinted up the steep road outside our basement apartment.

"What?" I asked.

"Your dad died," she said simply, without prefacing the news with, "I'm sorry."

"How did he die?" I inquired.

"Well, you know he was in a long-term care facility for many years, and he had a brain injury from years ago," she reminded me.

"Yes, I know, I realize that, but how did he die?" I asked again.

"Aspiration pneumonia," she replied without hesitation and with clinical certainty. I looked out the basement window that had a sliver of a view to the cloudless afternoon sky.

"Thanks for letting me know. I'll call my sisters."

"Okay," Island Aunt responded.

Neither of us pursued a longer conversation. The necessary information had been exchanged with the blandness of binary code. I didn't ask about funeral arrangements and she didn't divulge the plans, if there were any at all. After a brief silent period, we bid each other goodbye.

Sometimes the shortest silent periods between two people are the most awkward, and the closure of my conversation with Island Aunt had been one of them. When I pushed the red button on the receiver to end the call, I realized that silences between two people as punctuation during conversations about uncomfortable topics don't always stem from a lack of concern, empathy, or disinterest. Both my mother and father's families ended conversations with me after the murder, and I'd had decades to understand that their silence hadn't been due to indifference. They just didn't know what to say. Their disappearance also didn't mean none of them cared about me, either. It meant they also didn't know what to do. With nothing to say or do, walking away was the natural next step in my relationship with them.

As if I were at his grave reading his epitaph, four words engraved in stone flashed before me: Husband, Father, Brother, Murderer. With his death and burial, I could carry on with my life, unencumbered by the past. I pictured Dad's optometry card with "DECEASED" in capital letters scrawled diagonally with a red pen over the three-by-five index card. Even though his eyelids were closed and would decay with the rest of his body, he had lost his vision years ago when he stopped seeing the world as a reasonable man. I knew a diagnosis of aspiration pneumonia meant he had developed inflammation in his lungs and airways as a consequence of inhaling foreign material such as food, vomit, saliva, or some other liquid. I didn't know what had happened to Dad's physical remains until I asked Middle1 many years later. Unlike Mom's, his body had been buried in the family plot in the old cemetery above Somewhere Small.

Alone with my thoughts, I lifted my legs and hugged my knees against my chest. I took a deep breath, and as I exhaled, I rose from the couch and walked to the kitchen. I put the kettle on to make a cup of tea and then returned to the living room, sat on the floor, and stole another glimpse of the sliver of blue sky before making the calls. It was around three in the afternoon when I keyed in Eldest's number and leaned my back against the couch. The phone rang several times before she answered. I panicked when I detected a slur in her speech. Why did she sound drunk at three o'clock in the afternoon?

"You sound tired. How are you?" I asked her.

"I just woke up from a nap," she slurred.

I had never known her to take naps or to be much of a drinker. But she had seemed depressed in recent years when the beginning of her adult life had not resulted in marriage and motherhood.

"I wanted to talk to you about our dad. Island Aunt just called me with news that he died," I explained.

"Oh," she replied in a voice devoid of anger, sadness, or even relief, which surprised me because she had often expressed disgust with any mention of him. Her reaction to Dad's death was no different than if I had recited a randomly selected obituary from The Urban City newspaper. I leaned forward, as if doing so would increase my powers of perception to decode the reason for Eldest's slurred speech.

"What are you up to these days?" I asked, hoping that as the conversation continued her voice would return to normal.

"Not much. I'm not working, and I don't go out much."

With those few words from Eldest, my hope disappeared as quickly as a snowflake landing on wet pavement.

"I gotta go," she announced.

Within two minutes, Eldest wanted to end the conversation; although it was brief, we had just spoken more than we had in the previous five years.

Even though it was warm in the basement suite, the palm of my hand holding the receiver had become cold and clammy. Cross-legged and hunched over on the living room floor, I stared at Eldest's phone number while I replayed our short conversation in my mind. Had she been taking tranquilizers to calm the anxiety from the existential angst she may have been feeling or to assuage life's disappointments in general? My intuitive responses to the questions were "No" and "No." But what was the reason then? I didn't know what was happening to Eldest, but my fear about her fate was an elephant in the room that was also sitting on my chest. And before drifting off to sleep that night, I could have sworn I saw a black balloon burst. And it didn't contain benign air, either. An inky sludge sprayed above me and rained blackness on what had been a perfect summer day. I knew Eldest's slurred speech had nothing to do with drugs, alcohol, or residual grogginess from an afternoon nap.

I also knew her slurred speech had a more troubling explanation because of what I experienced while we spoke. It felt as if I were doing somersaults on one of the many lawns along MerryAnna Crescent in Somewhere Small. While we talked, my eyes were not closed and I wasn't lost in a reverie about gymnastics. They were wide open and fully dilated; if anyone could have looked into them as I held the receiver to my ear, they would have wondered what on Earth had made me so afraid and so sad. I didn't know the reason either, but I was about to find out.

I did call Youngest and Middle1, but I have no recollection of my conversations with either of them.

Because of the tumbling sensation in my stomach after my conversation with Island Aunt, I decided I wanted to talk to Dad's physician directly about the events surrounding his death. Subjectivity, denial, shame, and many other things cloud the truth sometimes. And it was time for the sun to shine on objectivity. Specifically, I wanted to know how The System would code Dad's underlying cause of death. My aunt told me the truth about Dad's primary cause, but the truth resided beyond the primary or even secondary causes and in the oldest branches of our family tree. I called her back and asked for Dad's physician's name and phone number and decided to call him over the lunch break while attending a medical informatics conference the next day.

Dark&Angry drove me to the terminal where I caught a ferry to The Urban City centre. He didn't open my door and hug me before I made the journey across the inlet. We had stopped kissing and hugging each other several months before, and for us to feign affection in the midst of a personal crisis would have been a depressing one-star performance. Besides, I had already discovered that placing any trust in him during a period of emotional vulnerability was tantamount to putting my savings into the hands of a thief. We had stopped playing our roles in the couples' paradox.

It was a radiant day in The Urban City, yet my mood matched that of the squawking seagulls circling the ferry as it headed south. I sat down in a seat near a window with a view to the west. I squirmed and fidgeted but lacked the energy to stand. My stomach fluttered while I walked at a fast pace to the conference venue. When I crossed the same waterway going in the other direction later in the day, the events between crossings would cause me to insert an addendum to the chapter of my life called "What I thought about my dad." And I hoped the chapters following "The Truth about Dad" would tell stories about the last half of a life that had been filled with kept promises and truths that didn't take decades to be unveiled.

I sat in the morning lectures as if listening to them while tethered to a lawn chair at the bottom of a pool. At the beginning of the lunch break, while holding my breath, I waded to the lobby and heard the voices of the hundreds of other attendees as the mumbling of zombies. I spotted the only vacant telephone booth in the reception hall and walked quickly to reach it before someone else beat me to it. I had never noticed just how shiny the receivers were on pay phones. Before lifting the receiver from its cradle, I removed the carefully folded piece of paper with the downward-sloping scribble of Dad's doctor's name and phone number. As I punched the cold metal numbers, I liked the sensation of my warm breath on my upper lip. But the warmth didn't stop it from twitching, and it didn't prevent the tic from spreading to my eyelids.

After three rings, a man answered with a professional salutation that calmed me. I introduced myself as Dad's daughter.

"How can I help you?" he asked.

"I want to know what happened to my dad."

Silence. The doctor knew what to say but didn't want to.

"You don't know?"

The lobby became still and silent as if a blanket of snow had fallen around me.

"Um, no. I don't." My mouth dried up the same way it had when I sat in a dentist's chair and a hygienist suctioned every droplet of saliva out of it. I placed my left hand on the wall to steady myself even though I was sitting.

"Your father died of Huntington's disease. The primary cause of death was aspiration pneumonia, but the underlying cause, which is what matters to you, is the Huntington's disease. I'm surprised you didn't know. We knew about his condition for a number of years."

He continued to tell me that the individual probability that my sisters and I carried the gene was the toss of a coin, and the probability that none of us had inherited it was one in sixteen.

"The way my sister talks now, um, her words are very slurred," I said.

His silence filled me with dread as quickly as water gushes into a culvert during a flash flood. I was no longer aware of where I was and didn't dare turn around to watch all the people hopping from venue to venue while eating sandwiches that spilled out of plastic wrappings. Instead, I stared at the number pad on the phone, as if focusing on something small would end the blizzard in my mind. Within an instant I wanted to run, hoping that if I ran far and fast enough I could quell the inner storm before it became a tornado that lifted me into a junk-filled chaos. The doctor remained silent, intuiting I had more to say about Eldest.

"She's different. She used to like people. Now she doesn't leave her house. Her friends have disappeared. She has worked hard since she left school."

I paused, waiting for some encouraging words from the doctor. My heart raced when the five-second wait became too long.

"Now she can't hold down jobs. She fell down the stairs recently and sprained her ankle."

I told him more about Eldest's behavioural changes over the years, that as a young woman she had been gregarious and socially exuberant, never one to shun planning a party or to shy away from attending one.

"These signs are ominous," he said in the voice of a father who needed to tell a child something she didn't want to hear. And like most truths, this one didn't need any embellishment.

Even though Dad's physician spoke few words during our conversation, the cadence of his voice was gentle and slow, and I assumed both were intentional — the gentleness to soothe me and the slowness to ensure I didn't miss a single word. But maybe he spoke in such a way to everyone when he talked about death because of a softening that had transformed him after years of attending to people during the winter season of their lives, like ice and snow that smooth jagged cliffs.

We ended the conversation with Dad's physician saying, "Good luck." When I hung up the receiver, it was still as shiny as when I had picked it up, but there were droplets of moisture where my hand had been. The man who signed The System's death certificate for my father was the archeologist who gave me the most important relic from my ancestral cemetery. His gift was the truth about Dad. But the truth just shifted the position of my burden from the past to the future. As a result of my conversation with him, it rolled up my back, over my shoulders, and into my hands. At least while it was on my back, I could still see, even though I could feel its weight throughout my body. But once in front of me and against my chest, its size obscured my view, broke my wrists, and blistered my hands. The news hadn't changed the uncertainty of my future, but the fifty-percent probability that my sisters and I carried the gene for Huntington's disease added a terrifying certainty I didn't know how to handle.

On the return ferry ride, I sunk into a seat on the shady side and looked at the still calm seas to the east. The sunny side would have made me sweat more than I already had, despite being in air-conditioned lecture halls for much of the day. During the ride, a fire erupted behind my solar plexus near my spine. If I hadn't known any better, I would have sworn my upper lumbar vertebrae had begun to burn after learning Dad's closest relatives had kept the family secret to themselves for years. Having coped with prior disappointments, I was certain I could cool it before the vertebrae crumbled, with my back becoming the shape of the electrical hazard symbol, the one that is crooked in the middle.

I didn't know what Huntington's disease was until I poured over medical journals and case studies of afflicted families. Other than the fifty-fifty individual probability, the disease is relatively rare, occurring in approximately 1 in 10,000 people; it follows an autosomal dominant inheritance pattern. If one parent has the disease, each of the children has a fifty percent chance of inheriting it.

Dad had been born in 1940, and just as he was developing symptoms in his mid-twenties, the famous singer/songwriter Woody Guthrie died from the disease. Ten years later, in 1977, the National Institute of Neurological Disorders and

Stroke supported studies to search for the genetic marker for Huntington's disease after the Commission for the Control of Huntington's Disease and Its Consequences (mandated by the US Congress) published a series of recommendations. Then, in 1983, researchers linked the gene responsible for Huntington's disease to chromosome 4. However, another ten years would pass before the genetic marker was discovered as a result of the collaborative work of fifty scientists from nine different institutions around the world.

In March 1993, the Huntington's Disease Collaborative Research Group declared victory when they found the exact location and nature of the mutation. In 1994, genetic testing for Huntington's disease became commercially available. Only one year later, Dad died. Had Island Uncle done us a favour by concealing the truth about Dad's condition? What if we had learned as children about the real problem with Dad and that we each had a fifty percent chance of inheriting it? The passage of an unknown amount of time was the only way we would know our genetic fate. Would we have lived mindfully during that period, fast-tracking our careers and exercising discernment in our relationships and other important life choices? Or would dread have been a constant companion that stuffed a sock in our mouths to stop us from telling someone an important truth? Would it have jumped in front of us before our eyes met those of a soul mate crossing our path and covered our ears before we reached an ocean to hear the crashing of waves on a beach? Would it have been the bitter residue that tainted every meal and been the first thing we tasted when we woke up each day? For me, mindfulness and dread would have taken turns, but I can't say for sure how long each would have reigned.

By the time we found out about our risk for Huntington's disease, Middle1 and Youngest had already been settled in stable marriages and each had one child, both girls. Eldest had been living on her own in a town west of Somewhere Small. And I was living in The Urban City and still attached to Dark&Angry. I had begun to view my life differently with the news about the possible genetic bomb ticking in my DNA. I learned about an interesting phenomenon while researching the facts about the disease. When children inherit the gene from their fathers, a phenomenon called genetic anticipation occurs, which means the offspring tend to develop the disease earlier in life than he does, perhaps as nature's way of ridding the deviant gene from the family gene pool. Eldest had already developed early symptoms if Dad's doctor had interpreted her slurred speech correctly.

After Dad died, Eldest moved back to Somewhere Small, and Youngest had been living in a town near there for most of her life. Eldest had isolated herself for months, and when Youngest reconnected with her, the physical symptoms had extended far beyond slurred speech. Eldest's gait was unsteady. In fact, people with early stage Huntington's disease are often mistaken for being drunk; she was also experiencing uncontrollable jerking movements throughout her body and her facial expressions were contorted. Several appointments with a local neurologist confirmed Eldest had Huntington's disease.

Middle1 and Youngest proceeded immediately with genetic testing due to their family situations. If they had inherited the disease, each of their daughters would also have had a fifty percent chance of having it. I tried to ignore my possible fate of physical, emotional, and mental degeneration that would likely start in the next few years, given the mere three-year age difference between

Eldest and me. I needed to end my relationship with Dark&Angry but lacked the fortitude given the events that transpired with the news of Dad's death.

I got the gentle nudge six months later to end the relationship, but in the most unexpected way. While with Dark&Angry, I met a woman who had become a spiritual mentor and I attended evenings hosted by her to discuss various topics about healing and spirituality. The woman was a believer in astrology but I hadn't investigated the subject enough to form an opinion about it one way or another. Like many people, I'd read the horoscopes in the newspaper on days when I was bored or desperate for a sign (credible or not) that a difficult period would end, or if I had forgotten that change was like The Big River in Somewhere Small. She'd had a "reading" by a well-known Vedic astrologer who had been visiting The Urban City to meet clients in person. What on Earth was a Vedic astrologer? As opposed to what? A Chinese astrologer? A Western astrologer? In the end, I didn't care what type of astrology he practised. In a state of disarray, personally and professionally, I decided to have a "reading," hoping that my "chart" indicated a better future. Seeing my life piled in a messy heap around me and carrying a burden that I couldn't see beyond, I sought the services of someone I thought might know more about my future than I did.

I drove to my appointment with The Astrologer on a rainy February evening after work. When I arrived, I knocked on the door repeatedly, but no one was there. Maybe his absence was a sign my fate was too difficult or troubling to talk about and he could not find a comfortable way to tell me what he saw in the planets, their houses, and constellations associated with my exact birth time in Somewhere Small. He called in the evening with an apology, explaining he needed to visit someone unexpectedly in the hospital, and we rescheduled the appointment for a few days later.

When I arrived at the door a second time, a casually dressed man in jeans and a white shirt smiled widely as he shook my hand. He was a handsome man in his late forties and looked ordinary, with the exception of his eyes, which reminded me of knots on the pine trees back in Somewhere Small.

"Please come in, my dear," he said warmly. "It's cold and damp out there."

I walked behind him into the entrance of a house built on the bank of a canyon. I dismissed my impression of his eyes as he escorted me into the hallway where original art from around the world hung on the walls. The living room windows opened out onto a balcony overlooking the dense green forest.

"Would you like to step outside for some fresh air and a view to the canyon before we get started?"

"Sure. I'd like that." But I secretly thought he must have had bad news for me since he was inviting me to relax even before the reading.

Once on the balcony, I stepped up onto a wooden bench overlooking a steep descent into the canyon lined with evergreens and dressed with a sheer cape of fog. I closed my eyes. The misty air caressed my face in the waning hours of the day and I felt the tension in my body disappear as the dewy dust landed on me. After taking in a few deep breaths, I was ready to face the man inside. I returned to the living room where he led me to a sitting area with two wooden chairs facing each other.

"Please sit down," he said, motioning for me to sit in the chair closest to the balcony. He sat across from me and handed me two pieces of paper, which were incomprehensible until he gave me an overview before he conducted the reading.

"Vedic astrology uses your exact time and location of birth to determine the placement of planets in constellations using the fixed zodiac. It also uses dashas or periods to predict influences during different times of your life. But keep in mind, these are influences and probabilities and do not predict your life because of the free will we all possess."

A fine liability clause, I thought. And did I even have the correct information about the time of my birth? The certificate I had received from The System indicated I'd been born at 6:45 a.m. Six forty-five seemed a little too precise a time to be accurate. Perhaps I was born a few minutes earlier or later, and maybe I even entered this world at 6:45 p.m. Having worked in the field of health information and its management, I knew the incidence of errors associated with the collection of personal health data was as chronic as the diseases The System managed. Should the "a" in my time of birth have been a "p"? I'm certain the data collector who entered my information into the database didn't call Mom to validate what the hospital had submitted. Certainly a data entry error by The System would have changed everything about my destiny according to Vedic Astrology. I took comfort in the data collection error rates and free will, regardless of what he had to say.

"So I see Vedic astrology says I'm a Pisces, not an Aries?" I asked.

"Yes, that's correct. And you also have Jupiter in conjunction with your Sun. You will have good fortune in foreign countries, and you will do much work in hospitals or government institutions."

My curiosity was piqued by the accuracy of his first observations.

"Between the ages of five and six, you were traumatically separated from one or both of your parents," he said.

"Yes, that's true," I replied, dumbfounded.

"Are you in a relationship?"

"Yes."

"Does he abuse you?"

"Not physically."

"Don't worry. You'll be out of it soon," he claimed, not knowing that I had already been secretly planning my exit from the relationship with Dark&Angry.

"Good to know my fate is in agreement with my free will."

"And you should think carefully about getting married before you enter your forties. Your placement of Saturn with Venus doesn't bode well for success in relationships before you enter your major Saturn period."

He continued. "Your father—you have had extended periods of separation from him."

"How do you see that?"

"Although Jupiter and the Sun are favourably combined in your twelfth house, the Sun is the father and he's placed in the house of confinement and hospitals."

"I see. Yes, I've not seen him since I was five. What about my mother? What does my chart tell you about her?"

"You were in a Moon period between the ages of five and six. And the placement of Mars and Rahu in your fourth house indicates violence and trauma. Your Mars is debilitated in Cancer. And it's the house of the mother and early childhood."

He told me many other trends and possibilities about my future, and even specific details, but I have not lived long enough to know whether what he said is accurate or not. At the end of the reading, The Astrologer accompanied me to the door. He draped my coat over my shoulders.

"Would you like to have lunch with me tomorrow? I'm here for a few more days."

"Oh, sure. Why not?" I responded. I didn't consider a lunch date with him as cheating because I didn't find him attractive in a romantic sense.

Driving home from my meeting with The Astrologer, I knew it was shame that was fogging up the windows of my personal life and I lacked the will to wipe them down to see that my life could be better outside the walls of the house I shared with Dark&Angry. For much of the relationship, I believed the likelihood that my life would be worse was higher than the possibility it could be better if I ended it with him. Dark&Angry and I had experienced a short spring when we met, and I couldn't claim there had been a summer at all. Within six months of dating, fall had begun and swiftly turned to winter. By the end of the last year of our prolonged winter together, I couldn't share the same bed with him and had resorted to sleeping on the floor of our living room to avoid being close to him physically during my blank slate period between 3:00 a.m. and 7:00 a.m. Even in the unlikely scenario that he could draw on it, I wasn't taking any chances to give him the opportunity.

The Astrologer turned out to be a catalyst that expedited my breakup with Dark&Angry. Over the lunch date, I learned his eyes had not been hiding an important unresolved issue from the past. Burning embers simmered behind them glowing with anger toward his biological mother who had given him up for adoption. He told me the story of his loneliness in his adoptive parents' home growing up as a single child. But he'd met his best friend early in his childhood, and the spiritual brother he found had given him the beginnings of a community to belong to and an inkling that his destiny involved rebuilding a foundation with a spiritual family rather than a biological one, until he was old enough to marry and have children of his own.

The following night during dinner with The Astrologer, I tried to imagine us in various stages of physical intimacy, but my thoughts certainly could not have been converted into an erotic novella. Perhaps our beginning was exactly how a healthy relationship should begin. After all, I had been intensely physically attracted to Dark&Angry when we first met, and by the end of our relationship, he tasted like sauerkraut, smelled like a swamp, and acted like a beast. Therefore, was it not possible for my physical attraction to the Astrologer to develop, given first impressions of emotional, spiritual, and intellectual compatibility? I was willing to find out.

When we arrived back at his temporary home after dinner, we made our way to his room, where we reclined on his bed in a cuddly embrace. I hadn't been touched or hugged tenderly by a man for too long. The carpet flooring I slept on was softer than Dark&Angry. The Astrologer made me feel content, and I'd even go so far as to say loved, simply for being me. No man had ever made me feel that way, and in that moment, the ventricles of my heart relaxed.

Talking in a whisper about many things, The Astrologer and I began to kiss. However, the kisses didn't set off an episode of tingling vertigo like when we kiss someone with whom we feel an intense physical and soulful connection. When this rare event takes place, the lovers experience all seasons. In spring the lovers are the tulip and the daffodil whose blooms brush up against each other, as if cheek-to-cheek. With the arrival of summer, they are kites that float, dance, and flutter in a flighty summer breeze. In autumn, the lovers become two maple leaves in flight after being torn from the tree, formerly the umbilical cord that fed them. The tango has begun as the lovers dip and rise with the wind as their music. In winter, the lovers are two snowflakes, clinging to each other as they make their meandrous descent to a blanket of snow below. But flowers, kites, maple leaves, and snowflakes fall to the earth eventually, marking the end of their blissful journeys.

I hadn't experienced all seasons in my kisses with The Astrologer, but I was instantly alarmed when I looked at the clock to discover two hours had passed since we tucked ourselves into his bedroom. During the drive home, I predicted correctly that Dark&Angry had been trying to figure out where I was even though his concern stemmed from his loss of control, not from caring about my personal safety.

Before meeting The Astrologer for dinner, I had lied to Dark&Angry about my plans for the evening. I said I would be working with my boss on a presentation. Arriving home, I found out that he had located her number and called her when I hadn't returned home by 11 p.m. I wanted to go to work the next day, shut my door, and avoid looking directly at anyone for the week to dilute my embarrassment. Yet in the process I had received exactly what I needed, which was the final push to end my relationship with Dark&Angry. Although I hadn't been unfaithful to him in the complete sense, I told him about my evening with The Astrologer and that we needed to separate. He received the news as if it were a letter from The System telling him his house insurance had expired, and he proceeded without pause to write down tasks to renew it. His first words were: "Do you think I can make it on my own?" I had viewed Dark&Angry as an adventure companion only; therefore, I wasn't offended by his question. But I didn't ask him whether he thought I could fix my bike on my own.

There were no tearful declarations of love and the loss of it in the early morning hours of Monday. We had already separated. The disentanglement of our hearts was a simple procedure since the strings that had attached them were flimsy and worn from the moment we said hello to each other at the gym. Neither of us had space in our hearts for authentic intimacy. We had both become too angry and too disillusioned by love's unpromising odds. I made an entry into my lessons-learned archives to not move in with a man who is living with his parents when I meet him. I told myself I would end up being an extension of his mother's apron strings, and that extension would never transform into lingerie once it reached the bedroom.

The pièce de résistance with Dark&Angry came a few days later when the reality of our impending breakup had made its way to his angry core. In one final panic-stricken moment, he threatened to kill me if I left him. This threat left me with the disturbing realization I had attracted Dad's psychological twin. Obviously, my relationship with Dark&Angry had ended with some serious feedback: not so fast, soldier, you've got some learnin' to do.

I made the same decision as my mother to move out of the house I shared with my abuser, but unlike "That House," my temporary home at my friend's house was located on the second floor and required a key to enter the building and another one to enter the suite, which meant I slept well. I also made the decision to placate Dark&Angry. I paid the rent at our apartment for the month while he packed his things.

When I finally mustered the courage to end my relationship with Dark&Angry, I understood the meaning of epiphany, which until then I associated with a questionable episode recounted by flakes or cult members. On the day I moved out for the one month period, I drove to a grocery store a few miles away and sat in my parked car before running my errands. I watched people go about their business. I watched children laugh and skip alongside their mothers. I watched lovers hand in hand with bags of groceries filled with ingredients to make dinner together. My body may have been four hundred miles west of Somewhere Small creating The Good Life, but my spirit had not similarly matured. I was still the lonely girl from Somewhere Small looking for somewhere to belong and someone to love me. The latest man I'd found was a reflection of the kind of man I thought I deserved.

After one month away from my apartment, I added "thief" to my description of Dark&Angry when I discovered he had stolen my antique fishing reel and neoprene waders. At least he hadn't taken any of my books. Unfortunately, I hadn't tidied up other loose ends with Dark&Angry after he moved out, which ended up costing me. We broke up in May; in August, while on vacation with his new girlfriend, he was in an accident and claimed his passenger was me, because the vehicle insurance had still been in my name after our separation. Although the insurance company representative had heard countless stories of women who had been similarly taken advantage of, they could do nothing because the insurer was the liable party in the event of an accident. For the next five years, I wrote off my higher insurance premiums as bad debt, embarrassing but forgivable line items in my tax-deductible expenses.

After the break up with Dark&Angry, I asked my doctor for a referral to see a psychiatrist who specialized in trauma since the soldier strategy wasn't really working. Fortunately for me, I had a friend who knew him and was able to bypass the one-year wait list. Seeing him for the first time was tantamount to meeting a very wise soul who peered into the deep, dark crevices of my being. There was nowhere for the soldier to hide anymore. His eyes were fiercely blue and penetrating. Could I actually look at him directly and face what I had avoided for so many years? Yes, I was ready. But before I embarked on my journey into healing with modern psychiatric medicine, I had ventured into the esoteric eastern domain rather unexpectedly during a series of guided meditations with The Astrologer, who offered me a seat at his one-day workshop while he had been in The Urban City.

The group participated in four exercises, with the last one focusing on forgiveness. The meditation began with an instruction to close our eyes, take a few deep breaths, and then imagine, simultaneously, a beam of light descending from above and penetrating our heads and a thick cord anchoring us to the centre of the Earth. Then The Astrologer had us envision walking along a lush path, filled with a chorus of birds and splashes of colour from exotic flowers and plants. After walking along this path for a few minutes, he told us to imagine a bridge leading to the other side of the path. We were to envision a guide on the other side of the bridge who would escort us to an encounter with the person (or persons) we wanted to meet during the meditation.

The form of "Jesus" was waiting for me on the other side of the bridge. I was not a Christian and I hadn't developed any affinity to Jesus (or any other religious icon), yet "He" radiated pure, unconditional love, one that embodied absolute acceptance—no judgment for the mistakes I made in my life, no judgment about my present and future human weaknesses and struggles, and no expectation that I had to forgive anyone or anything, then or ever. What was, what is, and what will be didn't matter to "Him." I basked in the presence that loved and honoured me for all I had been, who I was in that moment, and who I would become in all remaining moments of my life. There were no clocks in the realm, and the past, present, and future were one.

"Jesus" held my hand as we climbed several wooden steps. Making the last step, we walked out into a vast meadow nestled in a valley. A waterfall that resembled swelling cumulus clouds emerged from the mountains to the north and descended below the meadow. To the south, a jagged snowy peak rose behind the meadow where my parents were picnicking on a plaid blanket stretched out on an open grassy area. Dressed in clothing from the sixties, they were engaged in lively conversation and laughing flirtatiously with each other. This view of them happily residing in what I had imagined as some dimension in The Great Unknown ignited a rage that had been dormant for years. I thought, *Oh, how nice it is that you are blissfully happy in The Great Unknown. I'll just leave you two be so that you can continue your little party while we plod on to suffer through the radioactive wasteland you left us in.* I didn't care if they were in The Great Unknown after having been absent for so many years. But I wondered why Dad was not in Hell while Mom danced in a garden with the prince—no, the king—she should have married in the first place.

When the meditation was over, The Astrologer asked everyone to share the details of their visions with the group. With each story, the all-too-familiar cinch tightened around my chest when I could no longer avoid the uncomfortable emotions that percolated to the surface during the meditation. I was the last one to tell my version of what I saw while light streamed into my head from above and a network of roots anchored my feet to the centre of the Earth. Getting to the part about "Jesus" and the absolute and unconditional love he expressed made me cry uncontrollably in front of a room full of strangers.

Despite the emotional release in the moments following the meditation, I was not yet ready to forgive either of my parents. "Jesus" had remained a silent, numinous presence throughout the experience. There was no verbal exchange between "Him" and me about my readiness to forgive. He looked at me with a non-judgmental acknowledgement that the time had not yet arrived. Of course, that state was perfectly acceptable, and no conditions followed as to when, how, or if I ever needed to forgive them at all.

Although I was about to engage in a dialogue with a wise man who was a professional in traditional western medicine, I had already learned about a different kind of communication that was possible but lacked a rational explanation. The dialogue that occurred was of a mysterious sort, one involving a messenger of The Powers That Be. The incident happened in November 1996 while I was working at The Trauma Registry in The Urban City, a few weeks after a social evening with my spiritual mentor and some of her friends. My spiritual mentor had been a Reiki master and she announced her intention to teach the practice in three levels to those of us who were interested. The word *Reiki* is derived from two Japanese words: "Rei," which means "God's wisdom or the Higher Power" and "Ki," which is "life force energy." I questioned the authenticity of the practice and was hesitant to pursue a path that appeared to be an ill-defined art rather than an evidence-based science. However, I had received "treatments" from her friend and, during them, noticed a relaxation sweep over my entire body. My friend used to metaphorically compare Reiki to a chestnut and how the practice was like water and nutrients necessary for a seed to grow into its full expression. She recommended I ask for a sign about whether I should take the class, given my skepticism.

When I left my friend's apartment, I looked skyward and flippantly demanded, *Okay, give me a sign, and I mean a real one.* After my incantation, I released thoughts about signs from The Powers That Be and carried on as if receiving anything after such a command was reserved for fairy tales and fantasies. I walked along the long narrow concrete path away from my friend's apartment to the street where my car had been parked. The night sky was dark and dreary and dripping. Sitting in my car, raindrops dotted the windscreen and blurred my view to the outside world. But I started the engine, turned on the wipers, and when I put on my glasses before driving home I was happy that I once again saw the outside world in sharp images and couldn't mistake shadows for people. After tucking myself into bed and falling into an easy slumber, I did not encounter enlightened messengers in the dormiveglia before the morning alarm went off. The surprise I got came in broad daylight, not from an ambiguous scenario in my subconscious while I slept.

On a late afternoon, while walking back to my car that I had parked on a residential street ten minutes away from the hospital, what happened was as unambiguous as anything I could have imagined and it happened while I had been standing at the northwest intersection across from The Urban City hall. Waiting there to cross the street heading east, I noticed a young woman standing at the corner opposite me because she was dressed in clothing similar to what the Amish typically wear. I crossed the street to where the young woman was standing and with my back to her, I waited for the light to change. I felt a tap on my shoulder and I turned around to find her staring at me.

"I have something for you," she stated matter-of-factly.

"Oh?"

She held out her open hand. Sitting in the centre of her palm was one shiny chestnut. I took the chestnut from the messenger's palm and squeezed it in mine.

"Thank you," I said, then turned around and waited for the walk sign to cross the street.

I didn't interpret the episode of the woman with the chestnut as a message for me to pursue becoming a Reiki practitioner. Instead, I learned that important information could be conveyed by strangers in the most unlikely and improbable circumstances, if and only if I was willing to receive it. Despite my sarcastic request to The Powers That Be as I walked down the stairs of my friend's apartment building, they were more than happy to supply me with an irrefutable sign. They grant requests, even rude and presumptuous ones. Apparently The Powers That Be lack egos while they conduct their business. No one can dispute the chestnut story was a rare event, but perhaps it had nothing to do with The Powers That Be. Maybe it was the one in all the moments of my life that would be so.

But I did contemplate the existence of The Powers That Be when I was a child and periodically sensed the presence of warm hands on my shoulders. I could have misconstrued the touch for the sensation of a light spring breeze, but it normally happened on unusually still and calm days. It also occurred when I was alone in a quiet place, lonely in a loud place, and sometimes when I was about to do something that scared me. Could the light touch have been Mom's way of communicating with me from The Great Unknown? If she had appeared as a translucent version of herself, perhaps she thought I would have become too frightened or consumed by fear that my ability to see her apparition was an early sign of the same insanity that afflicted Dad. She used her invisible hands because she didn't want me to become paranoid. She wanted to reassure me when I needed comfort. And the gentle touches would do just that.

But I had become an adult with a complicated life, one too crowded to allow space for childhood innocence and belief in improbable events, until the young messenger presented me with a chestnut in the palm of her hand when we met in front of the city hall at a busy corner in The Urban City.

CHAPTER 16

DISSECTING EMOTIONS WITH PSYCHIATRIST #2

One thing you can't hide – is when you're crippled inside.
John Lennon

And with a complicated life, I occasionally fantasized about being someone with a psychiatric disorder that allowed me to compartmentalize my existence as Middle2 and leave her world from time to time. In my work as a health information consultant, I often needed to refer to various coding manuals to investigate how information about disease, diagnostic, and medical procedures were coded for research and statistical analysis. I was intrigued to find a disorder in The Diagnostic and Statistical Manual that caused dissociation from oneself. Depersonalization disorder is the sudden sense of being outside oneself, observing one's actions from a distance, as though watching a movie. I had often experienced fleeting periods of feeling I was recounting the story of someone else's life when a new friend asked me about my family. I never did tell Psychiatrist #1 about my mental meanderings and considered she may have reached a different conclusion if I had. With a more extensive look at related problems, I really wished I'd had dissociative identity, formerly known as multiple personality disorder, particularly if I could command at will a transition between or among personalities, if there were more than two. Of course I had other requirements: only one person could talk at a time; after all, there must be healthy boundaries between personalities. All others would have perfect vision since corrective eyewear for more than one would be expensive, and we would need to see things clearly. Most importantly, no one could have agoraphobia, and I'd go so far as to say everyone would need to love to travel because I would want no obstacles to jet away to Faraway Places, and I wanted no drama among us while exploring them.

As I continued my research, I concluded my ideal disorder in the dissociative memory grouping was dissociative fugue, one where a person can create physical distance from her real identity. I could also adopt a new identity in a new location. In the diagnostic description of this disorder, fugue events typically only last a few hours, or in rare cases, a few months. Most people don't remember them, and I would request that option too if I had the choice. Leaving the fugue world would be like closing a door to a favourite hide-a-way known only to me, and what went on behind that door would stay there.

My reveries ended as soon as I finished scanning the sections in the manual. I idealized diseases I'm certain contained a brand of misery worse than the one I had been experiencing, because as much as I dreamed about leaving the reality that was mine, there was no control in the disorders I imagined having. I needed to face being me, a me whose vision of the future and experience of the present had been clouded by my unresolved feelings about the past. And Psychiatrist #2 would be the man who would help me part the clouds, but not before the release of claps of thunder, flashes of lightning, and pelting rain.

Psychiatrist #2 was not like most of his peers. People referred to him became patients only after a lengthy questionnaire was completed; he assessed the responses, and conducted a final interview with the subjects to make a final determination about whether he believed his type of therapy could help them. With one look at him, I believed he knew where my spirit was broken, and he had a type of extrasensory vision that didn't need luminol to see blood stains the unaided human eye couldn't. He could find dormant or hidden wounds because his emotional surveillance system was as sensitive as radar that can track UFOs and planes in the night sky.

My interview with him began with a pointed question: "Why are you here?" I recounted a short history of the last day I saw Mom and Dad and my time in the foster homes. I told him I thought I'd dealt with my childhood by becoming a functional, healthy adult until I met Dark&Angry. With that answer I entered therapy two weeks later.

Seated in a creaky wicker chair, I noticed a lone box of tissue on the stand to the left of me as Psychiatrist #2 set up video equipment to record the sessions. When he sat across from me, there was no avoiding his steely blue eyes, given the close proximity of our chairs.

"How did you feel when Dark&Angry threatened to kill you?"

I stared at him blankly and became uncharacteristically mute. "Come on, tell me, what sensations did you feel in your body when Dark&Angry told you he would kill you if you tried to leave him?"

"I didn't feel anything. I thought about the irony of attracting an angry man and committed to avoiding my mother's fate. I began making a mental list of things I needed to do to leave Dark&Angry but included a list of my behaviours to appease him before I changed the locks on the apartment we shared."

"I see. So you associate feelings with a to-do list?"

I started to cry. It was easy to be a girl and cry when I was angry. Good girls didn't get mad without being labelled bitches. But Psychiatrist #2 wasn't interested in helping me perpetuate my good girl image.

"So you want to take all this misery to your grave, is that the plan?"

"No," I answered.

But there was a big difference between saying, "No," and doing what was necessary to avoid being ensnared in a coffle of my ancestors' ghosts until I entered The Great Unknown. Mom had taken a whole lot of misery to her grave, and any misery that remained buried in my psyche wasn't nearly as bad as what accompanied her. And what did it matter anyway if I took misery to my grave? I'd known plenty of cantankerous crones in Somewhere Small who smoked, drank, swore for decades after their retirement, and then died in the quiet pre-dawn hours of the coldest day of winter. The difference between the grumpy old people in Somewhere Small and me was that they were outwardly angry, knew it, and didn't care. They told people to fuck off, whether it was to the bus driver who drove into a puddle, soaking them; to the evangelists that wouldn't take "no" for an answer when they requested a brief chat with them about the importance of having Jesus as their saviour; or to the skateboarder who nearly knocked them down on the sidewalk. And when they couldn't tell people to fuck off to their faces, they raised their middle finger without hesitation, even in front of their grandchildren. Psychiatrist #2 was trying to teach me how to become a grumpy old woman from Somewhere Small. But being a bitch was only one of the problems I had with expressing anger. I had plenty of evidence it destroyed relationships and led to murder.

Therefore, I had decided to avoid it altogether. The problem was that avoidance didn't get rid of it and it wasn't like chlorine that evaporates from water over time. Repressed anger is as silent a killer as undiagnosed hypertension. Before I met Psychiatrist #2, I was fit enough to outrun anger because I obsessively hiked the hills on the north side of The Urban City. Sitting in the wicker chair across from the man with the penetrating eyes, I couldn't run anywhere.

"You know, you are obviously an intelligent, capable woman, but you do realize you're still a kindergartener when it comes to your emotions? You're emotionally retarded."

His assessment made me laugh.

"Oh, so you think this is funny, do you?"

"I've never been called retarded."

"Tell me how you felt. Tell me," he tried again.

My rage had been a captive sleeping lion, but Psychiatrist #2 woke him and opened the cage.

I lowered my head and closed my eyes, coaching myself that the man before me was trying to help me, not control me. Psychiatrist #2's skill at uncovering my rage exceeded my ability to play the good girl. I took a deep breath as if the air would cool the heat growing in my belly, but instead, it had the effect of a fan on crackling kindling. The heat began to burn in my solar plexus and it spawned a vicious attack on Dark&Angry in my imagination. I began beating him with a bat and delighted in watching and listening to his agonizing pain as he wailed and begged me to stop. In the middle of the attack, Dark&Angry transformed into my dad and me into the little girl waiting for him under the stairs in The Little House. I surprised him this time with a delicious attack, ending with his broken and bloodied body before me. The assaults would vary each week. Sometimes I beat him to death with a bat, a club, or a hammer; other times, I gored his neck with the viciousness of a ravenous lion and sawed his flesh with the hacking force of its carnassials, but more often than not, I sliced Dad's throat with one clean and effective stroke and luxuriated in watching the blood gush out of his neck while feeling satisfied the score had been settled.

After a few sessions, Psychiatrist #2 asked me to recall for him the events after the dinner hour at "That House" on March 28, 1968. He wanted to know how I had been feeling while staring out the square mesh screen door and begging The Powers That Be to do something to help Mom who had been screaming and begging Dad, "Please, please don't do it." He wasn't interested in the nature of my pleas to The Powers That Be. He wanted to know about the sensations in my body. My chest had become tight as if someone were pushing the middle of my back into a wall. My legs were weak, but not weak in the way they used to get from running around the many grassy fields and up the steep roads in Somewhere Small. Looking out the mesh door, my legs had become weak because I was scared.

Psychiatrist #2 also guided me back to Mom's bedroom door on several occasions. He didn't want the details about what she had been wearing or how far the pool of blood extended beyond her body. He was still interested in how my chest and legs felt as I raced to her door and saw her lifeless body for the first time. My first thought was, *What chest and legs?* I had left my body just as Mom had left hers. Then, instead of something pushing my back into a wall, something heavier than the combined weight of my grandfathers sat on my head, causing me to buckle and curl into a ball at my mother's feet. I desperately wanted to go where she had gone.

But I was also angry with my mom and proceeded to lecture her as if I were her middle-aged mother and she a twenty-four year old sitting on our couch while I paced in front of her and interrogated her about that night.

"What the hell were you doing going on a date with another man when you had a crazy ex-husband who had threatened to kill you? Were you trying to give him a reason to follow through with his promise? And why were you on the phone with your sister-in-law? If you hadn't been, you might have heard him arrive and been able to escape through the back door. You claim to have loved your children and did everything to save them, but did you really, given the choices you made that night?"

"You didn't have to die, Mother. You didn't have to!" Regressions that included my mother always ended with a similar protest that was sometimes a question intended to make her feel guilty, as if she were still alive, living a parallel life somewhere else but able to hear my words and thoughts: "Do you know how many birthdays you have missed? And what do you think about the surrogate parents we had who were supposedly chosen because they were adults who knew how to foster our care?"

My throat burned and my chest ached as I looked at Psychiatrist #2 during my proclamation to my imaginary mother, as if he could somehow channel her or The Powers That Be with a sensible response. He used to look at me and pause before saying, "You look sad, Middle2." Each time he said those words, he remained silent and gave me permission to cry for as long as I needed to.

The sessions with Psychiatrist #2 were not just an emotional catharsis for rage and sadness—he planted seeds of wisdom in me, and through my passage in life, worldly experience would cultivate their growth. He said that all relationships are superficial until the people have resolved a conflict about an important topic. But, like much sage advice, the gift of time was required to recognize and embrace that truth. Discussing my failed relationships with men, he also counselled me about the importance of relationships outside of romantic ones. Romantic partners fulfill a meaningful part of life's journey, but as we get older, friendships, creative interests, and generosity of spirit to those less fortunate are as rewarding and possibly more important to our happiness and contentment. He also predicted that my relationship with my Wise-But-Drug-Addicted Girlfriend would not survive as long as I continued to search and pursue an authentic life. He believed that one drug-addicted friend would be too many for me eventually.

In my sessions with Psychiatrist #2 I had found a reason why I didn't want to take my misery to my grave. Misery had made me want everything in life to be black and white. It also made me anxious because I wanted certainty and guarantees no one or any thing could give me. And the more misery I acknowledged with Psychiatrist #2, the more I started to see colour and uncertainty as creators of possibilities that didn't exist in a black-and-white world. Releasing the anger was a dragon breathing fire on my past. And with the fires came tears of surrender that heralded in newness that springs from nothing. I walked on the burnt and crispy ashes of my past that steamed and sizzled as my tears fell on them. But The Evil Tree couldn't ensnare me anymore because the dragon's breath had burned all of it, the tangled leaves, the knotted branches, and the twisted trunk, all the way down to the tips of its deeply buried roots. I saw beauty in the lustrous blackened remains and joy in the shiny green sprigs that grew shortly thereafter.

Even though The Evil Tree had become a charred heap that returned to the earth, my digging was incomplete. I needed to decide whether I wanted to know if the flaw in Dad's DNA also existed in mine.

CHAPTER 17

CHROMOSOME 4

Like nuclear power, genetic engineering is not a neutral technology. It is by its very nature too powerful for our present state of social and scientific development, no matter whose hands are controlling it. Just as we would say, especially after Chernobyl, that a nuclear power plant is just as dangerous in a socialist nation as it is in a capitalist one, so I would say the same thing for genetic engineering. It is inherently eugenic in that it always requires someone to decide what is a good and a bad gene.
Linda Bullard

Suicide is man's way of telling God, "You can't fire me, I quit."
Bill Maher

I continued seeing Psychiatrist #2 for the next year, and part of my therapy revolved around discussing the issue of whether or not to be tested for Huntington's disease. From time to time I would play an inane game with myself to assist with the decision-making process. While driving in my car on a known route I would picture three intersections and instruct myself that if the traffic signal was red at all three, The Powers That Be were recommending I not be tested; and similarly if all were green, I should proceed. No definitive result presented itself to me. I was not ready to make a decision, and even if the silly experiment had worked, I'm not sure I would have acted on the advice. Given Eldest's early onset, my symptoms would appear within the following three to five years if I carried the gene. The state of my DNA would speak for itself within a short period without the requirement for testing. I had already waited two years since Dad died. Surely I could continue sitting on the fence, but would I again become Humpty Dumpty and have another big fall?

I thought my approach seemed reasonable until I continued reading detailed articles from the medical journals about the inheritance patterns of the disease and found out about the grey zone, that annoying and ambiguous section of the black and white palette. Many situations in life present with at least one shade of grey, and the inheritance patterns of Huntington's disease were no exception. I learned that the severity and age of onset depended on something called the number of CAG repeats an individual inherited from the affected parent. The larger the number, the earlier the onset, and the grey zone contained five shades numbered thirty-six to forty. From my perspective, they all had the same name: "Ignotus," which means "unknown" in Latin. I liked my term for the grey zone because it sounded like an unpalatable type of pasta.

The longer I wondered about the state of my DNA, the burden of not knowing grew heavier and the space in my mind where imagination resides dimmed to the flicker of a solitary candle at the end of its wick. And once the wick dimmed to a smoky redness before becoming black, I knew if darkness filled my mind for too long it would attract bats and spiders. I finally made the decision to be tested when the anxiety of not knowing became greater than the fear that I carried the gene, which happened when I found out both Youngest and Middle1 had been tested and both were negative for the disease.

Statistically I thought I carried the gene because the probability that three out of four of us didn't have it was only one in eight, even though my individual probability was still fifty percent. When panic set in, my brain became a mass of pool balls spinning inside my skull. The path of the balls became a convoluted maze I couldn't have retraced. "Did I have it? Did I have it? Did I have it?" could be heard with a pool stick striking the cue ball that scattered the others in all directions. As they collided and ricocheted, they all boomed their libretto: "Yes, you could. Yes, you could. Yes, you could." When the cacophony ended and a period of calm ensued, I became obsessed with only one question: How would I face life knowing the Huntington's gene might someday trigger a destructive path through my brain? Not knowing my genetic fate had narrowed my perspective, as if I was a pedestrian in a sprawling new metropolis in some faraway place I had been excited to explore, but I had to walk down its seediest and scariest alley first with no guarantee I would make it out of there alive.

"I'm going to be tested," I announced to Psychiatrist #2 during our first session in January 1997.

"I'm surprised," he responded. "Why now?"

"Because if I have it, I'm not sticking around to wait for my brain to shrink to the size of a walnut."

On January 13th, 1997, I had an appointment with a geneticist. This man saw his patients on The Island southwest of The Urban City at a medical clinic inside the largest hospital there. As soon as the ferry departed from the terminal south of The Urban City, I gazed out at the strait and took the deepest breath I could of the cool, moist air. The day was gloriously sunny but stayed in my car for the duration of the journey. I reclined in my seat, closed my eyes, and tried to focus on the rumble of the engines and the gentle sway of the sea. But I couldn't keep my eyes closed for long. I stared at the ceiling of the car deck. It became my temporary anchor, just like the horizon is for seagoers with motion sickness. Introducing a visual element to my distraction gave me something to do.

I was in a numb hypnotic state during the drive to the hospital. I focused on the dotted line separating the two lanes to the south and stayed in the rightmost lane. I was in no hurry to reach my destination, but I didn't want to be late either. I kept to the speed limit. There was no need to rush. During the drive, I didn't let my gaze wander to the countryside. I wanted no reminders of a happy time in my life while I completed my post-secondary education on The Island years earlier.

Island Friend was waiting for me at the clinic when I arrived. I took my seat, looked at the other patients, and wondered what genetic dice had landed them in The Geneticist's office. On the wall of the waiting room hung a picture of a little girl who had a genetic disorder called Rett Syndrome. Children with this disease never have a normal life developmentally, cognitively, physically, and socially; clinical indications are that they have little to no self-awareness. The blessing with Huntington's disease was most people who have inherited it often have the opportunity to live an unrestricted life for some or much of their adulthood. The curse was they would someday become conscious of their slow and debilitating demise.

"Hello," a warm Scot said, extending his hand to greet me in the waiting area. He wasn't wearing a white coat and his attire was business casual. Even though he was dressed in calming shades of blue, I still noticed the clinical intensity brimming in his seaweed-coloured eyes. "Have a seat," he said, pointing to the same kind of medical bed as in my family physician's exam room. But the one in his office didn't have a cover made from the same material as toilet seat protectors in public washrooms, a set-up that didn't worry me. After all, he didn't do pelvic exams.

I watched him write something in what I presumed was my medical record, and then he approached me.

"What day of the week is it?" he asked.

"Tuesday." What a relief. I could answer the first question. Although if I had been unable to answer it, I probably would not have been there at all.

"Count backward from one hundred." I didn't have to close my eyes to concentrate as I began. He stopped me at ninety.

"Repeat the numbers back to me in the order I say them."

I avoided his eyes and gazed at the blank beige wall to the right.

"Five, twenty, six, one, twelve, forty, nine," I recalled.

"Move your eyes from left to right." My eyes met but didn't lock with his at the midway point of the exercise.

"Move your eyes in a clockwise motion."

Concentrating, I stretched my eyes as far as I could, seeing the room as a hula hoop. And unlike the command to move my eyes to the right and left, I could not catch a glimpse of him watching me.

"Now move them counterclockwise."

This time I noticed my medical chart to the left, and the black ink on the top page became spiders scurrying around the page. I hated spiders again.

My eye sockets and the surrounding muscles seemed tired as I followed his instructions, but I couldn't tell if I had completed them without setting off an alarm in him. The Geneticist was a middle-aged man and had seen thousands of patients during his career. Consequently, through observation, he reached conclusions quickly—not because of a direct channel to The Powers That Be, but because he had refined powers of observation he was comfortable writing in indelible ink.

"We're done," The Geneticist declared, without looking in my eyes. Hadn't I read somewhere that people are either lying or need to avoid another person's eyes when they're aware of an uncomfortable truth they don't want to risk revealing with a look? He handed me a laboratory requisition that I would present to the phlebotomist who would take a sample of my blood. As we left the office, he rested a hand on my back and said, "Good luck."

The phlebotomist swabbed the crease of my left arm more gently than others had done in the past. And before inserting the needle she looked into my eyes without uttering a word, with the type of gaze I hoped was like the one I gave disabled people whose paths I crossed on the streets of The Urban City. I'd had several blood samples extracted for various regular checkups over the years. But this time was different. When she applied the tourniquet and inserted the needle, I became mesmerized as my blood swirled into the test tube, with the black and white clock chanting its clinical "tick, tick, tick," in the background. What would the blood have to say about the state of my IT15 gene on Chromosome 4? How many CAG repeats had I inherited from my parents, specifically from Dad? Would the result definitively tell me I would develop the disease if I lived long enough, or would I become a member of the Ignotus Club? The test results are known within one week of the lab receiving the sample, but there was a requirement in The Urban City for patients to receive counselling for a month to discuss the potential emotional impacts of either a negative or positive result. I would receive my results on February 13, a Thursday. Not that I was overly superstitious, but I was glad I wouldn't receive the news on Friday the thirteenth.

I stayed at my Island Friend's house for the night after the appointment with The Geneticist. During the night, I dreamt about my DNA—not in its true form as a double helix molecule, but as a set of building blocks, each one containing letters of the alphabet. Each building block grew in size at a preternatural rate as some invisible force continued to stack them one on top of the other. I also dreamt about Eldest's DNA. The building blocks of hers were smaller and didn't stack as highly as mine did. I woke up to a foreboding sense that I carried the gene, and that The Powers That Be had begun to prepare me for the bad news.

However, I returned to The Urban City still feeling calm and resolute because my future had already been determined at the moment of conception. There was nothing to be done but remain fully present in each moment until I knew my results. My efforts at equanimity failed shortly thereafter through a series of events that reinforced my conclusion after waking up from the dream.

One week after providing my blood sample, Eldest planned a trip to The Urban City for an assessment by a neurologist at the university. Youngest's in-laws had driven her to the city and during her visit she would bunk with me in my studio apartment. When I saw Eldest, my heart sank, and I developed periods of intense vertigo as if I had been planted on a pony of a merry-go-round, unable to stop. No official diagnosis of Huntington's disease had been made, yet she exhibited the early signs. Her voice slurred when she spoke, her limbs jerked uncontrollably, and she walked as if inebriated. On the first night, while Eldest slept in my bed, I listened to her toss and turn until the nightly tranquilizer took effect. My heart was thumping to the words of a shaman whose advice drummed "face your fear." My body ached as if I had been bedridden with a fever, causing me to toss and turn throughout the night. I also woke up several times as if an alarm had gone off, reminding me to hold my breath and remain perfectly still until I could assure myself Eldest had not left my bed.

The next day, Eldest and I drove to the university for her appointment. Two other patients in more advanced stages of Huntington's disease were also waiting for their assessments. They had been confined to wheelchairs, and despite the anti-spasmodic medication, the uncontrollable jerking motions hadn't stopped. As soon as Eldest was called for her appointment I sought out the nearest bathroom, sat in the corner, and cried—not only for Eldest and me, but also for the others in the waiting room. The worn polish on the concrete floor and the ceiling vent blowing out cool air made the room cold and clinical. A pink clear liquid filled the soap dispenser, and taped above it was a torn piece of paper with a reminder to "wash your hands for your safety and the safety of others." The mirror above the sink even had a four-point instruction set of a proper hand wash. There were no signs of love and beauty from the outside world, no plastic flowers on the sink, or Anne Geddes' photographs on the walls to remind visitors that, despite the solemnity of the circumstances that had brought them to the clinic, flowers still bloomed and babies were still being born.

Driving back to my apartment after the appointment, I decided I couldn't stay with Eldest for the remainder of her visit—I called a friend and asked if I could sleep in her spare bedroom. Seeing Eldest was like watching a scary movie. She was the villain who looked human but could transform into a monster at any moment. But I wasn't watching her on screen in a movie theatre and chewing nervously on popcorn. It was daylight and the monster was sitting in my living room, obsessed and asking repeatedly when we were going to get pizza and coke for lunch. I lied by telling Eldest I had to go to work and that I just couldn't take the time off to spend with her. Besides, she was going to spend one day with one of her high school friends and then she would drive back to Somewhere Small the following day with Youngest's in-laws. Two days later, after Eldest left my apartment, I returned home from my friend's to find the red light flashing on my answering machine with a "2" on the display, indicating I had two unheard voice messages. A work colleague had called wishing me well, and one of Eldest's high school friends screamed about how ashamed I should be for abandoning Eldest during her time of greatest need.

Youngest also called me after she visited Eldest back in Somewhere Small.

"How could you leave her alone like that? She's your sister," she said sternly.

"I'm sorry," I replied, sitting on my bed with the phone to my ear. I could feel my pulse quicken in my sweaty palm.

"Eldest has some happy news about her life and you might think about calling her, if you care that is."

"Of course I care. How can you even say that? I'm sorry I couldn't be there for her while she was here in The Urban City, I really am," I stammered. "I'm happy she has exciting news. I'll call her." Youngest and I said goodbye to each other cordially but coolly. Pushing the "End" button on my handheld phone, my chest contracted in the all-too-familiar prelude to a cry.

With a soggy tissue crumpled in my left hand, I held the phone in my right one and dialled Eldest's number.

"Hello," she answered groggily.

"Hello, Eldest. It's Middle2."

"Why are you calling me?" she yelled, surprising me that her tone could change so quickly.

"Youngest told me you had some happy news. I just wanted to find out what it is and see how you're doing."

"You hardly talked to me when I was in the same city as you. Why the hell do you care what's going on in my life now that I'm not there?" Eldest continued to yell.

"Eldest, I'm sorry," I said quietly.

"I'm getting married," she announced flatly.

"Oh! Congratulations! When's the wedding?"

"May. And you won't be invited. *Aaaaaand*, I never want to see you again," she replied and hung up.

I learned from Youngest that Eldest had met her fiancé at a community program created to take disabled adults out on day excursions. He was disabled from a type of Muscular Dystrophy and they continued to build a friendship over several months following their first meeting.

After hearing the message from Eldest's friend and talking to Youngest and Eldest on the phone, I sat on my bed and wept again. I wanted to believe my mom would have hugged me after looking compassionately into my eyes if she had known I avoided being Eldest's caretaker during her medically required visit to The Urban City. But that's one of the problems with how we see people we love who have died too soon. We brand them as saints who would forgive anything we do. But it didn't matter how forgiving spirits and entities were in The Great Unknown. I was in the land of the living where I had been labelled bad and weak. I had failed a decency test and joined the growing list of humans that had forsaken Eldest. Maybe I deserved to have Huntington's disease to strengthen my ability to carry psychological burdens and to endure physical and mental disability. And in a hushed conversation among The Powers That Be that took place before my conception, they had determined Huntington's disease would be an ideal component of the lesson plan.

After my conversation with Eldest, I hid in bed for two days until my discomfort became an angry dog that bit my ankles and chased me out of the house. I decided to venture in the direction of the dead-end street that was only a five-minute walk from my doorstep to begin my indulgence in planning my suicide if I carried the gene. At the time I lived in a place with many circular or meandering streets. When my need to escape was acute or I became paranoid about needing a backup plan in case my neighbourhood's dead end became inaccessible, I would flee in my car and try to find another perfect, private dead end. In those moments I was my dad's daughter. Driving around The Urban City that drizzled and dripped endlessly that February, I tried to figure out what would be the most painless way to slip away. If I kept enough of the sleeping pills Psychiatrist #2 had given me, I could start with those to relax myself, and while waiting for them to take effect, I could pump the carbon monoxide exhaust into my car and recline in the driver's seat while waiting for liftoff into The Great Unknown. I wasn't afraid to die if it mirrored what happened in one of my dreams. In April of 1996, during the stay at my friend's apartment following the breakup with Dark&Angry, my vision occurred, which only made sense months later. It was a brilliant sunny day and my friend and I were walking in the middle of an airport runway. We both understood without speaking to each other that I was to lie down on the left of the dashed line and she on the right. Once settled, we were to shut our eyes. As soon as I closed my eyelids, I could hear a plane approaching. My nervousness kept pace with the heightening roar until it became thunderous and caused my body to vibrate uncontrollably. As the plane swept over us, I exploded like a star-shaped firework to become both everything and nothing as I dissolved into the infinite expansiveness of the blue sky. In August, my friend was diagnosed with metastatic breast cancer and she died the following year, a few days before Diana, Princess of Wales.

Although the blue ovals prescribed by Psychiatrist #2 turned off my dreams as a tap does a water faucet, I woke up often every night, startled each time as if someone had slunk up behind me and tapped me ever so slightly on the shoulder. It was February in The Urban City, a notoriously dismal month that began with a collective countdown to the number of days until spring break. I dispensed with a countdown that year, but my Wise-But-Drug-Addicted Girlfriend kept a continuous supply of red licorice in a kitchen drawer normally reserved for chocolate, and we played marathon sessions of Crib to temper the dread I wore like a pair of dirty socks I couldn't take off.

I decided I might as well employ my default behaviour when the wait and the weather were threatening to test my patience and drown my hope. I fled to Somewhere Sunny, a coastal city two thousand kilometres south of The Urban City. I booked my stay at a Victorian hotel across from the sea, where the shimmering horizon would remind me it was an illusion because the ocean carried on beyond it. And life would carry on beyond my current crisis whether I continued to live or not. I was a mere droplet in the sea. I was larger than a water molecule and much smaller than the volume of any wave. But the truth was, quantifying myself in such a way didn't really matter in the grand scheme of things. Whether I was a droplet, a wave, or the whole sea itself, I was still at the mercy of powers beyond my control, just like the sea was at the mercy of the gravitational forces of the sun and moon. I was changeable and impermanent, and subject to things beyond my control, regardless of how big or small I was.

During the plane ride I read a little blue hard-covered book called, "Heal Thyself" by Edward Bach. The book described physical and mental ailments from the perspective of resolving karma. In the section about diseases where people lose their cognition and ability to control their movements, Bach theorized that those so afflicted had abused their power by exerting control over others without their permission or with ill intent. Affliction with an ailment that immobilized a person physically and mentally was a corrective measure, a resolution to the disharmony and in keeping with the laws of nature. His theories made me curious, but my curiosity suffered a sudden death from the notion I could have been an abusive dictator in other life-times. I was having enough difficulty reconciling the events in my current life. What was the point of such conjecture when I couldn't verify my evolution over multiple lifetimes? And even if I could as a way to accept a difficult fate, the facts of my life situation would not change from a new awareness. Admittedly, my perspective could have changed, but this life was tormenting me enough and I didn't need to feel guilty about one or more other lifetimes of bad behaviour. The little blue book was an interesting and provocative read, but I was no longer in the mood to ponder the unknowable.

The clouds dissipated as the plane made its way south of The Urban City. Somewhere Sunny was warm and soothing. Once off the plane, I hurried out of the airport to get a glimpse of the perfectly blue sky, and as soon as I did, my body responded as if I had sunk my toes into warm beach sand and stretched myself out like a solar panel needing to be recharged. Once booked into the hotel, I decided the normally off-limits in-suite snack bar was there for my uninhibited enjoyment. I basically told my internal critic chirping, "Don't eat that junk," to "Shut the hell up." I sat on the royal blue carpet in front of the mini-bar and worked my way through the treats without any care about the cost or the caloric consequences. I started with the Oreo cookies and worked my way through the chocolate bars and ended with the nuts. But the snack bar could only satisfy me for so long. Although feeling shaky on my feet, I needed to leave the hotel room.

Beauty oozed out of everyone and everything in Somewhere Sunny. And even though the sun made the surroundings shimmer, everything appeared threateningly ephemeral, as if at any given moment, all things could disintegrate, leaving me in a void with nothing to cling to. Imprisoned in a tenuous reality while walking the streets of Somewhere Sunny, I questioned whether people noticed my strange disequilibrium. But unsteady and unstable people walk among us all the time. I was just another in the crowd, one example of the natural state everywhere.

I wanted to get on the Ferris wheel but couldn't be certain I wouldn't leap impulsively from my seat in a moment of desperation. I couldn't do that to the people enjoying the beauty of the pier. I walked to its farthest edge many times during my brief stay in Somewhere Sunny; without fail, on each occasion, I thought about jumping off, but again reminded myself about the time and expense to save me. Equally disturbing was the idea that if I did drown, someone would have to drag my limp body back to the beach. Plus the logistics of getting me back to The Urban City would have been a hassle for The Systems in Somewhere Sunny and The Urban City. The worst thought was that I would become a coroner's case and be subjected to the autopsy protocol.

On my final day, I spent most of my time wandering aimlessly through the local shops surrounding the hotel. When I arrived back at my room in the evening, there were several voice messages from my Island friend, each with an urgent plea to call her back immediately. By the frantic tone of her voice, I thought there must have been an emergency of some sort on The Island. I called her back to learn she had received an unexpected message from her mother, which was odd because she had already entered The Great Unknown. When Island Friend and I were studying at the Island University, her mother had been like one to me. She was wise but also radiated a serene beauty from her daily practice of T'ai Chi right up until her death from ovarian cancer a few years earlier.

That afternoon, Island Friend had driven to her sister's house for dinner. When she walked into the house, she found her sister ashen and in shock, staring at the hallway entrance Island Friend had just walked through. My friend was terrified by the look on her sister's face, which could only mean something disastrous had happened. Her sister told her she had just seen their mother, who had yelled out to her, "Middle2 doesn't have the gene for Huntington's disease, she's just supposed to think she has it." Island Friend and I later hypothesized about why her mom's spirit had appeared to her sister rather than to either of us. Her sister had always been the calm, rational presence in our lives, coupled with the fact she was a devout non-believer in spirits, ghosts, and all things metaphysical. Island Friend and I weren't ardent believers, but we were curious. If Island Friend had claimed such a sighting, I would have dismissed it as a hoax she had conjured up to calm me; and if the spirit had appeared to me, I would have interpreted any vision of otherworldly beings as a side effect of the sleeping pills or an affirmation that Huntington's disease had begun its siege in the area of my brain responsible for such things. For the remainder of my trip, the ethereal appearance of Island Friend's mother had become the cozy blanket I wrapped myself in when I crawled into bed each night, even though I remained convinced about my genetic state with respect to Huntington's disease.

When I returned to The Urban City, fog hovered over it like a mushroom cloud. Even now, years later, it's still hard for me to admit I was going to commit suicide if I carried the gene for the disease. It still feels like a shameful action, marking me as weak and unable to cope with the reality of a physically and mentally debilitating disease. I couldn't look it in the eye and declare that my fighting spirit would prevail no matter how bad things got.

Psychiatrist #2 asked me how was I going to end it all. As I revealed my death plan, I thought I detected traces of dismay in his sympathetic eyes. After a few moments of silence, I asked him what he would do in my position. He didn't know. I was relieved. Even a man who had heard every possible horror story about pain and suffering was human and he could not say how he would react in the same situation. But I was also disappointed. Somehow I wanted him to reclaim the courage I had lost by saying he was certain I could cope with bad news. His liturgy would continue: "With the Human Genome Project, science is on the cusp of being able to splice genes and eclipse the bad ones. Scientists have been genetically engineering bacteria since the 1970s. Much progress can be made in twenty years. Middle2, you need to have faith. Anything is possible…"

The Cinderella myth dies hard. Another man was not going to rescue me from my new misery. In the meantime, I continued to survey the neighbourhood for a quiet and private place to die. I needed the privacy to prevent someone from appearing who would talk me out of it, and the quiet as a way to commune with God, if one existed, to have mercy on my soul and welcome me with open arms into The Great Unknown without judgment for lacking the courage to surrender to my fate with grace.

February 13 arrived soon enough. My Island Friend made the trip to The Urban City to accompany me to my evening appointment with Psychiatrist #2. I cried when she arrived with a white, thick terry cloth bathrobe as a gift for me. I prayed if I wore it in my car, my deathbed, the white would somehow purify me as some form of embalmment that prevented me from burning in Hell. Included in the gift was a little blue velvet bag with three stones inside, one inscribed with Courage, another with Strength, and a third with Hope. I lacked all three, except for a small measure of hope that with the end of my physical being, someone who needed the cherished stones would receive them through a benefactor acting on my behalf. I didn't need to bequeath them to Eldest because she already personified all three.

Island Friend and I reminisced about life and discussed its big questions while we drove for most of the day. During the last half-hour of the drive we sat in silence. When the dread of the next couple of hours tightened its grip around me, I stole the occasional glimpse of the sound and saw the island mounds as portals to other realities I could paraglide to, and as soon as I touched down on them, I could dump my consciousness as easily as dropping the wing, harness, and accessories I used to get there. Before long, the hidden sun slid beneath the horizon and night fell as it had the previous day and the day before that. The islands and my fantasies faded away. I watched the raindrops fall as softly as tears on the windshield and the wipers sweep them away. Once back in The Urban City, neither of us had much of an appetite and decided to wait for dinner until after the appointment with Psychiatrist #2.

The office manager always kept the national radio station playing in the background after she left the office. My friend and I sat down in the empty waiting area to discover a special program on requiems was playing. The requiems filled the air as we waited, and no matter how many deep breaths I took, I was dizzy in the same way I used to get when I got up too quickly. After twenty minutes, we heard Psychiatrist #2's office door open. As soon as the patient before me left the office, he called me in. My genetic fate was no longer some abstract concept. However, having accepted the imminent end of my life, an eerie calmness washed over me as I walked into his office and plunked myself into the wicker chair as usual. I didn't engage him in any idle chatter. Instead, I stared out the window at the bridge that descended into the darkness of The Urban City park while he prepared the video camera.

"What will you do if your results are positive?"

"You already know," I answered.

"You haven't changed your mind?"

"Not unless all the medical texts are mistaken about what Huntington's disease does to people who have it. I'd be crazier than I already am to live like that. I don't see the point, frankly."

"I see," he said with the same sympathetic look he gave me just before I started to cry at the end of my regressions that led to killing my dad and talking to my mom.

"The Geneticist faxed me the results of your genetic testing," he said.

In that instant, all the lights in the building went out, which happened frequently at 7:00 p.m. during previous appointments. But that night the darkness startled me and sent my heart racing. My heart didn't lie. I was afraid again. The lights came back on as quickly as this thought darted through my mind.

"You do not carry the gene for Huntington's disease," Psychiatrist #2 announced, and he handed me two pieces of paper. I read them both, with Psychiatrist #2 watching me as I did. The first was the fax cover page, and the second a detailed analysis of the findings. At the bottom of the first page was a short note written by The Geneticist: "The attached results show

that she IS NOT AT RISK of developing Huntington's disease."
I had inherited fifteen CAG repeats from Mom and seventeen
from Dad, both being nowhere near the zone of uncertainty.

When I had finished reading the report, I looked up at
Psychiatrist #2.

"What will you do now?" he wanted to know.

"Live, I hope."

I needed to reverse my prescribed terminal state by finding
a purpose, a reason for being. But the truth was, I didn't know
what it meant "to live". At the end of our session, we left the
little alcove that housed the wicker chair, his round-back chair,
and the video camera. Clutching my paper results (which he
counselled to guard for insurance purposes), I walked to the
door with Psychiatrist #2 and we entered the waiting area to
find Island Friend's fingers stuck to her mouth. The requiems
had stopped. Looking at me, she could tell she wouldn't have to
help me get dressed in the white robe she had brought me and
pray I would take T'ai Chi lessons from her mother in The Great
Unknown. After she hugged me, she flew into Psychiatrist #2's
arms. Watching them in a warm, tender embrace, I realized I'd
never hugged anyone that way. But I made a promise to myself
that I would one day.

Island Friend and I left Psychiatrist #2's office arm-in-arm to
the elevator.

"You don't have Huntington's disease," she chanted, tugging
my elbow each time she did.

"Yes, but Eldest does," I repeated in my mind with each of her
chants. I watched the round black buttons light up as the elevator passed each floor down to the ground.

"Let's go eat!" she interrupted.

Just how was I supposed to jump up and down for joy as if I had just won the DNA lottery when I hated The Powers That Be for the cursed fate they had doled out to Eldest? Each time I thought about her future, I felt a stab in my heart like a nail being hammered into the very centre of it. If any event reinforced life's injustice, it was that she would have to face a challenge more difficult than any from her youth. Why her? The best questions lead to others or have grey answers. Eldest would never become a mother, but she would eventually be one of The System's adult infants.

As Island Friend and I walked arm-in-arm into the restaurant, two men at the bar who were eagerly eyeing us mirrored each other's nauseating chuckle that had me thinking their combined brain size was much smaller than that of a newborn's. We ignored them. Over dinner, we talked about hopes and dreams, even though I still felt morose and hadn't begun to extricate myself from the self-imposed death sentence that lacked space for any entries beneath "The End". The two men were still at the bar as we made our way to the exit, their level of inebriation more advanced, which had eliminated any possibility of social grace.

"Hey, are you the two lesbos who came in here a while ago?" said the one closest to us.

"No, but I see you're the same obnoxious drunks we ignored walking in here," Island friend quipped. I laughed out loud for the first time in thirty days.

At my apartment later that night, I lay in my bed, unable to sleep as Island Friend snuggled up beside me, her breath soft and shallow, an indication that her subconscious was not tormenting her. I couldn't give mine a chance to hold me in its grip and toss me around like a rag doll. When I did nod off, it reared its ugly head like an arrogant and nosy neighbour who scolded me in the same tone I had lectured my mother in during one of my sessions with Psychiatrist #2.

"How dare you, Middle2? How dare you think about taking the cowardly way out of your life if you carried the devilish gene whose pitchfork poked out of your family crest?"

Even though I turned away from her and started to walk away, she had the ability to lift herself with her house and yard as her stage and walk backwards in front of me to continue her performance.

"You're a self-righteous little bitch, you know that? People have suffered, people still suffer, and they will continue to suffer. Why do you think you're so special you can just walk away from pain when you've reached some arbitrary threshold determined by you?" She stopped pointing her finger and put her hands on her hips while continuing the lecture as she paced back and forth on the lawn.

"Things don't work that way, Middle2. You're supposed to learn how to react to all circumstances with grace. You should know this by now," she continued.

"Here, put these on for size, you cow," I hollered, as I threw my shoes at her. She put them on and tied the laces. "How comfortable are they? Why don't you take a little stroll in them and give me the blister count at the end of your walkabout," I shouted to her, making a speaker with my hands cupped around my mouth to make sure she could hear me.

I took a deep breath in preparation for giving her a lecture of my own. But I woke up in a sweat before I could deliver my rebuttal. Island Friend's breathing was shallower by then, and the only other sound I heard was the "tink" of the electric heater on the wall beside my bed. I lifted my arms and cupped the back of my head with my hands.

I didn't get the chance to escort the neighbour through my ancestral cemetery to show her the plots of two of my cousins who had died as broken-hearted teenagers, and Dad's brother who had also died of complications from Huntington's disease. And leaving the cemetery, I would have also told her about my cousin with schizophrenia.

I imagined how the conversation would have continued.

"I can't wear these shoes," she whined. "You pronate, I supinate. The differences in our feet don't lend themselves to sharing footwear, even flats or running shoes."

"Oh, give me a few minutes. I'll go find shoes belonging to someone who supinates," I'd insist. If she had the ability to lift her household and plant herself in front of me when I tried to walk away from her, surely I would have been capable of manifesting shoes that met her requirements.

"No, no, dear. I can't waste time waiting for you, even if it is only for a few minutes," she replied. "I have other things to do."

"Yeah, sure you do. Of course. Far be it for me to detain you," motioning with my hands for her to get on her way. A siren in the distance shook me out of my reverie. Island Friend took a deep breath. I turned away from her and stared at the glass butterfly attached to a mini-light in the electrical outlet across from the bed. It flickered ever so slightly. I lay still for what seemed like hours but fell asleep again sometime during the quietest time of the night. But I didn't dream about the neighbour.

I can't say for sure whether I would have reclined in my car with sleeping pills and carbon monoxide as my chosen protocol for entering The Great Unknown if Psychiatrist #2 had told me

I carried the gene. But I certainly had planned to do it before he handed me the two-page result. The fact that I thought about doing it at all made me want to hide in the darkest corner of my house for an indefinite period of time. And if I did re-emerge into the world at some future date, I wanted to be someone other than Middle2.

After Island Friend left The Urban City, I studied the two-page lab report; anger surged in my gut as if I'd been reliving my rage toward Dad for killing Mom when I looked at the header of the report. Driving to my next appointment, I practised what I would tell Psychiatrist #2 once he turned on the video equipment and sat across from me.

"You're a bastard, and I don't need you with an alphabet behind your name telling me I'm emotionally retarded." And I wouldn't have stopped there. "You think you understand suffering, don't you? How would you have felt if I couldn't wait any longer two nights ago? What if I'd carried out my plan a few days early? Huh? How would you have felt? Would you have taken any misery to your grave? Probably not. Because in reality you don't really give a damn about your patients."

Arriving in the parking lot outside his office, I stepped out of my car but I didn't walk like the downtrodden pathetic orphan from Somewhere Small. I was aware of a lightness of being and a quickening in my step, while I imagined the puddles in the parking lot as squares I could hopscotch, with my left and right feet taking turns stomping down on each of them. And I would say out loud, "Now *that*'s alacrity!" as I opened the door to the building where Psychiatrist #2's office was.

A few minutes later, seated across from Psychiatrist #2, I initiated a different conversation with the man who knew the most intimate details of my life.

"You received my lab results two days before my appointment," I confronted him. "I guess torture is included in the treatment plan, is it?" I said, looking into his eyes.

"That wasn't my intention."

"I convinced you I had the disease, didn't I? And you decided to punish me for the misery I caused you."

"Oh sure," Psychiatrist #2 laughed. "Actually, The Geneticist and I both didn't think you had it, but we couldn't tell you what we thought."

"And you also decided you couldn't tell me when you knew, it appears." Tears filled my eyes. Another man I'd come to trust had disappointed me.

"I'm sorry," he said and stopped there.

Of course, suffering begets narcissism, and it occurred to me months later that I wasn't the only hard case he had been dealing with at the time. The truth was, he only dealt with hard cases. In all likelihood, during those two days, he'd counselled a few patients who'd tried to commit suicide, parents of children who had, or spouses whose husband or wife hadn't come home one day and never would.

My annoyance grew with each session when he continued the habit of asking me how I was feeling as soon as he sat down across from me. One night I didn't give him the chance to ask me the question.

"How are you?" I asked while he was preparing the video equipment.

"Oh, so you're finally beginning to see the inequity in this relationship," he responded as he made his way to the chair across from me.

I was ready to leave the wicker chair in search of an equitable relationship.

Psychiatrist #2 helped me recover enough pieces of my spirit for me to begin envisioning a future. He packaged these pieces into a box, much like a jigsaw puzzle, for me to take away and later decide just how to put them together. With each session, he helped me build the border that acted as a womb to my self-discovery. Once the border had been built, the sessions with him needed to end and I could complete its interior, or not. Leaving Psychiatrist #2's office after our last appointment, I experienced flashbacks to my early years in Somewhere Small, to the days when I had become swept away in flights of fancy while running on the expansive grassy fields of my first schoolyard. In those moments, I knew without a doubt that anything was possible, regardless of my life circumstances in The Alcoholic Foster Parents' house. While at their home, I bobbed inside the bottles they were drowning in, but I was the genie that could and would squeeze out of the impossibly small bottlenecks. Even from inside the bottles, I could see the amorphous shapes of the trees and the hazy rainbows on stormy days. Despite the blurry views, I knew I'd eventually become a grateful witness to clear images of the world's beauty. And that time had finally come.

By the end of the year, I set out on my first trip to Faraway Places. Yes, I had decided that an important subtext embedded in my incantation to "live" called me to leave my native land, to explore the world I lived in, to see its splendour. The world was no longer the miniature plastic globe on the windowsill of my grade seven classroom, and it was no longer an object I could only experience through my finger tips. The world was much bigger than its replica and I was ready to walk along its many paths.

CHAPTER 18

FARAWAY PLACES #1

The hero's journey always begins with the call. One way or another, a guide must come to say, "Look, you're in sleepy land. Wake. Come on a trip. There's a whole aspect of your consciousness, your being, that's not been touched. So you're at home here? Well, there's not enough of you there." And so it starts.
Joseph Campbell

Like learning how to ride a bike, most of us need to crash and hurt ourselves a few times in relationships before finding one that doesn't leave us bruised and battered. When we find the right one, we know it isn't perfect but we don't become emotionally shattered every time all hell breaks loose. This brings me to love #3: BuddhaBound. Let me start by saying he was attractive and a self-ascribed "evolved soul," which perhaps all by itself should have been a burning red flag. Most evolved souls are too busy trying to solve big problems rather than telling the world how advanced they are. And if he had in fact been an exalted being, he wouldn't have been talking to me on planet Earth. Instead, he would have already graduated to the realm where The Powers That Be operated. But I had developed an interest in meditation and he had written a book on the subject, which made me assume he was at least on the path to enlightenment. It didn't take long to figure out our definitions of "evolved" were as different as salt and pepper. His understanding included the ability to sit in the dentist's chair to have his mercury fillings replaced without the need for anesthetic; mine revolved around his ability to live independently, which meant he could also pay his own bills. At age forty, he still lived with his mother; this should have been more than a red flag—it should have been a fire alarm sending me on a marathon in the opposite direction, and dialling Relationship 911. Clearly I'd developed a case of amnesia about the lesson I had added to my romantic archives about refusing to date men who still lived with one or both parents, regardless of the halo they spun around their heads while expounding on their altruism.

He also appeared more interested in finding a partner who could partially fund his creative projects and technology toys than someone with whom he could build an intimate relationship. I became certain his angelic self-assessment was delusional with his disclosure that he had ended his marriage by telling his wife he was going to the library to conduct some research for the book he was writing. He did go to the library alright, but he failed to tell her that it was located on an island in the middle of the Pacific Ocean three thousand miles away from The Urban City. At one point, he tried to convince me he deserved to be in relationships with people who supported him financially, affording him the freedom to focus exclusively on his spiritual and creative pursuits.

Finding such people was his good karma for lifetimes of devotion to God. While he basked in the glow of his identity as an enlightened being, I continued grappling with my emotional disability by making a plan to remediate it.

I thought making a solo trip to Faraway Places might advance it because social science gurus agree all good relationships begin with the relationship we have with ourselves. What better way to improve the relationship with myself than by taking a trip to Europe, somewhere I'd never been? And given Eldest's fate and my one-month walk down the path toward death's door, it was time to disinter the memories of my globe spinning days in my little elementary school surrounded by unflappable poplars.

And after the chestnut experience orchestrated by The Powers That Be, I had to believe they had not made a mistake by dropping me in Somewhere Small. Perhaps some combination of Mom and Dad's genes created wanderlust in me and life circumstances intensified its expression over the years. What began as my toddler adventures in the neighbourhood surrounding The Little House to find the cats and dogs that wandered about, progressed to staring at the plastic globe on the classroom windowsill only a few feet away from me, as if it were a boy I liked but needed the safety of the space between us. But when puberty activated my wanderlust, I could no longer stop myself from approaching the globe and running my fingers over the countries and oceans. I placed the tips of my little fingers in the middle of the Atlantic or Pacific Oceans, spun the globe, and saw my future glimmering in the reflection of the fluorescent landing strip along the Arctic Circle. Sometimes I spun it counterclockwise, and other times in a clockwise direction. My heart raced as the countries blurred into a psychedelic gyrating mass that hypnotized me. I tried to focus on the equator as it slowed, allowing my attention to turn to the northern hemisphere two times out of three since just over two thirds of the Earth's land is above the equator. As much as I loved water, I didn't want to be a plastic bottle bobbing in the middle of an ocean in the southern hemisphere.

I let the prospect of adventure guide me when I snuck from my seat to engage in a spin session with my little round friend. In the seventh grade at my elementary school, I had begun a clandestine dialogue with my constant companion—and what a companion it was. The globe stimulated all my senses as it slowed and finally stopped, with my gaze landing on some Faraway Place. From time to time, my eyes settled on my native land, and in particular on Somewhere Small. On those occasions, I spun it again to remind myself about free will and probability. I could change the outcome by trying again, and the likelihood of my eyes landing on the same spot with a few consecutive spins was low.

I regarded the outcome of the conversations with my companion as good news when my eyes fixated on a Faraway Place I already wanted to visit. Those moments were as glorious as watching the setting sun in Somewhere Small, because as soon as it disappeared from my view, it would rise in every place around the world within twenty-four hours, and some of those places were ones I already knew I wanted to see. The most thrilling thought about the sun was that within twenty-four hours it would rise and set in places I didn't yet know about. I sometimes doubted whether I could escape the clutches of Somewhere Small or muster the willpower to do it, yet I continued to twirl the globe anyway. I believed my dreams dripped oil into the hands that threatened to hold me captive in Somewhere Small. But there was an equally potent property of dreams that I discovered while jogging around the fields and through the trails of Somewhere Small. Dreams asphyxiated doubt, and as they grew, my doubts began to choke and I fully expected they would cease to have an air supply long before I made my entrance into The Great Unknown.

Although I tried to conduct my business when my teacher was otherwise distracted, I caught him watching me from time to time and all he did was smile. Who was he to deny my self-taught lessons in geography? He did what a teacher is supposed to do besides educate us on the fundamentals of reading, writing, and arithmetic—he fostered curiosity and creativity in his students.

During those elementary school days, I didn't think about how I would earn enough money to make such trips, with whom I would take them, or the sequence of my adventures. Somewhere Small had The Big River running through it, and that river dumped into an ocean with currents that eventually carried its contents to Faraway Places. I would become The Big River one day, but the details didn't matter. I just needed faith. Having faith in a dream is quiet, yet more potent than talking about hopes. Hope is often riddled with doubt, but faith is the ultimate time traveller who already sees the dream as a reality. Even a prisoner can build dreams from within his cell where there are no views to the horizon or to the heavens. She just needs to envision her future as the truth with the same conviction of Galileo, who knew before everyone else that the Earth revolved around the sun.

And at the age of thirty-four, nearly twenty years after my grade seven teacher taught me that dreaming and wondering were as important as geometry and algebra, my most anticipated exercise to satisfy my curiosity still related to a form of geometry. It involved the lines, circles, triangles, and parallelograms created from tracing the steps I would take in Faraway Places.

My adventures began on October 1, 1997, when I left The Urban City for the first time to explore another continent. Walking into the international terminal and looking up at the display of departing flights, I smiled as if it contained a list of new friends I would become very fond of. Once I stored my luggage in the overhead bin, I reclined in my seat on the airplane as if leaning back onto the chest of a man I wouldn't just like. He was one I would fall in love with.

Arriving early in the morning after the red-eye flight to Heathrow Airport, I had seven hours to wait before the connecting flight to Nice, France. The terminal where our plane disembarked was old, dark, and dreary, and renovations to Terminal 5 had not yet been conceived. The thought of staying in the depressing place and trying to get some sleep on a hard bench made me feel more exhausted than I already was. I decided to take the train to a small town a few miles east of the airport. Once I arrived, my first stop was at the local library to send emails to both Island Friend and BuddhaBound, telling them I'd arrived safely at my first destination and was eager to explore the quaint British town a few miles from the airport.

Leaving the library, I decided to search for a pub offering vegetarian dishes. I thought the odds of finding such an eatery were not in my favour; however, what happened next would delight me more than two eggs over easy and a mimosa. Half a block into my search, two gentlemen—one eighty-four and the other in his fifties—approached me from behind. They each hooked one arm in mine as if getting ready to lift me over a gaping hole I'd be certain to fall into without their perfectly timed rescue. Their demeanour was playful and fun, and filled with intentions to be the cheery town mascots for a naïve traveler. The fifty-something-year-old was avuncular, and the older of the two, a wise grandfatherly type.

"You must need breakfast, my lady," said the uncle. "But we need to make a stop first. Even with money in my wallet, I want to make sure we have enough. One never can tell how much anything's going to cost when a woman's involved," he added.

"Don't worry," I replied. "I'm not much of a breakfast eater and I'm Scottish, even with other people's money." I decided to exclude the Irish and Swedish influences or the fact that I liked fine champagne and five-star hotels.

"Not always true, young lady," he said. "Lasses are frugal, you're right. Until you're divorced from one."

I chuckled and smiled at the grandfather as we made our way into a horse-betting establishment.

In the first bet, the uncle won four hundred pounds. The grandfather shook his head at the incredible stroke of good luck, and with one look at my wide eyes he bent over in a paroxysm of laughter. He was one of those people whose entire body shook when humour took hold of him. Going back outside with my hosts, I wondered what we would talk about over breakfast but was already certain I wouldn't need English breakfast tea to warm my belly.

Within a minute of sitting down at a table in a pub across the street, the grandfather took my right hand and opened it to expose my palm. Staring into it like a gypsy gazing into her crystal ball, he ran his crooked index finger over the straight unchained line spanning the middle.

"You'll never lose your mind," the grandfather said with wide eyes as if he had just solved the anagram "sane to the end" whose individual letters overlaid the line separating the upper and lower sections of my palm. "But watch that heart," he warned.

"Bring us three glasses of fresh-squeezed orange juice," asked the uncle of the waitress who'd arrived at our table.

"What's wrong with my heart?"

"Nothing physical," the grandfather assured me.

"Bloody hell, good fellow, leave the poor girl alone," piped in the uncle. "We want her to have happy memories of us," he added, smiling and taking my other hand in his. "Besides, you and I just might find we are of the same lovely mind," he sang, searching for my heart in my eyes.

"Maybe you should read your poetry to a relative," I said, looking into the grandfather's eyes.

"Don't mind him. He likes drama," the grandfather said with a sigh. "You'll live in California, by the way, my dear. And you have Tinseltown in your blood, whether you like it or not. I imagine you don't. But get used to the Americans. You'll spend a lot of time with them."

"Oh, and what in my palm tells you that?" I wanted to know, withdrawing my left hand from the uncle's.

"It's not in the lines. I just see things when I touch peoples' hands. It's no different when someone else with the gift looks into the leaves in a teacup. Images just come."

I looked into my empty cup and only saw loose leaves in a moist, untidy clump.

The uncle had remarried, but as a writer he was perpetually in search of a muse, and the grandfather had not been fortunate in his romantic fate. He'd met the perfect woman fifty years earlier but she died before they could establish a union with The Simple Life as its banner. He'd had no worldly aspirations as a young man. He wanted to settle in a little town with his princess, buy a house with her, and raise a family. He reminisced about the many opportunities over the years, but none quite measured up to the young beauty he'd fallen in love with years before. Despite the early loss of his only love, the grandfather's gait was on the verge of being a skip, the corners of his lips didn't droop, and his worldviews weren't cloudy, even though his vision was from cataracts. But had he developed an unhealthy idolatry of the woman he had deemed perfect in every way? This version of the tragic love story has always struck me as especially unkind because he who remains is haunted by the impassioned memories of new love. It's easy to imagine how the bliss of blossoming love becomes suspended in the exalted realm of fantasy. True love endures all seasons, not just the radiance of the early days. And as the weather comes and goes, the love and respect for each other deepens because of the storms they've weathered together. He didn't get to find out whether his deep infatuation would have evolved into true love because his was also a fairytale, but one that ended a little earlier into the plot than "Cinderella." But like most fairytales, his and Cinderella's ended in the spring of love, not the winter. In him I recognized a kindred spirit whose heart had been bent out of shape in the same way as mine.

The two gentlemen insisted on accompanying me back to the airport so that we could continue our conversation about life and love. In our goodbye at the entrance to the departure gates, we hugged each other as if we'd been lifelong friends, and yet when we parted with hands raised in the final goodbye as I walked away, we all knew our paths were parallel lines that had crossed each other's for the first and final time. Our instant and easy rapport inevitably led to conversations about life's most important topics. They were members of my tribe, the people with whom I could develop an emotional intimacy I had never known.

The first leg of my trip landed me in the south of France where I enjoyed traipsing through the old section of Nice, adjacent to the Mediterranean seaside. I was convinced the taxi driver who brought me to my hotel had been a discontented man who'd not followed his dream of becoming a NASCAR racer and evidently prided himself in his ability to navigate the busy streets as if he were one. I had become complacent from fatigue, and if my first night in a Faraway Place was going to be my last, at least I had begun the journey.

Arriving at the hotel, I found it charming in its old world character. The room was filled with antiques and the floor-to-ceiling windows opened to a landscape artist's paradise. I smelled the bygone years in the room and communed with the guests who had also slept there, some solo like me, and others curled up with their lovers after having roamed the cobbled streets of the romantic city by the sea. With the spirits of many in my room, I wasn't lonely.

In the middle of the night, I woke feeling abnormally thirsty, and when I turned on the light, a myriad of cockroaches dispersed like fireworks and disappeared into the nooks and crannies of my abode. I had become accustomed to living in places where nocturnal activities scared me. But cockroaches didn't frighten me like spiders and people did, so I happily drifted off to sleep again once I satisfied my thirst, fully expecting my roommates to re-emerge after the lights went out.

I wandered the streets of Nice for a few days before heading to Munich to visit BrotherLove's aunt whom I'd met a few times during the twelve years we were together. Like BrotherLove's mother, she had been another woman whose company made me feel warm inside, as if I had just finished drinking a cup of hot chocolate. She worked as a forensic psychologist and we enjoyed intense conversations about relationships and life in general. She'd had one son, a talented artist but also a troubled soul who medicated his pain through drugs and alcohol no matter how much his mother loved him and prayed for his redemption. Like many of us who can't find solutions to problems through our own will and actions, she sought faith in an object, and in her case it was one she had found in a Faraway Place. During a vacation to the South Pacific, while wandering through a museum, she spotted a female Day Protector spirit whose purpose was to prevent illness and disaster. She found the piece too expensive and decided not to purchase it while there, but once she had returned to Germany, she decided that need trumped the price tag. When it arrived several weeks later, she hung the piece above her dining room table for the mask's protective qualities to radiate throughout her home and beyond, to the places her son found himself in.

Munich needed a Day Protector to rain softness on its centre. There was a ubiquitous depression in the city, except in the historic centre where artisans operated their businesses and sold their products. During one of my excursions, I saw exit signs to Dachau, and even though the reservoir in my heart where grief resided was no longer at capacity, I couldn't face the thirty-thousand ghosts there. BrotherLove's aunt and I discussed the psychological residue she also believed was real and palpable in the city she had lived in for most of her adulthood.

I experienced melancholy's high tide when it was time to say goodbye to her at the train station after my one-week stay. Yet again, I had met a kindred spirit with whom I shared the same intellectual and emotional connection I had with the British gentlemen. But with her I could add another element to our connectedness. We were women whose spirits were broken in the place that makes people empathetic. But she had found a way to use her sensitivity to help others, whereas I had positive thoughts filled with good intentions that lacked an outlet.

The next leg of my trip had me travelling from Munich to Venice by train. I met two older couples during the journey, one en route to The Vatican City and the other heading to my much-anticipated destination. I had planned to disembark at Verona to visit some of the churches and languish in the memory of Romeo and Juliet, but I decided Venice in its entirety would be my church of choice. And as we approached the historic city, I no longer wanted to partake in the memories associated with tragic love stories. The thought made me tired.

My first view of Venice is one of the most enchanting moments in my travels to Faraway Places. We arrived on a Saturday night as the sun was setting and the city was bustling with activity along the Grand Canal. The couple and I stood with our jaws agape after uttering, "Wow," in unison as the gondola approached its final drop-off point.

Making our way to the entrance of the Piazza San Marco filled me with great expectations. The narrow passage to the plaza opened into an expansive marvel that was the square. Its perimeter was lined with trattorias whose relaxed and happy occupants were ensconced in animated conversations while musicians around them played an assortment of tempered classical pieces.

The couple pleaded ignorance about how to find their hotel and asked me to help them locate it, and if I was successful, they wanted to treat me to dinner. With little effort we found it and later enjoyed pizza in a modest cafe in the square. The feigned incompetence was their way of wanting to be my temporary parents. I think they also sympathized with my solo status in a romantic place. I didn't disclose my sadness to them but wondered if they had caught a glimpse of my watery eyes as the train approached the arrivals platform.

On my second night, I decided to venture out and have a glass of Prosecco in one of the many quaint eateries. I chose a small trattoria called "Alfredo's" where I could write postcards with pictures of gondolas and the Piazza San Marco to Island Friend and BuddhaBound. Within a few minutes of being served and finding a pen in my purse, I was invited to the table occupied by the owner, his manager, and a mother-daughter duo. I sipped on my drink while they inundated me with questions about my profession, marital status, and what I did for adventure in The Urban City. The men wanted to see a photo of BuddhaBound.

"He's too good-looking to be trusted," the bar manager said, shaking his head. "You realize he's probably having an affair right now," he continued, smiling widely at me as if he were telling me something utterly splendid about my future. The women and the owner laughed uproariously as if he had just told them the funniest joke they'd ever heard.

"Don't listen to him," the mother said, slapping him coyly on the back of his head. "His optimism's disappearing faster than the hair on his head."

"If he is, I have the next reason to break up with him," I responded, laughing. But no one else seemed to think what I said was funny. *Oh, well*, I thought. I took another sip from my glass and enjoyed the sensation of bubbles tickling my upper lip.

"I could give you another reason," the bar manager suggested. "We could discuss it over a nightcap back at my apartment."

"Oh no, I suspect you're a better host to a crowd."

The owner crumpled his red napkin and placed it over his mouth to stifle his laughter, and the women looked at each other and rolled their eyes. I wasn't sure if their reactions were due to the bar manager's final question or my answer to it.

I savoured the curvy streets and antique surprises of Venice but I avoided the majority of tourist attractions due to the lengthy waits. I absorbed the beauty of the city filled with ancient buildings that reminded me of osteoporotic women who still radiated elegance despite being clothed in wrinkled, torn, and faded dresses. Would I become Venice as an old woman whose hourglass midsection has ballooned to that of gnocchi, and whose brow has creased from indulging curiosities and pondering puzzles? I can't predict my future, but I do aspire to be the old woman who knows grace and grit are more important than physical beauty and that mystery is as important as knowledge because it's what kept me thirsty over the years.

During my daily jaunts, I became enamoured with Murano glass, and like BrotherLove's aunt, I needed a symbolic piece that held my hopes for the future. I chose a clear glass statue of two lovers embracing, but his and her forms were also still distinct as individuals. The glass was speckled with gold flecks that would glitter even at night under the faint glow of the city lights in The Urban City. I bought the piece as a symbol of the kind of love I wanted to give and receive in my lifetime; having recently imbibed the energy of the Day Protector, I was sure its powers had begun to manifest with my statuesque find in Venice. I wanted a love that glittered like the gold flecks in "The Lovers," and one that could endure periods of darkness. I wanted another who honoured the individual as much as the couple, and independence as much as cooperation. I wanted one who didn't lose sight of the parts comprising the whole, yet he could appreciate wholeness without needing to dissect it. We would learn significant things from our individual journeys and from the one we created together. And having met him, I would come to know that he had the courage to open his eyes in periods of darkness, and during them he had experienced some of the most magnificent visions, having lost his attachment to things and even to himself sometimes. And he wouldn't need me to believe he can do anything. He will have reached that conclusion already. I suppose if I had to say one thing about him, it would be, "There's a man who's calm in the desert, during vertiginous sandstorms and hallucinations from dehydration. Staring into the high noon and midnight skies doesn't scare him, and infinity is provocative because he is certain that interesting things thrive beyond boundaries, and the most important things have no boundaries at all."

The day I left Venice to make my way back to the train station for the scheduled departure to the south of France I experienced the natural phenomenon of *acqua alta* as I approached St. Mark's Square. I took off my socks and shoes and waded through the cool waters that had flooded it overnight. The annual flood not only meant the high tide had arrived, but also that my tears had begun to flow from having to leave the most memorable place I had ever been. On the gondola back to the city's entrance, I had my last chance to admire the unique grandeur of the historic wonder that had welcomed me for a few days. As we glided through the canal, I silently said goodbye, and I fully intended to return one day, but the next time with the charming company of another silly romantic who would be as awestruck as I had been rounding the corner that opened out into the square. And in keeping with "The Lovers," we would enchant each other with our individual memories of the place and create new ones together.

Arriving back in Nice, I was eagerly anticipating the departure for Corsica where I would spend the final leg of my five-week trip. I was due to take a ferry there, but when I arrived at the terminal, an attendant informed us that the ferry had developed a mechanical malfunction and the scheduled departure for the day (and possibly the next couple of days) would be cancelled. I had woken up with a sore throat that morning and wondered what I would do for accommodations that night, but more importantly, how was I going to get to Corsica, if at all? The attendant mentioned ferries were still departing on schedule from Genoa, nicknamed "The Superb One" because of its former glory in the twelfth century when numerous notable landmarks had been built.

Fortunately, I had begun a conversation with an elderly couple who had a vehicle and offered me a ride. If we left immediately, we would make the final sailing of the day. And so began the second most terrifying car ride of my trip. The man might have been elderly but his ability to navigate the traffic at high speeds while completely composed astonished me. It had been a warm October afternoon in the south of France, and not one bead of sweat bubbled up along his hairline as he gripped the wheel and flexed his entire upper body while leaning slightly forward. His wife reclined in her seat, crossed her arms, and sighed with what I would describe as a midlife resignation. While gazing out at the aquamarine view to the south, she entertained me with stories of their daily life together. With the window open and the wind barely moving her stiff curls, I could still hear her sigh heavily between topics, which I hoped meant she was just tired, and not bored with her life or suffering from a pre-heart attack bout of indigestion. I spent the next two hours developing a throbbing cramp in my right hand from squeezing the door handle, while my fever and sore throat continued to remind me the flu was settling into my bones. Oh, my God, I dreaded what I expected to be one of the longest nights of my life.

Arriving at Genoa's ferry terminal, we had a short wait before boarding the boat. Whatever glory remained in The Superb One, I found no evidence of it in the terminal's toilet facilities, which consisted of a rickety hut built around an open sewer pipe descending into the bowels of the city. Shortly after boarding, I found my cabin and collapsed into my bunk. The gentle sway of the sea distracted me from the fever and body aches by lulling me into a deep sleep. The unsteady and changeable sea soothed me, because when I woke up the next morning to the voice of the captain announcing our imminent arrival to the port in Ajaccio, it took a few seconds for me to remember just who and where I was. My kindhearted travel mates taxied me to my seaside apartment that had a view to the milky Mediterranean. Stepping into my new temporary home, I luxuriated in the cooling effect of the ceramic tiles under my feet since they had not been spared the effects of the worsening fever.

I found the spotless apartment by the sea charming, with its décor comfortably minimalistic and modern. I stared at the photos on the walls and studied the artifacts the owners had collected from their excursions to Faraway Places. My throat had become lodged with what felt like multiple tiny razor blades, a sign that I had just entered day one of what would become two weeks of coughing fits, a ruddy nose, and a garbage can full of snotty, crumpled tissues.

I spent the first two days accepting my fate by being appreciative that I had arrived in an idyllic location to recover. I pulled back the blankets and deeply inhaled the scent of freshly laundered linens before slipping between the crisp sheets. I lowered my head onto the feathery pillow and, noticing how still and quiet the island retreat was, a pang of loneliness stirred in me. The feverish ache throughout my body made me think about what would happen to me if I died alone on the little French island in the Mediterranean. Would anyone even know how to find me? I had left the villa address with BuddhaBound and he was due to pick me up on my arrival date, so I presumed he would investigate in the event I didn't return on schedule. I dismissed my thoughts as absurd. If the authorities arrived after BuddhaBound's inquiries and a coroner was called to come, zip me in a bag, and ship me back to The Urban City, so be it. This was a matter of fate. What displeased me the most was the burden my sudden death would be for someone back home. And if BuddhaBound didn't help, who would? I had close friends and blood relatives back in The Urban City but could not say for certain whether any of them would take charge. And it really wasn't due to a failing in them or their lack of commitment to me. It was due to my inability to give genuine hugs and to believe that my personal relationships could be anything other than superficial and transient. Exhausted, I dug into my bag for *The Tibetan Book of the Dead*. As I tried to comprehend the bardo, my consciousness faded to darkness as the Mediterranean lapped softly on the beach below my cocoon.

When I could no longer bear the bardo or my loneliness, I sought refuge in the collection of music in my villa by the sea.

Some of the instrumental pieces reflected my loneliness, but they were a source of comfort rather than misery, because I believed the composers must have created them from having also experienced it. Knowing I had companions in my isolation made it easier to endure, even though I knew they were dead. Closing my eyes while I listened made me forget I was Middle2 because images of glaciers, snow drifts, rivers, and seas faded in and out of a field of darkness. They reminded me of my own composition: mostly water. The musical geniuses and the pictures warmed me, evaporating my feelings of separation, and releasing them into the air we all breathe.

Corsica was deserted, its European homeowners and summer travellers having returned home for the winter. I was determined to find a way into the city to rent a car so that I could explore the island no matter how much I ached, hacked, and sneezed. I decided to walk the ten kilometres to the car rental location. After all, I had just spent the last three days in bed; despite how poorly I still felt, I would muster the energy to get there. And if I lacked the physical energy, my will to have a car would be the motivating force to reach the destination even if I had to resort to crawling on all fours. I hadn't factored in the weakening side effects of fever, which made me feel as if I had been in a fight that left my entire body feeling bruised. I had the will but it didn't invigorate me. Within a kilometre, I decided the only way I was going to get there was to ask for help because the terrain was hilly and the roads lacked paved shoulders that would have made crawling a painful and perilous choice. I had done plenty of hitchhiking during my youth in Somewhere Small, and I chose the same method for the first time as an adult. Within a few minutes, a boisterous young Frenchman offered me a ride and dropped me at the front door of the rental establishment.

My relief at having arrived at a place where I could purchase freedom lasted less than a minute. I'd forgotten the photocopy of my driver's license in The Urban City, and without it, the agency could not lend me a car. Fortunately, the Frenchman was a generous gentleman and drove me back to the seaside villa where I made a call to BuddhaBound who immediately travelled to my apartment in The Urban City to fax a copy of my license to the car rental agency.

The following day I was expecting to repeat the hitchhiking sojourn back to the agency but the French couple that drove me to Genoa decided to pay me a visit. Telling them about my predicament, they once again extended their kindness by driving me to the town where I picked up the car. It never occurred to me that people whose acquaintance was new and undoubtedly short-lived would think to pay me a visit for no reason other than to see if I was on the mend. I needed to alter my expectations about the kindness of strangers.

My first excursion in the car involved driving along a windy and dusty road into a park where I had researched hiking trails. Not well enough to do any hike yet, I decided to scope it out to see what it looked like. Within a few kilometres off the beaten path, I became instantly alarmed by serious men in camouflage who were armed with guns. The island had recently experienced civil disruption and I feared I had just entered a war zone. I turned around without finding the hiking trails and made a visit to the neighbours' house to inquire about the men. The couple laughed at my fears of a civil uprising, clarifying that duck hunting season had begun and the citizens of Corsica were as serious about it as their ongoing fight for sovereignty and freedom. The men in camouflage reawakened my fear of entering The Great Unknown while in a Faraway Place. I wasn't afraid to die, even if it was alone. But I was afraid of entering The Great Unknown without having learned how to be with people between the first hello and the last goodbye. I was afraid I would enter The Great Unknown without having told the people who mattered to me I loved them. And yes, I was afraid I would never muster the courage to apologize to my sisters for failing to help Eldest when she needed me the most.

Although I hadn't trespassed very far into a soldier's war zone in the park, I didn't feel the same way when I joined the neighbours in their house for dinner the following night. Their house was too quiet. There is as much war in silence as there is in overt acts of violence. The couple moved stiffly around the kitchen while doing their best to engage in conversation about bland and benign topics. Even the children, who were eight and ten, seemed to carry an unshakeable and burdensome load as they played games in the background. The woman of the household carried an even heavier one. Her voice droned in a depressed tone as if to add the subtext to each spoken word: "We may live in paradise, but sweet Jesus, take me away from this God-forsaken place before I slit my wrists." It wasn't too long before I found out the God-forsaken thing was her husband and not the island. He flirted shamelessly with me and undoubtedly with many of the single women who crossed his path in the busy summer months.

During the dinner hour, as he fawned over me, I became embarrassed by his behaviour on her behalf and refused to indulge him in the silly game he ended up playing by himself. During the meal my fever returned, not because of the virus, but because of the social situation. Thank goodness a coughing fit struck me shortly after the freshly baked apple pie arrived on the table; I had an easy excuse to retreat to the cold ceramic tiles and crisp white sheets.

As I made my hasty exit from their house into a narrow passage leading to the backdoor entrance of my apartment, the husband invited me to go chestnut picking the following day. Having been afraid to venture into the mountains by myself because of the warnings about wild boars, I longed for a chance to see some of the terrain with people who knew it well. I accepted the invitation given my limited social options; besides, walking with people is not the same as sitting at the dinner table with them. On a walk, looking them in the eye would be optional and distractions from unpleasant topics easier to achieve.

Once behind the closed doors of my apartment, I craved a bath before crawling into bed, even though I hadn't exercised or even remotely broken into a sweat that day. I needed to wash away the residue of war and heartache that filled the house next door. Towelling myself down while getting ready for bed, I wondered if the couple had ever had a bath together and tenderly washed each other's backs while giggling over shared intimacies spoken in hushed voices. Meeting the British, Italian, and now French strangers over the past few weeks had provided me with some refinements to my list of "undesirables" in my ideal romantic relationship.

Before returning to *The Tibetan Book of the Dead*, I stared at the ceiling and thought about how a man could treat the woman who had borne his children that way. More importantly, why hadn't she demanded more from the man who had become her husband and was the father of her children? Or did they have an agreement that he could carry on as he did as long as he didn't put his dirty hands on her more than once a month? And if such an agreement existed, how on Earth did their early romance devolve to such a state? Or maybe their life together hadn't started out that way. Maybe they had loved and lost their First Loves, and within a few years after they met each other, they had mutually and concurrently reached the conclusion they had found an acceptable mate.

I regretted accepting the invitation from the previous night to go chestnut picking when the neighbour appeared alone at my doorstep in the morning, freshly showered and chirping as merrily as the birds. His wife hadn't been feeling well (I couldn't imagine why) and the children were more interested in their books and games than heading out into the hills. I remained at a safe distance from him and asked as many questions as I could think of about the history of the island while we rummaged through the damp mix of leaves and dirt for acceptable specimens. I feigned fatigue after about an hour and he promptly accepted my weakness as a reason to turn back.

After the outing, I was ready to leave the island paradise but needed to amuse myself for three more days. Between day two and three, a wicked storm descended on the Mediterranean, causing yet again another disruption in the ferry schedules. I assumed the storm would pass quickly and the skies would be clear and the seas glassy within twenty-four hours. The palm trees slapped the roofs and the waves flooded the beach, but the storm's duration didn't follow the normal patterns. It was recorded as the worst in fifty years, and after twenty-four hours, the commuter planes between the mainland and the island also stopped operating. The day before I was to leave, the storm still raged. I made a decision to travel back to France by plane, assuming the normal flight schedule resumed by then. Despite the still-stormy skies on my day of departure, the flight crossed the Mediterranean uneventfully, and within two days I had returned to The Urban City.

With my first solo trip to Faraway Places, my wanderlust became the cherished bleach of a maid's cleaning supplies. It was the ultimate cleaner, the product capable of dissolving the most persistent stains, the tool in my arsenal that could make anything clean and bright and white again. But bleach, like travel, is a temporary cleaner. Many stains return, and the ones that reappear gradually are the most insidious because they darken slowly enough to be barely noticeable.

BuddhaBound was the first stain to reappear and darken quickly. Once home, I conceded to his persistent requests to move in with me after six months of dating. Another flag I ignored (this one even had a skull and crossbones) was his unrelenting sobbing that started when I said I really didn't think we should live together as the date drew closer. He still moved in but we only lived together for just over a year until I suggested he make another trip to a library somewhere. Apparently Buddha had already been calling him repeatedly in the preceding few weeks, and he departed to India for a much-needed spiritual retreat two days after he moved out.

CHAPTER 19

NICE&NEUTRAL

The hardest part of growing up is that you have to do what is right for you, even if it means breaking someone's heart. Including your own.
Unknown

Clearly, meeting men in the usual fashion wasn't really working for me, including dating men from my native land. Or perhaps I was meeting men in the usual fashion for women my age but I was experiencing a different version of "love is blind." I was unable to see healthy men who lived in The Urban City and were compatible with me. The more important issue was that I belonged in all the places I had visited during my travels to Faraway Places #1 more than I ever had in The Urban City. Even Somewhere Small was more like home because of the nostalgic attachment to the place I was born, and its physical beauty suited my innate disposition as a nature-loving tomboy. Therefore, the available foreigners who had moved to my country would have been like ships I needed to politely salute as we crossed paths, while I orchestrated my search for home in a Faraway Place. And it didn't matter whether Forever After was possible with any of the foreigners I met in my native land, because they had found home in a country I never would. With that analysis, I began Internet dating with men who lived in Faraway Places.

The first man I met online was from New Zealand and worked as a fisheries biologist. He was obviously intelligent, having earned a doctorate in biology. He was educated. Check. He also exhibited a sense of adventure, suggesting we meet on a heart-shaped island between Christmas and New Year's Eve that year. He was romantic. Check. He also insisted on separate sleeping quarters until we became friends. Unbelievable. Check and bonus marks! He wanted us to explore the island together while we talked about our mutual hopes and dreams. Did this man exist or was he a virtual character from some other world inhabited by perfect beings? My optimism ran high during the hot July while we engaged in long narratives over email.

However, things spiraled downward within a couple of weeks. When he sent me a photo of himself, I searched in vain for a hint of attraction to him, first by focusing on different parts of his face, and then by imagining his profile. I tried but couldn't see myself with him, beside him, holding hands, hugging. My imagination remained a tabula rasa when it came to envisioning scenes of physical closeness with the biologist. Yet, according to his biography, he was an excellent match for me, and our communications were stimulating and thoughtful. The berating progressed to lengthy diatribes of self-loathing about my lack of depth, which usually occurred during the fourteen-kilometre drive to work through the congested core of The Urban City. It wasn't that he didn't match a mental image of the person I had conjured up during a fanciful daydream. My superficiality was preventing me from finding a person with whom I could create and sustain a stable life because I couldn't appreciate the men who were good for me. Actually, my problem went beyond superficiality. I had the type of eye disease that made suitable men repulsive to me.

My neuroticism grew with each email communication between us. The more appealing he became emotionally and intellectually, the more I focused on how physically unappealing I found him. I never actually told him I wasn't attracted to him because I was so ashamed of my thoughts and feelings that I couldn't admit them to anyone. Even acknowledging them to myself was privately embarrassing. A month after we had met online, I looked in the bathroom mirror one night after I'd washed my face and brushed my teeth. *And just how attractive do you think you are?* I thought, staring solemnly at my reflection. *You haven't won any awards for beauty or any personality traits honouring your congeniality and sainthood.* No matter how much I engaged in this self-talk, I couldn't convince myself to book a flight and make the twelve-hour journey to meet the biologist on the heart-shaped island in the South Pacific.

The longer we communicated by email, the more I sensed his longing for us to fall in love without having met. I was worried the only serious relationships this man had experienced were with plants and fish, and any interest in him from a human female was ample reason to begin planning a life together. I became mute somewhere between, "I imagine us spending summers together camping," and "Can you believe it, I already have the names of my children picked out?" I wanted kids but with someone I also wanted to kiss, and I already knew I would never want to kiss the Kiwi, even before I saw his photograph. Although the South Pacific islands had been a desirable destination during my dialogue with the globe on the windowsill, the invitation was tainted: wrong man, wrong time. I didn't need to hire a hacker who could remove any evidence of my existence from his inbox. An ocean separated us and I was certain a gentle rejection would send a clear message he wouldn't rebut. I told him I thought we were incompatible. He didn't argue with the ardour of a certain man or propose an experiment to prove me wrong. I didn't hear from him again and assumed he returned to his books while searching for a woman who wanted him, maybe even just a little.

By this point I'd begun a conversation with another man also from New Zealand who presented himself as interesting, charming, and accomplished. He was an entrepreneur in the process of building an Internet business that allowed computer novices to build websites. I had always admired entrepreneurs because of the risk-taking and persistence required to succeed. The most compelling reason, though, was that entrepreneurs needed to believe in themselves when few others did because of their daring vision. And daring visions do not typically conform to rules or the status quo.

For several weeks we exchanged emails that revealed a depth to his insights and experiences, and he was a courageous man driven to extreme adventure. He had made several solo trips as a glider pilot and a sailor and avoided accidents, except during a crash landing while paragliding that sent him to the hospital for surgery to fix a broken shoulder. He took risks. He thrived on adventure. He had managed several photography franchises with his ex-wife. He appealed to me because I wanted to be more like him. When it came time to exchange photographs at my request

I sent him a recent one of me immediately but waited for several days to receive his. His slow response concerned me. Why was he hesitating? Was he worried about whether I'd be attracted to him? I finally received it and my instant impression was that he was not the physical type I was normally attracted to. Admittedly, I wasn't repulsed, but I thought of him as stodgy and conservative even though he had painted a different picture of himself, or perhaps I created the picture I wanted to see.

Why couldn't I find a man who was both interesting and physically appealing to me? Or did I need to revise my expectations and choose one as more important over the other? I ruminated obsessively about the source of attraction. The silent self-loathing about my lack of depth continued unabated. Walking around The Urban City, I scanned many men in coffee shops, department stores, and on street corners. I conducted an internal check about my attraction to them and summarized its nature as mysterious and unpredictable. Occasionally I crossed paths with a man who deviated from the physical type I normally found attractive. I prefer tall slender men, but sometimes found a short, portly guy appealed to me because of something else more important, such as a generosity of spirit, great wit, or a calming presence. And in the case of First Love, with one look at him, I had reunited with someone I'd known from another time and dimension, whose details were inaccessible in keeping with the laws dictated by The Powers That Be. But First Love was irrelevant; I needed to recover from judging my desire for someone based on a photo, and my recovery would be part of the cure for my poor vision. If someone had handed me a stained and dirty copy of *Crime and Punishment*, would I have tossed it in the garbage and dismissed it as unreadable because of its shabby covers without having discovered the beauty between them? Meeting another man from New Zealand presented a lesson for me, and damn it, I was going to learn it.

Besides, physical attraction cannot be the substance of a relationship. What would happen if one of us became paralyzed or in some other way afflicted, preventing us from being able to physically satisfy each other? Forever After requires a great friendship rather than an intense physical attraction to someone. I told myself both my head and my heart needed input into my romantic ideals: but frankly, more head, less heart needed to dictate my future choices. And perhaps it was time to find a true companion rather than search for the elusive and possibly non-existent grand passion. With my ruminations, The Evil Temptress had been lurking in the recesses of my mind, waiting patiently to be heard until she could no longer restrain herself.

Her high-pitched voice began to narrate what could only be described as the first paragraph of a great love story: "Oh, yes, the grand passion. The rare but sublime thing that has defied a wholly satisfying description, even by the literary giants, past and present. But after having watched her parents, who reminded her of Jane Eyre and Edward Rochester from one of her favourite novels, still laugh together like giddy teenagers with a twinkle in their eyes after more than thirty years of marriage no less, the young and despondently unattached Elizabeth knew it was possible. And she set out to find it, even if it meant travelling to the remotest places in the world. She had one true love and she would seek him until she found him, and once she did, well, the rest would be history for the storybooks her children and grandchildren would read." The Evil Temptress was bastardizing a beloved classic and I hated her for it. I told her to shut the hell up, or I would personally hunt her down and poke daggers in her eyes. She was silent for a while, but like all arrogant characters, she couldn't remain so for long.

But I wasn't a memorable character in a literary romance. Despite my lack of physical attraction to the second foreigner I had met online, it was overrated anyway and would likely doom a relationship (as per the prior precedent established with Dark&Angry); therefore, I might as well find a good companion who would be loyal and committed to me. Passion was intoxicating but unnecessary because it paved the path to suffering (as all drugs do), and I was done pursuing it. I needed a man who was Nice&Neutral with whom I could build The Simple Life and The Good Life.

In the summer of the year that I started communicating with Nice&Neutral, I had registered to attend the Maui Writer's Conference in August. Of course, he knew about my travel before I left The Urban City, and I suspected he was going to surprise me by showing up there to meet me. I was more excited about the prospect of attending the conference than about meeting him, which didn't bode well for our romance. I wondered if The Evil Temptress had been repeating her sweet little opening paragraph to me while I slept. It didn't matter anyway. She wrote fairytales with Cinderellas who meet their princes, and lord knows their character arcs bore no resemblance to mine. My story is about mature love, not about clichéd arcs of fictional characters.

My itinerary took me to a different island for an overnight layover before travelling to the conference the next day. Disembarking from the plane, I closed my eyes and inhaled the sweet, floral scent of tropical flowers and the warm air blowing from the south and caressing my bare skin. The little island was a balm that soaked into the core of my being. It was The Earth's Womb: a safe, secure place that protects, nourishes, and allows. Surely this utopia favoured romance in the same way fertile soil germinates the most fragile seeds.

I checked into my hotel room and saw a note on the floor that had been tucked under my door. It had been hand-written on a napkin adorned with a sunflower bursting with happiness on a sky-blue background. As expected, it hailed from Nice&Neutral who had checked into the same hotel earlier in the evening. Although the sentiment and delivery of the note was romantic and sweet, I was dismayed and depressed at the thought of meeting him. I sensed I wouldn't be attracted to him and it was in our best interests to avoid meeting. He would be travelling back to New Zealand within forty-eight hours and if we didn't get together before I left for the conference the next day, the opportunity to meet each other would slip away.

Brushing my teeth, I spit the toothpaste and my guilt about not wanting to meet Nice&Neutral into the sink, and watched them float in the tap water before it carried them down the drain. I undressed quickly, turned out the lights, and tucked myself into bed, with the soft neon lights casting a warm glow on the walls of the room. Perhaps fate would intervene on my behalf in the form of a tropical storm that would cause a power outage during the night, preventing the alarm from going off. And by the time I woke, I would have needed to dash to the airport with no time to knock on the door of Nice&Neutral. I tried to console myself with the truth that attraction couldn't be forced. And as a truth, it applied to everyone, not just me. We either are or we aren't, and I wasn't flawed if I didn't find him appealing. There was no need for my subconscious to provide clarity. There was no mystery. There was no confusion. There was no doubt. And there was no need for fate to stage an intervention. The truth didn't need costars.

There was no power outage in the night and the alarm went off at 7:00 a.m. I suppose I could have "accidentally" set it to 7:00 p.m. but I was excited about being in The Earth's Womb for the first time and exploring one of its islands for a day. My lack of enthusiasm about meeting Nice&Neutral did not dampen my need to be an explorer. I still wasn't excited about meeting him but it would have been disrespectful to pretend I didn't get the note even though he had made a unilateral decision to fly there. This man had flown all the way from his native land in the South Pacific to meet me in person. To avoid him would have been cruel and insensitive, whether he had consulted me or not.

I showered and got dressed, packed my things, and made my way to the floor where his room was located. As I approached the door, I knew he was inside because of the light spilling into the hallway from the gap between the door and the floor. I knocked and he greeted me warmly. At first sight, I still didn't find him attractive, but I wasn't instantly repulsed either. Not a great sign, but also not a dismal one. While we spent the day together, during the moments when we were sitting on the beach, I found myself incurably exhausted. When I finally surrendered to the fatigue and lay down, I fell promptly asleep, which for me was unusual particularly after I had slept so soundly the previous night. A true gentleman, he changed his position to protect me from the sun for two hours. I reasoned the fatigue had resulted from the three-hour time difference between The Urban City and The Earth's Womb rather than from boredom.

Before boarding the plane to the island where the conference was being held, we had an early dinner together. I was astonished he carried no credit card and didn't have enough cash to pay for his portion of the meal. What adult would travel to another country without a credit card or sufficient cash to purchase a meal? But I dismissed the sign and sympathized with his status as a struggling entrepreneur who had the courage to do what most people never would by getting on a plane to meet a woman from another country all in the name of pursuing love. His was a romantic and risky gesture. I should be blessed rather than cursed by such hopefulness. Nevertheless, I was still bothered by his lack of common sense about finances during a trip far away from home. I was not looking for a man to pay my bills, but I wanted one who could pay his, and if we had a future together, I wanted us to share the responsibility.

I don't remember our first goodbye at the airport to catch my flight to The Earth's Womb, but I do remember feeling energized when the plane took off from Honolulu to Maui. I can't remember what we talked about when we met, during the afternoon on the beach, or over dinner.

The distraction of the writer's conference temporarily relieved the underlying nervousness about my budding relationship with Nice&Neutral. My inner coach told me to calm down. There was no real pressure for me to make any decisions about beginning a life with this man. Besides, he lived thousands of miles away from me and the relationship would evolve slowly, or time apart would be like water poured onto a burgeoning fire. I counselled myself he was a good fit for me: several years older than I with three grown children, he was mature and had learned lessons from being a father, businessman, and survivor of divorce.

Our friendship grew as we continued to chat over email and by phone. And was friendship not the most assured way to form a long-lasting relationship with a romantic partner? Despite my practical rationalization about why he was the perfect man for me, I continued to have nagging doubts because of the fatigue that came over me when I talked to him from thousands of miles away. How was it possible for me to feel exhausted talking to such a nice man? Perhaps I had simply been unaccustomed to a drama-free relationship, and as time passed I would view the stability with him as a healthy and necessary step to building a comfortable future.

Nice&Neutral convinced me a visit to The Urban City for a few months would help solidify our relationship. I agreed and he arrived that year just before Christmas. I had already planned to attend a ten-day silent retreat between Boxing Day and the New Year festivities. I stayed overnight with Island Friend before driving to the lakeside retreat, a two-hour drive to the north.

"You don't love him, Middle2," she said, washing the dishes that night when we were alone in her kitchen. "No woman, and I mean *NO* woman, would leave a man she loves during Christmas *and* not spend New Year's Eve with him. No one. If you don't believe me, do a survey and leave room for comments. Because I can guarantee you, there will be *lots* of them."

"You're being ridiculous. I planned this retreat *months* ago. Are you suggesting I should have cancelled something I've wanted to do for years, just because I'm dating a man? You're right. I don't love him. How can I love someone I've only known a few months?"

"You'll tell me one day," she said, flicking the water on the tips of her fingers into the sink. "So, how often are these retreats anyway?"

229

"I didn't check. They're all over the place. I wanted to come here."

"Hah! *Seeeeee!* You could do this retreat when he's back in New Zealand in a few months. And you wouldn't have to come here either. You know I'm right. But nope, *no, no, no,* you decided you just had to do it now."

"I think you're just missing the point. Besides, he doesn't care that I've gone away. He said he'd just work."

"So let's see if I've got your current romantic life figured out. You want to be on an island in a location where you can't even make a phone call to your new boyfriend to wish him Happy New Year and maybe talk about what you want to do to each other when you get back? *And* you think he's okay with it all, even though he said he'd *'just work'*?"

"Oh, Jesus, you're worse than I am. Can you just stop with the analysis?"

In the morning, Island Friend and I hugged each other and I settled into my car for the drive along a winding road into the mountains. By the time I reached the summit I had entered dense fog that made its home among the trees for much of the winter. Being in the mountains draped in a winter fog calmed me.

I was the last of seven women sharing a small cabin to arrive at the camp. Our cabin was large enough to house three bunk beds, our luggage, and a foam mattress in one of the corners, which would become my sleeping quarters for ten days. There were windows on both of the corner walls and conifers filled my view. When I stood up, I had glimpses of the lake and the path that bordered it. The windows out to the world reassured me that at the end of the period of confinement, physical freedom would be mine again. But first I needed to liberate myself from the mental prison by letting go of the cascade of thoughts flooding my mind. Walking meditations during our unstructured time were not permitted. I could not stroll along the path and take snapshots with my eyes to scroll through when the confinement became intolerable. But views from the windows sufficed because their glass was clear and clean. I couldn't talk, but I could see the beauty around me and I preferred the lake view in the mountains to the sea view in The Urban City. I didn't miss Nice&Neutral, and if our relationship endured, we would celebrate New Year's Eve together the following year. Island Friend and I clearly had opposing views about romance and she didn't know me as well as she thought she did.

The first three days of the retreat made me increasingly anxious about my relationship with Nice&Neutral, but I kept working at remaining in the present moment. I began to observe the minute details of the bark and pine needles on the tree outside the window, without having a torrent of thoughts buzzing through my mind like frantic flies trapped behind a closed window. I realized that up until that point in my life I'd never truly been fully present anywhere or with anyone, except when I was bicycling, swimming, or singing.

During childhood rides, I easily recalled a searing pain of knives slicing the big muscles of my legs as I cycled up one of the many hills in Somewhere Small. Yet without fail, each time I dismounted whatever bike I happened to be riding, I was elated. The freedom of having a way to travel around Somewhere Small connected the high points on a curve that unambiguously demonstrated my improving faith over time. Being in water created a different but equally pleasing effect. I loved floating on my back with my eyes closed, and while my awareness scanned my physical body, I dissolved into a watery world where boundaries were limitless and where I felt at one with all that is. I caught a glimpse, consciously this time, of being everything and nothing at the same time. Singing came naturally to Eldest and me. Alcoholic Foster Mother's mom used to have us gather around her to sing after dinner from time to time. Even though I was nowhere near water during the postprandial choir sessions, I had already learned in elementary science classes that the human body is comprised of more than fifty percent water. During Christmas, as my awareness dissolved into the watery vibrations of the vocal cords, our first foster grandmother's smiling face encouraged us to let our voices be heard. She had been the countervailing force against Alcoholic Foster Father who said, "Kids should be seen and not heard" so often that he should have just hung placards on every door in the house and saved himself the bother of verbal reminders.

After the ten-day silent meditation, my re-entry into routine life began with the ferry ride to The Urban City. During the journey, I focused on the horizon when I panicked about the reunion with Nice&Neutral back at my apartment because I would never become the full moon rising above the horizon. Nor would I become joy, having lost my awareness of my identity as Middle2 while I sang, swam, or cycled. I would never be like the fiddler as long as I was with Nice&Neutral. The pace of my life quickened once back on land where I made a twenty-minute drive to my apartment. Parked outside, I watched Nice&Neutral walk toward me with a bouquet of flowers. I felt neutral seeing him again, with neither a leaping delight nor a sickening dread. Neutrality is a positive quality of a mediator trying to facilitate peace between two warring nations, but not to describe a reunion between two lovers separated and silent for ten days. I viewed him as a friend coming to give me a warm welcome in a public place, not as a lover I couldn't wait to unite with in a private one. I tried to coax a shiver of passion as he made his way toward me, but only the winter wind drifted up my spine as we embraced. Passion sprung from rhyme, not reason, from the heart, not the head. There was no route from my head to my heart with Nice&Neutral. No poetic verses sprung to mind when I walked along the many rivers in the mountains on the north side of The Urban City.

With the new year underway in The Urban City, I led my normal life routine by waking up at six-thirty, getting ready for work, and departing for the day. Without fail, each day on my return, Nice&Neutral was sitting at my desk in front of his computer, toiling away in his familiar attire of sweat pants and a t-shirt. Nice&Neutral had arrived in The Urban City with only a few clothes and no personal funds. He adapted quickly to being a guest without responsibilities, and in the six months since we met, we had already settled into the life of a married couple with standard routines and reversed roles. And despite his claims of building a solid business for himself, the notions of grandeur lived mostly in his head without any real evidence he could or would become an independent businessman who did not need my financial support. However, I was determined to build confidence in him. With his impeccable work ethic, I convinced myself the seeds of success would sprout and bear fruit eventually. I just needed to adopt the faith of Middle1, who was married to a farmer. No matter how many droughts and downpours ruined the crops, we would reap the rewards of a bountiful harvest in the future.

After a few months together, Nice&Neutral returned to his native country in the South Pacific, which left me relieved and able to relax, like a dog that can curl up again in its favourite resting spot when an unsettling noise has stopped. The idea of being the person in the relationship to earn and manage money working at a boring job left me with transitory but recurring chronic fatigue. Was The Simple Life making me ill? When Nice&Neutral returned to his homeland, my fatigue disappeared and we continued our long-distance email communication with the occasional phone call. Within a couple of months, we agreed I would visit the South Pacific for twelve weeks. Nice&Neutral's native land intrigued me, even though my gaze never landed on it and I hadn't decoded its Braille-like bumps as a desirable place to visit when my fingers ran over it on the plastic globe.

After three plane rides, I finally arrived at my destination, where I received a spectacular welcome. As a pilot, Nice&Neutral was friends with many other pilots throughout the country. One of them picked me up at the airport and treated me to a thrilling helicopter ride over the land surrounding the airport. I had never been in a helicopter with the pilot maneuvering it like a roller coaster. I found out much later that his brother had also inherited the need to explore beyond the boundaries of the transportation safety regulations. He routinely flew under bridges and too close to cliffs. I smiled hearing stories about such men. Within minutes of my arrival, I knew I would leave the semi-colon-shaped country with fond memories of its rugged and pristine beauty. New Zealand was a country with exquisitely fresh air and filled with poplars whose sleek forms rose to the heavens and looked like blazing cobs of corn against the blue winter sky. Yet I knew I would look forward to leaving and probably not return there in my lifetime. Not only did I need a kinship with people, I also needed to feel at home in the lands I visited. Experiencing either would stir a desire to return, but neither eliminated it for future consideration, unless fate landed me there again for some reason. Although physically beautiful with warm, hospitable people, my temperament changed into the shape of the country while I was there. I became a semi-colon in the middle of a wrinkled, blank page.

I arrived in the winter season and Nice&Neutral had rented a small house that was a deep freezer, only bigger. The only source of heat was a fireplace in the living room, which we stoked all day long and into the evening. Fortunately, though, Nice&Neutral's business partner and his wife's dog would accompany me on lengthy daily hikes, which were a welcome distraction when my feet got cold enough that I couldn't think about doing anything else. It didn't take long for Jack the Dog to become a whirling dervish whenever I put on my coat and laced my hiking boots. This transformation made me laugh each time and I never got bored of his unbridled enthusiasm as we headed off into the mountains. This simple routine filled me with joy and energy as I tried to navigate my way in the first Faraway Place I thought was beautiful but less comfortable to me than my native land. Nice&Neutral seemed more confident and self-assured in his homeland, assuaging my fears about his hermit-like tendencies in mine. Although awestruck by the physical beauty of the country, I found the culture retrograde and the ubiquitous poverty con- sciousness depressed me. Because of my impressions, I felt abnor- mally introverted, as Nice&Neutral had behaved in The Urban City. But the hikes with Jack the Dog prevented my somber mood from freezing and becoming lodged in an unreachable place.

The other aerial treats Nice&Neutral arranged exhilarated me. On one occasion, I joined a group for a hot air balloon ride. Once the whoosh of the helium being injected into the balloon was complete and we were five thousand feet above the land, we glided in a surreal peace over the unspoiled land above and around Queenstown. I was in the world but not of it, far enough above the Earth to marvel at the expansive beauty below me, but not high enough to touch the wings of angels.

I also joined a small group for a helicopter tour to the top of the highest mountain nicknamed after Captain James Cook who circumnavigated the islands in 1770. The hard-packed snow glistened under the crystal-blue sky of the southern hemisphere, and it was quiet on the top of that mountain. The beauty rattled me because I wanted to do things that enchanted me in my day-to-day life. I wanted to be joyful in fulfilling a purpose that was mine; being in the natural beauty of Nice&Neutral's native land didn't show me the way, but it encouraged me to continue search-ing for it. Beauty, like love, makes us brave. Observing life and appreciating the Art of others are no longer enough. We don't just admire pretty flowers anymore. We learn how to paint them. And we don't just study maps. We pack them and triple-check they are in our bags before heading to the airport.

As the end of the trip drew near, the days got longer and the temperatures warmer, which also melted my mood. Nice&Neutral and I returned to The Urban City, but first made a two-week visit to a small island north of his native land. The geography of this island stunned me. Black rocks littered white sandy beaches opening to crystal clear aquamarine waters teeming with lumi-nescent fish. Wandering through the villages above the resort, I admired the reverence with which the native people honoured their deceased family members, and in particular, their maternal figures. Floral wreaths decorated the graves, along with heartfelt messages and memories of the imprint the women had made on the family. Although North American culture did not include backyard burials, the practice in some places and cultures healed me in the same way I anonymously grieved local or world events that resonated with me. I didn't know the whereabouts of my mother's ashes, but being in a Faraway Place with customs that expressed devotion to female figures altered my attitude about the past and the actions I could take in the future to honour my mother. I could find a tree, a rock, or a resting place in one of the many parks of The Urban City and visit it on her birthday or on the anniversary of her death. While there, I could recite a poem I had written for her, or any number of other things. I had choices, and there were as many ways to celebrate her life as my imagination would allow. I didn't want to plant a tree in the backyard of my home because I considered myself a nomadic citizen of the world, but The Powers That Be and fate weren't preventing me from carrying out a plan to celebrate her. I was.

Back in The Urban City, we settled into the same routine we'd started in the South Pacific, and I returned to the same contract work I'd left behind. Work distracted me from Nice&Neutral's daily practice of toiling at his computer without leaving the house. Yet again, I'd found myself a stable life with a home and someone who cared about me, just as I'd done with BrotherLove, but doubt buzzed around me like the mosquitoes did on humid summer nights in Somewhere Small. It didn't take long for them to bite me repeatedly until the itching became unbearable. I finally realized what had been troubling me: I had taken on the male role in the relationship, and I couldn't bear it. I had become the sun and Nice&Neutral the moon. I was suffering from a lunar eclipse, hiding in the shadow of a bigger and more powerful Earth because I lacked the motivation to change my personal circumstances. We mutually agreed Nice&Neutral would return to the South Pacific to be in his own environment where known business prospects could be nurtured.

After two weeks, he called me from the hospital to let me know he had cut off the distal phalanx of his left thumb and the surgeons could not reattach it. The mishap delayed his return to The Urban City to allow his thumb to heal sufficiently for him to travel. I was interested in the symbolic meaning of Nice&Neutral's thumb accident. Kinetically, the thumb is known for its opposition properties with respect to the other digits. Talented mechanically, Nice&Neutral could build or fix anything. I'd heard of Louise Hay and her book *Heal Your Life* and looked up her interpretation of the symbolic meaning of losing a thumb. According to her, it was associated with "losing the frantic race to prove oneself." The rational explanation was he lost part of his thumb due to inattention while using a saw, a common accident. And in the end, the esoteric meaning had no merit beyond what Nice&Neutral thought, regardless of what Louise Hay hypothesized or how interesting her analysis was to me. I didn't tell Nice&Neutral about her interpretation of the loss of a thumb because our relationship didn't include discussing the esoteric meaning of losing digits or battles of any other type for that matter.

Nice&Neutral returned to The Urban City with a positive attitude about his accident. He was grateful it didn't involve his entire hand or arm. And I needed to be thankful for the life I was building with him and to support his quest to be an entrepreneur while I reclaimed my lunar identity. My professional life had started to gain momentum again, and although I didn't wake up rubbing my hands together in anticipation of the day before me, or sing "An Everlasting Love" while I showered, my personal circumstances could be much worse. Adopting an attitude of thankfulness for what I had would help me be content. "Damn it, just be happy, Middle2" became my new mantra. I was thirty-six years old, and the time had arrived for me to be mature, responsible, and sensible about my life decisions. I repeat: Nice&Neutral was warm, sensitive, kind, affectionate, and gentle. So what if the above was a list of adjectives rather than a sonnet expressing my undying love for him? And so what if I had to be the one to go out into the world and make a living while he struggled with his fledgling business venture? I reminded myself each morning as I brushed powder on my brow that my circumstances as a married woman could be intolerable and would have been with both BuddhaBound and Dark&Angry.

I wasn't Cinderella, sweeping chimneys and mopping floors, and I was earning a better annual income than most people do in their lifetimes. So what if I hadn't found my prince? Big deal. Princes were mythical characters without credible biographies. I envisioned Cinderella on her deathbed and knew it was time to let her go. Despite her imminent departure into The Great Unknown, I still longed for a knight. At least I had made progress since my childhood because I didn't imagine him saving me from a group of bandits, lifting me onto his trusty steed with one hand, and whisking me away in the direction of auspicious pink skies at sunset. But I did prefer it if he wore armour, as long as it had a few scratches on it. In fact, the more, the better. One who has survived the trenches could also survive the two types of blows in life. They can be the knock-down this-is-going-to-kill-me type: the person with whom we found Forever After dies suddenly; the house burns down; we face a life-threatening illness on a day that began like most others. They are the bullets of fate, shot at us

239

from an unknown location. Nothing prepares us for the this-is-going-to-kill-me type. The other kind are the tap-tap-tap kind that cause bruises, starting with ones we don't notice, and progressing to ones we see getting dressed every morning and forget about by breakfast. But eventually, the repeated bruises give us headaches and lower back pain that we manage with over the counter non-steroidal anti-inflammatory medication, which we keep in the car, at work in our desk, and by our bedside table beside a glass of water. The tolerable bruises and aches are taps from the soul whose knocks we have ignored for months, sometimes even years. But the minor injuries aren't generic like the medicines used to soothe them. They're warnings that tell us we've closed the door to joy. The tap-tap type become the knock-down blows when The Powers That Be introduce a this-is-going-to-kill-me kind when we fail to make necessary changes on our own. The fact is, the bruisings and the knock-downs can both kill us, but if they don't, we have a choice about how to live after them. Whether we like it or not, life is about the growth that comes with the phases in the cycle of suffering: shock, sadness, anger, resignation, fulfilling a duty to oneself, and then to others. I wanted a knight who is steady during life's this-is-going-to-kill-me blows, points out the bruises on my back that I don't see, and reminds me of the ones I try to forget about.

With Cinderella's last breath, I had developed a new form of heart disease. It wasn't fatal but it was chronic, with willpower and resignation its management protocol. Despite my self-prescribed treatment, Cinderella haunted me in my sleep with dreams of First Love, and while awake, with taunts from young happy lovers laughing and kissing in public. I was convinced they were still enjoying the blush of their honeymoon, with boredom and complacency the neighbourhoods they would soon move into. And when I bickered with Cinderella's ghost during my hikes in the mountains, she would simply disappear, letting me rant, while Mother Nature patted me on the back saying, "There, there, dear. I'll be here for you always." In the meantime, her ethereal highness had fluttered away into the southerly wind in search of another victim strolling by herself on some lover's lane.

With the death of Cinderella, Nice&Neutral and I decided to get married after a year and a half of dating. We made the wedding a low-key affair since both of us were not interested in spending copious amounts of money on one day of our lives. We agreed to save the income we had been earning to buy a house or an apartment that we could invest in for several years. We arranged for a civil service in the room of an upscale hotel in the hub of The Urban City, with only a few close friends present at a ceremony that included vows we had written to each other. We both agreed that the premise of marriage excluded Forever After. And if one or both of us stopped growing as individuals, we would decide to respectfully separate. We wrote our vows out of a practical approach to living, not from a united front based on a 'til-death-do-we-part commitment to one another. We were friends. With my practical approach, I tucked Kahlil Gibran's often-quoted poem into a folder labeled "Favourites in an ideal world, but not applicable to me."

When love beckons you, follow him,
Though his ways are hard and steep,
And when his wings enfold you yield to him,
Though the sword hidden among his pinions may wound you.

And when he speaks to you believe in him,

Though his voice may shatter your dreams

as the north wind lays waste the garden.

For even as love crowns you, so shall he crucify

you. Even as he is for your growth, so is he for your pruning.

Even as he ascends to your height and caresses

your tenderest branches that quiver in the sun,

So shall he descend to your roots and shake

them in their clinging to the earth.

Being married to Nice&Neutral couldn't seriously wound me because my love for him swam in shallow, clear, and protected waters where storms or floods weren't possible. My heart did not plumb the depths with his; therefore, no matter what the outcome, I would not drown in a puddle of sorrow from losing him or be crucified and left with a searing pain in my heart. And certainly, the contents of my garden would not become a disheveled mess after some silly poetic north wind tore through it.

We chose our wedding rings together, went shopping for my version of a wedding dress, and rented a tuxedo for him. I chose a full-length green skirt and a black sequined sheer top. The day of the wedding I spent at a local spa having my first facial, getting my makeup done and hair swept up for an event that could have easily been a charity ball. After the wedding, I had intentions of shortening the skirt for other occasions, but they never arrived, or somehow the outfit seemed unsuited or inappropriate. We chose simple gold bands, mine with three rows of small diamonds. Again, we took the practical route where the rings were concerned. There was no grand gesture of sentimentality behind them, and wearing them simply connoted the symbolism of being a couple socially.

After the ceremony, we went to a local seafood restaurant a few blocks from the hotel where we would stay the night. The eatery was beautifully decorated with Christmas lights tastefully wrapped around the many plants and pillars throughout the interior. I had invited friends from different phases of my life. We ate our meals at a cozy round table, which pleased me, since circular things symbolize unity. I knew they also symbolized eternity, but it was too long to be relevant.

In bed in our hotel room on the eighteenth floor, after my new husband had gone to sleep, I lay on my back, arms folded across my chest in what a passionate bystander would have described as a mummy's pose. I reminded myself: Husband #1 was warm, sensitive, kind, affectionate, and gentle. So what if I was the provider? Even without Husband #1, I would need to provide for myself, and even with children I'd vowed to never depend on a man financially. Nevertheless, I couldn't shake the loss of Cinderella. Her death made me depressed. What began as an unrelenting need to sleep in until mid-morning on any given weekend grew to hating to get out of bed on weekdays at 6:30. The bed had become a magnet, and my body the iron ore clinging to it. No matter how much I exercised and ate well, I could not battle the chronic fatigue. I even went to my doctor to see if I was suffering from some kind of terminal illness. I didn't know what to do, and as it turned out, didn't have to ask, either. Help came to me in the most unexpected and unusual way on New Year's Eve in 2001.

I had met Gay Hair Stylist in Psychiatrist #2's waiting room. During the long waits for our appointments, we forged a

243

friendship. Usually there were three of us in the waiting room on the day of our appointments. Gay Hair Stylist and I would compare sessions while the third of our convivial little trio would sit back with his head against the wall and his eyes closed, apparently oblivious to our conversation, until his therapist arrived and escorted him away. Gay Hair Stylist's appointments really did mirror the stereotypical view I'd developed of the psychiatrist/patient relationship. He really did lay stretched out on a couch while recounting dream sequences or life events from the previous week without any probing about their psychological impact on him. If Psychiatrist #2 had practiced this form of therapy, I'd still be seeing him on a weekly basis. My dream sequences alone would have kept us busy indefinitely.

That New Year's Eve, Gay Hair Stylist had invited us to a party one of his friend's was hosting. We arrived at our friend's house early since he'd promised to give me a makeover. I'd been conservative my entire life and decided it was high time to adopt a dramatic look, if only for a night. Before my friend got started on my new look, he gave Husband #1 and me a "brownie" to get the party started. I had never had a "brownie," cookie, or any other tasty treat with hallucinogenic ingredients, but he assured us the effect would be mild.

A new hairstyle was the first step of my makeover. When I looked in the mirror after his primping, teasing, and spraying, I hated my thick hair for the first time in my life and could not believe it was possible to transform it into the size and shape of the pumpkins we used to harvest during September in Somewhere Small. Thank goodness Thanksgiving had already come and gone because he may have persuaded me to let him dye it orange.

I ate another one of the tasty treats before we moved into the makeup and wardrobe phases. Looking in the mirror to put on my eye shadow, I felt odd, as if the bathroom were getting smaller at a preternatural rate. Soon I became stuck in a psychological prison, and I saw a door in every direction I looked whose brass locks all turned to the left into the locked position. No matter where I went in his apartment, the world looked small and crowded, even though I was the only one in it. The Gay Hair Stylist attended the party and left Husband #1 and I alone for the evening. I paced my friend's living room floor and watching the blinking of the city lights and traffic ten stories below me, I knew Husband #1 was around me, but I didn't want to run to him for solace or any form of reassurance. Hours later, Husband #1 and I were well enough to leave Gay Hair Stylist's apartment and we drove home in silence. Once there, we snuck into our rented townhouse like two teenagers who didn't want our sleeping parents to know what time and in what state we had arrived home from our New Year's Eve party. We undressed and slumped into our bed without saying goodnight to each other or doing other more intimate things a happily married husband and wife might do to celebrate the first day of the New Year.

As usual, Husband #1 rose from bed the next morning before I did. I met him in the living room with a cup of tea and we both asked each other how we were doing, as if we had just met but felt awkward having just spent the night together. We celebrated New Year's Day with a shared gratitude that sleep had released us from the psychological prison we had entered the night before, but we still didn't toast our togetherness with hopes and dreams as a couple for the coming year. We shared laughs together occasionally, but only when we pretended to be our Jimmy and Jenny characters who had lisps and only cheerful dispositions.

As the months passed, Jimmy ceased to be entertaining and his appearance became a fly buzzing around my head wherever Nice&Neutral channeled the character. I lacked faith in Husband #1 and he was experiencing a solar eclipse that prevented his light from becoming earthbound as long as I was his wife. I had married someone I liked but didn't love. And I had an inkling of the difference between liking and loving someone. A wide and deep valley separates Like and Love, two ecosystems as different as one can imagine.

In the days that turned into months following the brownie incident, I could no longer avoid the truth: my dreams had been collecting dust in the suburban tomb I shared with Husband #1. But a cold north wind blew the dust away at an uncomfortable rate, sooner than expected, and certainly under less than ideal circumstances. Before the year ended, I received a knockdown blow.

CHAPTER 20

REUNITED AND IT FEELS SO GOOD.
OR DOES IT?

That first love. And the first one who breaks your heart. For me, they just happen to be the same person.
Sarah Dessen

First loves can fuck you up.
Tara Kelly

I was still married to Husband #1 when I renewed contact with First Love. The circumstances surrounding our electronic reunion were uncanny. At the time, I was taking a technical communications course at one of the local universities in The Urban City and was working on an assignment with another student who partnered with me for the duration of the course. For each assignment, one person completed the research while the other distilled, wrote, and edited the content. We had been working on a piece where it was my turn to be the writer and editor. It was 2002 and our job involved describing and providing an example of a business that provided a service or product in an emerging technology. Her father died after she started the research and she needed to travel by plane to the east coast of the country for his funeral. Due to the unexpected circumstances, we switched roles. In my search for relevant companies, I came across a link containing a press release about First Love in a new role as CTO for a small company in Silicon Valley. I sent him an inane email about the lightning speed of the last twenty-five years, and because of the length of time that had passed since we had seen each other, I asked if he remembered me. He responded after about a week, and in the few short emails that followed, we agreed to try to meet in San Francisco if I travelled there for a yoga retreat in a small community north of Silicon Valley during the Labor Day weekend in six month's time.

In the meantime, I was becoming increasingly resentful of my role as the sun in my marriage to Nice&Neutral. One year into the marriage, I developed the habit of pretending to be asleep when he lightly touched my back long after we crawled into bed most nights; when he hugged me tightly from behind, I complained about being too tired to turn around to face him. I was making no progress in my romantic relationships when I conducted a review of my history before forcing myself to get out of bed on my thirty-ninth birthday. I had recognized I couldn't have a successful romantic relationship with a brother (BrotherLove), a father (Dark&Angry), a woman/son (Husband #1), or a leech (BuddhaBound).

Months passed, and I had no communication with First Love during the period after my private decision to forego the yoga retreat, because I hadn't changed my work situation and Husband

#1 and I had just moved into less-expensive accommodations. And although we had reduced our expenses, we couldn't afford for me to take a vacation, even for a few days. His declaration was specific. But he insisted if he could secure a contract with a businessman who ran a custom furniture store, the milestone would be a clear sign I was supposed to attend the retreat. If he could earn one thousand dollars by the following Thursday, that sum would be a nod from The Powers That Be for me to attend the retreat.

I had no expectations because I also needed to be able to use my Air Miles to book a return flight since I did not want to spend several hundred dollars on air travel to Silicon Valley. Given the low odds of the thousand-dollar goal and the need to use my Air Miles for the plane ticket, I would focus on finding other work as a positive step in my professional life, rather than plan a frivolous trip. But my dreamscape added an element of drama to all the reason and logic prevailing during the day. In the following week, I dreamt Husband #1 and I were living in a glass house set high on a rocky outcrop that led out to sunny blue skies and a calm sea. As I took a long and steady look out of the perfectly transparent floor-to-ceiling windows at the horizon, time accelerated. The sun sank behind storm clouds that appeared as quickly as the billowing darkness from an unexpected massive explosion. And behind the explosion, a tsunami appeared, heading in our direction.

Husband #1 worked tirelessly to secure the contract with the carpenter. While I was at home on my computer on Wednesday before the Labour Day weekend, he attended a third meeting in what he hoped would lead to signing a contract. When I heard the apartment door open and close with no hello, I assumed he was disappointed with the outcome of the meeting. I stayed at my desk.

"I did it," he yelled behind me. "And you, my wife, are going to California."

"Really?" I said, turning around to face him.

"Yes, REALLY!" he yelled, jumping up and down.

"I don't know if I can use my Air Miles. The retreat's only two days away."

"Look, I think you need to do this," Husband #1 insisted. "Just try and let's see what happens."

As soon as I finished booking my flights to San Francisco, the phone rang.

"Who's calling?" I heard Husband #1 ask from the living room.

He came into the office and handed me the phone. "A high school friend for you." Husband #1 left the room while I chatted with First Love.

"Hello. It's been a long time. But your voice hasn't changed."

Neither had his.

"Who answered the phone?"

"Oh, that was my husband."

"What are your plans for the weekend? Are you still coming to The Bay Area?"

"Yeah, as a matter of fact I just booked my flights."

"Where's the retreat?"

"In The Grass Valley."

"You'll like it there, but it'll be hot."

"It's okay. I'll cool down when I get back to San Francisco."

"Will you call me before you go back to The Urban City?"

"Yeah, sure, it'd be fun to see you. It'll be hard to summarize the last twenty-five years in an evening, but we liked to talk. I don't imagine that's changed."

"We liked to talk to each other and I hope *that* hasn't changed," he said. "I'm looking forward to it."

"Okay, I should go," I said.

"Bye. See you in a few days."

Hearing First Love's voice reminded me about Forever After as if it were a card I'd discarded at age sixteen, when I came to believe it was stamped with "FATE" inside a circle consisting of the letters: T, R, O, U, B, L, E.

I arrived at The Grass Valley lodge close to midnight, and after checking in, I walked behind the attendant who looked like The Hermit in a deck of tarot cards when she raised a lantern and carried it at a perpendicular angle to her torso to light our way as she guided me along a narrow path consisting of cracked clay but lined with willowy grasses.

The next morning, I wandered around the retreat grounds and took several deep breaths of the hot, dry air. The rolling hills were scorched from the sun that had been baking them for days. The spindly grasses undulated and crackled in the afternoon as the breezes swept over them, while sand clouds swirled upward toward the highest point complete with a giant Buddha statue, the poised protector that watched over the land below it. The winds escalated as the weekend progressed due to the record-breaking afternoon temperatures, but no matter how many sand-storms obscured Buddha, or how hot it got, I knew he couldn't be carried away by the wind or burned into an unrecognizable heap of charred remains. Resting on the hill, he was a strong and steady presence in The Grass Valley.

The three-day retreat passed quickly, and despite participating in many yoga classes and eating fine vegetarian food, my body was stiff and tense. I had chatted with Husband #1 several times during my stay, each conversation a tacit attempt to reassure each other our relationship was as resilient as the tall grasses, unbreakable despite the fierce winds that flattened them temporarily or their exposure to the sun that baked every molecule of water out of them. I never thought about the possibility of fire, but in hindsight, it was the real threat to The Grass Valley. Then again, burnt remains provide nutrient-rich ash for new growth.

Driving to San Francisco, the sizzling temperatures plummeted as I neared the ocean. I made my way to the hotel where I stayed for two nights before returning to The Urban City. Once in the neighbourhood, I stopped at a local delicatessan, picked up some food, and settled into my hotel room. During my drive back to San Francisco from The Grass Valley, I had reaffirmed my decision to go home without speaking to or seeing First Love. My biggest fear was that visiting First Love again would expose the infertile ground we inhabited. Infertile ground can flourish again with enough care and attention, can't it? Cactuses grow in the desert, and they have for millennia. My marriage might have been a fledgling cactus in the middle of the Sahara, but it could survive because Nice&Neutral and I had imbued it with sufficient will to live.

Having always loved San Francisco, I woke up feeling excited to wander up and down the hilly streets and meander through the lanky buildings converted to intimate galleries. When I walked into the entrance of the first gallery, I immediately noticed a striking woman sitting at a spacious antique desk to the right. The Gallery Lady had hazel eyes with witchy powers of perception to see into broken spirits, and the more broken the spirit, the more acute her vision. The Powers That Be had endowed her retinas with infrared cameras she could turn on at will to view the past, present, and future dark nights of peoples' souls. But we were in a public place and people like her didn't use those kinds of powers in public places. I wanted to escape her presence as quickly as possible to avoid her eyes, the seasoned sales pitch, or the probing questions about my tastes in art. I wanted to enjoy the works in peace as a way to prolong my solitary state while managing the growing uneasiness about my imminent return to The Urban City. Seeing her terrified me as much as if I had just seen my grandmother's ghost appear right before my eyes.

I ran up the six flights of stairs to get her out of my sight. I was relieved when I arrived on the top floor, where I was the sole occupant. I sat in a couch in the middle of the room and opened a Russian painters' history book with the dimensions of a place mat. As soon as I calmed myself enough to concentrate on the words, I heard the soft footsteps of someone approaching me from behind. I glanced up to see The Gallery Lady smiling down at me. As I looked into her eyes, the pit in my stomach returned. I wondered if it was possible for someone to develop an ulcer in under five minutes. The muffin I'd eaten for breakfast had settled into a lead ball that would find a permanent home somewhere in the lining of my stomach, to become a yeast-filled cyst that could burst without warning.

We've all met one or more of her type in our lifetimes. She had the radar to detect a particular kind of torment plaguing the gallery visitors. She knew implicitly the solo ones with crinkled brows walking through the door on a weekday must be especially troubled—otherwise, why were they not at Ghirardelli Square, eating chocolate and buying miniature replicas of the Golden Gate Bridge? They must be looking for messages in Art to salve their pain. And beauty does heal, beauty in Art and beauty in people. The inquisition was about to begin and there was nowhere for me to escape. I was on the top floor and any excuse to pre-empt a conversation before it had even begun would have been futile.

"You look as if you like to walk and it's such a nice day out there," she said.

"I just spent three nice days in The Grass Valley hiking in the hills and doing yoga. I need a different kind of therapy today."

"By the look on your face, it's not working."

"I'm tired from the heat. Record-breaking temperatures on all three days."

"So I heard. What brings you to San Francisco?"

"I'm just passing through on my way back home."

"We're proud of our gallery, but it's not in the tourist brochures."

"I like art and have never been much of a tourist."

"Did you leave your husband back home?" she asked, likely after noticing the wedding ring on my left hand.

"Yes, and he paid for me to be here in the first place."

"What a nice guy."

"Yes, he is."

"I married an ambitious one, but a mean one. You're fortunate."

"Mine's neither."

"He must be lacking something, given how much you're twirling your wedding ring as if you're getting ready to take it off."

The remainder of the conversation with The Gallery Lady acted like a truth serum after her remark about my wedding ring. She probably also detected my lips turned down a little with the mention of Husband #1. Or perhaps I turned away from her and stared morosely at the coffee table lined with books about dead artists. I don't remember.

"Do you have friends here?"

"No. Well, he's not a friend anymore. Someone I dated from high school lives here, but I haven't seen him for twenty-five years."

"Ah, the high school sweetheart."

"More like the high school disaster, but yes, it started out that way."

"Are you going to see him before you go home?"

"I need to focus on my marriage, not search for ghosts in haunted houses."

"Ghosts? They usually relate to the inanimate energies of the dead or generic things we are afraid of. Which is it for you?"

Oh, Jesus, was I really having this conversation with a stranger in a gallery on Geary Street in one of my favourite cities? But I'd never see her again, and perhaps by being honest with a compassionate stranger who had no emotional attachment to me or to my romantic past, present, or future, I would reach conclusions and take actions with a calm and rational mindset once I returned to The Urban City.

"The state of your marriage is independent of whether you see First Love again or not. Because you're afraid to see him, you need to do it. Seeing him again is not going to change the fact that your marriage is weak." She looked at me sympathetically, but I didn't need her sympathy. Even if I thought I did, as soon as I left the gallery it wouldn't matter anyway, because it wasn't going to solve my marital ache. I sought solace again in the book cover about dead artists, but what I really wanted then was to be roaming through Ghirardelli Square and tasting its finest chocolate.

Although spacious with ceilings at least twenty-five feet high, the room collapsed to the size of a cardboard box. Relief from my claustrophobic surroundings required a quick decision. I needed to see First Love, whether I wanted to or not. As if on cue that her job with me was done, as soon as I made this decision, a flood of people arrived on the floor, and The Gallery Lady politely dismissed herself.

"It was nice to talk to you," she said. *At least it was 'nice' for one of us,* I thought.

I wandered aimlessly around the gallery for a few minutes but left when I decided to find a computer to email First Love, saying that I could meet him in the evening before flying back to The Urban City the following night. I walked back to my hotel room by 5:00 p.m. but didn't want to wait all evening there if we weren't going to meet. In the email, I asked him to call me between 5:00 and 6:00 p.m. if he wanted to arrange to meet. The phone rang at exactly five o' clock.

"Jeez, you don't give a guy much leeway," First Love said. "Where are you staying?"

"On Lombard near Van Ness."

"I'm having dinner with my kids, but I'll be free around eight." My heart stopped racing when I found out he had children. Careful with his words, First Love gave me parsimonious and clear instructions to his house, and if I couldn't find it, I thought I would have been the one who'd made a mistake writing them down.

After we hung up, I got into the shower and lathered my hair into a foamy bouffant. I enjoyed the pleasing effect of the warm mist inside my chest as I inhaled and considered what First Love and I would talk about during our reunion. But I was certain we wouldn't focus on the happenings in Somewhere Small under The Willow Tree, and by the end of the evening, when he closed the door behind me, I would take all of my heart back with me to The Urban City.

During the drive, I distracted myself with a National Public Radio presentation about the aftermath of 9/11, which was still gnawing at the United States' collective psyche. Being immersed in the radio program made the drive pass too quickly. When I arrived in the neighbourhood, I found a restaurant offering takeout dinners. While waiting for my order, I called Husband #1 from a payphone in the parking lot and told him I was on my way to First Love's house for a visit. Seemingly blasé about my evening plans, Husband #1 told me to enjoy my reunion and that he was looking forward to seeing me when I got back to The Urban City the following night.

I admired Husband #1's philosophy about relationships. He used to compare a marriage to knitting. Each person held a needle used to co-create a pattern consisting of knit and purl stitches — knit being loyalty and purl being commitment. And the wool they used to knit their individual lives together needed to be resilient enough to handle the stretches and strains that prevented it from tearing when one or both needed more space between them. And as long as the two worked together and someone didn't decide to let the stitches slip off his or her needle — or one didn't get a pair of scissors and sever their design — they would be all right.

Picking up my order, I could no longer procrastinate meeting First Love. It was getting late on what would be a work night for him, though I remembered he liked the night, too. We were owls whose eyes got bigger and better long after the sun set.

The thought sent my memory to warm summer nights riding our bicycles to The Janitor and The Bingo Player's house. First Love was a gentleman. He always escorted me home after our clandestine sessions along The Big River that made me forget who and where I was. We took turns leading the ride beneath the orange neon streetlamps that hung like commas above us as we rode on opposite sides of the solid yellow line. First Love and I knew how to be together and apart, even as teenagers.

Although the restaurant was only a few blocks from his house, it had grown dark and there were very few streetlights in his neighbourhood. I also found it difficult to locate the numbers on the houses. I ended up knocking on the door of a house I knew was the wrong address, but I hoped the occupants knew First Love and where he lived. A petite woman holding a puppy resembling a black ball of wool stuffed with Mexican jumping beans answered the door. As soon as I asked her about First Love, she raised her thumb in the direction to my left, which I thought was a bit abrupt and terse, but I was a stranger after all.

Off I went next-door, where I hesitated before knocking. When he answered the door, I still found him attractive, and as soon as I entered the house, my eyes quickly shifted to a woman sitting at the kitchen table in the far end of the house. I immediately thought she was his wife, which he clarified when he introduced her as a long-time family friend he'd met several years before as professional colleagues. He escorted me to the table where his friend was sitting and pulled out the chair for me at the head of the table. I avoided looking into the eyes of First Love and instead focused on opening my takeout.

First Love had not outgrown his charming politesse. He set my place at the table with a napkin, cutlery, and a plate so that I wouldn't be eating my dinner out of a box. Moody jazz played in the background while the three of us exchanged polite but superficial conversation about our lives. First Love's friend had been born and raised as a southern belle and her skills as a diplomatic guest were perfectly refined as the third person in the presence of two adults who had been high school sweethearts and not seen each other for twenty-five years. Before I arrived they had been enjoying dessert, and as a result I didn't feel as if I were being rude by eating my meal in front of them. At least I had the distraction of vegetables on my plate to help me digest the strangeness of seeing First Love again.

After we had covered the topics that told us enough about each other, I mentioned the curt interaction with the woman who lived next door. Both First Love and his friend burst out laughing and in between chuckles he told me she was his ex-wife. With the revelation he was no longer married, The Evil Temptress chimed in like a record that had a scratch in it and kept repeating, "Oh, what a night. This, I gotta see." I shook my head to interrupt her absurdity but it didn't take long for the news to travel to my belly. And despite my meal being a simple vegetarian ratatouille, my stomach gurgled as an accompaniment to The Evil Temptress' chant.

Shortly after the disclosure about the identity of the neighbour, First Love's friend announced she needed to leave. He accompanied her to her car while I continued to pick at my meal at the kitchen table. I surveyed the kitchen and living room and smiled at his children's photographs on the refrigerator. A few minutes later, I heard the front door creak. Without saying a word, First

Love walked to the kitchen sink, and with his back to me, he rinsed the dinner dishes and put them into the dishwasher.

Even doing dishes, he was a graceful man. He placed the plates in perfect alignment in the dishwasher and dropped the silverware into their cubicles, leaving enough space between them to ensure each and every one would be sparkling at the end of the dry cycle. I stared at his long and still-lean torso and followed his slender fingers and the elegant movements they made as he periodically shook the water from their tips. I liked the shape and size of his hands and noticed his body hadn't changed much, though I could not describe the subtle changes that must have taken place over the years. We dated during the summer months of Somewhere Small where clothing was only necessary for discretion and public civility. Twenty-five years later, First Love and I had grown up, and he was dressed in loose-fitting business attire and I in casual summer wear. I was married. And he was otherwise involved. Therefore, no exploration of his body to build a mental map of his middle-aged shape would take place. And I would sit at a safe distance from him to create a barrier to temptation.

His voice snapped me out of my wandering reverie.

"So you're married?" he asked with his back to me.

"Yes. And you're divorced?

"No. Separated, actually."

"What happened?"

"I didn't like being treated like the furniture after having three kids, so I found romance outside the marriage."

With his back still to me while drying his hands, his head seemed to lower a little and his voice hinted at a sadness and anger as he summarized life with his wife. They had welcomed three children within five years, and by the seven-year mark, he craved the odd stolen date night with an unknown destination but a known romantic one. He wanted what I saw and heard at The War Bride and The Canadian Soldier's house even after thirty years of marriage, and he had found the seeds of it with another woman while he was still married. I squirmed in the chair at the head of First Love's kitchen table when I found out how his marriage ended.

The Evil Temptress continued her narration in earnest when First Love excused himself to go outside for a few minutes. "By the way, never mind Elizabeth and Jane and Edward, your story is unfolding beautifully. How absolutely darling. You're in the part where fate has reunited you with your childhood sweetheart after a prolonged period of separation. You two had spent twenty-five years in the requisite distance phase of two hearts that still beat as one. Even Jane and Edward weren't separated for that long! And here we are. First Love is in his moody, tragic phase, and like the modern man he is, he's even doing dishes. And look at you. Aw. You've been on your quest to assert your courage and individuality for years without too much success yet, but it's okay. A good heroine's gotta have a compelling arc with memorable plot points to satisfy her audience. The way it's gone so far, the love story between you and First Love doesn't include fires and the irreversible loss of senses—and we already know you're no heiress—but nevertheless, your reunion is novel-worthy, Middle2. And fate has been extraordinarily helpful in some ways. I personally couldn't have written a more improbable sequence of events. Admit it, Middle2, you're in awe of the perfect planning abilities of The Powers That Be, and you believe their organizational skills deserve some kind of worship, perhaps even a religion, in their honour."

Just what I needed, a new religion. The Evil Temptress clearly was confused about the kind of story this was, but her summary to this point did amuse me, I must say.

It didn't matter that I noticed the beginnings of an internal quiver, an apprehension about First Love's predilection for prevarication and promiscuity. The internal quiver stopped briefly as I scanned his lithe backside while he scrubbed the dinner dishes and I sipped on a glass of wine he offered me. As if under a spell, an ambitious ride down memory lane began with a warmth diffusing through my chest and continued with the poignant television scene involving Cinderella and her prince staring lovingly into each other's eyes. Before long, her face mutated into mine, and her prince's into First Love's, whereupon I lost all awareness of the jittery feeling, because I had once again found myself entangled with First Love under the swaying branches of The Willow Tree.

CHAPTER 21

FIRST LOVE PRIVATE REUNION

The magic of first love is our ignorance that it can never end.
Benjamin Disraeli

When First Love finished cleaning the kitchen, we continued our conversation in his living room where we sat side by side with jazz still playing in the background. Talking to him was easy, and so was being with him in moments of silence. Our reunion made me want to walk with him as long as it took to find a new tree for us to get cozy under. Maybe it would be a maple tree, like the name of the street he lived on. Within the first five minutes of our conversation, I could see the reasons I'd married Husband #1 stacked before me like a house of cards that collapsed from being exposed to the sweeping movement of a magician's cape.

"Tell me about your husband."

"He's a nice guy." *Nice* was too close to neutral, but I lacked the will and a dictionary of doting terms for Husband #1 didn't exist.

"The only words you can find to describe the man you're married to are, 'he's nice'?"

I had a husband problem. The truth was bad enough coming from a stranger in a gallery, but coming from First Love made me sad. I watched the candle flicker on the wooden chest while I rolled my paper napkin into a tube with one hand, and held the crystal glass filled with auburn liqueur in the other. No matter how slowly I sipped my postprandial beverage, my throat didn't stop burning that night.

When First Love excused himself for a minute, the truth throbbed inside my chest. How I felt with my husband was not how I wanted to feel about the man I was married to. I wanted to be alive in conversation with him; I wanted to feel physically attracted to him; I wanted to love the way he smelled; I wanted to know his heart: his hopes, his dreams, his fears, his passions; I wanted to support him in his quest to be all that he dreamt of being, even if his answer was "I don't know yet;" I wanted to travel the world with him, exploring cultures, lands, and peoples; I wanted us to read our favourite books together and snuggle up to watch movies on Saturday nights; I wanted us to fight respectfully when we resolved problems, ending them every time with "I'm sorry," and "I love you;" I wanted to maintain a deep and unwavering respect for him. And during the low points, when we didn't like ourselves or each other much, we would still wish each other a good day when we parted and hug when we reunited.

I wanted to "do love," which meant certain things about how I wanted to behave in my relationships. I had never done love before and instead, avoided it and its poisonous territory. It was a nature's paradise, but I avoided it because of the untold number of predators masked as candy-coated fruits and voluptuous flowers, where the biggest and boldest of both were the most seductive and the most dangerous. Why would I risk loving someone else when the two people who created me disappeared forever from my life in less than half an hour? And the only other people I had loved were First Love, who abandoned me, and The War Bride, who decided I was a bad person and unworthy of her love for using the word "alacrity" in a letter she had no business reading in the first place. And then, of course, my inability to hold onto the keepsakes of love—the opal from BrotherLove and the sapphire from The War Bride—was evidence of my problem with doing love. I was inept at keeping the tokens of love from people. If I couldn't prevent the loss of symbols of love given to me as gifts, what faith would the people I love have in me to cherish them? And how would they be confident in my ability to hold our love in the palms of my hands and not let it slip through my fingers through careless action or inattention?

In doing love, aren't we supposed to plumb the depths of our experience and actions with others? In doing love, we adorn it with cherished relics collected from our many and varied explorations beneath the surface of life. The number and nature of the keepsakes we gaze at when it's all said and done become our personal mythology that answers the question, "How deep was it?" How deep was our love? Well, my love hadn't been very deep, because I'd either lost or gotten rid of the things collected from my romantic relationships. I have never put a photo of me with a romantic partner anywhere, on any wall, any desk, and not even tucked in a compartment of my wallet near my credit cards to ensure I saw it every day.

When First Love returned, he sat a little closer to me on his couch and filled my glass with more liqueur. There was no need to continue talking about Husband #1 because the problem was clear and the solution didn't involve First Love. The conversation didn't revolve around romance. We talked about travel, books, and his children, whom he clearly loved.

At two o'clock in the morning, we weren't tired yet.

"Let's go for a drive," he said, slapping his hands on his knees. "I wanna show you the city view from the mountains."

Sinking into the driver's seat of his burgundy sports car, he opened the rooftop; within ten minutes we were climbing a narrow paved road lined with redwoods and lush ferns. The lanky redwoods swayed in the wind and serenaded us with a continuous hush as we made our way to the summit. An image of Cinderella unpinning her hair in the carriage that was no longer a pumpkin jumped out at me and I could hear her murmuring something about wind running its fingers through her hair. Clearly the quantity of alcohol I'd consumed was causing me to hallucinate. At the midway point, First Love pulled the car into a lookout point and asked me if I wanted to drive.

"I don't think so," I replied, not because I didn't want to, but because I didn't have my driver's license with me.

"Don't disappoint me and start acting like a girl," he teased me. The odds of the police being in the hills above his neighbourhood were low, so into the driver's seat I went, though I still drove cautiously, which didn't have anything to do with being a girl. If we'd been in an accident, the night would have ended with another unpleasant reality—although I'm fairly certain his ex-wife would have smirked while looking at herself in her bathroom mirror the next morning after hearing news that we ended up in a ditch.

We returned to his house to have a nightcap of Grand Marnier or Cointreau. Did we have one of each? With the verbal part of our reunion complete, we kissed, but I didn't have enough time to know whether the experience spanned four seasons, because sanity slapped me on the shoulder.

"I need to go. My husband doesn't deserve this," I said. I shook the closeness I'd just experienced with First Love off me as I smoothed out my clothes.

First Love sighed deeply. "That's sweet." He got up from the couch and escorted me outside. He hugged me with only tenderness, and he gave me a kiss on the cheek before I got into my car to drive back to San Francisco.

"Drive safely," he said, closing the car door.

I drove back to San Francisco at the speed limit, but the highway lights and bulletin boards appeared in fast-forward motion. I gripped the steering wheel more tightly than I needed to, and a burning pain grew in my shoulder blades as cars zoomed past me on both sides of the lane I was travelling in. I opened all the windows to disperse the flash of memories bombarding me from the evening with First Love. The circulation of the warm air from the San Francisco Bay only increased the frame rate that they appeared before me. I resorted to turning on the radio to find a song I could blare, hoping that playing it loudly enough would scramble the images, or better yet, send them into the windy bay that would carry them away to a place where I could never find them. The first song I tuned into was "Just My Imagination." I punched the power button of the radio, and coached myself to calm down. I tried to focus on the simple act of breathing, which had reliably pacified me in chaotic phases of my life, thanks to the prescription from my family physician in Somewhere Small. But what I really wanted to do was keep driving and turn east as soon as possible. And once I reached the Atlantic Ocean, board a ship with an officer waiting to present me with papers for a new identity in some Faraway Place. And it didn't need to be one I wanted to visit, either. It just needed it to be one I could escape to. I needed some bleach for the nasty stain that was developing, and I needed it fast.

I wanted The Good Life and The Simple Life with someone, yet after spending an evening and most of the night with First Love, my husband was not the person I wanted to be with when I closed the curtains to the outside world after the sun set. He was not the one I wanted to talk to about my fears, frustrations, hopes, dreams, and dark thoughts. He's not the one I wanted to run back to, sharing with him the wondrous things I'd discovered about some Faraway Place I travelled to without him. As long as I was with Husband #1, the door to my passions and secrets would remain under lock and key, and no matter how much I wanted to avoid getting divorced, I would never express love in its full spectrum as long as I was with him. I could hope for that day to come, but with a lifetime of tomorrows it never would, because the window to that door held a blurry image of a man whose eyes didn't match Husband #1's.

Thank goodness the growing brightness in the east in the pre-dawn hours of a new day had fully restored my sanity by the time I reached the parking lot of my hotel. I believed The Powers That Be supported my reunion with First Love, not for me to become his lover, but for me to realize my mistake in marrying Husband #1. But ultimately, the decision to see him was a matter of choice after my talk with The Gallery Lady. The hand of fate didn't pluck me out of my hotel room in San Francisco and plant me squarely at the doorstep of First Love's house. I made that decision, got in my rented car, and drove south with his perfectly

delivered instructions in tow that led me to his unlit neighbourhood. Maybe, just maybe, The Powers That Be were returning
my Forever After card to me, and "T-R-O-U-B-L-E-D Fate" had
faded from its surface over the years.

Driving past an advertisement for a telecommunications
company that read, "Near or far, *hear* we are," I knew I wanted
a man who could go the distance with me and didn't leave any
doubt about his commitment to me, no matter how far away
we were from each other. It wouldn't matter if we were half a
world apart because neither of us would feel the separation in our
hearts. A happy life with First Love would remain theoretical and
abstract, rather than a personal example that I would write about,
one that The Evil Temptress could use as inspiration for another
great love story, or one that resuscitated Cinderella and sentimentality when I drank wine. But meeting First Love gave me a goal:
I wanted to learn how to do love. Love as a noun is defined as "a
strong feeling of affection and sexual attraction for someone." As
a verb, the definition is "to feel affection and sexual attraction for
someone." I needed to create my personal definition, because for
me to do love required the expression of feelings toward someone
and actions that showed him my sincerity. And sometimes the
most loving act is silence. The thought of doing love made my
chest feel the same kind of warmth as if I had just rubbed it with
rose oil infused with menthol.

I arrived back at my hotel room in the early morning hours
when ambitious business people in San Francisco were already
waking up to the first day of business after Labour Day. I quickly
prepared for bed and slipped under the covers, only to be completely terrified by a knock at the door.

"Who is it?" I asked.

"The police, ma'am." What? The police? What did they want with me in the middle of the night? Oh, my God, was I about to be arrested in a foreign country for something I did while driving back to San Francisco?

I opened the door to see the female officer looking concerned.

"Are you all right?" she asked.

I was perplexed. After all, she must have been able to see I was absolutely fine.

"We received a call from your husband. He was concerned you hadn't made it back to your hotel safely."

"Thanks for checking. But I'm fine, really."

"Okay, well you enjoy the rest of your stay here. We'll let your husband know. Goodnight."

Tucking myself back into bed, I stared at the opaque floral curtains with a small opening between them that let in a narrow pane of light as a new day definitely dawned.

Husband #1 must have panicked when he hadn't received a good night call from me, even though we had already said goodnight to each other when I called him from the telephone booth outside the restaurant near First Love's house. Perhaps he had intuited the reunion took a friendlier turn than he would have liked. As I reached over to turn out the lamp on the night table, the phone rang.

"So I guess this means you made it safely back to your room?" First Love said.

"Yeah," I replied. But with a wider definition of "sure," I was anything but.

"I received an email from your husband, reminding me *you* are *his* wife," First Love continued, with a chuckle.

I might have been Husband #1's wife, but I wasn't his chattel. That thought irritated me more than the hum of the fridge in my room.

"He also alluded to your new profession if your marriage ends. Apparently, you're gonna be a nun." And that thought was funny.

Husband #1 wanted to convince First Love that if I became a divorcée, my devotion would turn to God and not to another man. And in particular, not to him.

CHAPTER 22

THE SIMPLE LIFE COMES UNDONE

The first step to getting the things you want out of life is this: Decide what you want.

Ben Stein

Flying home to The Urban City, I couldn't sit in my seat after the plane reached cruising altitude. I paced the narrow aisle on the Boeing 737 until once again forced to sit for landing. I knew my marriage was in trouble, but I wanted to work at it, even if my husband's eyes didn't match those of the man in the window in my mind that presented a blurry image of my ideal mate. I had accepted the safety of The Simple Life with Husband #1 but a complexity infected it after my reunion with First Love. Even without the First Love problem, my life with Husband #1 wasn't what I wanted.

When I arrived home, I told my husband what had happened with First Love, including that we kissed, and that I wanted a deeper connection like the one I'd felt with him. My husband listened without judgment and even seemed compassionate. He didn't stomp and holler or storm out of the house. Maybe he'd had a First Love who tempted him during his marriage to his first wife. After my disclosure, I was relieved for having been honest, but the guilt of having kissed First Love and wanting to do more with him nagged at me. In an even nobler act of selflessness, my husband gave me carte blanche to sleep with First Love if I needed to as a way to resolve my feelings about him and the marriage in general. But he didn't want to know about it if it happened. Who would make such an offer? Someone of great nobility—or someone with low self-esteem.

First Love and I continued to correspond via email. At the end of a business trip a week after our reunion in San Francisco, he found out his maternal grandmother had died unexpectedly; he would be returning to Somewhere Small to attend her funeral. We decided to meet again at his Cabin Retreat an hour away from Somewhere Small after the funeral, where we would spend the weekend together.

The route between The Urban City and Somewhere Small passes through lush meadows that climb into rugged mountains before it descends into sub-desert plains and rises again into a mix of deciduous and coniferous forests. Along a straight stretch at the summit of the first mountain pass of the drive, I was alarmed to hear a police siren behind me. I assumed he was racing to a scene ahead, but in fact he had been pursuing me. I was about to have the second encounter in a month with a police officer. After he issued me a speeding ticket, I sat in my car for a few minutes until he drove away. I got out of the driver's seat to stretch my arms toward the blue sky and inhaled as much of the crisp air as I could force into my lungs. The river below me glistened under the autumn sun, with the currents twisting and turning around each other like silver ribbons. I understood the officer's recommendation to "slow down and be safe" on the road, but not where my life direction was concerned. I'd been doing those things for too long and for far too much of my adult life.

The Cabin Retreat was located on the far side of a lake nestled in one of the mountain ranges east of Somewhere Small. First Love and I both arrived there after sunset in the pitch-black desolation in front of the glassy lake we needed to cross. Summer had ended and all the vacationers had shuttered their places for the winter. During our time there, we did the things we loved to do together: play games, listen to music, talk, and otherwise communicate with each other. The communication that occurred on the living room couch and in the adjacent bedroom of The Cabin Retreat lacked the intimacy of a committed couple because there were too many others in the room with us (my husband, his girlfriends, and his ex-wife). At the end of the three-day visit, he headed east and I headed west at the fork in the road above the lake. From the rearview mirror, I watched his rental car move in the direction opposite me and then disappear as mine rounded a corner of its own. I thought this second reunion would be the final good-bye to First Love, even though being with him reawakened my need to find an intimate union with a man. But for that to happen, I needed to enter the hazardous area, the no-safety zone where the risks were as high as the rewards that would come from pursuing love differently than I'd done in the past.

During the eight-hour drive back to The Urban City, I had plenty of time to think about the conversation with my husband once I arrived. I didn't plan the entire conversation, but I knew the final outcome: I'd be getting a divorce. I would not be able to continue a physical relationship with my husband after experiencing three days of the kind of union I'd dreamt about having with a man. I broke the news to my husband as honestly and gently as I could, but ended up needing to use a more direct approach after he wrapped himself in denial a few days later. Eventually I told him I wasn't in love with him the way I wanted to be and that I was sorry. I told him I hoped he would find a companion who adored him the way I wished I did.

Within a few weeks, my husband left The Urban City to return to New Zealand. During the drive between the apartment we had shared and The Urban City, unspoken words became nervous tension that filled the car and suffocated me. By the time we reached the downtown core, Husband #1 and I had started to argue and I became afraid to drive him all the way to the airport. I asked him to get out of the car downtown. Looking into each other's eyes and saying goodbye, I knew Husband #1 and I would not see each other again. When he stepped out of the car, my heart opened like the blossoming tulips in spring, even though a downpour was pelting their velvety petals.

The sun was setting as I made my way across the bridge back to my home on the north side of The Urban City. I was crossing over to my newly single life as a woman in her late thirties. I should have known the marriage was destined to end when I reflected on the key events before, during, and immediately after our wedding. When I first met Nice&Neutral, the lack of internal excitement or romantic glee at the thought of meeting him should have been enough of a warning. And feeling energetically depleted on our first day together in The Earth's Womb should have been the next big sign telling me to walk away, regardless of how "nice" he was. I couldn't foretell my life, but I knew that I wouldn't repeat the mistake I had made with Husband #1. I would not marry a man I felt neutral about.

In the post-mortem of my marriage, I summarized it with several reminders classified as, "Don't get married again if…:"

· The night before your wedding, you just can't stop drinking that bottle of Gewurztraminer you opened after your "last supper" as a single person.

· Later in the bathtub, you can't stop crying when you think about the otherworldly connection you had with your First Love.

· You forget to put on your engagement ring before leaving for the church to meet your beloved. You reason it's only a ring, after all; marriage is about commitment, not about a silly piece of jewelry.

· At the altar, somewhere in between uttering, "'til death do us part" and "in sickness and in health'" you feel a fleeting nausea you attribute to the overconsumption of wine during the previous night's "last supper."

· Also at the altar, you experience flashbacks of scenes in "Runaway Bride" but you see yourself instead of Julia Roberts in the horse getaway sequence.

· On your wedding night, you both get undressed slowly while complaining about your aching feet. You get into bed on one side and your beloved on the other. You fall asleep mid-sentence while repeating to your groom how tired you are and which body part hurts the most now that you're on your backs.

· You forgot the lingerie your bridesmaids gave you as a wedding present. Given how tired and achy your body is, it would have been a waste of space in your overnight bag anyway.

· Also on your wedding night, after falling into a deep sleep, you find yourself in a sexy and wildly satisfying dream with "the one that got away." Somehow sleep made all the aches disappear.

· When you wake up the next day, the very beginning of your wonderful life together, the first thought entering your mind is, *Man, I need some exercise*, followed by "Honey, do you know where my running shoes are?" Laced up and in spandex, you are so very grateful for sleep's restorative effect.

· During your first run as a newly married woman, you stop listening to silly love songs after having trouble breathing when Van Morrison's "Have I Told You Lately" starts to play.

The worst sign I married the wrong person happened during my first meeting with the lawyer to formally begin divorce proceedings. Sitting erect in her blue suit with a notepad and pen in hand, she was ready to gather the facts she needed from me.

"What day did you get married?"

"Oh, um, let's see." I looked to the left corner of the ceiling as if a fly I would find buzzing up there would jog my memory. "It was a Friday, I remember. Well, this is awkward. Sorry."

"You're joking, right?" she asked, staring at me with a stunned look. "Well, this is a first. Do you remember what month it was at least?"

"December. I wanted to get married between Christmas and New Year's Eve. It's my favourite time of the year."

If I remarry, my wedding dress will not suffer the same demise the green satin one did. In the evening following our wedding night, when he and I returned to our rented house on the north side of The Urban City, I rolled up the dress and stuffed it into a green opaque plastic bag as if preparing it for the upcoming weekly waste disposal. I didn't throw it over my shoulder, march down the stairs, and dump it in the normal pickup spot for garbage collection, but instead, tucked it away in a rarely opened closet. I also didn't deliver it into the loving and capable hands of my Iranian seamstress who could have transformed it into a party dress for some future celebration. The seamstress route seemed premature and the closet one sensible, at least for the time being. We later moved to a townhouse where I found another rarely opened closet to stuff it into, and when I closed the shuttered doors, promptly forgot about its whereabouts until the next move a year later.

The green satin dress suffered a dramatic demise in the same home where my marriage ended. Three years later following the lengthy divorce from Husband #1 (who had gone undercover Down Under), a friend and I were having a glass of wine on a Saturday night. On the topic of rituals and their importance in cementing key milestones or life events, we agreed divorce should be celebrated for the positive impact the partner had on our lives. With that, she asked me what had happened to my wedding dress. I walked to the hallway closet to retrieve it from its raised (albeit undignified) state on the top shelf.

With the bag in tow, I returned to my friend in the living room and dumped the crumpled contents onto the carpet. Although the bag had been hidden away in three different closets since my wedding day, seeing the dress in a dishevelled heap on the floor pricked at the loss of Forever After with Husband #1. Meanwhile, Cinderella had been stretched out in a supine position on the carpet beside me, with her palms resting on her temples. She hated the end of a love story, even a passionless one.

My friend was a counsellor by profession and could intuit my sadness without a cathartic commentary. She asked me if I wanted to keep the wedding dress, noting that it carried with it a psychological bond to Husband #1. In that moment, I channelled my inner seamstress, one that lacked talent for designing dresses using tape measures, sewing machines, and needles, but one who had superlative skills with the tools of her trade: a pair of scissors, several small white plastic garbage bags, wine, and candles. My friend topped up our glasses as I prepared for the procedure. Cinderella refused a sip of wine from my glass, turned away from us, and took on the fetal position. But we quickly forgot about her as the ceremony got underway.

Scissors in my right hand, I picked up the dress in my left hand and decided on an inside out approach to its coming undone. The lacy lining was an easier target, and as I made a few incisions, I dispensed with the scissors, figuring my hands were more than capable of completing the tearing phase of the job. Besides, being a tactile sort, I enjoyed feeling the pre-tear tension followed by the release accompanying each rip. My friend became my coach, asking me how I was feeling as the cutting got underway. As it turned out, I didn't need much prompting to purge my feelings with a little early encouragement from her. In fact, she ceased to exist once I started cutting the outer satiny layer with my shears.

"Don't you just love the sound of that? Metal cutting satin."

And with each tear of the lacy lining, I yelled, "Yeah, that feels goooooood," as if I were with a man in my bedroom, not a female friend in my living room.

During the ceremony, I received a phone call from First Love who already knew about my plans to have dinner with my friend. I walked out to my balcony with a view to the west side of The Urban City, and shook my head when I mistook a cloud for the ghost of Cinderella, and two twinkling stars as her eyes.

"What are you ladies up to?"

"Not much. We're going through some old clothes," I said, admiring the scissors in my hand.

"You two sure know how to have fun on a Saturday night," he laughed.

"Wine helps."

"I just wanted to say goodnight. I'm going to a late movie."

"Oh, what are you gonna see?"

"Not sure yet."

"Well, enjoy it, and I look forward to your review tomorrow."

"Okay, 'night."

"Night."

Before walking back into my apartment, I looked back up into the sky and was relieved to see that Cinderella's ghost had disappeared. We continued to fit the remains of my wedding dress into plastic bags that we stacked by the door of my apartment. Once we were done, I filled our glasses with white wine and we raised them like Lady Liberties with torches. The name of the wine we had been drinking became the inspiration for the toast. "See ya later," we said in unison.

After dumping the bags into the garbage bin, I returned to my apartment and fell into a visionless slumber after concluding that although I still liked Husband #1's marriage metaphor, the design I will choose with my next husband will fill me with anticipation, and the sound our needles will make as they cross over each other's will excite me.

I dozed for the entire morning the next day after waking up with a headache, not from having drunk too much wine during the "See Ya Later" celebrations, but from having placed too much hope in what I knew had been a hopeless situation the moment

I'd met the man who became Husband #1. I was suffering from hope withdrawal, but I finally left my bed after I woke up from a dream with Cinderella singing, "Reunited and it feels so good, reunited 'cause we've understood, there's one perfect fit, and, sugar, this one is it…"

CHAPTER 23

REUNION CONTINUES WITH FLAGS AND FLAMES

His ex is still in the picture (#66).
He openly admits to being unfaithful to an ex (#85).
He takes phone calls during your date (#14).
He checks out other women when he's with you (#67).
"96 Relationship Flags Every Woman Should Know"
– by Guyspeak, Friday, May 13, 2011

After our reunion at The Cabin Retreat, First Love and I communicated via email periodically. As Christmas neared, he needed to make several business trips to a large city south of The Urban City, where I would meet him. During the visits, he repeated his doubts about being able to commit to a monogamous relationship because he needed sustained, intense passion and was afraid of being taken for granted—two circumstances he could not tolerate. But in keeping with my difficulty in doing love, I reasoned I could also enjoy his company and our physical intimacy without becoming too attached. My long-distance relationship with him would be the quiet valley I would cross before entering love's territory. In the meantime, I could relax and enjoy myself with my First Love while walking through the uncomplicated and easy valley.

Six months into our reunion, First Love and I decided to take our first trip together on a cruise in the Caribbean Sea. Cruise ships weren't a desirable travel option for me because of the limits naturally imposed by the itinerary and the herding mentality required to ferry a few thousand people from one port to another. But First Love convinced me of the merits of the cruise company and the nature of the holiday. The ship only accommodated one hundred guests and there was an equal number of polite and overly accommodating staff whose sole reason for being was to cater to the guests' every whim. I was uncomfortable with the overly servile nature of the cruise that had staff pull back the bed covers each night, place chocolate hearts in the centre of the pillows, and offer to serve everyone drinks in the far reaches of the ship twenty-four hours a day. However, the limited number of people on the boat and the unstructured options for meals and activities convinced me I would probably enjoy myself. I would also be able to take jaunts around the outer decks to gaze up into the starry night without the distraction of urban noise and city lights. And the sound of the engines, the wind, and the waves would lull a water-loving being like me into a sea-induced serenity.

When we arrived at First Love's house after he picked me up from the airport, I noticed his other more modest, family-oriented vehicle was vacant from its usual resting spot under the maple tree. In addition, the leaves in the vacant spot had been collecting there for at least a few days. I ignored the mystery of the missing

car and focused on going away together to a romantic destination as a way to celebrate our ongoing reunion and shared sense
of adventure.

Landing on one of the small islands in the Caribbean Sea, we
were welcomed with open arms to its shores, the breaking waves
calling us as a friend would, with curled fingers signalling to come
for a visit. Once we settled into our cabin, dined on fresh fruits
and salads, and sipped on the requisite inaugural rum drink,
we took our first excursion on a catamaran for an afternoon of
snorkeling in the impossibly clear aquamarine waters. Normally
careful in the sun, I made the painful mistake of not wearing a
sun shirt. I ended up with a second-degree burn on my back and
spent the remainder of the vacation covered up and slathering
vitamin E on it twice a day. I had a hard time believing I could
be so stupid. Blue eyed with fair skin and unaccustomed to much
sun exposure since my childhood days of swimming in the pools
and lakes around Somewhere Small, I let myself get burned.

When we returned to First Love's house after seven days on
the luxurious cruise, the four-door family suburban vehicle was
still missing from its dedicated spot. I finally asked him about it.
First Love's answer reminded me I still had a tendency to avoid
conversations about topics whose content would disturb me.

He had lent his practical car to his photographer girlfriend who
was a struggling student. First Love and I had not committed to
an exclusive relationship and this girlfriend was in an incompatible phase of life. Even without the exclusivity agreement, my
loyalty loving soul was dumbfounded that First Love could have
sex with another woman before we departed on our romantic
reunion together. The difference between his other girlfriend and
me was that she was a student and I had entered the professional

world with a bank balance of The Good Life; therefore, I could afford a trip to a Faraway Place.

During a walk in the neighbourhood, as I reeled about his ongoing relationships, First Love assured me that he could buy me a house where we both could live. I believed him, but I didn't want his house. I wanted his whole heart, but I doubted it would ever be available, at least to me. I doubted the sincerity of his words and adopted the belief that I, too, was one of his playmates. But I was also afflicted with incurable optimism.

One month later, on my fortieth birthday and during a romantic dinner at a seaside restaurant, First Love announced that he had ended his romantic relationships with other women and was prepared to commit to an exclusive relationship with me. I couldn't tell whether the internal quiver was due to pessimism or elation.

First Love and I settled into The Good Life with each other hundreds of miles apart, with me living and working in the Urban City and he in Silicon Valley. Our life was anything but simple. But the flexibility of my work schedule as a consultant allowed me to travel back and forth between The Urban City and San Francisco to visit him and maintain my professional life back in my native land. We agreed to avoid a separation of more than two weeks, and we would never spend our birthdays, Valentine's Day, Christmas, and New Year's celebrations apart. We would continue our long-distance relationship until his children graduated from high school, which meant that in ten year's time we would find a way to share a house in the same city. Then we would create The Simple Life but still fulfill the needs of our adventurous souls.

In the spring and autumn, First Love and I made one or more trips to the Cabin Retreat. We spent our happiest times there. We enjoyed listening to First Love's collection of music. Then there were the marathon Scrabble games, skinny-dipping at dusk with the moon rising in the east, bocce games in the sandpit above the beach, and sitting together, comfortably quiet, when both of us had immersed ourselves in a delicious book on some afternoons. On really hot days, we could take breaks from whatever we were doing to cool off in the lake or step out onto the balcony to admire and talk about how grateful we were for being able to experience the pristine beauty of our childhood playground. First Love often sought peace in the night sky and spent hours on the balcony gazing up at the Milky Way. I have never been able to look at the sky for too long, and I can't attribute my discomfort to the fast-moving storm clouds I watched from the porch of the Little House in Somewhere Small. Whether it's the perfectly blue summer sky or the speckled dark one at midnight, I inevitably become terrified because it's just too big for me to ponder.

First Love and I normally flew separately from our respective cities to the U.S. border town and then made a three-hour drive to the Cabin Retreat. Before beginning the journey north, First Love set up his iPhone to play the latest episodes of "Radio Lab," which covers various topics about social experiments and scientific discoveries. Being with First Love during these short drives altered my view of road trips. Gone were the days of staring out the backseat windows for sixteen hours between Somewhere Small and the Prairies. Gone were the days of having to take turns with my sisters for a window seat and getting dizzy from the second hand smoke and Roy's wailing. Road trips with First Love to the Cabin Retreat were no longer something to suffer through like the flu. On the days I woke up knowing I would be reunited with First Love by sunset and holding hands with him in the rented car, I could tolerate the worst dreary day in The Urban City. And such were the days of my life, days I would remember for the rest of it, confirmed to me by a "Radio Lab" podcast of an interview with a Nobel laureate who explained exactly how my brain would imprint my cherished memories into its neural network.

When First Love and I travelled together, we relished serendipity like a child who has discovered a secret doorway she can't wait to walk through with wide eyes and wandering hands. During one of our trips, we had a six-hour layover at a small airport. Rather than watch the inbound and outbound planes at our gate, we rented a car and drove into the city and the surrounding mountains to satisfy our curiosity about how the locals lived. Our eyes sampled the French and South Pacific flavours on display in the shop windows, and as we made our way into the mountains along the mucky, rust-coloured roads, we waved at numerous locals tending to the hens and gardens outside their homes that were the size and shape of our car garages back home.

Despite our shared sense of adventure, I struggled with trust issues from the beginning of our relationship, compelling me to suggest we end it at least once a month. I argued the distance between us would be too challenging, when in fact what I really grappled with was his ability to be faithful to me. I thought I couldn't meet his needs, not because I didn't have a host of things to offer him, but because he needed the affection and attention of more than one woman, a conclusion based on history rather than on an acute predictive power. My uncertainties fuelled his, which heightened his compulsion to be seen and recognized by beautiful women wherever we went. In times of duress, we could not reassure each other. First Love needed assurance of his desirability and I never unpacked my suitcases when I arrived at his house.

We both longed for a constant and passionate romance with a best friend, but best friends trust each other and we didn't. Could we with time?

On Easter weekend a year after we'd begun our exclusive relationship, First Love flew me to Paris in style. He used his much-prized Virgin Atlantic Air Miles to treat me to a first-class seat. I tossed and turned in the full-length bed under the violet glow of the cabin lights. I sipped on champagne and tried to watch several different movies but found myself unable to concentrate for long. When I landed in Paris after a brief stop in Britain, First Love met me in the arrivals area, hugged me tenderly, and gave me the kind of kiss a romantic man would when he greeted the girlfriend he hadn't seen for a few weeks. It was my first trip to Paris and I remember thinking that it seemed both familiar and foreign, the way some places do when we visit them. My history with France had begun years earlier in elementary school when our instructor played the guitar and sang us "Aux Champs Elysees" after showing us pictures of it and The Eiffel Tower. And, of course, it was the native land of The War Bride, the woman who transformed me from a scrubby tomboy into a lady.

While on the train, First Love told me we were going into the country south of Paris to spend the evening with friends he'd become close to when he lived there years before. We met the woman of the couple in the city centre to board the train that would take us to our destination. I felt an instant camaraderie with our hostess who was our companion for the short ride. She was warm, chatty, and striking in her looks, not in the sense of extraordinary beauty, but in the contrast of her eyes, skin tone, and hair. Like many French women, she had an air of elegance, even when dressed casually in jeans and a t-shirt. During the ride, we discussed romance and the possibility of being faithful to one person for life. Up until that point in the conversation I had remained silent, staring out the rectangular windows and watching Paris disappear as we travelled south.

"We've been together for over twenty years, and I've come to believe a couple can be devoted for a period, but not a lifetime," she said, without any sign of sadness that I could detect.

First Love slapped me playfully on my right thigh. "What do you think?" First love asked me. He didn't have to caption it with "See, you've just received confirmation of what we experienced people know."

"I don't know. But yes, I hope it's possible. I can't speak from experience. I can only speak from a hopeful heart." Exhaustion overcame me and I leaned on First Love, resting my head on his arm.

When our male host picked us up at the train station, the entire town must have known he'd arrived by the booming hello he gave us, the kind politicians give while stumping in front of cheering crowds. When First Love introduced me to him, he wrapped his arms around me hard enough to give me an adjustment to my thoracic spine, and no matter how hard I tried to avoid taking in a mouthful of his hair, which flew around his head like a spray of ruffled feathers as he turned this way and that, I decided to give up because soon I'd be enjoying a glass of wine and goat cheese.

After a short drive, we arrived at their country home that was old enough and big enough for the local ghosts to convene for the occasional meeting with The Powers That Be. We drank wine and engaged in desultory conversation as we prepared food in the kitchen. By early evening, we had switched from Sauvignon Blanc to Merlot and nibbled on cheese, fruit, and deliciously baked breads from the local merchants. The wine became my heating pad, remedying the chill from exhaustion, and by the time we finished the feast of duck and traditional French condiments, I was swaying from side to side—not from enjoying the beat of the background North African music the host had turned on before we sat down, but from the prelude to a fainting spell that was about to tip me over. First Love sat close to me with his arm around me, providing the lean-to I needed during the meal.

After dinner, as the party got livelier and the host began to bounce on a stool while he played the piano, First Love sensed I had become one of the wilting plants in the corner; he whispered in my ear that if I needed to go to sleep, he would help excuse me for the night. He led me upstairs to a bedroom in the farthest corner from the living room below. He tucked the blankets up around my neck and kissed me on the forehead before tiptoeing toward the door. Within seconds, I plunged into the deepest reaches of sleep where it was too dark to dream.

The next morning, First Love and I returned to Paris for the Easter long weekend. Many of the museums were closed, but we did visit a cosmopolitan bar on Saturday night, where all the beautiful people in Paris gather in their fancy attire to meet their fancy friends and imbibe fancy drinks while taking molecular-sized bites from the centre of impossibly small plates.

I never felt secure with First Love when we were socializing in places with a bounty of beautiful women. He always seemed to be on the lookout for someone who would flirt with him. This behaviour made me moody and uncommunicative, but I always tried to convince myself I was the one with the problem. During dinner dates, when his flirting with waitresses became intolerable, I made a habit of retreating to the bathroom. While washing my hands, I often looked in the mirror and gave my reflection an admonishing sneer. First Love's behaviour wasn't like the water on my hands. I couldn't shake off the effects of his actions, but I could dry my hands with alacrity, crumple the paper into a tight little ball, and drop it in the bin beside the sink on my way out.

First Love and I earned respectable salaries in our professions, and the bounty of The Good Life during the early days in Somewhere Small showed me money could solve many of life's most difficult problems. But it could not solve one of the basic tenets of Forever After: Trust cannot be bought or sold with a bank balance. Trust's currency is comfort. And I wasn't comfortable opening the door to my heart and letting First Love wander through its fragile spaces. Without trust, The Good Life's appeal loses its luster. The Good Life doesn't resolve a lack of trust, just like a new coat of paint doesn't prevent rotting wood from turning to pulp. Without trust, The Simple Life is never relaxing, even with all the material riches of The Good Life. But the luster can take some time to fade, especially when its original sheen is unspeakably alluring and brilliant beyond all expectations.

First Love organized a trip for us to Bora Bora after I told him I thought everyone should see the place dubbed the most beautiful place on Earth. He had been on Club Med excursions before and convinced me we would enjoy a similar experience in Bora Bora, because all aspects of accommodation were taken care of—from food, to drinks, to various activities around the island. We departed on the vacation from San Francisco and thirteen hours later we landed on the main island before boarding a small plane to reach our final destination on the small island in the South Pacific. The short flight was only thirty minutes long at a cruising altitude of five thousand meters. Although in a sleepy daze from the red-eye flight, I still marvelled at the turquoise waters surrounding the constellation of little islands below us. A remote and tropical paradise awaited us. Upon landing, we were ferried along the coast for a fifteen-minute boat ride to reach our accommodations. Once we checked in, we were escorted to our self-contained rustic cabin, which had high-beamed ceilings and overlooked the ocean just a few hundred feet away. The common area was designed as an open space as well, with thatched roofs, no walls, and only steps away from the tepid waters. We settled in comfortably into our temporary holiday quarters.

My favourite memories of the holiday involved water, though it didn't serve as a rinsing agent to wash away my angst. Halfway through our vacation, First Love and I decided to wade into the ocean that stretched out like a blanket of black satin shimmering under a nearly full moon. A reef provided a protective barrier around the island, which made me feel reasonably safe in the water, at least from losing a limb from a shark attack. However, there were still several dangerous creatures that could hurt us. I was afraid of the shy stonefish that remained hidden unless stepped on. But we took the risk of being chair-bound for a month while the pain subsided. First Love walked much farther ahead of me into the ocean. I tried to manage my fear by focusing on the beautiful view before me and the silky warm water against my legs as I glided away from the shoreline. The water only came up to my waist, even after having walked a hundred meters from land. At a certain point, a paroxysm of terror overtook me, which caused me to turn around and bolt back to shore as quickly as possible. First Love continued his leisurely exploration in the shallow waters before meeting me back on land. The uneasy combination of fear and comfort in the South Pacific seas mirrored my conflicted feelings about First Love. He had enticed me, just as my favourite element had, and I was unable to resist the temptation of being an explorer in the waters surrounding the most beautiful place on Earth.

My second favourite memory occurred during the last excursion we took before heading home. A group of us were ferried to a location where there was an opening in the coral reef surrounding the island. As soon as I mounted my snorkeling equipment and allowed the currents to guide me, the nautical Gods hypnotized me with the images of an aquatic kaleidoscope that made me forget about the troubles above the surface and back on land.

Throughout the entire ten-day trip to the most beautiful place on Earth, First Love and I walked on different paths periodically, but together or apart, the paths had several sections with loose gravel, and many of those sections were in places where we had to go downhill. And when we were together, either in our cabin or out on an excursion, a quiet melancholy dimmed my view when we were looking at something exquisitely beautiful or laughing with a group over a shared joke. And for the next three months, the internal quiver that had begun on the first night of my reunion with First Love became worse just before the full moon. We had definitely created The Good Life for ourselves and with each other. But I began to wonder about the growing complexities and complexes that infected what appeared to be a promising Simple Life, making it toxic, not unlike a bacterial infection that becomes systemic and life-threatening, with treatment that is also complex and perhaps unsuccessful.

During the plane ride back to San Francisco in the middle of the night, The Evil Temptress lectured me in a raspy voice during a period of turbulence in the middle of the Pacific Ocean. "You know, I have a problem with how this story's going. Why do you have to mention your fear of sharks, and the 'internal quiver' that, quite frankly, is becoming annoyingly redundant at this point. No one is going to read a story about love that compares it to death and disease." And I had a problem with The Evil Temptress and her attachment to the spring season of romance, like the British uncle I had met during my trip to Faraway Places #1. I wanted to tell her that she caused disease by casting her love spells, and it was more important to dispel them, not perpetuate them.

CHAPTER 24

THE TRUTH ABOUT FIRST
LOVE AND ME

*As I grow older, I pay less attention to what men say. I just watch what
they do.*
Andrew Carnegie

*Why, if it was an illusion, not praise the catastrophe, whatever it was, that
destroyed the illusion and put truth in its place.*
Virginia Woolf

*Your task is not to seek for love, but merely to seek and find all the barriers
within yourself that you have built against it.*
Rumi

A very wise woman once advised me how important it is to listen
carefully during the first conversation we have with someone new,
romantic or otherwise. Yes, what people do matters according to

the wisdom of Andrew Carnegie, but we will get an indication of their future actions based on what they say about the past. The first few words have adequately informed us if we have listened well enough. The wise woman said people are more likely to tell the truth before either party has made a huge investment. As a truth, it is often riddled with paradox. We think our knowledge of someone is directly related to the length of time we've known him or her, but our first impressions often come to bear months or years later as a disturbing déjà vu.

Six months after we began our exclusive relationship, First Love announced he had accepted a position in Los Angeles but would commute between there and San Francisco where he would maintain his home. Two months after he started his new job, I met him in Los Angeles on a February evening. We had made plans to eat dinner with Blonde Bombshell and her husband, who lived there at the time. During dinner, I developed a headache behind my eyes that the white wine and charming dinner company couldn't cure. Between the main course and dessert, I retreated to the restaurant bathroom.

While lathering the soap in my hand, I searched the eyes in the mirror above the sink. I didn't think I had ever stared into my eyes for as long as I did that night, and in doing so, I got a glimpse of what lay behind my irises and in the depths of my pupils. The more I searched, the calmer I became; I had the distinct impression I was accessing a place where only the truth resides. Looking down into the sink as I washed away the soapy lather from my hands, I took a deep breath and made a decision to confront First Love about a suspicion that had been growing for several months: I believed he was still seeing his ex-girlfriend.

Once back at the apartment, he went to his bedroom to pack his suitcase for our return flight to San Francisco the following day. No longer able to restrain myself, I walked down the dark hallway to confront him in the bedroom. He met me in the middle of the hallway where I stopped him.

"I need to ask you a question," I said.

He sensed the seriousness in my tone, put his hands on my shoulders, and encouraged me by saying, "Sure, of course. What's happening?"

"Did you sleep with your ex-girlfriend before she left for New Zealand?"

"Yes," he said, then clarified: "We had a one-time thing to say goodbye before she left."

I wondered if it had been on the night he picked me up from the San Francisco airport and insisted on changing the sheets without my help and having a bath before we went to bed together.

In bed that night, unable to sleep, I thought about my personal dream language. For me, when a major disruption is about to occur, I often dream about tidal waves approaching me from a safe enclosure. For several weeks prior to First Love's confession about his ex-girlfriend, my subconscious haunted me with disturbing aquatic scenes. Sometimes, I watched a tidal wave approach me as I gazed out the windows from inside a luxurious seaside home; other times, I clung frantically to a buoy being tossed about in choppy waters; and occasionally, I found myself rowing furiously in a lake under a starless sky, with my current location and final destination unknown.

The following morning over breakfast, First Love appeared uneasy, as if he was waiting for the right moment to tell me something. Maybe he wanted to wait until I'd had a few bites of breakfast before breaking more bad news to me. I wasn't prone to vomiting in the worst of circumstances, but I wanted to vomit, not because I felt nauseous, but so that I could ruin the outfit he had put on to travel back to San Francisco.

"Our one-night thing was actually a nine-month one."

"So I've been coming down here for nine months while you've been carrying on with her?"

"Look, I don't want to spend my life with her. I just like the way she makes me feel."

"I seem to have read an article once that said most men marry women that make them feel good," I said.

I got up from the table with my plate, scraped the rest of my breakfast into the garbage, and quietly went about packing my things for our plane ride back to Silicon Valley later that afternoon. On board and at cruising altitude, I chewed on the green straw of my gin and tonic and stabbed at the lime long after the glass was empty. When the plane began to descend over the mountains to the west of San Francisco, I closed my eyes, wanting to be a bird soaring above the peaks and into the valleys for as long as I wanted. But even if I had been that bird, I would have needed to return to the land eventually.

I assessed my own behaviour and what part I might have played in his departure from the relationship. My frequent suggestion that we end our relationship made him insecure. I apologized profusely to First Love each time, but when my insecurities about his commitment to me as his exclusive partner resurfaced, I'd threaten again, as if being with him gave me an obsessive compulsive disorder to flee. Our hearts parted the first time this happened around the glass table on the deck at his house on Maple. From that point forward, our hearts had become two magnets with their north poles facing one another. But if I could unpack my bags with First Love, we could have a beautiful and rare relationship that would last the rest of our lives. A few months after First Love and I decided to stay together as a couple, I was still chewing on his disclosure about liking the way his ex-girlfriend made him feel, unable to swallow it or spit it out.

"What does it mean when a man likes the way a woman makes him feel?" I asked him one night when we were sitting together on his couch watching *Love Actually*.

"She makes me feel as if I can do anything," he responded without any hesitation. With that, I believed it was just a matter of time before he would find another to fill the need in him or to return to his ex-girlfriend. I saw this truth in the place behind my eyes that I had accessed for the first time in the restaurant bathroom before confronting First Love. He needed external validation from at least two women, and I doubted I had ever been one of them, or would be, because he never once said he liked the way I made him feel, and the majority of times we were out socially, he inevitably ended up flirting with at least one woman in the room.

But I convinced myself that we had a special kind of bond. We were childhood sweethearts, after all, and that powerful young love was potent and could trump any obstacle. First Love would realize eventually what I already knew: our love was the entire suit of spades. Spades were the ultimate workhorses, and with enough of them, I could dig through the dirt and find my way to the two of hearts, which symbolized my union with First Love.

But I questioned the prospect of the two of hearts after a dream I had about First Love four months later. In it, he and I were facing each other on the shore of a beach, with a dense fog rolling in from the sea, threatening to engulf us. First Love looked melancholy, his normally vibrant eyes dull and his movements subdued and slow. Without saying a word, he turned around and an arm of fog wrapped itself around him. I watched him disappear into it and made no effort to follow him because I knew two things: I couldn't penetrate the fog and I didn't want to even if I could. When I woke up, my chest had constricted as if someone had wrapped a bandage around it tightly enough to prevent the pieces of my broken heart from spilling onto the floor.

In 2008, three years after the breach of trust, I took a sabbatical from my consulting practice for several months to write a screenplay; during that time, I lived with First Love at his house south of San Francisco. We both found happiness in the daily routine together during this period, but First Love said something odd to me over breakfast on a hot summer day while we were sitting out on the balcony. He questioned whether I could live with someone at this stage of my life after having been independent for the last few years since my divorce. Had First Love forgotten that I had spent twelve years with a boyfriend I'd met in high school, and that we'd lived together for most of it? In fact, I'd really only lived by myself for a total of three years since I'd graduated from high school. On what basis had he formulated this idea, since the facts of my life contradicted what he was suggesting?

First Love was insinuating that my independence made me a poor candidate for a live-in relationship; however, I would reach a different conclusion that had nothing to do with me, but did involve dog hair and an earring. First Love had an allergy to cats and dogs, yet I found dog hair on his bedspread and throughout his house. One of his colleagues had a dog and would occasionally bring her to the office; as a consequence, I ignored the persistence of the long hairs, noting that animal hair is easily transported from one place to another and also has the irritating property of being particularly clingy. But the niggling continued because of its presence on the bedspread. Before long, I would learn about another potential source of the dog hair.

First Love's and his ex-girlfriend's children attended the same schools, which meant news about the activities in the other household would spring from the mouths of First Love's children, presenting me with pieces of a puzzle I would toss into my brain's detective unit to consider with previously collected evidence. I learned through the children that First Love's ex-girlfriend's family included a dog with long white hair. When the children visited the ex-girlfriend's house, perhaps they had been in the vehicles that brought the hair back to First Love's home a few kilometres away. Even though the children sometimes stretched out on First Love's bed to watch a movie, my intuition informed me the hair ended up on the bedspread via a person who was not one of his children. The Powers That Be were all too willing to provide me with information to support my instincts, even though it had upsetting implications and disturbing consequences. On a Sunday afternoon, I asked First Love if we could add support to the sagging middle of his bed. When we removed the mattress, I found a woman's earring.

"Where did this come from?" I asked him, turning it over in the palm of my hand as if it were a coin I was getting ready to toss. If heads showed up, he was a cheater. What I actually thought was that the coin had two heads.

"The box fell on the floor a while ago, and I guess I missed it." The earring had been the stray, the outlier, unnoticed as it fell from somewhere. I just happened to believe that somewhere involved the earlobe of a woman who had recently been in his bed. And so began the next level of insecurities, which intensi-fied over the following three years due to happenings that made my intuition scream like a Geiger counter held near the site of a nuclear disaster.

While dating First Love, I dreaded Halloween ever since the time we went to a house party in San Francisco. He'd dressed up as a freakish gynecologist donning a ghoulish mask and gloves that endowed him with long and flexible fingers. A few times throughout the night, I found him chatting with women, the ones who were attractive and dressed in stereotypically provocative costumes of nurses, librarians, and rock stars. He took particular joy in undulating his fingers at their eye level while they laughed coquettishly. I refused to concede to the antics of the jealous, insecure girlfriend. I was better than that. And First Love had made the promise to me about fidelity. Of course, promises can be broken. In fact, I'd broken more than a few in our relationship during moments of emotional fragility when I doubted his com-mitment to me. In the first year, I'd broken his heart each time I told him I thought we should break up. I'm certain my brittle promises to First Love led to a build-up of dusty residue, and no amount of loving displays of affection could sweep it away entirely. The tears he shed each time cemented the small amounts that remained; within the first year together, a thick coat made his heart a little more rigid and closed. As a consequence, First Love was also less likely to press the knit against his chest when he needed comfort during times we were apart. The truth was, First Love and I just weren't very good at reassuring each other.

First Love and I spent Halloween apart in 2011. His office was located in an edgy section of San Francisco, and by the end of the day, I decided not to ask him about his plans for the evening, refusing to be the girlfriend whose polite inquiries were really veiled with a thick but transparent coat of suspicion and mistrust even the most far-sighted idiot could see through. And First Love was no idiot. When evening approached and we had our brief chat after work, neither of us mentioned Halloween, as if it were just another ordinary day. That year it fell on a Monday and I wondered just how much trouble someone could get into on the most fun adult holiday that fell on the most boring day of the week. In my mind, the probability of getting into trouble varied depending on the day of the week the adult fun day fell on: hump day, maybe, Thursday probably, and Friday or Saturday, most certainly. In any case, even if in the following year, circumstances prevented First Love and me from being together, Halloween would fall on a Wednesday, a relatively safe day. Although First Love and I made a habit of calling each other to say goodnight every night we were apart, that year neither of us made a call on Halloween.

Self-deception is an insidious creature, like a snake with a penchant for cinching its victims' waists at night. While asleep, it wraps itself a little tighter around their cores, making it slightly more difficult to breathe with each passing day, until one night they have a nightmare about not being able to breathe at all. No matter how hard they gasp for air, their diaphragms are paralyzed.

When I woke up on the morning following Halloween in 2011, I had trouble taking a deep breath. It turned out the snake could extend its squeezing activity in the daytime, too, when First Love called me just before noon. My belt tightened one notch when we ended the call. I replayed the conversation in my mind and stopped at the part where he disclosed he had just arrived at work after taking a shower at a fitness club close to his office. That piece of information was a yield sign telling me to pay closer attention to conversations with him and to become more observant about things that made my internal quiver quicken when I visited him at his home in Silicon Valley.

The evidence grew as slowly as the fullness of a piggy bank does, until one day its owner notices that it's full after months of adding a few coins here and there. And while the piggy bank filled, the truth formed crystals that periodically dropped down to my heart, clanking and making all kinds of screeching noises along the way. The crystal that dropped into my heart nearly a year later was unusually large and caused a gaping wound as it made its way there.

Within a few weeks, the air turned crisp just before Labor Day in The Urban City. First Love and I usually spent Labour Day together, but in 2011, we took separate weekend vacations. A friend of his had travelled to meet him in San Francisco to take a few jaunts together on motorcycles, with First Love riding the one he owned and his friend taking out a rental for the weekend. A girlfriend and I had decided to go on a day hike in a park north of The Urban City. It was one of my favourite trails of the many surrounding The Urban City because of the three glacial lakes hikers reach at different elevations. Each lake serves as a reward for the hard work required to complete the hike in one day. The glassy turquoise lakes stretch out beneath the rugged glacial peaks, allowing the awestruck viewers to catch their breath, only to have it immediately taken away again at the first glimpse of both through the spaces between the evergreens.

Before picking up my friend to make the three-hour drive to begin the hike, I walked a few blocks from my downtown apartment to a local grocer to buy snacks for the hike. While wandering the aisles, I decided to call First Love to see how his plans were unfolding with his friend. He didn't answer his cell phone and I left a message, giving him an update about my hiking plan for the day. We had always agreed that when we called each other, if we didn't answer, we could always leave a voice message. Within a few minutes, he returned my call; after we said our initial hellos, he asked me if I had listened to the update about his motorcycle trip.

"What update?" I asked. My first thought was that First Love had left a message for someone else, probably his ex-girlfriend or some new one, but had forgotten it hadn't been for me.

"Never mind, I'm still dim from getting up early," he said.

Not enough sleep? Well, why not? First Love rarely had trouble going to sleep after he tucked himself into bed, unless he had a pleasurable distraction that made him not want to. However, his pleasurable distractions also involved novels. But doubt gets tired after a certain number of benefits have been granted.

I learned the following day that within the first couple of hours of the motorcycle ride, First Love had taken a fall resulting in one or more broken ribs. He had nearly gone over an embankment and only mentioned it the following day as a casual comment during a phone conversation. When I probed for details, First Love refused to talk about it. When I saw him a week later in Silicon Valley, he still had difficulty breathing and walking without wincing. He had shut me out of the events prior to and following the accident.

Following Labour Day, I made a decision to purchase a property in The Urban City after growing tired and frustrated with paying more to rent a small, noisy downtown apartment than I would for a mortgage. As an adult, I made many important decisions in the month of September. I suppose the month set off an alarm in my internal clock about going back to school to learn the next of life's lessons. It took me the better part of a month to find the place I wanted to buy. I closed the deal at the end of September and moved into the loft on December 1, 2011.

On the weekend I took possession of my new home, First Love came to The Urban City to help me celebrate. We stayed in the apartment on a blow-up mattress with a sleeping bag and a few candles, which I thought was a romantic form of urban camping and a memorable way to toast the milestone. The first night he arrived, we decided to walk to a French restaurant and have dinner as a way to begin the weekend. The place had already gained popularity and we had to wait a few hours before a table would become available. First Love and I strolled down the street to a quaint café where we decided to order an appetizer and a cocktail.

A while later back at the bistro, the place was still abuzz with happy patrons enjoying a night of fine food, conversation, and Edith Piaf's voice serenading us in the background with her soft and throaty ballads. The only reservation we were able to secure was at the bar, where we chatted with the people who ended up sitting down next to us. Enjoying the conviviality of the European eatery, we ordered a bottle of wine and discussed many things with our first set of bar mates. The two men were a couple, one a physician in training, the other an artist. They had been finishing their meal when we sat down beside them. One of the men had been a customer of the software developed by the company where First Love worked. The man was from Germany, and First Love was understandably pleased and proud that a random person he'd just met knew about the company he worked for and raved about its primary product. As the couple left, the German fellow and First Love exchanged business cards, with the German promising to call First Love if he visited San Francisco in the future.

"Do you actually think he'll call you?" I asked First Love. "People tend to do these things as polite gestures, not promises."

"I have more luck with beautiful women when I give them my card," he said, wiping the corners of his lips with his white napkin.

"Oh, yeah? And how often does that happen?"

"Once in a while."

"In bars, you mean, or what?"

"Different places. But mainly in bars and airports." *Isn't this just ducky?* I thought, but asked instead, "Do they ever call you?"

"Yeah, sometimes."

By this point in our relationship, I'd stopped sulking when First Love said things I didn't like. I had learned how to be inquisitive but still didn't ask the full complement of questions a prosecuting lawyer would have in this scenario.

The hairs on the back of my neck reacted to our conversation about business cards as a spider does when it detects the vibration of a predator on a distant thread of its web. I didn't have the facts at my disposal, but my body registered the information with an increase in the frequency and intensity of my internal quiver. I didn't need all the facts—I received the news as if my coronary arteries had suffered a spasm from the quiver that had migrated upward from the deepest part of my solar plexus. The response in my body told me everything I needed to know. We finished the excellent bottle of merlot First Love had chosen and the waiter brought us our bill. We were done.

During our walk back to my loft, talking about other subjects, First Love asked me what I wanted to do to make my loft feel like my home. But I was capable of only so much creativity, and its channels were clogged with scenarios about First Love's encounters with his new business connections. I could have written an erotic novel in a weekend with my guesses about their business conduct, but erotica is supposed to be fun and exciting, and needless to say, includes "happy endings." I had no trouble with the beginning and middle, but the endings were invariably messy, and all of them involved something getting broken. My focus was narrowing on First Love's actual extracurricular activities, and between American Thanksgiving and Christmas, this focus would shrink to the diameter of a pin.

That year, American Thanksgiving had only taken place a few weeks before my arrival for the Christmas holidays. We weren't able to spend it together because I needed to be on the east side of my native land for a business trip. While I assumed First Love was eating turkey, I was spending the evening over a glass of wine with a colleague in the lounge of our hotel. Change was definitely in the air when my colleague confided over pre-dinner drinks that she was leaving her post permanently to pursue personal travel and other ventures. I wondered if my life would also take a dramatic shift in the new year.

I never found out how First Love had spent American Thanksgiving: I didn't ask and he didn't tell. Being a football fan, perhaps he spent it on his couch to watch a few games. First Love was extroverted and enjoyed participating in traditions, which made me speculate he spent it at one of his friend's. He was free to do as he pleased, since no one owns anyone, and I was proud of myself for continuing to be the mature girlfriend, travelling along the tidy road above the bumpy, crooked path of my insecurities. I had become a wary truth-seeker since Labour Day, and as such,

I was spending much more time on the high road. I can't say I enjoyed the view, but the path below had become a prison, with its potholes and pests that had distracted me from looking straight ahead most of the time.

I arrived in San Francisco for Christmas on December 22 that year, a late arrival for me compared to previous years. First Love and his children hadn't decorated a tree and he hadn't wrapped the red rope lights around the balcony banister that overlooked the bedroom we shared. First Love wasn't excited about Christmas that year. But I sensed his lack of enthusiasm had a broader scope than Christmas: the sparkle in his vibrant brown eyes had waned, and his usually airy, light-footed gait was noticeably slower. Over the years, we anticipated Christmas like most children do. We couldn't wait to buy the tree and decorate it while listening to a compilation of Christmas songs sung by Nat King Cole, Frank Sinatra, and Bing Crosby; we'd sip on hot chocolate after we strung the lights, hung the tinsel, and cheered when we turned on the lights for the first time.

First Love was also the kind of man who liked to shop for Christmas presents at a casual pace in one of the outdoor shopping districts near his home. We spontaneously separated when we each had ideas of our own about what presents to purchase next and looked forward to meeting at the French pastry café for an afternoon latte and a chocolate croissant when we were done.

As soon as I settled into First Love's house upon my arrival, I went to the fridge to find the bottle of white wine he had chilled for my arrival. When I opened the door, deception was flashing its red beacon on a plastic container filled with cranberry sauce. It had been pushed aside on the second shelf and had reached the midway point of its journey to the back, like other unused things do in closets, fridges, and cupboards. My stomach turned, not because I hated the sweet red stuff, but because I believed it had come from his ex-girlfriend's house as part of the leftover package he had gone home with on Thanksgiving. And maybe that wasn't the only thing he took with him. Did he have pumpkin pie, too, with the traditional dollop of whipping cream—and perhaps a postprandial roll in his ex-girlfriend's rose garden?

First Love came into the kitchen as I opened the lid to see it had not yet turned mouldy.

"What's this from?" I asked, turning around and raising it so that I was sure he could get a good look at it.

"Oh, it was left over from our Christmas party at work," he said, turning around to get two wine glasses from the cabinet just outside the kitchen door.

I put the lid on the container and placed it onto the shelf exactly where I'd found it. He stood beside me and took the wine from the side door compartment, opened the bottle, and poured a modest amount into our glasses on the counter.

I wanted to believe him but didn't. His company didn't fit the profile of one that would serve turkey dinner in a warehouse. Pizza, beer, and bourbon were the standard consumables for the staff who toiled away at their cubicles in the open space, and having attended the previous year's Christmas party, I knew turkey dinner would have been a surprising deviation from the barroom style. His explanation didn't fit. Plus, when First Love and I had started dating years earlier, the same plastic containers with leftovers from his ex-girlfriend filled his refrigerator. As it turned out, I was no longer excited about Christmas, either.

"Come on," said First Love, carrying our glasses into the living room. "Let's watch the Grinch."

I had been a resident of Whoville my entire life, even living with The Alcoholic Foster Parents. But now I was like The Grinch—not because my heart had become two sizes too small, but because it had shrunk to the size of his from the activities that had started squeezing it on Labour Day. I didn't want to stop Christmas like the Grinch, but I did want to be with the stolen presents and dropped into the abyss at the top of Mount Crumpit and emerge back in the world only if I was armed with an unlimited supply of nepenthe.

Deception only has so many tricks up its sleeve. Eventually the space gets crowded, the sleeve tears, and the little devils spill out in an assorted and colourful mess. Just like the seasons can't be forced into being, neither can the truth, until the scales tip in its favour when the threshold of undeniability is reached. Nearing the threshold, I needed my multi-hour walks on a daily basis to treat the dizziness that plagued me if I sat at my desk in the alcove for too long. As the days passed, my pace quickened, and I needed to shake my entire body periodically like a duck does after being below the surface of water for too long.

On the last day of my Christmas vacation with First Love, I spent much of the day scanning business receipts in anticipation of the much-dreaded fiscal year end. First Love and I argued about finances associated with the Cabin Retreat, and during a late-afternoon walk, we spent much of it in silence, where normally we would talk about many topics and he would stop to take photographs along the way. In the evening, he dozed on the couch while I retreated to my computer in the alcove, busying myself with preparations for returning to my personal and professional life in The Urban City. We went to bed, our backs a safe distance from each other's while the haunting and melancholic songs of

Bevinda echoed in what seemed to be a hollow bedroom. First Love slept when he was sad and sometimes wheezed throughout the night from an asthma attack. But I tossed and turned, unable to get comfortable or stop my mind from playing Toni Braxton's "Another Sad Love Song." At 2:11 a.m., I left the bed we had shared for nearly ten years and moved to the spare bedroom where his children normally slept when they were with him. I found comfort and quiet there and slept until 6:30 a.m. when the phone alarm went off. He made his coffee to go, and I made my tea. We drove to the airport listening to global news rather than discussing the local problem of "us." Arriving at the airport, our kiss goodbye told the truth about the state of "us." We kissed each other on the cheek as if we were business acquaintances rather than each other's Forever After. We had both started building a vision of our lives that didn't include each other.

I waited at my gate to board the flight back to The Urban City, and no matter how hard I tried to distract myself with the news and views of the takeoffs and landings outside, a single thought from the part of my brain that knew fear continued to prod it with an insistent index finger: *Could it really be over?* Belted in my seat as the captain taxied the plane to the takeoff runway, I thought for the first time, *Yes, it could be.* When the captain announced, "Attendants, prepare for takeoff," the woman behind me started puking and didn't stop heaving until we landed.

Back in The Urban City airport, I took the train to my office where I had a short break with the colleague who was already preparing to leave her job in two month's time. When we finished visiting, we left the café and walked for a few blocks, stopping at an intersection where we said goodbye to each other with a hug. When we parted, I stared up into the sky filled with dark and pillowy clouds. The sight of them made my legs weak as if I had just heard upsetting news. I recognized that feeling in my legs all too well. Life as I knew it was once again coming to an end.

The normal communication patterns between First Love and me changed dramatically that January, 2012. I had moved into my loft and spent the month sleeping on the blow-up mattress while I planned to have it modestly renovated, including the bathroom First Love and I had torn apart. Many nights in January I had a recurring dream about First Love. I saw him standing in front of a fire blazing behind him. He seemed oblivious to the inferno moving toward him, and no matter how loudly I yelled out to him, he remained stationary and expressionless.

I developed the flu during the first week after returning to The Urban City and rationalized the feverish nights were causing the fiery dreams. Throughout the month, he communicated in an emotionless, apathetic, and business-like manner, which made me an angry old dog ready to pick fights with him. But instead of picking fights with him, I called upon the assistance of The Powers That Be on January 31 for the second time in my life. I wasn't sure how many "signs" I had been allotted and decided to save however many were remaining after the chestnut sign for life's serious questions.

To prepare, I sat in my new brown leather chair that sat at an angle beside the hissing gas fireplace and took a deep breath.

"I want the truth. If he is not fully committed to me, tell me now. I want to know," I said out loud. My words echoed in my barren apartment, as if The Powers That Be were restating them and giving me an opportunity to change my mind. Uttering my request calmed me and I sat in silence without feeling compelled to edit it. I wanted to be in a committed relationship, and if First

Love hadn't been faithful to me, I wanted to move forward with my life without him.

The following week, our conversations continued to be perfunctory and pricklier than the thorny stems of a rose bush. For the first time in nearly ten years, First Love and I did not speak to each other for three days. On Thursday in the morning, via email, we agreed to chat in the afternoon after we had both finished our work for the day. I was meeting a friend at a local hotel at the end of the day for a glass of wine. Before leaving the office, I retreated to an empty meeting room to make the call to First Love.

"I can't talk for long," he announced after I said hello to him. "I need to go pick up my daughter from school." I had become an acquaintance of his that January. He no longer called his youngest child by her name with me. She was "his daughter."

"I think we should break up," spilled out of me, unable to bear any more terse conversations.

"That's my sense, too, even though I feel panicked about it," he replied.

"Okay, well, I guess you should go pick up your daughter, then." We said goodbye and hung up.

We had the worst kind of goodbye. Our voices cracked when we took turns saying one simple word to each other that would cause a cascade of complex emotions for an indefinite period. Ending the call, I stared at my cell phone in disbelief that First Love and I had ended our ten-year relationship over the phone, just like that.

Walking back to my desk to pack up my belongings for the day, I didn't think it was possible to feel panic and relief in my heart at the same time. In one beat I was relieved my relationship with First Love was over because of my growing certainty about his infidelity and with the next several, dread flooded my chest cavity.

The sun was setting as I made my way to my friend's hotel room. Opening the door, she gave me a hug and handed me a glass of red wine. She returned to her double bed and I plunked myself down on the other one. The tears streaming down my face made my friend bolt upright as if a fire alarm had just gone off in the hotel.

"What's wrong?" Detail-oriented, she asked a parade of questions for the next two hours. I don't remember my answers or how my body felt. But as I got up to leave, I scanned the cityscape to the north, with the background of the mountain summits, snowy and bright under fluorescent lights. I knew I would become the lonesome nomad wandering through the trails at night on the north side of The Urban City, if only for a time.

Driving back to my loft, I tossed the steel ring studded with dewy little diamonds First Love had given me five years earlier out the car window. There had been no explicit promise associated with the ring when First Love gave it to me, but I had hoped the gift came with an intention of Forever After. But intention is only a seed, and the seed of our union failed to germinate and sprout for all to see because we poisoned it as much as we watered it over the years. I loathed John Donne and other poets who revered circles as symbols of eternity. They were theorists who seduced us into believing in the possibility of Forever After. Their pretty words and perfectly drawn images belonged in a Utopia as ridiculously fictional as Cinderella and her prince. Circles are a fine geometric form, but frankly, they have no place in the domain of the heart, even if its vessels are round.

During my drive to work the morning after First Love and I broke up, he left me a voice message to inform me he would be flying to The Urban City to discuss our breakup face-to-face. I emailed him and told him not to come because I had other plans for the weekend. Later that day, during lunch, when I walked downtown to mail First Love the keys to his home and vehicle, I stopped midway across the bridge to send him an email asking him if he'd been unfaithful to me with his ex-girlfriend.

He replied right away: "Yes."

He said he wanted to tell me in person by flying to The Urban City and to give me some of my personal belongings. I didn't care about my personal belongings that were associated with my life in Silicon Valley. I told him to send them to a second-hand store since I viewed them as either broken or stained.

I interpreted my January dream of the blaze behind First Love as a precursor to our relationship going up in flames. After the truth emerged about his infidelity, I didn't have any dreams of being engulfed in a haze of denial, trying desperately to find someone or something to hold onto while wandering aimlessly among the ashes. With his one simple email response to me confirming what I had suspected all along, my view of the relationship metamorphosed in an instant; I saw it based on how things were, rather than how I wanted them to be.

A month after our breakup, I drove to a mountain lookout with a southern view to The Urban City. I reclined my seat and looked beyond the lights of the bridge descending into the blackness of the city park. I closed my eyes. An image of two lovers facing each other and raising two gold cups to toast their celebrated union shattered before me, leaving one of a man and a woman walking in opposite directions on a cracked and barren wasteland under a stormy, moonless sky. She wore a black dress with a high collar and a skirt that dragged behind her. Three swords pierced the middle of her back. She held a black blindfold in her left hand and an indigo lamp shone from her forehead, lighting her path. The man had the head of the devil and the body of a lean athlete. He wore a purple, richly textured coat with a fur collar and a leopard loincloth. A halo shone high above him, but it wasn't clear where its resting place would be. I couldn't see the couples' eyes, but I'm certain they contained murky sections.

The images vanished as quickly as they had appeared because of my obsessive need to return to replaying ten years of scenes and conversations between First Love and me. First Love had told me the Truth on the first night of our reunion on the Labour Day weekend about what he had to offer me. When we reunited at his home after the yoga retreat, sitting next to me on his couch with the orange glow of a lamp warming me, he said: "You know I can't give you what you need." Even though we had talked about growing old together many times during our relationship, the most important thing he'd said to me that night was still true — but I didn't want to hear it then.

The truth stood at my bedside every morning, dressed in ratty and wrinkled clothes. I hurled profanities at it before getting out of bed, but only after ignoring it by turning over and going back to sleep for an hour before re-entering the world as a zombie. Driving to work, I would crank up the volume of my car radio and belt out the words to Gloria Gaynor's "I Will Survive," or The Stampeders' "Devil You," while pointing my index finger as if it were a knife I was threatening to use. It didn't take long for the sadness to erupt in equally dramatic fashion by the time I got home and was listening to romantic songs such as Madeleine

Peyroux's "Someone Like You" while walking up thirteen flights of stairs to a friend's apartment where I had been staying temporarily. Usually by the time I reached the seventh floor, I had dropped whatever I was carrying in a careless heap and sat down on the cold concrete platform separating the two floors. I sobbed, I yelled, and I swore as if I were acting out a breakup scene in front of my lover and an audience.

But by spring, the time had come to stop recycling my anger and sadness. I disconnected my heart and mind from First Love's during my long walks along the many paths on the north side of The Urban City, paths running along the bulging rivers that raged like my emotions had. Where the rivers emptied into the sea, I watched my dreams about Forever After with First Love float away with the ocean currents. He would not be my lover and companion for the rest of my life. As I let him go, my lightness of being frothed like egg whites being whipped to meringue. I also began to notice the sweet signs of life: giggling children chasing after their puppies in the park, young leaves unfurling on the trees that had been naked all winter, and the resolute crocuses bobbing in puddles after a heavy rain. I could smile again at new lovers, drunk and dizzy in love, blind to the world, because they saw everything they needed to in each other's eyes.

CHAPTER 25

SELF MATTERS

Our lives begin to end the day we become silent about the things that matter.
Martin Luther King Jr.

I lost two important people before my relationship with First Love ended. One was a close friend I'd met at my first job when I returned to The Urban City after bidding goodbye to The Island years. She had been born on Halloween, and in the fifteen years since I'd met her, we often made a ritual of having dinner delivered to her house while we handed out candy to the neighbourhood kids.

I received a call from her shortly after I'd arrived home from work on a hot Thursday afternoon in July 2004. She had just finished dinner and begun to experience tightness in her chest and an ache in her jaw. Our houses were only a few miles apart, and when I arrived to pick her up and escort her to the hospital, she anxiously approached the car, holding her chest, and looking ashen. Her appearance made me worry she wasn't suffering from heat exhaustion or anxiety provoked by a stressful home life. She had previously talked about the inherited heart disease in her family that had prematurely killed several members on her mother's side. But a recent stress test and additional blood work showed her to be in fine health.

Once we arrived at the hospital, two tests were conducted right away when the doctor examined her: an electrocardiogram and blood work to measure the presence of cardiac markers. Both tests would determine whether or not she'd had a heart attack. She was admitted to a hospital bed in the emergency room while we waited for the results. I went home to my apartment across the street and got ready for bed while I waited for word from her.

Just before midnight she called to inform me the results of both diagnostic tests confirmed that she'd suffered a heart attack and she was scheduled to have a consultation with a cardiologist the following day. I visited her before work the next morning but arrived when the cardiologist was still discussing the results with her. The cardiologist informed her she had a blockage in at least one of her coronary arteries and she would likely require an angioplasty in the best case scenario, more invasive surgery in the worst. But an angiogram would be conducted first to diagnose the seriousness of the blockage and the extent in general of her heart disease. The diagnostic and corrective procedures would be conducted at the hospital specializing in cardiac care located in the centre of The Urban City.

The next morning, I visited her before getting on with Saturday errands. When I dropped off some of her belongings, she was talking on the phone to her family in the eastern part of the country. I sat down to read the newspaper for a few minutes. But after about half an hour I needed to meet a mutual friend so I mouthed to her we would stop by later. As I made my way to the door of the hospital room, she looked at me with an expression I translated as, *Take care, it's been nice knowing you.* I dismissed it as morbid paranoia. I didn't tell our mutual friend who would have agreed with the morbid paranoia label, but would have enhanced it with "crazy."

We went to a matinee showing of *The Corporation* in the afternoon, and as soon as the movie ended, we brought her supper before our dinner party with a different set of friends. As soon as we arrived at the hospital, we noticed a flurry of activity around our friend's hospital room. The head nurse shooed us away. Our friend had had another heart attack, and the doctors had decided to expedite the angiogram procedure. They were preparing her to be transported to The Urban City hospital and we left the hospital concerned about our friend. My friend and I drove a short distance back to her apartment for the dinner party she was hosting. We'd made arrangements with our friend's son to keep us apprised of her condition during the evening.

Within a couple of hours, the son called with news that a cardiac surgeon had been called to perform emergency heart surgery on our friend because they could not stabilize her. He told us she'd had to be resuscitated twice and they were very concerned about whether she was strong enough to survive the surgery. We were crestfallen. The dinner party was over promptly and my friend and I hurried to The Urban City hospital to keep vigil with our friend's son. As we rounded the corner of the street a few blocks from the hospital, I sensed a vacancy, as if our friend had travelled to a Faraway Place at an impossible speed. I believed she had already begun her journey to The Great Unknown. The sad thought erased any embarrassment about the earlier premonition when my friend said goodbye to me with a look.

"She's gone," I said.

The two words left my lips as swiftly and automatically as a mouthful of tea that cannot be contained in the fit of a coughing spasm. As soon as we arrived on the floor where our friend was, another mutual friend had already been waiting for us. When she saw us, she shook her head.

"She's gone," the woman yelled.

A nurse escorted us into the procedure room where our friend's lifeless body lay on a gurney. Fortunately, she was still draped in her hospital gown. Our friend's essence, the part of her that animated her body and mind, was gone, leaving her lifeless shell still and at peace before us.

With the death of my friend, I arrived at the service, prepared to speak publicly about the positive impact she had made on my life. I stood before the group and read a segment from Kahlil Gibran's piece on death:

> *Only when you drink from the river of silence*
> *Shall you indeed sing.*
> *And when you have reached the mountain top,*
> *Then you shall begin to climb.*
> *And when the earth shall claim your limbs, then*
> *Shall you truly dance.*

Although I recited this piece to the audience with a heartfelt farewell to my friend who loved to dance, I could not lift my eyes from the paper in my hands because I was embarrassed at the thought of becoming a sobbing mute in front of a group of strangers. I had mustered the courage to get up in front of the audience, but I could not look into a single pair of eyes in the congregation. I was not yet ready to be publicly vulnerable when my sad eyes met those of many others who were looking directly into mine.

I had a dinner conversation with my friend two weeks before she died. We used to enjoy Thai dinners at the modest little eatery when we needed cover and comfort from the rain-soaked Urban City during the winter, but that Saturday evening we were celebrating the end of a radiant summer day. During dinner, we talked about how to honour people we had loved and lost. At the end of our conversation, my friend reassured me about the nature of love. When we have loved someone, our hearts create space to hold the brand of love we experienced from having known them, and when we lose them, our hearts don't shrink with the loss, because love is always expansive. And all of us are supposed to leave this life with open hearts, regardless of the number of sorrows and disappointments we have endured. Our hearts don't become larger with love, but their vessels do dilate, allowing its essence to course through our veins and impregnate every cell with its goodness. She had become the wise elder who had spoken the truth with a calmness, clarity, and certainty that made a believer out of me.

It made a believer out of me even though her resilience waxed and waned in the face of a devastating betrayal she'd experienced in her marriage. After nearly twenty years together, her husband had moved into their basement apartment because she could no longer endure the painful lack of intimacy between them. Before my friend married him, she suspected he was gay and asked him directly about it before the wedding. He convinced her she was the person he loved and she was the one he wanted to share his life with. Once they were living in separate quarters in their house, my friend ached for the truth she knew he'd been hiding from her for years. In a final confrontation, she entered the basement and begged him for it. If truth is a buoy and deception an anchor, with his admission, my friend's heart sprung from the bottom of a river and sprung to the surface with a newfound freedom. Following their divorce, she pursued lifelong interests and rebuilt a social network, but her marital history hung on every wall and sat in cardboard boxes in her kitchen until the day she died. Although her life flowed like The Big River running through Somewhere Small, she often had trouble avoiding undertows and escaping eddies.

The System's death certificate for my friend classified her primary cause of death as coronary artery disease. She had suffered from high blood pressure for many years and her genetics indicated a high probability she would also die from the disease. I'm neither a geneticist nor a cardiologist, but I do believe a contributing factor to my friend's death was a broken heart. Even though she had forgiven her ex-husband and herself for closeting the Truth before she got married, the pain from the deception in her marriage haunted her periodically. My friend taught me a different lesson than my colleague whose two babies had died from a fatal genetic liver disease. She taught me about the danger of allowing someone else's words to have more power over us than our own.

The other person I lost while reunited with First Love was my Wise-But-Drug-Addicted Girlfriend. She did not die, but I needed to let her go after twenty years of friendship. During that period, several people had persisted in leading her to the professional help she needed to overcome her addictions and mental illness, but the power of both was greater than her personal will. When I started to feel unsafe around her, I ended the friendship. Time validated Psychiatrist #2's prediction about the outcome of my relationship with her. It took that long for me to release my belief that her life could be different if enough people loved her. Having dreams for other people and becoming a supporting character in their dramas were ways I avoided conceiving and pursuing mine.

CHAPTER 26

ELDEST

Despite the enormous suffering Eldest endured in fifty years of life, she had indeed been the elder of her sisters, leaving us with a legacy as towering as the skyward poplars that still grace Somewhere Small.
Middle2

As the oldest of four girls, Eldest likely forced us into various corners of The Little House and "That House" when she thought being neither seen nor heard was required during the noisy periods in rooms with closed doors. Eldest became our mother when Mom wasn't available. And as long as Dad lived with us, Mom's availability was limited.

I could never understand why Eldest cried every day on her way to school. We would all accompany her to the doors of the classroom as a way to comfort and reassure her, but her grumbling never ended. Eldest had started an early rebellion with The System, beginning in elementary school. Perhaps as a child, she had some inkling that she would spend the last seven years of her life back in it, not as a blossoming bud, but as a fully dependent adult.

Eldest and I lived together in The Alcoholic Foster Parent's and The Janitor and The Bingo Player's homes, which made up eight years of our childhood, with each year filled with more than four seasons and particularly long winters. Intense moments are engraved in our memories as "Look to This Day" was on the backside of the silver heart First Love gave me, but some explode our current reality, firing our thoughts in all directions. The fragments from the day Eldest moved out of The Bingo Player and the Janitor's house orbited my head but never entered my memory bank. I may not remember much about her last day at the final foster home we lived in together, but I could enumerate a list of sorrowful milestones by the time she reached seventeen years old. She had become an orphan at age seven. She had been excommunicated from Alcoholic Foster Father's house at age fifteen for disclosing his extramarital affair to Young Pretty Foster Mother. She had again been banished from The Janitor and The Bingo Player's house because of the personality conflict between her and The Bingo Player. When she learned how to drive and purchased her first used car, Eldest had become the caged bird that couldn't stop squawking after timed releases allowed her to fly above the acidic air in Somewhere Small. But on her graduation day from high school, The System and The Bingo Player no longer had the right to lock the cage door. Eldest didn't turn around when she fled the smoky coop for the last time.

But less than eight years later, Eldest had begun to exhibit the early signs of Huntington's disease, which caused her to dissociate from her close friends and family for several years before we learned that her depression had nothing to do with her disappointing life circumstances and everything to do with a fatal flaw in her DNA.

Eldest was the martyr in her generation of our family. The suffering she bore as the oldest child in our family taught Middle1, Youngest, and me about grace. In the early stage of the disease, when she became unusually moody, angry, and reclusive, we learned to honour her life choices. Once we found out the truth about Dad's cause of death, and when Eldest was correctly diagnosed, she surrendered to the next step in her difficult destiny. Youngest recounted a conversation with Eldest once her diagnosis had been confirmed. Given a choice, Eldest would have carried the burden of Huntington's disease, because Youngest and Middle1 had become mothers. When Youngest bemoaned the sad truth about Eldest's condition and asked, "But why you?" Eldest responded with a simple, "Why not?"

Three of the four of us would have the opportunity to pursue dreams that filled our fanciful heads when we were children. What we accomplished would be due to some measure of fate and free will, but Eldest's fate had been sealed and her free will eclipsed by a gene I thought of as a terrorist. With the first signs of the disease, fate had begun to wrap a straitjacket around her. And as time progressed, it would tighten as she moaned and kicked, not out of a conscious protest, but because she couldn't help herself, even with the drugs The System prescribed her.

In August 2010, Eldest was admitted to The Poplar Pavilion long-term care facility, undoubtedly given the name because of the eponymous trees lining the borders of the hospital wing. With each visit I saw the arboreal perimeter as a prickly, wired fence, the kind surrounding prisons. And the poplars around Eldest's prison were getting taller every year. It was only when I started to see them as the gateway to The Great Unknown that I stopped being afraid to enter her room.

Poplar trees grow quickly and require little water or coddling. According to the Native American tradition, the spirit of the tree symbolizes possibilities, the manifestation of dreams, and all life experiences become golden just as the tree's leaves do in autumn. When the wind sways the lanky branches and flutters its leaves during the fiercest storms, the tree's spirit whispers reassuring things about lost memories and dreams, and it doesn't topple over because of its deep roots. The spirit of the poplar is also a reminder that we are never given a wish or dream without also being given opportunities to make it a reality. I hoped the whispers comforted Eldest and she gained strength from them during windstorms. Perhaps she even mistook the golden autumn leaves for the sun. Each time I left her room after a visit, I wanted the poplar spirit to tell her that even though she hadn't been able to fulfill her dream of becoming a mother, she had been like one to Middle1, Youngest, and me at times in our lives when we needed one the most. Dreams are fulfilled, but not always in the ways we expect. When Eldest knew the truth about what was happening to her, particularly in the middle of the night when she writhed and moaned, I prayed that the poplar spirit channeled the voice of our mother who would sing her the lullaby she liked the most when she had been a sad or sick little girl.

Eldest's deteriorating brain tormented her physical body with uncontrollable twitches and restlessness until she died. Her only relief came from the pharmaceuticals prescribed to her by The System. What did people who had Huntington's disease do in the nineteenth century when The System had no remedies to offer them? Did they lose their minds from the never-ending twitching and jerking, or did the deterioration of their brains protect them from knowing what was happening to them? Surely the defective gene also created some mechanism that mitigated the mental and physical wretchedness of the disease it caused. And if it didn't, perhaps the unfortunate ones thought it best to find the closest Big River before they forgot how to get to it, where they could wade in one last time without looking back to shore.

In the late stages of her disease, there was one problem The System's drugs had not been able to temper. While she slept, Eldest's writhing caused her to gouge her hands and arms, regardless of how finely manicured her nails were. Had the whispers of the poplars become chants of the Devil—or worse, had the Devil whisked her away to some hot and hellish inferno where he spun her round and round? Eventually the staff wheeled Eldest's bed to the nurses' station because, even having restrained her, they weren't sure they would find her safely in her bed the next day. Her mind receded into a gradual dementia with periods of psychosis. As her condition worsened, people who cared about her looked into her eyes and knew when she recognized them or when her awareness had slipped away. When the light in her eyes began to dim like the setting sun, where did she go? Did she enter a dreamlike state, reliving scenes from her life, or did her mind become a jumble of disconnected thoughts and fleeting feelings short-lived enough to prevent a prolonged period of agony? In the early stages of the disease, Eldest had been all too aware of her difficult fate while she could still walk, but would the brain degeneration eventually cause her to lose awareness of what was happening to her? I couldn't become the puppeteer in *Being John Malkovich* to know what she experienced when the light in her eyes had dimmed and she didn't react to seeing me, as if she were asleep with her eyes open. During the last few years of her confinement, the effects of Huntington's disease became a slug, leaving a sinewy trail of mucous, dissolving the parts of her brain that made her like no one else in the world.

Eldest's husband dutifully visited her every day in her room and wheeled her outside one or more times a week, more frequently during the summer months, which were her favourite. An avid sports fan, he was able to watch television, which undoubtedly helped him cope with the diminishing companionship of his wife, the one he had taken for better, for worse, in sickness, and in health.

On November 6, 2010, while shopping for Christmas presents in The Urban City, I received a phone call from First Love who in turn had received one from Middle1, that Eldest's condition had become critical due to an infection, and her departure to The Great Unknown was imminent. I had changed my phone number since having spoken to Middle1 in 2005 and had given her his in case of an emergency. Just before 5:00 a.m. on November 7, Youngest sent me a text informing me Eldest had died. I went back to sleep but woke with a start that caused panic until I remembered the reason for it. I did not spend that Sunday the way I had expected to.

Middle1 lived in the Prairies and I in The Urban City, which meant we both needed to travel to Somewhere Small immediately. Due to winter conditions, I didn't make the eight-hour drive or fly from The Urban City to the airport in Somewhere Small, because flights were often cancelled due to the unpredictable weather and difficult landings in the valley. Instead, I drove across the border to the south for three hours to fly out of the nearest large centre from The Urban City.

Driving from the north side of The Urban City into the city centre, the world moved in slow motion no matter how fast I was going. That day, The Urban City was both familiar and foreign. I noticed the buildings and street corners that had fed my mind with a banquet of happy memories from the two decades I'd spent there. But I also sensed I was driving through a foreign place, because the familiar had become lost in the swirling emotions caused by a once-in-a-lifetime event. And the swirling emotions became animated around me because my mind needed a bigger place to hold all of them at once.

It was a damp grey day that Sunday in November when I drove down Main Street of The Urban City, yet I imagined heat waves rising from the pavement, pink petals from spring cherry blossoms raining down on me, and butterflies chasing things I couldn't see. I was drawn to people who reminded me of Eldest — someone who walked like she used to, someone else whose body was shaped like hers, and the many people who smiled, because she had done that often when she was in a crowd.

For what remained of my life, I would remember exactly where I was when I found out Eldest was getting ready to enter The Great Unknown and when she did less than twenty-four hours later. Few events in life are imprinted in our memories with date, time, and where-I-was-when-that-happened stamps. Life-changing events, such as the death of someone I care about, focus me. They act as lenses with specific functions. I see things that matter to me more clearly; things that aren't as important as I thought become faded, and the outdated or outworn disappears altogether.

During my drive south of The Urban City, the highway became the fine line separating me from the real world to the east—one that would continue without Eldest in it—from the reel to the west that had begun to play her biopic. The highway signs that appeared, showing me the number of miles to my destination, marked major milestones of Eldest's life: the smiling girl who played outside with no jacket in the winter; the grumpy girl who always wailed on the walk to school; the curvaceous teenager with the ready smile and effervescent personality; the woeful graduate who pined for the boyfriend who dumped her; the sad young adult who failed to find lasting happiness with a man; the young woman who struggled with her self-image because of her addiction to food; the Eldest of four sisters who gracefully accepted her fate at having been the sole heir of the delinquent section of DNA; the debilitated adult who became as vulnerable as a newborn, though unlike a newborn, she didn't have her entire life ahead of her.

Youngest and Eldest's husband kept vigil at her bedside during the last twenty-four hours of her life. They took turns holding her hand while the other nodded off for brief periods. The moment that we take our last breath is as poignant as when we take our first. The people present at our arrival are not usually the same as the ones that say goodbye to us. But we can be sure that our greeters and our good-byers have been significant to us, even in cases where the relationship survived periods of estrangement and strain. On our deathbeds, they may still have conflicted feelings about us; they may love us a little or a lot. But we can be sure of one thing: their feelings for us are not neutral.

Youngest talked about the moment of Eldest's death two years after she died. She had been the one holding her hand when she took her last breath. Youngest and Eldest's connection when our mom died, and then again at the moment of Eldest's death, is an interesting one to me. Eldest placed Youngest on the top bunk bed when she and Middle1 left the house to find help when Dad stormed into Mom's bedroom. As a seven-year-old child, Eldest made the best decision she could to protect Youngest from harm. Youngest couldn't protect Eldest from harm, but I have no doubt her presence calmed Eldest as her breath slowed before stopping altogether.

First Love flew from Silicon Valley to meet me at the airport three hours south of Somewhere Small. Normally our trips to Somewhere Small from that airport were joyful occasions because they included travel to the Cabin Retreat. But this trip was somber and we spent most of the drive in quiet reflection about the upcoming events to celebrate Eldest's life. Driving up to the summit of the final mountain pass, we encountered a blizzard that forced us to crawl along the winding highway until we reached First Love's mother's house. I reclined my seat, settling into the slow pace and the silence of the night, and First Love started the perfect playlist of gentle jazz. I closed my eyes to find an image of Eldest's face on the inside of my eyelids. The picture of her was the last time I looked in her eyes during a visit to Poplar Pavilion where I could still see the light in them, as if she still knew who she was, where she was, and that I was her sister. The visit marked the last time she said, "I love you," which made me hopeful she had forgiven me.

Over the phone, I had agreed to meet Middle1 and Youngest at the funeral home the following day. We had not seen each other for nearly fifteen years until I drove into the diagonal parking spot in front of the funeral home where they stood waiting for me at the front door. Youngest, Middle1, and I greeted each other cordially and warmly, but not with the affection that only grows from seeing each other for many years and sharing events and the memories made from them. As soon as we entered the building, the funeral director shook our hands and expressed his sympathies before leading us to a meeting room with an oblong table that looked like it belonged in a boardroom. He sat at the head of the table. Middle 1 and Youngest took seats on one side, and Eldest's husband and I on the other. Sitting around a table with our host to complete The System's paperwork, I sensed an unspoken agreement with my sisters and her husband. We had gathered to make decisions in the best interests of Eldest and do what we could to give her a tender and respectful goodbye. When we discussed the agenda for the funeral, my heart pounded like a child's feet stomping in the middle of a temper tantrum. I wanted to remember Eldest alive for a while longer before completing the paperwork required to enter the details of her death into The System's databases and transfer her pension payments to her husband. But matters of the heart didn't belong around the boardroom table.

Eldest wanted to be cremated, and we needed to choose the type of wooden container for her body. We also needed to provide medical information about her physical body to determine whether she could be cremated at all. If a person has had radiation therapy for bone cancer within two months of their death, they can't be cremated because of the radiation hazard. And if a person has a pacemaker, it must be removed because it becomes explosive when exposed to high temperatures.

When it came to selecting the coffin, we couldn't choose the plain plywood option, even though we knew it would disintegrate within seconds. It looked like a box a mechanic would use to keep his tools stored in a dark, dingy corner of a garage. Even though it would become ashes in under a minute, we believed choosing the toolbox version would have somehow defiled the last step of caring for her physical remains. Instead we picked one with a richly textured carving on its exterior that we thought also symbolized the complexity of Eldest's life. We also decided to play music from her favorite 1980s pop bands at the beginning of the reception, to commemorate the short-lived happy period during the two years following her high school graduation.

Once the arrangements had been made for her funeral, we walked to a coffee shop in Somewhere Small to begin drafting her eulogy. We didn't need caffeine to stimulate conversation, since we had much catching up to do having not seen each other for fifteen years. We each shared memories about Eldest, who never failed in her responsibilities of being the eldest child and took on the role of parents for us when she could. Middle1 and Youngest both talked about the support Eldest had given them during and after the birth of their daughters, and I told them about Eldest's open door in my periods of existential angst when I returned to Somewhere Small during my early university years.

The next evening, we gathered at Youngest's house to create a collage of photos representing Eldest's tree of life. We placed individual photos of our parents at its base, since we had never been given photos of them as a couple, before, during, or after their marriage. Making our way from the roots to the outer branches of Eldest's collage, we chose photos of her progression from childhood to her teenage years and into adulthood. We didn't include any photos of Eldest in any of the foster homes because her happiest moments were with her friends. Most of the photos had been taken outside, and she was smiling in all of them, except in the one of us with our mom sitting on the front door steps of The Little House. The photo had been taken on a sunny day, but maybe on a morning before Eldest had to go to school. At the top of the collage we placed a photo of Eldest confined to her bed in Poplar Pavilion, and we left empty space above it, providing room for her essence that might have survived the ashes.

When we gathered in the funeral home a few days later, we sat in the reception area to receive guests as they arrived. I became mute because of the stinging in my throat and chest when The Bee Gee's song "How Deep is Your Love," sang out from the speakers. Within seconds after the song began, I regressed to my bunk bed in the still of the night at The Janitor and The Bingo Player's house with Eldest sobbing in the single bed across from me. She played the song repeatedly after her first serious boyfriend broke up with her. Until that period in her life, Eldest had always been jovial and talkative. We never saw her cry in the light of day when her heart was breaking. I suffered in silence and solitude during much of my childhood, and as I looked at Middle1 and Youngest in the reception area that day, I wondered if they had too.

We had two surprise visitors enter the greeting area: Mom's twin and her youngest sister. Middle1 had maintained a relationship with Mom's twin over the years. As soon as she saw our aunt walk through the door, she burst into tears, with Youngest and I following suit. But we composed ourselves as more guests continued to arrive. The other guests entered the service area door adjacent to the reception room where we were. Consequently, we didn't know exactly who had arrived to bear witness to the memory of Eldest's life.

Middle1, Youngest, and I all contributed to giving Eldest's eulogy, but instead of suffering silently, we all openly cried in front of people who had known Eldest for most of her life, many of whom I hadn't seen in over thirty years. We spoke genuinely to the congregation about the essence of Eldest, what she valued, and what made her unique.

We concluded Eldest's eulogy with her most powerful messages that came from her silent presence at Poplar Pavilion:

1. Accept your life. And when things are tough, never give up. Paradoxically, "accept your life" is a short, sweet sentence comprised of simple words, but to truly accept your life is not very easy during the most difficult challenges. Eldest accepted every stage of her illness with grace and hope. When she started to have difficulty walking, she accepted the wheelchair, and instead of staying inside, she still smiled during daily walks with her husband pushing the chair behind her. When she could no longer be cared for at home, she accepted having to be in the hospital for the remainder of her life, without complaining or bemoaning her fate.

2. Each day is an opportunity to meet a new friend. Wherever you go, talk to strangers. You may learn some of the most important things from them.

3. An open heart is the conduit for love to flow within and without. Don't let disappointments contract your heart permanently. Giving and receiving love are natural human actions, regardless of the sadness, cynicism, or pessimism that temporarily constricts them.

4. Don't be scared. Try new things. See what happens. Life can change in an instant, causing you to change direction unexpectedly—but a bounty awaits you, regardless of the initial impression of the change, for better or worse.

5. Keep plants in your house. They are symbols and reminders of life. Watering and pruning them is good for your heart, because in those actions you are nurturing life.

6. Help others as much as you can without expecting anything in return. But only keep close friendships with people who energize you and leave you feeling optimistic about life's possibilities.

And finally,

7. Keep smiling. The first thing people noticed about Eldest was her smile. A genuine smile is an indicator of an open heart. There are fake smiles, too, and it's important to learn how to recognize them. If you don't see a person's crow's feet when they smile, it's fake. If they're not old enough to have crow's feet, if their eyes don't get smaller when they smile at you, the smile does not stem from joy.

When the service for Eldest ended, some of the guests in the audience came to talk to us. I stayed at the front of the service area for the entire duration of the reception talking to various people, many of whom I hadn't seen for many years. The Janitor was the first to come and greet me. Much older, but still jovial and kind, he gave his condolences and finished with an update that The Bingo Player's diabetes had been acting up and she couldn't make it to the funeral. But she did happen to be down the street playing Bingo at the local legion hall during the service. Given the demise of the relationship between Eldest and The Bingo Player, I didn't think Eldest was sobbing in The Great Unknown because our third foster mother didn't attend her funeral.

Throughout our lives, information about our mother has appeared like rainbows do, surprising and beautiful endings to grey, moody skies. We saw a few rainbows at the funeral home. Alcoholic Foster Mother's brother came to me after the service and told me something very touching about Mom and us. He said she used to take us for a walk every day and he often saw the five of us together walking over one of the bridges connecting the city of Somewhere Small to the neighbouring residential areas on the other side of The Big River. And one of Mom's sisters also gave us a card from their eldest sister who could not attend the funeral because she was recovering from hip surgery. In the card, she told us that Mom adored us and fondly referred to us as her "four blonde beauties."

Leaving the funeral home once all had been said and done, I hoped our parents would have been proud of our goodbye to Eldest. We didn't have the opportunity to say goodbye to Mom or Dad through the ritual of a funeral. It was one reason why I didn't do goodbyes very well, either. I hadn't learned how to eulogize anyone. When my relationships ended, I left without a goodbye conversation about why the relationship mattered at all, what I valued in the person, and why our paths needed to separate. When my relationships ended with the living, I simply walked away without honouring them before letting them go, not even privately. It has been much easier for me to say goodbye to the dead than to the living, but with Eldest's funeral I vowed to improve my goodbyes to those who have not yet entered The Great Unknown. And in my heart I would know the difference between a good one and a bad one. Bad ones mean they don't happen at all. Good ones mean I don't necessarily give him a hug when we say goodbye. I will have stood by some big river, put him and his belongings in a hot air balloon, along with the broken pieces of my memories of him, before untying it and watching it drift away until it becomes a speck and then nothing at all. And after its disappearance, I wouldn't experience the warmth of menthol or the pain of frostbite in my chest. I would stand in silence for a few moments and bask in a peace that comes from having said and done what was necessary for closure.

When First Love and I drove back to the airport south of the border near Somewhere Small, we boarded planes going to different destinations, his to San Francisco and mine to Seattle. Bending over a chair outside the security gates to put my winter boots back on, I remembered the birthday card Eldest had given me on my twenty-first birthday. The words of the poem "Footprints" were inscribed on a background of footprints along a shoreline. The poem was composed as dialogue between someone and the Lord; the person asks the Lord why there is only one set of footprints when he went through particularly difficult times, implying that he was alone during them. But the Lord replies, "It is during those times that I carried you." Eldest's path in this life had been a difficult climb in stormy weather rather than a stroll along a sandy, hospitable shore. And there was only ever one set of footprints and they were hers. But by the time the plane landed in Seattle, I realized it didn't matter whether I believed the message in "Footprints" or not. What mattered was that Eldest probably did, and I hoped she was right.

Unlike our mother's ashes, whose location remains unknown to me, Eldest's ashes rest on the bedside table in the bedroom of her husband's apartment in Somewhere Small, with his and her wedding rings sitting on top of the urn. I want to scatter a portion of her remains on the surface of one of her favourite places in the mountains surrounding Somewhere Small, called Champion Lakes. Not surprisingly, its name reflects exactly what she was. Despite the enormous suffering Eldest had endured in fifty years of life, she had indeed been the elder of her sisters, leaving us with a legacy as towering as the skyward poplars that still grace Somewhere Small.

CHAPTER 27

THE TRUTH ABOUT DAD'S SISTER AND HER HUSBAND

The sins of the father are to be laid upon the children.
Shakespeare

Mom's two sisters attended Eldest's funeral, but there was a notable absentee: Dad's Sister's Husband, the man who had driven us away from "That House" after the murder. If Eldest had died ten years earlier, I would not have expected him to attend, since he wasn't a blood relative, and we hadn't maintained contact with him during our childhood growing up in Somewhere Small, despite his many attempts over the years. But five years before she died, I learned why we mattered to him, and why I thought he would have joined us in our goodbye to Eldest. His need to know about the state of our wellbeing confused me as a child; I'd classified him as one of the slippery weirdos from Somewhere Small, but I realized I had labeled him as such in error after he contacted me through the social media site classmates.com.

I joined the site on the twentieth anniversary of graduating from the high school in Somewhere Small as a way to search for a few childhood friends I wanted to contact. But he was not one of the people I had intended to find. He sent me a message several weeks later asking me how I was doing and where I lived. We exchanged phone numbers, and during a short conversation we agreed to meet at his home since we lived within a short distance of each other but in different suburbs of The Urban City. After our visit, I no longer viewed my uncle as a slippery weirdo. His attempts to visit me during our childhood were his way of honouring the legacy of a woman he referred to as the best person he'd ever met.

He told me she had been his best friend since they were in kindergarten, which explained his sincere attempts to see us. Talking to me at his dinner table, my uncle told me about the nights Mom used to sit with medical textbooks she had borrowed from the library to find a reason for Dad's erratic behaviour. I could imagine how the textbooks probably towered over her while she sat, her shaky fingers thumbing through the pages for many consecutive nights after she had put us to bed. But the book she really needed was the one she didn't have, which was probably a blessing. If she had discovered the truth before she died, she would have had four more reasons to worry.

Dad's Sister lost her brother and her best girlfriend on March 28, 1968. She inherited the guilt of being on the phone with Mom during the murder, the shame of having a brother who was a murderer, and a father who was his accomplice. She also inherited the sorrow of having four orphans in her home while she was pregnant with her second child. The events on that spring day scrambled Dad's sister's emotional DNA. From that point forward, she could only read words like "mood" and "live" from right to left so they became "doom" and "evil." And one or more letters in words that used to have happy associations were altered to become like dreary, distant cousins: "family" became "famine," "home" was "hate," "dad" transformed into "dead," and "heart" morphed into "apart." The things that should have healed her didn't. The sun made her sad, kindness enraged her, and sleep was the playground for her tireless demons that stampeded the corridors of her psyche. Worst of all, she couldn't see beautiful things anymore, because a veil of sorrow had blindfolded her.

My uncle nearly died during surgery just before Mom's death, and my aunt's nervous breakdown strained their marriage, but they attempted to save it by moving to The Urban City. Although optimism sat as a calm passenger while the family of four drove west, it became deathly ill by the time they reached The Urban City. Raising two toddlers, relocating to a new city, and being a homemaker didn't reset my aunt's equilibrium. After her period of depression, she had volatile fits of rage, terrifying him to the point where he could only sleep if he kept a knife under his pillow just in case the demons provoked a particularly violent episode.

Ultimately he could no longer sustain any semblance of order in the marriage, and he had also become increasingly concerned about the safety and wellbeing of his two children. He rebuilt his life as a single father, with little involvement from Dad's Sister. He proudly talked about his role as a father and provider for his children, and I admired him as he described their life together while he raised them to be independent adults. His daughter remained steadfast in her estrangement from her mother, and she has since built a stable relationship with a loving husband; together they are raising three children. His other child, a son, did not share the same happy fate of his sister.

A sensitive soul, he suffered through a tempestuous relationship with his mother. Dad's Sister would coax him into her life with a lullaby filled with promises of a sentimental reconciliation, followed by a period of bonding and building. But it wouldn't take long for the soothing sounds of a lullaby to become venomous spit that spewed out of her when she drank. They repeated this cycle for many years until he was in his early twenties but still lived near her in a city halfway between Somewhere Small and The Urban City. He had found a job as a taxicab driver, affording him many opportunities to salve his pain with the favourite analgesic he sipped from a water bottle.

One night, shortly after his girlfriend had broken up with him, he had a few drinks before his night shift. Unluckily for him, he was in a minor car accident that landed him in jail for driving under the influence. His mother taunted and shamed him for his irresponsible behaviour after his release. He later committed suicide by hanging himself in his bathroom. Dad's Sister's Husband had the unenviable fate of finding his only son and eldest child's lifeless body. My cousin had finally given up the desperate lifelong quest to receive unconditional love from the woman who gave him life. When his pain medication had become a source of shame, death became the only solution guaranteed to permanently end his suffering.

Dad's Sister's Husband adored his son who had inherited his mother's brown eyes and the demons lurking behind them. Even his father's consistent and doting love couldn't assuage the pain of being repeatedly abandoned by his mother. My uncle's heart broke in too many pieces to count, and he spent ten years in therapy with a psychiatrist who helped him piece them back together.

The night before I found out about my Dad's Sister's death, I had a dream about a grim reaper. I had been following a man dressed in a brown cloak, his faceless head locked in a downward position. A shovel sat comfortably on his left shoulder as he marched toward a destination in a cemetery where dewy grass was still sparkling like a carpet of diamonds from the rising sun. Above him swirled a willowy essence, like the vapour that rises above a hot cup of coffee. Intrigued, I followed the cloaked man whose cape billowed behind him as his gait quickened. The evanescent cloud continued to spin above him until he arrived at the plot he had been seeking. As soon as he lowered the shovel and started to dig, the cloud evaporated as if on cue by the snap of fingers I couldn't see. I woke up with a start, not from the snap of the invisible fingers, but from my alarm clock jarring me with the news that a new day had dawned and it was time for me to join it. Before opening my eyelids, I knew the dream meant that someone in my family had died. I didn't know the identity of the newly departed one, but would find out later that morning before my stomach started complaining it was lunchtime.

In the morning, I carried out the normal routine of getting ready for work and walking down the street to fetch a ride from my colleague who worked in the same building. During the drive, I was initially reluctant to talk to her about it because of my perception that she would have thought I had lost my left-brain during the previous night's sleep, but I decided to tell her about it anyway. She was British after all, and even the staunchest pragmatists among them believe in ghosts and other metaphysical things. I didn't care that the weird story I was about to share could travel at the rate of the corporate grapevine consisting of thousands of ovaries whose offspring would likely land in the inboxes of the busiest gossips. And I could suffer an embarrassing and possibly fatal professional demise from forwarded messages. It was easy to tell her the outlandish story because we had cried together many years before that day. When I met her years earlier in her office, I'd asked her about the photographs on her desk of two children whose faces I didn't recognize. She paused before telling me they were her children who had inherited a fatal liver disease that caused their deaths as toddlers. We cried when she told me they both died in her arms. I thought about her and her two babies many times after our hushed emotional conversation in her office. And I admired her bravery for risking becoming pregnant again without knowing whether her future babies would carry the gene. Her family thought she was foolish for getting pregnant again. But she didn't care. She knew without a doubt her future children would be healthy. And they were. Her story still makes me think about the unpopularity of decisions that come from the inner voice that knows things the rest of the world doesn't.

My colleague didn't laugh about the dream, but she did when I told her I was certain it meant someone in my family tree had died. I think she believed my reasoning abilities had become grossly impaired from the mushrooms Snow White's Dopey made me eat during the rapid eye movement phase of my sleep the previous night. We said our usual goodbyes getting out of the car once we'd parked at the office building. I arrived at my desk and got into the usual routine of work without thinking much more about the grim reaper.

Later in the morning, I received an email from Island Aunt telling me about the accidental death of Dad's Sister. She died from kidney failure as a result of taking one of The System's pain-killers with an unknown quantity of alcohol to try to numb the pain from a broken hip.

Dad's Sister and her son took the unresolved to their grave. Being the only female in a household of men after her mother died, it was easy to imagine her isolation. But an important matter had been resolved before my aunt entered The Great Unknown and that matter involved giving her daughter the gift of certainty that neither she nor her children would suffer from the genetic curse of Huntington's disease. As for my aunt's son, by the time he had reached his twenties and had begun forming romantic relationships with women, it was even easier to believe his primary cause of death stemmed from his belief that he was unworthy of the consistent and loyal love of a woman. But what I imagine is not necessarily the truth. And although their relationship and their fates were also none of my business, I still had a tendency to meddle in idle speculation about the dead.

The upside of pain is the strength earned from surviving it and knowing it's possible for peace to reign again. Dad's Sister's Husband grew stronger after the loss of his only son, as did his daughter from the loss of her only brother. Dad's Sister and her son weren't weak, but they were sensitive. And the downside for the sensitive ones among us is their difficulty in finding peace after pain — not because they don't want it, but because they hide in places it can never be found.

PART III:
FLOW

Never give up, for even rivers someday wash dams away.
Arthur Golden

In rivers, the water that you touch is the last of what has passed and the
first of that which comes; so with present time.
Leonardo da Vinci

CHAPTER 28

FARAWAY PLACES #2

Travel brings power and love back into your life.
Rumi

Nine months after my relationship with First Love ended and I settled into my newly single routine, I could look up into the blue sky and begin dreaming of another life—a life without First Love. I had found peace wrapped in the arms of Mother Nature in The Urban City and wanted to celebrate it in places that didn't guarantee peace, but did ensure discovery and adventure. I decided my next contract needed to stand in line behind Faraway Places #2, because fate could snatch our dreams without warning. And it doesn't always return them to us or keep them safe while we have our backs to them, out of necessity or distraction. Many a dream has fallen out of the clumsy clutches of fate and taken a downward spiral, free-falling with no dream catcher to rescue them.

My conclusion about fate and its effect on dreams set me on a path to Barcelona, the South African Bush, and Dublin.

It was a blustery day at Heathrow Airport on the first day of my journey to Faraway Places #2. During my twenty-four hour layover, I spent the night at a lovely private inn only a few miles from the airport. I booked into my room at the reception desk where I had the heart-warming experience of completing my check-in with staff whose personalities were staler than bread that looked pleasing at first glance, but was mouldy on the inside. But the boutique hotel hallways meandered in a nonlinear way that pleased me, yet at the same time made it hard for me to find my room without having to ask someone for directions. Normally I would have been happy to wander in my surroundings with curiosity as my guide, but we were both tired. Once I arrived in my room, I quickly dispensed with my new Calvin Klein bra, which had begun to dig into my ribcage somewhere over Greenland. I tucked myself between the crisp white sheets that I wished smelled like jasmine instead of bleach. The departing flights roared above the inn but I found soporific comfort in having the United Kingdom's version of "Who Wants to Be a Millionaire" playing in the background. Eight thousand kilometres and an ocean separated me from The Urban City where the scenes of the last ten years of my life had replayed in my mind for months, and I was content to lie down in a bed other than mine, with foreign accents and new surroundings to pacify my romantic misery. I could breathe deeply again without the weight of sorrow on my chest.

The highlight of my Heathrow layover en route to the first leg of my trip occurred when the diminutive but fast-talking servant appeared at my table in the hotel restaurant. He reminded me of the character Vizzini in *The Princess Bride*. He was an affable elfin man, and I was convinced that honeysuckle flowed through his arteries and veins because he was adorably sweet and made me feel like the honoured guest at a special family gathering.

The next morning, I made my way by cab back to Heathrow Airport to begin my journey to the first of three Faraway Places. The vitality of Barcelona energized me after the short stay at Heathrow's Airport. The Gaudi architecture was at its gaudy best with the blue skies in the background. The layout of the city and the inconsistent placement of street names made it difficult to navigate the streets at times. Although well-rested after my first night there, I found myself strangely overwhelmed by the bustling traffic, so much so that I needed to return to my room briefly within ten minutes of leaving the hotel to study the city map again. My inability to communicate in Spanish made me feel isolated, as if I were walking around like a hyperactive gerbil in a bubble, allowing me to see out, but making me invisible to the outside world.

On my last night in the city, while walking along Las Ramblas, I found a small venue advertising a flamenco performance that evening. I bought a ticket and sat at a nearby outdoor café to enjoy a glass of sangria until the doors opened. When the host brought me to my chair in the corner seat of the first row, I was relieved to be off my feet despite the reliably comfortable cushion of my Patagonia sandals. Sinking into the chair, my feet and legs sighed in unison. I sipped on champagne while scanning my surroundings. Chairs were arranged in a semicircle around a small raised wooden stage, scuffed and worn from the many performers who'd had their way with it. The arched ceiling completed the warm roundness of the venue, giving me the impression I was in a womb and about to witness the conception of a glorious life. Once the performance began, it didn't take long for beads of sweat to spray off the dancers' heads and hands as they twisted and turned in dramatic fashion with their arms and legs lifting and twirling in harmony with the music. At the height of their performance, my eyes welled with the realization that I had already lived half my life but had not expressed my Art with unrestrained abandon and unwavering commitment.

They wore fiery colours compared to my mostly black garb with muted shades of other darks. I had committed my existence to reason and practicality while they practiced and perfected storied moves. The difference between them and me was that they were expressing and performing their Art for the world to see; I was pacing while dreaming about mine behind a closed curtain.

The ego and one's Art are archrivals. Art requires no audience to experience the disembodied ecstasy of being true to one's spirit, while the ego needs the world to clap. Art closes its eyes and summons sincerity and truth; the ego smiles at itself in the mirror as it pumps up its chest, its mood and ability to perform dependent on the opinion of others. Truth and sincerity filled the flamenco venue on Las Ramblas. Spain was nowhere near the Prairies I had visited in my childhood, where I first witnessed the power truth and sincerity could have on a man. The toothless fiddler bore no resemblance to the perfectly coiffed and brightly costumed dancers. But what they had in common was a soaring spirit that comes from the joy they feel when expressing their Art.

It's important to learn from the masters, but not be shackled to them and their ideas. Producing one's Art involves mastery of the lessons of forefathers and then mastery of individual expression. The highest individual expression of one's Art is often a lonely pilgrimage because one is called to enter unknown territory, risk the disfavour of one's tribe, and experience the loneliness of isolation. But journeys into the unknown, disfavour, and loneliness teach the most important lessons: fervour in the solo pursuit of one's Art and detachment from what others think about it.

After the flamenco show, I took a leisurely stroll back to the hotel, stopping periodically to admire the work of local artists on display under makeshift booths along Las Ramblas. Back in my bed on my last night in Barcelona, I closed my eyes with images of flamenco dancers darting through my mind. Before falling asleep, warmth blossomed in my belly, as if the percussive tapping of their shoes created the friction necessary to light a waxy, white wick of a candle that had been waiting patiently for that very moment.

I had some extra time before the departing flight to Johannesburg and decided to make my way down to the arrivals area to charge my iPad before boarding the plane. While the device was charging, I watched people rather than read a book. I'm rarely bored at airports because my heart registers my memories of special interactions between people during goodbyes and hellos. The majority of the exchanges at Heathrow that day were what I'd consider neutral. But I also witnessed a wilting flower spring to life after receiving a restorative amount of water from the woman he had been waiting for. A man spotted his beloved in the crowd of weary travellers after what I suspected had been a long flight from India. He was happiness personified. With a modest bouquet of flowers in hand, he dashed along the rope separating the passengers from their rides, ducked under it, and raced toward her. Unaware of his proximity, he startled her and didn't give her a chance to recover before he wrapped his arms around her, picked her up, and twirled her round and round.

I have never missed someone that much to express such unrestrained joy at seeing him walk through the arrivals door of any airport terminal. I was certain the day would come when I would give a man I love such a welcome, in keeping with my practice of doing love. I would run to him and hug him as if nobody were watching, and if one or many were while I made a silly lovesick fool of myself, it would be their problem, not mine.

Boarding the plane to South Africa, I was eternally grateful for an aisle seat, given the size of the man who had already taken his seat next to mine. He was from South Africa, and an affable, gentlemanly sort, endowed with an enormous, athletic physique. He was also handsome, and he had auric eyes that flashed under the yellow glow of the nightlight above us. Of course, I didn't mind when our arms and legs accidentally touched one another's while the crew prepared for takeoff. Testosterone seeped out of all his pores, and I was happy to absorb the odd molecule from his bare forearm when it brushed up against mine.

The gentleman sitting directly in front of me was bigger than the one beside me, in that he was both heavier and taller. He was restless throughout the flight, reclining then straightening his seat frequently. He got up several times to retrieve something from his bag in the overhead compartment. His uneasiness made me jittery, like a cat with a jumpy tail, every strand of hair along its spine looking like little soldiers standing beside each other, getting ready for battle. I was on high alert without knowing why.

Unable to sleep during the night, I watched two movies beginning with *The Best Exotic Marigold Hotel*. When the hotel host said, "There's an Indian saying that it will be all right in the end, and if it's not all right, it's not the end," I wondered if the trip I was about to take would be the end, because by the time we reached cruising altitude I thought everything in my life felt all right. Time and tears had resuscitated me after the breakup with First Love and I was on a flight high above a continent that included many countries on the list of places to visit before I entered The Great Unknown. The second film I watched was *Act Like a Lady, Think Like a Man*, based on the book by comedian Steve Harvey. I approved of a dating probation period, denying access to everything from the neck down until a man has proven he's worthy of a pass. The kind of man I wanted to be with would not pout at the suggestion, at least not in front of me.

Johannesburg's O.R. Tambo Airport is not London's Heathrow. There are no immigration cards to fill out, and my South African seatmate suggested half of the attendants might be asleep at their posts. As it turned out, none of them were asleep, and they were not as relaxed as he had predicted. The guard whose wicket I ended up at wanted to know exactly why I was in South Africa and thoroughly checked the pages of my passport to see where else I had been. Within a few minutes, he appeared confident I had not arrived in the country to conduct or participate in some nefarious activity, and allowed me to proceed into the country.

In the baggage claim area, I found out what the man in front of me had been retrieving from his bag in the overhead compartment during the flight. He was at least a foot taller than I was and he stood outside the boundary of my personal space, but I could smell the alcohol on his breath. We engaged in idle banter while we waited for our suitcases to appear on the baggage carousel. He was from the eastern seaboard of my native land but spent three-month periods supervising drilling activities at a mine in Angola.

"It must be hard to be separated from your family for so long," I said, watching the carousel.

"Nope. The longer the better," he replied, with no hesitation. "She's a golddigger. Why would I want to be home for that?"

Silence was the best answer I could come up with to his first question.

"Isn't that the only reason women are with men?" he asked, staring down at me with an insistence I didn't pretend not to hear.

"No. But it's one of them, I guess." I omitted my trailing thought of, *Yeah and how many distasteful reasons do men have when it comes to their choice of a wife?* But I wasn't in the mood to philosophize about an incendiary topic with a strange, angry man, and in particular, a drunken one at an airport with armed guards everywhere.

"What are you doing here?" he said, assessing me as an opportunity to forget about his golddigger back home.

"Going on safari," I answered, still eyeing the baggage carousel.

"I'm staying at a really nice hotel for the night. Care to join me? I could show you a good time."

Yes—undoubtedly, he, the vodka, and I would have been a delirious threesome. "I need to get on a plane in a couple of hours, but thanks," I said.

With that, my little brown bag made its grand entrance from behind the rubber curtains, and I couldn't recall a time when I felt so overjoyed to see an inanimate object.

"Don't work too hard," I said to him and walked away to get my bag.

"Enjoy your safari," he yelled out to me as I made my way to the exit. People from my country were still polite, even after conversations about golddiggers and being rejected while under the influence of alcohol.

I lacked the patience to navigate the airport to find out where I needed to go to catch my next flight. However, there was no shortage of men waiting at the exit to help me find my way, which relieved me because the fatigue from a sleepless night and the excitement of being on my way to the South African Bush had made me exhausted and lazy about having to figure out the logistics of the flight to Hoedsprit. Of course, I knew this service came at a price, because that brand of friendliness wasn't free. I was willing to pay for help, from the least aggressive and friendliest man in the arrivals area. His assistance was courteous and more efficient than most services I'd received at other airports around the globe. As we approached the check-in desk, he began the marketing phase, which included a pearly white smile, polite light touches on my forearm captioned with how pleased he had been to help me, and that his living expenses exceeded his meagre wage. I admired his strategy. As I exited the baggage area, he approached me politely but was not obnoxiously insistent. Then he was helpful and efficient while treating me like a lady as he guided me to the national check-in gates. He touched me without undertones of desperation or vulgarity. His approach generated enough goodwill that I would have given him the same amount of money with or without the disclosure about his financial woes. Kindness combined with sincerity encourages generosity of spirit. He had done his job well. And although his strategy was as subtle as the message in the faces of the armed guards, I handed him ten Euros when we arrived at the gates for local flights.

The short flight between O.R. Tambo and The South African Bush landing strip was uneventful and restful. I remember very little about the flight because I nodded off for most of it. I knew I was in Africa as we touched down because of the zebra on the port side of the strip. As the plane taxied to the terminal that resembled a park information centre in my native land, I was boiling with excitement. Walking unsteadily down the narrow aisle with my baggage, I felt as if a magician had been spinning me around for fifteen hours and announced, "Here you are, once more," as he removed my blindfold at the plane's exit door.

The mid-morning sun had already been scorching the spare land around me, and I inhaled the scent of the earthy grasses and the dry heat curling off the asphalt, taking my first breath before embarking on my adventure in a grand Faraway Place. With my first steps on the new land, I had arrived home, finally. The Powers That Be and The Good Life had blessed me with a trip to my spiritual homeland. I entered the airport terminal where all the weary passengers wore vague looks of desperation as they tried to find their ride to their destinations in The South African Bush. Outside, I leaned up against the brick wall of the terminal after I couldn't locate a vehicle with the name of the lodge where I had reserved accommodations. The wall had absorbed the heat from the morning sun and it provided the perfect remedy for the shiver running through my body.

Once most people had found their rides, I returned inside the terminal to the information desk to inquire about my transportation. "Oh, there you are," the woman exclaimed when I gave her my name, as if she had spent hours looking for me. She accompanied me outside to a white SUV where a young guy sporting sunglasses and a khaki ball cap with matching pants stood on the curb and welcomed me with a smile as expansive as the Grand Canyon. He outstretched his hand and shook mine with an unexpected vigour. He put my suitcase in the rear compartment of the vehicle while I instinctively marched to the right side, which in South African vehicles is where the driver sits.

"You can drive if you want to. I don't mind," he said, and then laughed at my mistake.

"Oh, excuse me, I'm used to vehicles in my country," I said, walking to the other door. I regretted not taking him up on his offer since I didn't know if I would ever get another opportunity to drive in the South African Bush. But I was tired and wanted to be his passenger. Once settled into the vehicle, he removed his sunglasses, which unveiled the limpid eyes of an old and wise soul.

"How long is the drive to the lodge?" I asked, scanning the surroundings.

"About an hour," he responded.

"I'm so exhausted. I got no sleep on the flight here."

"You can sleep if you want to."

How could I sleep when the driver beside me would bring me to the place that had sat on the top of my must-see list for several decades?

"No, I'd rather take in the view."

"So, what made you travel here?"

"Watching *Animal Kingdom* on Sunday nights when I was little, and because life is short."

He smiled knowingly. I suppose many tourists had told him the same thing, and by now my response must have been a cliche.

"I don't know how long I have on this planet. When I heard about the serious illness of a colleague, I made a spontaneous decision to come here."

"Are you afraid to be here by yourself? You know, there are animals that could kill you with one bite."

"No. A quick death is appealing. Besides, bites from humans back home are worse," I laughed.

"I've been taking photos in the bush since I was a boy. I love it here. Do you love your work?" he asked. Nothing like covering serious life topics with a stranger halfway across the world from Somewhere Small. I was too comfortable with this stranger to lie to him or give an oblique answer to an important question.

"I like it. It's interesting. But I love writing. There's a big difference between liking and loving something, isn't there?"

He nodded.

"Are you married?" he asked me.

"Divorced. I liked my husband but didn't love him. It's important to like the one you're with, but there's gotta be respect and passion. And you've gotta think they're hot." I didn't have to twirl my hair. The wind created from the open windows did it for me.

Staring out at the landscape, I reflected on passion as we drove along a straight stretch. I hoped I would love a man one day, and that when we looked at each other, the light in our eyes would become brighter, and when we closed them during a hug or a kiss, sight wouldn't matter—we would feel the radiance of the other's soul warming our core; we'd feel the beat of each other's heart, steady and strong. We'd yearn to share our truths with each other, naked, in the light and in the dark. I hadn't met him yet, but when I did, we would be to each other what his lenses and cameras were to him: we couldn't imagine being apart for long because together we experienced a joy in being and doing that we hadn't experienced with anyone else.

"I would add one requirement," he said. "The person has to believe in God, because without that, well, I just don't know."

His comment made me think about The War Bride as a devout Catholic and her Canadian Soldier as devout in his atheism.

"Is it important to believe in him or act like him?"

"God saved me from doing very bad things. I need to be with someone who believes in him as much as I do."

We needed a respite from love and religion and I thought my next question would provide a speedy exodus out of serious life topics and into the mundane. I wanted his perspective on a day in the life of a ranger in the South African Bush.

"Other than the photo ops, why did you become a guide?"

"Because I love it. And I did it when I stopped needing my dad's approval. I'm happy. I've forgiven him through the help of God."

Would some future life circumstance cause him to forsake his chosen Father and revisit the one whose DNA he shared?

So much for the mundane. I didn't care, though. Dense conversations were my favourite kind, particularly unexpected ones with someone who was as direct as he was sensitive.

"I do love it," he continued, resting his left wrist on the steering wheel and letting his hand drop. "But it gets lonely out here sometimes."

I folded my arms and slouched in the seat. "As long as I'm here, you won't be lonely. I love to talk," I said, letting my head fall back into the depression of the headrest.

With his silence, I realized he wasn't lacking for people he could talk to about photography, the South African Bush, and their native lands. Staring out the passenger window after my faux pas, I found the stark land strangely comforting with its spindly leafless trees desperately seeking water.

"How hot does it get here in the summer?"

"Over fifty degrees Celsius. I can lose ten pounds in a day when it's that hot, but I would rather lose it doing other things."

"Maybe you should go work for Sports Illustrated. You know, you could have it both ways."

He laughed. "That's the plan."

Evidently he had envisioned his future and didn't need my creative input.

"Do you have kids?" he asked.

"No. I wanted them, though," I replied, gazing out at the barren landscape. "When the timing seemed right, fate said 'No'."

"You could still have children if you wanted to. Technology could help if you want to be a mother."

"Yes, you're right. Do you have children?" I asked him.

"No." He became silent after his one-word answer, as if not wanting to talk about his prospect of fatherhood.

"Do you want them?"

"Oh, yeah, definitely. But I'm not in a hurry to do that," he replied with a firm tenderness, as if he had envisioned himself holding a little girl with curly brown hair and eyes as limpid as his.

One hour elapsed quickly. Driving into the lodge, I already felt comfortable seeing the canvas tents and sitting area that opened to the river.

"Let me know if you get lonely," he said, parking the Range Rover.

"Sure. Maybe we can have a beer in the bar," I replied. He delivered my bags to the lobby where I received a hearty welcome from the hostess.

I'd never been nervous about travel to foreign countries, but the health risks of being in the South African Bush scared me. I didn't want to take the anti-malarial pills that the System's pharmacist handed me with an Encyclopedia Britannica of possible side effects. I was also afraid of snakes and insects, particularly those that hid in dark places. The hospitable manager didn't assuage my fears with her welcome, which included a diatribe about precautions.

"No baggage or clothing on the floor. Scorpions like them. We had one in the lobby two nights ago. And you must not walk unescorted to your tent in the morning and at night, for safety reasons. The space is open here. We had a zebra walk into the lobby not long ago. And you'll hear the lions and hippos close by," she warned.

I stayed in a canvas tent called Cheetah, situated about a hundred metres from the river. Opening the screen door, I smiled at the "Welcome Middle2," inscribed with leaves on the perfectly white duvet cover. Once I stored my bags and shoes as far above the floor as possible, I gathered up the leaves in my hands and resisted the urge to toss them in the air and release them like confetti to celebrate a momentous and rare event. I stretched out on the bed and naturally imagined myself with long, sleek legs and semi-retractable claws. Once settled, I enjoyed a brief nap before the first drive at 3:00 p.m. Ensconced in my tent, I felt at home as any cat would who'd found a quiet place to curl up, even though instinct dictated the need to keep her eyes open just a sliver. Despite having just arrived, I could not stop purring.

I was assigned to the safari vehicle driven by one of the other rangers at the camp for all of the drives. The contrast of watching flamenco dancers in Barcelona a few days earlier with sitting on a bench in a Land Rover in the middle of the South African Bush made me feel disoriented until we spotted a herd of elephants within ten minutes of leaving the lodge. The females and their calves mesmerized me while the guide explained their behaviour. They maintain lifelong bonds with other females who care for and protect the herd independently of the bulls who are primarily solitary and do not establish permanent bonds with the females or each other. (Oh, so First Love was a bull through no fault of his own.) The female dominated the herd, and their offspring thrived without the bulls. (And I would thrive without First Love with my tribe of feminine support back home.)

During my first night in the tent, I was awakened multiple times by the roaring hippos, the screeching monkeys, and multiple birds playing a symphony in the South African Bush. At one point, I lay awake for an hour to listen to all the foreign sounds that kept me in a state of wonder. The thought of dying in Africa did not bother me because I was in the remotest and most prized Faraway Place on my list. Even before landing in Johannesburg, I knew I would be sad to leave the place I was about to step foot on. Therefore, a painful, even gory death there was acceptable to me as long as it wasn't slow. Before my departure, I joked with several friends about putting my personal affairs in order in case I landed back in The Urban City in a box.

On the second day of the safari drives, we encountered a pride of lions whose heads were buried in the abdomen of a water buffalo they had just downed. We managed to get within ten feet of the feast, and even with my eyes closed for part of the lion's supper, there was little doubt about what was happening around us. I could hear and smell the gory death scene around us: the slurping of blood, the crunching of bones, and the putrid smell of stomach and intestinal remains as the predator-prey cycle of life played out before us. During the forty-five minutes while I watched with grim fascination, occasionally one of the lions looked up. Gazing into its light brown eyes, I laughed to myself, thinking that should the lions attack us (well, me in particular), there wouldn't be the need for a box or even a Ziploc plastic bag for my remains.

Throughout the four days at The Safari Lodge, The Ranger and I crossed paths every day at least once, with one of us politely asking the other, "How did you sleep?" On the second day at the camp, in between lunch and the afternoon drive (when I made a habit of sitting in the open lounge to read, chat with the other visitors, or scan the land across the river using a pair of binoculars) he approached me, handing me a small piece of white paper he had folded.

"What is it?"

"A love letter," he replied.

On the paper was a handwritten link to his photography page, and indeed it was a love letter, not from him to me but from him to his audience around the world. He loved his work, and it showed in his compositions. They told stories of timidity in the eyes of the newly-born, of threats in the jowls of lions and hippos, of speed in the torsos of cheetahs and leopards, and about tactics of hunters and the hunted. His photographs told me and everyone else about the beauty in life and death, beginnings and endings, and the flurry of activity that happens in between.

On my last night at the camp, our paths didn't cross. I was relieved we would not have that "beer" together after all, because I would have been sadder to leave the next morning than I already had been. Instead of making the early morning drive when I woke up the next day, I stayed in my tent to pack my belongings and sit out on the balcony to enjoy the view of the river and the sounds of the South African Bush around me before going to Dublin, where the air would prepare me for the damp conditions I would return to in The Urban City.

I wheeled my cases to the reception area to check out early so I could relax in the community seating area with my binoculars in hopes of seeing the elusive hippos I'd heard on the first night.

"What are you doing?" the hostess asked me.

"I thought I would come out early to settle my bills before leaving."

"But you're not leaving today. You have one more night with us."

I had misread the date on my itinerary. I returned to my cabin, lay on the crisp white covers on my bed, and slept as if it were the middle of the night. When I woke around noon, I watched an eerie vapour glide through the air as if Old Man Winter was exhaling in my tent. I watched it curiously as it made its way from my door to the bathroom before disappearing.

With the vapour gone, seconds later I became the frightened cat clinging to the canvas ceiling when a group of bonobos descended on my outdoor patio, thumping at the door and screeching with a hysteria that shook the foundation the tent was sitting on. The frenzy ended as suddenly as it had begun. I tiptoed to the door and snuck a look outside to see them huddled together on the neighbour's balcony. They scampered this way and that, which made me question whether the crazy activity was an omen. Yes, the bonobos' mischief foretold an agitation that would begin later that evening and last for several months because of my encounter with The Ranger on my final night in the South African Bush.

When our group arrived back at the lodge at the end of the afternoon drive, I decided to check my voicemail because of the twenty hours I would be out of communication as I travelled back to Britain before heading to Dublin. While I was on the phone, The Ranger plunked himself down beside me, looking as dejected as a dog that had been shooed away by its master. Getting off the phone, I sat down on the lobby couch beside him.

"Why do you look so sad?"

"There's just no pleasing those photographers," he replied.

"Look, there are always going to be the unpleasables wherever you go. The sooner you don't care what others think of you, the better your life will be."

I avoided looking into his eyes and instead stared at his lips, but then turned away and looked out into the blackness beyond the community deck. It was time to join the other guests for a pre-dinner glass of wine. "What you need is a back rub and a glass of wine," I told him as I got up to leave.

I wanted to talk to him for a long time, but the consequences of doing so troubled me. I didn't want to leave South Africa missing him. I had already spent the year recovering from the emotional turmoil of the breakup with First Love. Nine months later, boarding the plane to Heathrow, I was calm and centred and had constructed a pleasing new view of my life. After my trip to Dublin, I would be returning to the rainy season in The Urban City and I didn't need a new reason to make the days longer than they were going to be. I joined a couple from South Africa at a wooden bench overlooking the river for a brief conversation. The Ranger approached us a few minutes later while we were talking about our desires to travel to Faraway Places. It was a necessity for me, like The Ranger needed his camera and his lenses, and the sketch artist his pens and paper. The dinner bell rang then, and the South African couple and I sat at a table behind a fire pit while The Ranger sat upstairs with visitors from his afternoon tour.

After dinner, I retreated to my tent, and at 10:00 p.m. I prepared for bed by having my third bath for the day. Although the tub was large enough for me to stretch out completely, its size was the least-appealing quality. When I poured the foaming gel into the running tap water, it became a sudsy paradise with bubbles glistening under the yellow glow of the flickering light from the candles. Sinking into the warm water, the entire backside of my body tingled when it touched the bubbles. I didn't need Tibetan meditation music to relax me, because when I reclined and closed my eyes, images from the safari drives in the bush fanned before me in a display of postcards. But the slideshow stopped and I sat upright when I heard light footsteps outside. I emptied the tub and clapped my hands in the sudsy remains. Tomorrow would be another day, and I comforted myself with the thought that this would not be my last in the category of favourite adventures. I dressed and sat out on the balcony to read emails and the news before going to bed. In my periphery, I saw a shadow approaching me. When I turned around, The Ranger was walking toward me in his khaki outfit and woollen socks.

I rose to greet him.

"Have you seen the inside of one of these tents?" I asked.

"No."

"Come in then."

I opened the door and let him go in before me.

"Would you mind closing the blinds?" he asked, even though the screen door opened to the river and no one would be able to see us.

"Could you open this?" I asked him, handing him a bottle of red wine.

I felt him watching me undo the blinds. I was uncomfortable, but I was not a water buffalo unaware of the hungry lion behind it. Once done with the canvas drapes, I handed him two glasses that he filled. He gave me mine, and we raised them without looking at each other. I gave him a tour of my accommodations that ended in the bathroom where the candles still glowed. When we hugged, I knew in one breath that my short encounter with The Ranger would usher in longing and fear: longing for a romance with a kindred spirit, and fear that kindred spirits are a select few and I might not meet another one before I entered The Great Unknown. After our easy embrace, we stood in front of the bathroom sink and he lit a cigarette.

"I wish I could come to Dublin with you, but then what?"

"Nothing, and that's the problem."

And nothing was irreconcilable because of the generation, not the geography that separated us.

Later in the bathtub, surrounded by candles, I sat behind him and massaged his back as he described the devoted and constant love of his mother. As I ran my index finger over the tattoo on the middle of his back, he arched backwards and his spine cracked loudly enough to startle me. But that didn't discourage me from kissing the tattoo and uttering a silent prayer for him: *Be great, beautiful man*.

In our goodbye, The Ranger and I stood at the screen door of the tent; the view was serene blackness.

"Be successful," he told me. "And remember how fortunate you are. I haven't even left my country and you've travelled all over the world."

"Don't worry, you will."

"I will remember this night for the rest of my life," he said before turning away from me and disappearing into the quiet darkness.

The screen door squealed as I closed it. I tiptoed to my bed, tucked myself in, and rested my head where his had been only a few minutes before. In the deep dark silence of the South African Bush, I drifted to sleep after saying "I'll remember it too" out loud, hoping the silence of the night carried my words to his ears before he fell asleep.

During the next morning's drive, our vehicle ended up side-by-side with the other jeep The Ranger had been driving so that the entire group could watch a leopard perfectly perched on a horizontal section of a branch, as if it was the grand centrepiece in a museum. Wearing sunglasses, The Ranger and I looked at each other long enough to register the somber and sullen look in each other's faces. His may have been due to lack of sleep, but mine was from a melancholy that had settled into my heart like the dew drops had on the grasses overnight. Some things are just too beautiful to look at for too long, and within seconds I turned away from the leopard as I had from The Ranger minutes before. Instead, I wrapped my black scarf around my neck and bowed my head to look at the display screen on my camera to review the other photos I had taken that morning.

When the time came to leave Africa, the guide who drove me to the airport was jovial and kind, but rather than converse with him, I chose to engage in a silent goodbye to the country. Loneliness from having spent time at ease with a kindred spirit and saying goodbye to him shortly thereafter paled the blue sky above the desolate flatlands. Even though I wouldn't see The Ranger again, I still wanted to hold his heart in my hand and watch its cracks turn to gold, but it's not for me to know what happens to it or to him. But it is for me to decide what happens to my heart and me. And while The Ranger's kiss contained the beauty in all four seasons, I knew the quality of a kiss is only an indicator of love's potential. And kisses make up the periphery of true and abiding love, but mutual respect and commitment are in its centre. I should have been grateful for a rare and beautiful experience with a kindred spirit, but when I left his native land, gratitude was as far away as The Urban City, and when I arrived back there, it had travelled the same distance in the opposite direction. And I'm still not sure we will cross paths before I enter The Great Unknown. But time changes perspectives and circumstances. Gratitude for my experience with The Ranger might sneak up and wrap itself around me when I least expect it, then wrestle me to the ground and refuse to let me go until I surrender.

Indeed, I had fallen in love with Africa, and the love affair was about to end. Arriving back at the landing strip, I walked around the grounds of the terminal and made my way to the gate separating me from the tarmac. Peering through the mesh, I closed my eyes, praying that the searing midday heat would sink into my back and melt the tightness in my chest. The boarding announcement interrupted my prayer though, and the tightness stiffened in my chest. Once I was settled on the plane, within a few minutes an elderly gentleman originally from Italy sat in the aisle seat next to me and immediately began the story of his fifty-year marriage and his olive oil business, one he had been in the process of selling due to his failing health. The man ended our conversation with, "Life is shorter than you can possibly imagine," as the plane accelerated for takeoff. Once the plane was airborne, the Italian drifted off and I scanned the land below. The land beneath me might have been barren, but the conversations I had there were not.

As the plane flew over the multiple valleys, I thought about the conversation with The Ranger regarding the difference between Love and Like as the two sides separated by a valley. On Love's side, the view is wondrous, where residents can conjure up rainbows, fairies, and stardust. But make no mistake, demons and dragons wander in Love's territory too, though the residents only attract the predators if they are afraid for too long.

Love's side won't let them be consumed by complacency, either. While sleeping in Love's territory, if they've become too comfortable or a bit lazy, it plunks them on one of many magic carpets that are as ubiquitous as clouds. The carpet glides to The Threshold, hurtles through the turbulent skies in The Special World, and descends, bumping along a rocky plateau. The landing jars the sleeping travellers awake. Being in The Special World forces them to pursue their passion, because if they don't, sadness starts with a few aches, eventually becoming a burning fever. Love cannot support the sick for too long, because it doesn't offer emergency services. It does have an ample supply of tissue for the residents to weep from their losses and disappointments, but there is no equipment for treating the ones who have prolonged fevers. In this case, the long-suffering are solemnly escorted to the exit whose one-way path leads them down into the valley.

Like's residents are comfortable. Objects there are pale, lacking the vibrant colours of those filling the land of Love. People there have buried the wishful thinking from their youth. Their grand plans died a painful and sometimes prolonged death from the fatal injuries caused by sneers and jeers. It should come as no surprise there are more cemeteries than Art throughout Like. People in Like don't smile very much; they carry out their day-to-day routines at a languorous pace. Fortunately for them, the land of Love is always within reach; and there are enough shovels to unearth the buried treasures for the weary to reclaim them in their hearts. And if the shovels aren't a sufficient reminder, the dreams push daisies to the grassy surfaces where they bloom for much of the year. Love's residents have expansive spirits and they travel at night into the dreams of those in Like, enticing them to walk through the valley of darkness and up to their side.

Some choose to die in the valley of darkness, but most people spend time in both territories more than once in a lifetime. But when it's all said and done, the most satisfied have spent the majority of their time in Love.

Arriving back in London, I made my way to a day bed reservation to sleep before catching a late afternoon flight to Dublin. I did manage to sleep but found myself reeling about South Africa and the memories I'd collected there. I looked forward to getting on another airplane to a destination with no resemblance to the South African Bush. I spotted a rainbow over the horizon beyond my gate window and wanted to inhale its colourful spectrum to fill me with joyful expectations that would come to pass in Dublin. Surely to God, if there were one place on Earth where that was possible, it was in the land of limericks and leprechauns.

As soon as we landed in Dublin, I dismissed the hopeful interpretation of the rainbow. A miserable foggy cloak had been thrown over the city, and as I exited the airport to take a cab into town, my spirit whined about the damp chill no memory of the South African Bush could dry. I was sad and discombobulated and regretted the decision to include Dublin in my itinerary. Arriving at my hotel, even my room mirrored my emotional state. It smelled as if a wet dog had curled up on the bed all day and the floor was slanted, but at least in the direction that would prevent me from rolling out of the single bed onto the floor. I refused to let the climate in my room and outside stop me from exploring the immediate neighbourhood, even though I wanted to disappear in the bed with a book. I found a pub within a few blocks of the hotel and chatted with a couple of women visiting from California. They convinced me to take a day trip to the Cliffs of Moher on Guinness Day.

But before visiting the cliffs, I strolled through the streets of Dublin and visited some of the historical sites. The Kilmainham Gaol, a former prison operating as a museum, smelled damp. I made the tour on a drizzly day, but even on a sunny warm one, no amount of heat could have lifted the dankness that had seeped into its every stone from decades of sadness and torment. But there was light in the Gaol. Each of the cells had been constructed with a rectangular opening cut into the wall to give the prisoners a view to the sky as a way for them to commune with God during their confinement. My legs trembled during the visit to the Stonecutter's Yard where the executions of Irish prisoners occurred. English soldiers had been permitted to kill only one Irishman due to concerns about the impact on their psyches. How considerate. Many of the executioners had been teenagers or in their early twenties. Sand bags were placed between the prisoners and the walls to prevent bullet holes from damaging them. I wondered how any sensitive Englishman didn't wail in the night for the rest of his life for having the blood of even one man on his hands, just like my dad had done until the black mould reached the part of his brain that erased my mom and the murder from his memory. And the Irish didn't need bullet holes to remind them of the travesties in the Stonecutter's Yard, because memories are etched into the nation's collective psyche with the same ink used to craft The Book of Kells.

Tourists from around the world converged at the information centre near Trinity College to board a bus that would transport us to the west coast of the country for our visit to the cliffs. The bus wended its way through the verdant countryside, the ecological opposite of the South African Bush. Approaching the coast, we caught glimpses of jagged vertical drops to the Atlantic Ocean. Although Ireland's physical beauty and the peoples' kindness provided a warm welcome, stepping off the bus onto the parking area in front of the cliffs, I saw images of the South African Bush everywhere. A deceptive path of long grasses and dandelions snaked along its border and separated me from the Atlantic Ocean with only one careless step. Strolling along the path, I wondered how The Ranger would have captured the dramatic beauty around me. The cold wind twisted my hair into a knotted zebra's tail and my eyes became unfocused lenses that had me seeing things. Stones were the noses of hyenas sniffing the grassy clumps along the path; the cliff's outcrops were the trunks of elephants seeking the sea; and hippo nostrils and crocodile heads poked through the sapphirine sea, its waves slurping and bubbling around them. I even saw the crimson sun disappear beneath the horizon when the woollen red hat of another visitor dropped below the crest of the path in the distance.

At our last stop before making the two-hour journey back to Dublin, we stopped at a local pub where a band was celebrating Guinness in a grand manner by regaling an appreciative audience with beloved Irish folk songs. I stood in front of them capturing video and photos of the men bobbing and swaying in their seats as they played. Within a few minutes, an elderly gentleman approached me, carrying a small glass of Guinness in each hand.

"I know I will never see you again, but it's just not proper for a lady to stand alone in a pub on Guinness Day." I took the glass he handed me.

"Thank you, and cheers," I said, raising my glass to his but avoiding his eyes. While the band played, I glanced repeatedly at the bus driver who stood near the door. When he finally waved his hand as a cue we needed to leave, I thanked the man standing beside me for the beer. Even though we wouldn't see each other again, I was already nervous about his entry into my personal space, even if he couldn't help it because of the number of people in the room. My loneliness had ebbed briefly with the distraction of lively music among a group of feisty Irishmen. Its grip had been like a chiffon scarf worn tightly enough to threaten choking me, but being with people who valued connection of the heart and spirit, it surrendered for a few minutes to a light breeze that had coaxed its hand into the knot and loosened it.

The next day, I returned to London to catch my flight back to The Urban City. As the pilot guided the plane toward the runway for takeoff, I couldn't help but think of the bloody stains on the ground of the Stonecutter's Yard, with the ruddy remnants of human cruelty tainting the land of the sensitive ones. Stains were everywhere. Their shapes and colours might be different than the ones I had seen in my native land, but they represented life, and life was messy no matter where I went.

I no longer view travel as the bleach for life's blemishes, a necessary reprieve from the routines of The Simple Life and purchased with funds acquired through The Good Life. I want my life to be full of stains of different shapes, sizes, and colours from the entire spectrum, to complete the tapestry of my life. And I don't care if the final product looks pretty to anyone else's eye or not. After my travels to Faraway Places #2, I wanted to remove the rusty background that got that way because I could be more vulnerable with strangers I'd known for only a few days than with people I'd known for years. The stain arose from my belief that as long as I was in The Urban City, I would not feel a sense of belonging or find my people, my kindred spirits who transcended my DNA, the DNA that had resulted in pain and suffering and shame in Somewhere Small. Finding people in places as far away as possible from Somewhere Small wouldn't give me a sense of belonging. But being open wherever I went would, as would taking up my past into my hands as if it were a bouquet of dandelion heads topped with spheres of feathery seeds and blowing them into the wind.

CHAPTER 29

LET IT GO, LET IT GO, LET IT GO

Middle2: "What am I to do when the men I fall in love with are bad and the ones who love me are boring?"
The Powers That Be: "Read Rumi's quote at the begining of the chapter called 'Shattered Illusions'."

I didn't have Huntington's disease, but surely to God I'd inherited the gene that predisposed me to love men who were bad and feel repulsed by the boring ones who loved me. Thirty years and five loves later, I have begun to examine this thing called "romantic love," which I wished had an associated decision tree perfected by scientific methods as rigorous as the autopsy protocol developed by the global community of anatomical pathologists. My love life has been a series of experiments with the same holey outcomes as those in the organic chemistry lab, but they created cracks in my heart instead of holes in my clothes. I can easily replace clothing, but my heart is a different matter altogether.

Lasting romantic relationships require passion, commitment, and friendship expressed by both people. Two of the three might not be bad, but it's not enough—at least from my own, admittedly pothole-filled perspective. With First Love, I experienced passion and friendship with the obvious lack of commitment. With BrotherLove, we had both friendship and commitment, but not enough passion to sustain the attachment after twelve years. But to begin a relationship as teenagers or young adults without having experienced passion left an essential void in the spectrum of romantic love for both of us, and we would not find it in each other. And then there was Dark&Angry: we experienced all three qualities periodically, but never concurrently—and certainly never for an extended period of time, because we both lacked self-esteem. Psychiatrist #2 told me people who held unresolved anger and sadness often became depressed, and people who are depressed in the worst extremes become either homicidal or suicidal. Dark&Angry and I were travelling in opposite directions of the spectrum. He wasn't homicidal and I wasn't suicidal, but I knew our love was an empty ceramic cup with numerous cracks; it would eventually shatter after boiling water had been poured into it enough times. If I had remained with Dark&Angry, the effects would have been as toxic as slurping a teaspoon of antifreeze per day: not enough to kill me, but certainly enough to make me chronically ill.

The path continued with BuddhaBound. He didn't merit a full chapter, but reflecting on my time with him, he made me aware of an important pattern in my relationships with men: to be involved in a romantic relationship somehow required me to pay for the privilege financially, a belief I learned from being an entity with a unique personal identifier in The System as a foster child. My entry as a case in The System came with the requirement to track financial transactions associated with "fostering of my care" in three households. Being in one of The System's families necessitated an exchange of money. But financial transactions lack emotional involvement and therefore do not deal in the currencies of the heart, which include belonging and individuation, among others. As a child, The System paid for me to reside in each of the foster homes whether my emotional needs were met or not. Food, clothing, and shelter superseded being "placed" somewhere that supported my psychological wellbeing. The contract between The System and the three sets of parents did not include a list of my unique personal attributes needing care and attention, and I naturally learned to believe they didn't matter. I know children raised by their birth parents don't always get these needs met either, and I wasn't special in the category of neglect. In some ways, it was easier for children to be neglected by strangers than it is for them to be mistreated by their biological parents.

With the spectacular failure of my relationship with First Love, my faith in the ability to find an enduring love resembled the pattern of a sine wave with the peak amplitude of each cycle representing the optimist and the lowest point reflecting the not-so-positive pessimist. I vacillated between both phases in keeping with its pattern over time. And I never really stayed very long in the emotionally neutral positions where the curve met the time axis. The idealistic romantic in me struggled to keep my attitude on the straight line connecting the peaks of each cycle. But inevitably, I found myself unable to avoid the dramatic descents with some of my relationships. I needed a shakeup to toss me off the sine wave and send me into a free fall where I would eventually land in an upright position on a wave with low amplitude, offering me a leisurely glide where matters of the heart were concerned.

When I saw Jesus that day in the Guided Meditation about forgiveness during the workshop many years ago, the only therapy I'd received was from the chain-smoking grandmotherly Psychiatrist #1 who had been married to a sadomasochist. I interpreted my therapy with her as superficial. How could it not be? Was she really capable of helping me with the deepest aspects of my emotional disease, when a Category 5 hurricane had been brewing in hers? Yes, I had shed a few tears when she made the pronouncement at the end of our first series of sessions that I was "cool as a cucumber." In the end I didn't care about her "cool as a cucumber" assessment, or that there was no associated Diagnostic and Statistical Manual code. I didn't need a psychiatrist to provide me with a diagnosis for what ailed me. Defining my problem was simple, even though its solution was not obvious or certain. I was a broken-hearted twentysomething who had personally adopted several unhealthy characters. And what a cast of characters it was: The Lemon Picker from the Garden of Love (with credits being awarded to Psychiatrist #2 for making me aware of her); a People-Pleasing Addict (created as a result of being an orphan with the desperate need to belong somewhere, anywhere); The One with a Low Self-Love preventing me from finding and thriving in the land of Love (I had been psychologically glued to Somewhere Small, which was thousands of miles away from the land of Love, and I had no clues about how to create a map that would lead me there or what solvent would dissolve the glue that still stuck me to Somewhere Small); The Weak-Willed One in the face of adversity (not unlike a car with a three-cylinder engine that must climb a fifteen-percent grade hill;

it's not that I didn't want to make progress, I just didn't have the equipment that allowed me to reach the proverbial finish line); The Carrier of Family Shame, causing anxiety and a lack of confidence (further explanation is really unnecessary if you've read the previous chapters); and The Good Girl who habitually became aphasic in front of people who deserved a perfunctory "fuck off" (a symptom I became aware of during an appointment with my favourite physician between the ages of sixteen and twenty-one when he told me I was "too nice," which I now associate with the aforementioned People-Pleasing Addict searching for permission to enter whatever circle would accept me). I needed to exorcise these characters to see what remained, if anything. And in my case, I didn't solicit the services of a priest with assistants who restrained me during the fits of rage as the characters fought for their right to survive. Instead, I sought the more conservative and socially accepted route of modern psychiatry. The two options had one common element, though: there would be anger as my multiple personas fought for their survival, followed by sadness about the remaining ashes, and my naked, newly born self on stage for all to see. I didn't care that I was nude before the stage lights went out because I had become aware of a more profoundly troubling problem: I had no dreams, and therefore no reason to wake up. It wasn't until my sessions with Psychiatrist #2 began that I embarked on a journey to retrieve the pieces of my broken heart as the first step to building an authentic self I would not find in the ashes of the cremated characters.

After my breakup with First Love, it would have been easy for me to embrace the role of the scorned woman for an indefinite period. However, I had to take responsibility for failing to confront him about the numerous signs I accumulated during the many months before our relationship ended. I didn't want to acknowledge the truth that had been presented to me as clearly as crocuses and tulips are signs of spring. It was my responsibility to honestly evaluate why I decided to enter into and remain in a relationship with a man who could not commit to me. The truth was pretty simple, really: I didn't feel worthy of the loyal affections of a man.

Once the emotional storm of First Love's betrayal had cleared, I realized the person who was more difficult to forgive looked back at me in the mirror each night as I prepared for bed. I had slammed the door repeatedly on The Powers That Be that I'd relegated to a corner of a closet but whose calls could be heard as I slept, sometimes waking me, leaving me baffled and curious about what had shaken me out of the black slate of night. They hadn't given up trying to be heard, but they needed to resort to other means because of my decision to be deaf, dumb, and blind while awake. There had, in fact, been the catastrophic loss of the senses in my story, and I had to agree with The Evil Temptress about the uncanny potency of The Powers That Be and their sneaky ability to commune with my Self. And during my particularly troubling blind periods, they are most active when I sleep, because they don't need the help of my auditory and optic nerves to deliver messages to me. Now I try to commune with my Self while I'm awake because I need all the help I can get to be clear, since my eyes are still murky in some places. I place my fingers on my forehead and pretend to open its eye as if it had the same lids my eyes do. And once open, I imagine a violet crystal ball swirling in front of it, with the truth in the centre of the ball. And if I'm in a prolonged period of confusion, I open the largest eye I have that separates the two sides of my skull by placing my fingers along its centre and running them toward my ears.

I released the remaining vestiges of sadness about First Love when I could listen to "La Vie En Rose" from start to finish without crying at the point where Edith Piaf pines "C'est toi pour moi, moi pour toi dans la vie" (It's you for me, me for you in this life). We had listened to this song together for the first time during a cold grey drive to a romantic seaside lodge on The Island a few hours away from The Urban City. When we arrived there and completed checking into our room, we walked along the beach as the sun was setting. The clouds had parted, and the silky sand was reflecting the opalescent hues of twilight as we walked hand in hand or ran separately when we needed to celebrate our individual glee at being witnesses of such beauty. As I marveled at the fiery pinks of a winter sunset, the song lingered in my mind until the pearly sky turned to darkness, and returned to me throughout our relationship when another sunset reminded me of that autumn night.

After the winter of weeping, the spring flowers poked through the muck to bloom once again as they do. And by the time summer arrived, when I attended my heart check-up down by The Big River, I knew I had released First Love because I had returned to a love independent of him and anyone else. The new reality spoke of fidelity and loyalty and honour, beginning with the one who looked back at me from the river's surface.

Returning to physical places we shared together didn't suck me into a vortex of melancholy I couldn't escape. In the year of our breakup, I visited The Willow Tree above The Big River where we had become tongue-tied and otherwise entangled in each other. The branches would sway, dancing to the orchestral bliss singing out below. A web of thoughts and impressions ensnared me, but I didn't get tangled in it for long. I stood before the tree above The Big River and became an observer of the experiences sweeping through me. The memories were archived, but they no longer stole me from the present, sending me into the deceptively calm eye of a storm. My chest didn't tighten, my throat didn't burn in the usual prelude to a cry, and my stomach didn't feel like it was on a roller coaster without an operator. Being there during a heat wave surely would have triggered profuse sweating if I had still been angry or a chill if a maudlin memory had sucked me into its chilly undertow. I felt neither.

I walked below the tree to the shore of The Big River. The smelter above its banks no longer churned out the toxic smoke and acidic effluent it had during my early childhood in Somewhere Small. The poisoned banks of long ago were lined with trees and plants thanks to developments in environmental law.

Following the swift currents of The Big River, I no longer felt the reckless abandon to leap in and be swept away by what-ever current caught me. Instead, I glanced at various points of the river's surface—some calm, others swirling, and still others foaming with an enticing fervour. I concluded I didn't need to do anything other than witness the movements in the scene before me. With that awareness, I turned around, walked up the grassy knoll and under the overflowing branches of The Willow Tree toward my car. Driving away, my thoughts turned to First Love, a man who will occupy part of my heart forever, but that part is no longer broken. The cracks are filled, not with cement but with putty that is porous and pliable. Instead of breaking, our hearts get bent out of shape, returning to their original form after the cycle of grief is complete. Our hearts remember all shapes they have been, as stamps in our passports remind us of countries we have visited, and their pliability tells us that complete healing is indeed possible.

The first hello and the final goodbye to the people we have loved are like bookends, and what remains between them is the archive of our time together. In a proper goodbye, I snip the remaining vestiges of our entanglement. I untie the knots symbolizing the union, and let the individual slip away. A proper goodbye means I sit in silence and stillness beside some big river and allow my tears to flow and become one of its tributaries. A proper goodbye means I pick up the pieces of my anger piled in a disheveled heap and load each one into the basket of a hot air balloon; and when I'm done, I watch it drift away until it becomes a speck, and finally, nothing at all.

CHAPTER 30

PEACE WITH MOM AND DAD
IN THE GREAT UNKNOWN

I learned a long time ago that some people would rather die than forgive. It's a strange truth, but forgiveness is a painful and difficult process. It's not something that happens overnight. It's an evolution of the heart.
Sue Monk Kidd

If we have no peace, it is because we have forgotten that we belong to each other.
Mother Theresa

During my first night on safari in the South African bush when the angry roar of the hippopotamuses in the river beneath my tent woke me, I began an inquisition with my heart about my significant relationships: the long one with First Love and the short one with my parents. When the temper eased down by the river in the land where human civilization had begun, I contemplated my roots, and in particular the state of my heart where my parents were concerned.

But before getting to my parents, clarification about The Evil Tree is in order. The Evil Tree was a myth. It was not an entity following me from place to place and house to house, casting a shadow that foretold misfortune or growing a malignant and vampiric web of roots into the foundations of my homes or the ground beneath my wandering feet. The Evil Tree was our family tree and there was nothing evil about it. Our family tree tells an infinitely small part of the story of evolution and the laws of nature governing it. Every family tree contains mysteries in its DNA—some benign, some spontaneous, some known, some hidden, and some devastating to the individual and the family. And while it seemed to me the Devil lurked in our DNA, I only saw it that way because of how the mutation affected my family. My ego interpreted the defect as evil, but my spirit knows it is an outcome of the laws of nature.

I still don't like how the law corresponding to Huntington's disease played out in multiple generations of my family, but what else can I do other than accept the outcome and adopt a philosophy beyond the ego that is fond of classifying things as good or evil? Everyone suffers, so why would we be any different? The search for an answer as to why things happen as they do leads nowhere, regardless of how long one seeks a satisfying explanation. And joy and sorrow are inextricably linked. It's no coincidence we shed tears when we're in both states. And when we're deeply entrenched in one, the other is sure to follow. But denying grief is tantamount to putting the heart in a freezer. No matter how happy or sad I am in this life, the effect of time on joy and sadness is like that of the sun on the most brilliant of colours. It fades the intensity of both.

I knew I'd forgiven my parents when we gathered at Youngest's house two days before Eldest's funeral to create a collage of photos capturing the essence of her life. We designed a tree with roots that consisted of separate photos of Mom and Dad. Taken in the 1960s, the pictures were creased black and white, showing them in their prime; interestingly, both were standing in front of cars. We have no photos of them together as a couple, which seemed odd given they had gotten married and had become the parents of four children. But I supposed several photo albums existed and they might have suffered an ending not unlike that of my green satin wedding dress, but at the hands of one of Mom's siblings — or maybe her dad tossed them into The Big River. However, he was a Scot, and somehow I figured their destruction would have involved a fiery ending rather than a watery one.

In the photo of Dad, he was wearing a tight white t-shirt with jeans and standing in a James Dean pose, minus the cigarette and the fancy car. Pinning his photo to the board, I looked into the man's eyes, the eyes of my father. In his countenance I admired the proud, strapping, handsome man looking back at me. He had soft brown eyes where I imagined passion and vitality flickering as they danced in the murky crevices of his irises. I couldn't stop looking at his muscular physique, in particular his bare biceps, forearms, and hands. I no longer focused on his hands and the cascade of violent images that flashed before me: the cinching grip around Mom's Victorian neck; his hands trembling with an uncontrollable rage that no amount of sadness could temper; the hand that had spanked me because of my potty-training problems; the hand that gave me a chocolate bar on the last day we saw him;

the hand that carried the knife dripping with blood, leaving his sweeping signature between Mom's bedroom and the pavement where the blue station wagon had been parked. In his hands, I saw a man who had tenderly embraced my petite mom on many occasions before the black mould created by the defective gene on chromosome 4 began the insidious siege of his brain.

As Middle1 pinned Mom's photo beside Dad's, I saw them as the handsome young couple they were. It wasn't hard to envision Dad wanting to get to know her in the back seat of the car she was standing in front of, or inside the Corvair behind him. Mom epitomized femininity with her strawberry-blonde hair swept up in a bun and her slender but curvy figure on display in the white one-piece bathing suit she wore. Healthy amounts of testosterone raced through Dad's veins, with his angular jaw and bulky physique providing ample evidence, as did estrogen in Mom's veins, judging from the itty-bitty waist, which probably spawned wildly passionate fantasies in Dad involving his hands and the pearly white skin on her sinewy frame. The juxtaposition of their photos teleported me to the entrance of their personal archives.

The most popular version of Cinderella had been published in 1697 by Charles Perrault, which had no doubt infected Mom's psyche, whether through the collective unconscious or the annual rebroadcasts she watched on the television mounted on one of the corner tables her dad refused to dispose of after my grandmother's death. Of course, my dad had found his princess in the dainty blonde who had been all too receptive to his attentions. And Grandpa was no longer big enough to hide his darling bud that had blossomed into a shapely flower, with the local bees patiently buzzing around it. It was only natural that she wanted their attention. After all, it was a matter of survival.

Eyeing their photos, I could envision their mutual excitement with their first glimpse of each other at the community dance years ago, and the aching pangs of yearning for the next reunion as soon as they turned away from each other after their first goodbye. My eyes welled as I pictured their young love, filled with hopes and dreams and disappointments in some unimaginably distant galaxy. Four children within six years, a mortgage for The Little House, and a decent job up at the smelter had landed Dad in a pressure cooker without a release valve. And then there was the not-insignificant matter of his chromosome 4 that added an explosive power for good measure. Mom and Dad couldn't claim to be living The Good Life, given the expenses associated with supporting four small children. For that matter, The Simple Life had also eluded them, considering the tangled roots, twisted stump, and knotted branches that formed the skeleton of his and our family tree. And the System's rules permitting Dad's father to discharge his son from the psychiatric facility became the hand wielding a match that lit the element under the pot. Shortly thereafter, it began to hiss like the fuse of a bomb. I no longer saw them as the life-givers who'd made Eldest, Middle1, Youngest, and me orphans before graduating from elementary school. They had been young adults robbed of fulfilling their dreams, which had likely been as grand as my visions of travels to Faraway Places. They weren't like my cousin whose bud died prematurely because of a lack of nourishment, but they were two blossoming flowers on the family tree that had been violently shaken from it before they could ripen.

Looking at Dad's photo, I was no longer whisked into a blazing storm of primal rage that dominated my regressions with Psychiatrist #2 when anger morphed me into a lion. I now felt empathy for a man whose life force had begun to wane at the age when most people embark on a journey of individuality and self-expression. The twisted vine that was his DNA had corrupted his family tree long before he had been born, and there was nothing Mom, The System, or anyone else could do to fix it. Dad's destiny had been sealed from the moment of his conception.

I no longer resent the possibility that my parents might be partying on a plaid blanket in The Great Unknown, and I don't need confirmation during another walk with Jesus into the open meadow. I want them to see the universe around them and in each other, just as they had when my sisters and I were mere twinkles in their eyes. I want them to be swaying in each other's arms to "Put Your Head on My Shoulder" under a liquid silver moon, with their feet sinking into sand that glows in the dark as they dance. I imagine them meandering along some big river flowing with a glistening otherworldly liquid, one they can float effort-lessly in, without the need to tread water as we did in The Big River running through Somewhere Small. The consistency of the glittery balm is like amniotic fluid, allowing them to remain submerged for as long as they want, because the undertows that taunted us in The Big River aren't death traps in the rivers criss-crossing The Great Unknown. They are portals to other worlds, and getting caught in them is something to celebrate, not fear. Most importantly, if my parents exist somewhere in the universe, I trust they are holding hands as they explore celestial places, and those places are filling them with awe and wonder and everlast-ing joy.

CHAPTER 31

THIS LIFE

The privilege of a lifetime is to become who you truly are.
C. G. Jung

I don't want The Simple Life or The Good Life. I want My Life, which is not about the security that comes from the stability of The Simple Life and a healthy bank account with The Good Life. My Life is about being an explorer, not only of Faraway Places, but also in the scariest places I must face without leaving my home. My exploration of Faraway Places is a choice, but the exploration of the parts of myself I'd rather avoid often isn't, and it usually involves being in the valley between Like and Love for a while. Both forms of exploration are uncomfortable, because being open in such a way means I experience the ecstasy and emptiness of being human. I view My Life as somewhat of a juggling act requiring me to toss and catch balls of contrasting colours while navigating a narrow path separating opposites: joy and sorrow, pleasure and pain, forgiveness and hate. I have spent as much time on each side as I have walking the elevated and uneven path in the middle.

During moments of self-doubt that coincide with important life changes, I am more compelled than ever to focus on where other people are on their paths, and compare My Life to theirs, particularly those people who I naïvely think are happier than I am because of The Good Life they have created. But The Powers That Be boot me off my path onto the side of sorrow and pain until I remember that My Life is mine, their life is theirs. And following my purpose and expressing my Art fortify my life force, while comparing myself to others weakens it. Besides, why would any of us want to compare ourselves to anyone else when we already know there is no one like us?

My heart has survived multiple cracks on sorrow's side. I no longer seek ways to avoid new cracks by allowing myself to be paralyzed by uncertainty and loss, or to avoid scary people, places, or things. People I love will come and go from my life, but during our time together we sew fabric onto the patchwork of each other's lives. I cannot control many of the things that happen any more than I can stop the Earth from orbiting the sun.

The sudden separation from my parents and sisters as a child has made me anxious and scared about loss. In those moments, I've learned to place my left hand over my heart and tell myself that no matter what happens, all is well. The truth is that as soon as we say hello to someone, the goodbye to them is inevitable; we just don't know if it's a long one or a short one. Letting go is not the end. It's the beginning of something new and something better, even if it doesn't appear that way in the beginning. My Life isn't supposed to make me sad and cynical—at least not forever. And the things that cause me to suffer will also cause me to grow until I become the snake ready to shed the skin it has outgrown. Like the snake and its old skin, I need to let go of things that hinder my growth and invite a new phase of life that makes shedding the old necessary.

I've revised my theory about hearts. Not the part about the quest to return them to the state they were in on the day we were born, the state of openness and receptivity, with pure and naked vulnerability. But perhaps the cracks in our hearts are not filled with putty that's pliable and porous, because it can harden over time, too. Maybe they are filled with pure gold to ensure they remain malleable as new cracks form, which also allows old ones to shift and adapt as necessary. Then again, perhaps they are filled with putty first, and tears become the alchemist that turns them into gold. I need to remind myself to let my heart be born again and again. The heart of a newborn expects to be cradled tenderly and whispered to in a gentle voice about how improbabilities become more likely with belief and faith.

"I love you," is easily translatable into every language and is one of the first sentences a child learns. Saying it to someone with genuine tenderness and affection is hard for me. It's even harder to do when looking into his eyes, into the watery wells leading to his heart. When I tell someone I love him, I have sent an invitation from my heart, permitting him to dive into and meander through its depths with no guarantee that he won't leave it bent out of shape after the exploration. Letting someone into my heart means exposing my humanness, my sweetness, and the dark truths I haven't displayed to the world with banner advertisements. It means I entrust him with the public and private details of my biography, notably including the pretty and the not-so-pretty parts.

I no longer view The Garden of Love as an inhospitable wasteland, one I dare not enter. In fact, I've learned a few things about landscape architecture and created my own version of it, one that flourishes in the four seasons and survives in any kind of weather. First and foremost, my garden is hot enough in the summer season and sufficiently fertile to grow lemon trees, but I choose not to plant them in mine as a way to avoid tempting fate, for the same reason people don't walk under ladders.

My Garden of Love is naturally suited to perennials, and I've selected an assortment such that, whatever the season, some varieties are in bloom. Snowdrops pop up through the shallow layer of snow even before the crocuses. And the hearty hellebores insist on sprouting flowers as early as January. Baby's breath carpets part of my garden in the spring and foretells that warmer days and gentle rains are imminent. For those years with many tempests, I have planted yellow flags in the places that collect water, because they have the ability to survive floods. And the seed heads in the switchgrass planted throughout the garden become spangled with raindrops that I know will glisten when the sun peeks through the clouds again.

During periods of doubt or estrangement, I wander through the section filled with agapanthus, agave, and anemone, because I know they will be in bloom regardless of the season I find myself in. Seeing them, my tight chest relaxes, because I remember that love never dies. In my pessimistic periods, I visit the dead-nettles and the basket-of-golds that thrive in cracks between paving stones and at the edge of gravel paths where they produce dazzling neon yellow flowers in the spring. Love, just like these beauties, can blossom in the most difficult of circumstances.

And as much as I cherish animals, I have planted some species that are resistant to the nibbles of deer and rabbits, such as mead- owsweet. The Garden of Love resonates with beauty and harmony and the sweetness that comes with tenderness. So it stands to reason that animals would also be attracted to it and want to partake in its riches. Therefore, I made sure that they couldn't eat everything that grows there! On that note, my Garden of Love is filled with human edibles such as savoury, thyme, and rosemary, because I want it to be a source of vital nourishment if and when I, or the people who cross my Garden's path, need it.

Of course, there is a large rose garden in the northwest section that is meticulously pruned and weeded each year during spring and summer. Chocolate flowers line the perimeter of the rose garden as a sensual complement to the mouth-watering aroma inside its border. I periodically walk to this section of the garden, inhaling deeply while I pick a rose or two. And I couldn't com- plete my garden without evidence that nature honours the uni- versal symbol of love, which I've chosen to be none other than the bleeding heart.

My garden has a prominent location for symbols of the sun and the moon, the masculine and feminine. Such perfection rests in the tall and floppy sunflower that grows prolifically in both acidic and alkaline soils, not to mention that they are also resistant to deer and drought. And there is no better symbol of the feminine than the dreamy moonflower. It produces six-inch white flowers that open at dusk and release a sweet fragrance all night long.

The lawns are sprinkled with dandelions and no herbicide is used to kill them, since my Garden of Love is as unadulterated as

I can muster. I know they're weeds, but they grow yellow blossoms in the summer, and dandelion tea is a notable liver tonic. Even weeds have their uses; yet if they begin to overtake the lawns, I make a trip to the tool shed to find the little shovel to dig them out and calmly plant them in the botanical waste bin. I have placed a plastic tarantula on the door to the shed, not because I'm masochistic, but because I want to remember that even though spiders scare me, they play an important role in many ecosystems. I do hope the replica attenuates my fear of them before I enter The Great Unknown.

The red hot pokers, with their bold spikes of brilliantly coloured tubular flowers protected by sword-shaped leaves, guard the entrance to remind me that I can refuse anyone access into its premises. I can also remove a spike and point it at a trespasser or a fraudster while I politely but firmly ask them to leave.

And I have planted a few forget-me-nots in the corner of the garden that receives the most sun. When someone I love dies, I plant one in his or her honour. Cinderella's tombstone is erected in this same corner and is engraved with, "Here I remain, Forever After…" The Evil Temptress visits her grave periodically and can't help but weep from time to time.

If I were to become blind, I can always find my Garden through my memory of its magnificence or by following the intoxicating aromas of lavender, lemon balm, and lily of the valley that would lead me to it. And even in my blindness, I can envision that plaque above the gate of my Garden like the halo of an angel: "We are one."

Yet there are two most notable features of my Garden of Love. It is lined with poplars whose whispers remind me of the power of dreams. If I lose my faith for too long, powerful gusts whip through the branches, making the leaves cackle like a coven of witches, warning me that negativity is not inert.

My Garden is also situated near a big river, like the one running through Somewhere Small. Like The Big River, the pH of my garden river hovers around neutral most of the time; it's not acidic and it's not alkaline. But when it suffers an assault, balance is either restored by the adept hands of Mother Nature or what lives along it or in it ceases to be, because imbalance cannot be tolerated indefinitely.

Even though the water churns in the reverse direction when it rushes over boulders, it must flow southward eventually, for it also overcomes obstacles and continues on its path for miles until it fans out into the Pacific Ocean, losing its identity.

I am The Big River, too. I rise and fall with the seasons, year after year while navigating the swift currents, sometimes pausing to reflect during the slow meandering sections, to acknowledge that being is as important as doing. From time to time, I get stuck in eddies, creating the illusion that I am going around in circles. But The Big River's eddies don't stay in one place for long. Feeling stuck is an illusion, because like the moving eddy, I am making progress, even when it doesn't seem like it. Practising love and forgiveness has nourished my heart, opening it to give and receive. But in circumstances where forgiveness is as elusive as a young feather in a windstorm, I call on the grace and wisdom of the world's elders to guide me. With respect to doing love, I am flawed but still filled with promise. And promise doesn't imply the goal of being perfect at it. Promise means inhaling the nitrous oxide of kindness for myself and others, to open my vessels when sadness and disappointment constrict and harden my view of humanity. Promise also means understanding that "doing love" is an evolution of the heart—it might not be easy at times, but stagnation is harder. Over time, cracks form, putty fills them, I cry, and then my tears turn them into gold. Life circumstances might squeeze my heart, twist and bend it out of shape, but the changes are exercise, which benefits any muscle. During this evolution, my heart doesn't break with heartache. It changes and grows, not in size, but in its ability to endure the vicissitudes of life.

And like The Big River that dissolves into an ocean where it ceases to be, I will vanish into The Great Unknown one day, where I will become both everything and nothing as I dreamed long ago. Until then, I explore, I create, I wonder, I allow.

ABOUT THE AUTHOR

Karin J. Eyres has been a project consultant in Vancouver, Canada, for the past twenty years. She dabbled in writing screenplays, poetry, and short stories for many years, until the voices of her characters started to ignore her pleas to be quiet while she wrote bulleted lists in her project plans. When their voices became louder and more talkative than hers, she let them be heard, at first only for a few minutes, but then for several hours a day when she was no longer afraid of what they had to say or if anyone would care. She is currently working on her second novel.

CPSIA information can be obtained at www.ICGtesting.com
Printed in the USA
LVOW11s0236190915

454827LV00001B/34/P